NOT SO DONE

NOT SO DONE

A Sam Sunborn Novel

Charles Levin

Munn Avenue Press

First Edition

ISBN: 978-1-7352108-0-3

For Steve,

YOU SHOULD KNOW...

All the technology, science, locations, organizations, and global challenges in this novel are real and current today, except for a couple in development. Some names have been changed. Links and factual references can be found in the Author's Notes after Chapter 95. All the characters are fictional.

CONTENTS

"The Future fights the Past to produce the Present."
—Frank Einstein, Co-founder of Digital3000

"Americans believe death is optional."
—Woody Allen

"And you know something's happening but you don't
know what it is. Do you, Mr. Jones?"

—Bob Dylan, Ballad of a Thin Man

PROLOGUE

Remote control is a beautiful thing. In a darkened room, a black-gloved finger lifts the cover on the red switch. A few kilometers away, Angela LeTourneau struts down a sunny Parisian boulevard, arms swinging free like bird wings. *Oh, to be alive again.* Almost gone and then, a miracle. The million-dollars was a bargain, buying a new life, resurrection in a new body – a stronger, healthier, even voluptuous body. She is exhilarated by the morning chill in the air and the aroma of coffee wafting from the Café de Luna. The bright sunlight warms her face. Everything is alive. The breeze catches and lifts her long brown hair... but then a pain, a sharp pain like a knife to the temple. Something's gone wrong. A bug in the software. *Breathe.* Breathe deeply as the doctor said. *Was he a doctor? It will all be OK, right? Please.* She remembered something the doctor told her. "In her you will live, move and have your being."

The gloved finger flips the red switch. Angela takes her last breath and collapses to the sidewalk.

The Inspector hovers over the lifeless body, another victim of bodyjacking. The midday, late summer heat and humidity radiate off the macadam of Boulevard de Clichy. The acrid odor of the ripening corpse wafts through the air. Inspector Pierre Voleurdecor, "Inspector V" for short, started the UPDC, the Unité de Police de

Détournement de Corps — the Bodyjacking Police Unit — two years ago with the help of his U.S. counterpart, Renata Fermi.

New technology demanded new laws and skilled people to enforce those laws. Inspector V was a natural choice to head up the Unit after spending fifteen years in the Police Nationale's Antiterrorism Sub-Directorate or SDAT.. But he wonders every day if he made a dumb career choice. The incidence of bodyjacking, those stealing living bodies and implanting their own minds in those bodies, is growing at an exponential rate. The opportunity for terrorists and criminals to invade the bodies of otherwise healthy individuals, celebrities, and politicians defies national and international security.

V looks up from the body, slipping his sunglasses down from his forehead onto a disjointed nose. "Any ID?"

Paulette Goddard, V's assistant, sweeps the auburn hair from her eyes. "She had a passport on her. French named LeTourneau — no other ID. I sent it to Interpol to see what they have."

V stifles a cough. "Tenth one this week. This is très mal. Cause of death?"

"Notice the contorted look on her face. Like the others, looks like a stroke. And the hooked-shaped scar on her neck, just like the others too. The pathologist will confirm cause of death once he slices and dices."

"Nice image, Paulette. You've been hanging around Renata too long. Speaking of whom, where is she?"

"She's wrapping up a case in the U.S. Some terrorists tried to contaminate their food supply with the Dengue virus. That's all. Otherwise, she's just chillin'."

"Ah bon. Well, when she's free, we need her back here. Word is a well-known terrorist is driving this wave of bodyjackings."

"Yeah? Who would that be?"

"The current theory is Ahmed LaSalam, the Leopard."

"I thought he was dead."

"We all did." V looks down at the corpse, now attracting flies, "Just like this femme morte."

CHAPTER 1
BEING DIGITAL

Sam peers through his digital window, appreciating the abundant leaves of the 200-year-old oak wavering and shimmering in the September breeze. Although it's late summer, no window, no tree, and no Sam exist — not in a physical sense. The window, the tree, and Sam are all virtual, a collection of ones and zeros of Sam's creation.

"You're daydreaming, son. I can tell," Frank says.

"Hmm, yeah. As much as I try to recreate the real world with the feel of a warm summer day, the scent of Monica's perfume, or the feel of Evan's little hand in mine, I can only make pictures like this," Sam says.

Frank looks at Sam's virtual creation. "And you are getting good at it. Quite realistic. You know you can Skype anytime with Monica and Evan. They are very real."

"I know, but it's not the same. You have no idea how wonderful those few days were that I got to spend back in a physical form. Although it wasn't my original body, I could feel and smell and taste. The memory of my last night at home, lying next to Monica, fills me with both immense joy and a deep sadness," Sam says.

"I understand, but hey, I was alive once too. I had a wife and still have a daughter. My wife Susan is gone forever, but I still talk to Sarah almost every day. Yet, I'm not missing the aches and pains of getting old," Frank says.

"The whole body re-instantiation thing was a genius idea in principle. Yet, stealing another's body, no matter how desperate that body's owner's life, proved to be a mistake. Now the genie of your amazing invention has fled the bottle. Bodyjacking has morphed into a global criminal enterprise," Sam says.

Frank looks away and says, "I regret that, but you can't stop the engine of science. If I didn't do it, somebody else would have. At least we embedded blockchain into the technology so bodies and their owners could be tracked. We hold some hope of controlling the abuse of this technology."

"So now it's *we*, huh?"

"Yep, if it wasn't for you pushing me to get you back to save Evan from his terrorist kidnappers, none of this would have happened. So, you have skin in the game here too."

"Thanks, Dad. So now what? I'm stuck here and we have a bodyjacking crime-wave out there. What are you going to do about it?"

Frank grins. "I have some ideas on both fronts."

"Like what?"

"I can tell you now or tell you later."

"You're messing with me again, Frank. Why would I prefer *later* to *now?*"

"That's precisely the question, Sam. Because the answer all has to do with T*ime.*"

CHAPTER 2
TRUST

Ashaki stares, as if in a trance, at one of the three monitors on her desk at DHS's Manhattan Headquarters on Beaver Street. *What to do now?* She sold out her terrorist brother, Momar LaSalam, avenging his assault on her as a child. To be precise, he held her little arms down while their older brother, Ahmed, had his way with her again and again. Thanks to her recent actions as an adult, DHS agents Little, Hadar, and Fermi, with Sunborn and Einstein's help, cut Momar down. Still, she didn't want to stop Momar's intended attack. She just wanted to make Momar pay. Yet, the Americans must suffer for their drone attacks and senseless violence, which killed her parents and many other innocent Barinians. Those innocents weren't terrorists, but now their children are, including her.

Ironically, with her hacking skills, a phony resume, and bribes for references, she scored a job as a DHS analyst. Access to top-secret information will help her carry out a new plan while thwarting counterterrorism efforts to stop her. Yet, how long will her cover last before DHS or the Barinians figure out what she has done and what she plans to do? *Not long.* She needs supplies. Having hacked her way to millions, money is not a problem. However, a dedicated team with a shared vision will be harder to come by.

For recruiting, Barinians and their Middle Eastern allies are off-limits once they figure out she double-crossed her brother. *Think outside the box.* Her team members don't have to be from the Mideast. They just have to want to make Americans pay for something. *But what? Who could that be?*

Her eyes focus again on the screen. A CNN article about domestic terrorists, white nationalists. Hmm. They have a cause and sympathizers in high places. If the Americans ever really faced the truth, they'd realize a thousand more people die every year from domestic terrorists than from foreign actors like her. But the

Americans won't even use the term "domestic terrorist." It must be politically incorrect or politically protected. If DHS and the other sixteen Intelligence Agencies, including the FBI, devoted the resources and went after their own home-grown wack-a-doodles, they'd wipe them out in no time. *Maybe this is a convenient paradox for me,* she thinks.

Who could I contact? Could I really trust them? And why would they believe me? The answer to those questions may be that she exudes smarts and irresistible charm while being a world-class liar.

The late morning sun streams through the floor to ceiling windows at DHS headquarters on New York Avenue NE in D.C. The leaves will be turning soon. The aroma of morning coffee hangs in the air.

Rich leans over Michelle's cubicle and whispers, "I enjoyed last night. How about you?"

"It was OK," Michelle says.

Rich's face droops in mock disappointment.

"Just kidding. Don't be so sensitive. Besides, it was just a kiss," she says.

"Yeah, but what a kiss. Long, sloppy, some tongue. Just great."

"Rich, you're such a romantic. I think I need to get to know you better before this thing, whatever it is, goes any further. Besides, isn't there some DHS rule against fraternizing with subordinates?"

"Wrong on both counts. I don't think of you as a subordinate and you certainly don't treat me like I'm superior. I wouldn't label what this is as *fraternizing.*"

"You know what I mean. I'm still relatively new here. Just getting to like the place and the work. I don't want to blow it," she says.

"I won't let you. Besides, after bringing down the Cub, you're practically untouchable here." Rich is referring to their work together only a month ago that stopped Momar LaSalam, aka the Cub, from launching a nationwide biological attack.

"But it's still a mystery as to who tipped us off to his location, unlocked his computers, and kept us from being blown up," Michelle says.

"Yeah, and who supplied the biologicals, the weaponized dengue? Are they still out there? What's next?"

"Well, I guess it's our job to figure that out," Michelle says.

Rich touches the tip of his nose with his index finger. "Yeah, so stop sexually harassing me and get to work."

Michelle picks up her phone-book sized hardcopy of the DHS Employment manual and throws it at Rich, walloping him hard in the chest. "Read it," she says.

CHAPTER 3
VAN'S READY

The afternoon heats up as the sun rises above the tall pine treetops. Inside, Max Werner leans against the makeshift bar, takes a long deep toke on his Camel, gulps his frosted bottle of Bud, and blows a thin stream of blue smoke towards the ceiling. The smell of tobacco and spilled beer lingers. His grin widens as the "boys" amble into this rustic log cabin in the chilly Tennessee mountains. Looking through the window, he smiles at the various pickup trucks parked randomly on the dirt driveway.

As the screen door opens and slams shut, the Confederate flag nailed high up on the Lincoln log walls flutters above the shotgun rack. This cabin is Max's world, his little piece of heaven, man-cave, hideout, and war-room. The boys are mostly wearing white T-shirts and oil-stained jeans, arms competing for the most lavish tattoos. They filter in and take seats in the wooden chairs surrounding a beat-up, white metal kitchen table.

Max stubs out his cigarette on the wooden bar, collars his beer bottle and struts to the head of the table. *My army*, he thinks to himself and smirks. Still standing, Max bends over and places his palms flat on the table. Silently ratcheting his neck, he stares at each of the seven men one-by-one. "I'm ready to call this meetin' to order. This is a big day and tomorrow, God willin', will be the biggest day ever for NNN."

An older man, probably in his 70s, with gray beard stubble and the red face glow of a life-long Thunderbird man, coughs. "I vote we change the name of this here organization. Keep NNN but call it No – more Nigros Now."

One of the younger boys laughs. "I'd vote for NNJ – No More Jews."

Max takes a beat then slams his fist on the table. "Cut the shit. We're the *New Nationalist Network*. Respectable. We don't need no northern Jew lawyer coming after us and 'sides, *Nationalist* is no longer a dirty word. We want to do this thing tomorrow and have nobody be the wiser. You hear me?" Nobody moves. Max raises his voice. "I says, you hear me?"

The boys all nod at once. Max continues. "OK. You knows the money to do this doesn't grow on trees." He shifts his gaze to a middle-aged man with large black-rim glasses and red suspenders. "Riley, how's the sales this week?"

Riley opens a black ledger and scrolls down with his index finger. "Meth: fifty-five hundred, Oxy: twenty-two-hundred, girls: thirty-six hundred."

Max taps his finger on the table. "Why's the girls' number down?"

A young kid, Elroy, who looks too young to shave, jumps in. "Two of 'em got sick. Had to get rid of 'em. Got six new ones comin' this week. Mostly fifteen and sixteen. I got first dibs on the blonde."

"Keep it in your pants and take better care of those girls. We needs at least two thou a week from each. Understood?" Max says.

"Yes, sir. I'll make sure they're oiled up and ready to go." Elroy snickers.

Max stands up and moves towards the kid. He wraps his muscular arm in a choke-hold around the kid's neck, his USMC tattoo bulging. "You keep your paws off those girls. How many times I gotta tell you — you don't shit where you eat."

Elroy chokes. His face turns blue and his eyes start to move up in his head.

Max releases him. "You get my meaning now?"

The kid gulps in air and spits on the floor. "Yeah, yes, sir."

"Good." Max turns to the twenty-something man with the Marine haircut. "Van's ready? Equipment loaded?"

"Yes, sir. Ready to roll when you say."

"OK, it's about a fourteen-hour drive. You, Elroy, and Mags come with me." Max looks at his watch. "We leave at eight. I want to be in position when their session starts at eleven tomorrow. If all goes well, we'll press the button and be back here after midnight. John, pick up some pizza from the greaser's place in town and we'll all meet here tomorrow at two AM. Got it?" They all nod. "Good, let's do this thing."

CHAPTER 4
SCATTERED BODIES

At 11:00 AM, Nancy Lu, mic in hand, stands on the lawn of the Capitol Building on First Street SE, Washington D.C. "This is Nancy Lu reporting from the Capitol. Moments ago, members of the Congressional Black Caucus, the CBC, meeting in a secure room inside the Capitol building, were mysteriously stricken by some kind of attack. Staffers, who found the congressmen and women scattered about on the floor, describe some of the victims holding their ears, others coughing up blood. "Apparently..." Nancy pauses and looks away for a moment, "they mentioned a burning odor and eyeballs on the floor. Excuse me. I need a minute." Nancy puts her free hand over her eyes. She turns her head to the side, whispering to her producer, "It's alright, keep rolling..." She straightens up and continues, "We are now told that several are dead on the scene, but as you can see..." she turns and gestures towards First Street in front of the Capitol, "there are several ambulances. So hopefully, there will be survivors."

Nancy cups her hand over the earpiece in her left ear. "Wait. I'm getting a report that there were several children in a school group from California in the Caucus' meeting room at the time. Having won a competition to be on this trip, they were making a presentation to the CBC at the time of the incident. We're being told to call it an incident because we cannot be sure of the cause." She presses her hand tighter over her ear and trembles. "We're now told that several of the children have been either injured or killed."

Nancy turns to the side again, whispering, "I can't continue." She faces the camera once more with a grim smile. "Back to the studio and stay tuned for the latest updates. This is Nancy Lu, News 8."

Rich's phone vibrates in his pocket. *Michelle made me stop with the funky ringtone stuff*, he thinks. He checks the screen – *911*. He taps the icon, reads, jumps to his feet, and starts running down the row of office cubicles. Breathing heavily, he clutches Michelle's shoulder. "C'mon, let's go."

"What's going on?" she asks.

"Looks like an attack on the Capitol. We'll get a briefing on the way. Move!"

Michelle had been reviewing some CCTV videos on her computer. A grainy image of a woman with a baseball hat and scarf, standing in a dimly lit hallway freezes on her screen. Michelle rises to leave and turns back. She punches a key to lock the screen and jogs after Rich to the exit.

The following morning, Ashaki and Travis drive their rented Jeep fourteen miles up a dirt road in rural Tennessee. The sun is just breaking through the cloud blanket. Ashaki spots the fireman's helmet on the mailbox and turns right.

She has always been reluctant to get involved with American men. Having too much to hide, she wouldn't want to let anything slip in a moment of weakness. She made an exception with Travis Poole. He is an impressionable grad student in history at Hudson University in New York, seven years younger than her. They met at a bar. His rugged good looks and gentle manner got to her. Besides, the sex quenches her cravings. He also owns a gun, a Glock 19, which may come in handy on a trip like this.

They pull over in front of a rustic log cabin. When Ashaki opens the car door, she hears whooping and hollering from inside. The oaky smell of smoke from a wood fire is in the wind. *Gets cool at night in the mountains, even in September*, she thinks. She surveys the five pickup trucks parked at angles off to the side of the drive. "Travis, you stay here. If I'm not back in ten, come get me."

"Are you sure? I'd rather be there to stop something from happening, not pick up the pieces," Travis says.

"Don't worry. I'm a big girl and can take care of myself. Anyway, this is government business and I need to keep it confidential."

At the door, she takes a deep breath and knocks. Nothing. It's so noisy inside, maybe they can't hear. She pounds harder.

The door creaks open. A gaunt figure with a strapped T-shirt and bloodshot eyes flashes a toothless grin. "Well, looky here. Hello there, young lady. Are you lost? Would you like to come in, have a beer?" He chuckles.

"I would, but I'm not lost." She steps through the doorway and the room goes dead silent, all eyes on her. "I'm looking for Max."

CHAPTER 5
ELI'S TAIL

It's mid-morning, but Time doesn't matter much in Frank's virtual lab. Sam's still adjusting to the speed things happen here, thousands of times faster than in the physical world. Frank and Sam inhabit this "digiverse" filled mainly by electrons moving at lightning speed. Frank contrives computer-generated images of their old office, Sam's beat-up leather couch, the view of the river from the window, all to make Sam feel more at home. But it's not the same. Not like the physical world and being home with Monica and Evan, feeling the touch of her soft skin or seeing Evan's whole face smile.

"Frank, any progress on getting me back into a body again?" Sam asks.

"I told you I'm working on something. Take a look at this." An image flickers to life in Sam's virtual reality mode. On a steel lab table rests two cages. A white mouse scurries about in one cage while the other cage is empty. "We may be virtual, but the cages are real. Bart set them up for me back in our office. Bart, are you there?" Frank asks.

"Yep, cages are all set and hooked up to the new device I built to your specs. I think my furry friend, Eli, is ready," Bart says.

"OK. Sam, don't get your hopes too high yet. Here goes the first test of the time-based technology I've been working on. It may require many more iterations to get it right, but let's see what happens. Bart, step away from the cages just to be safe. In 3... 2... 1... "

Sam hears a low humming sound. "What's going on? I don't see anything."

"Be patient. Keep watching."

Taking a deep virtual breath, Sam focuses again on the cages. The mouse in the cage on the right stops moving and gradually blurs like he's out of focus. The bars of the cage still appear distinct, but the mouse's image becomes wavy like the heat off hot pavement and then Eli just disappears. "What? What just happened?"

"Keep watching," Frank says.

A small white haze forms in what had been the empty second cage on the left. Something amorphous starts to take shape. After a few more seconds, Eli appears fully formed in the second cage. Sam and Bart are speechless.

Frank smiles. "Seems that Eli has some magic powers."

"I don't understand. Is this like some *Star Trek* teleportation thing?" Sam says.

"No, or well, maybe sort of... It's more like I've found a seam in Time. By first digitizing them and then injecting something or someone into that seam, we can make them appear. In this case, it was Eli, the mouse. In your case, Sam, you're already digital, like a bunch of floating electrons. That gets us halfway there. It's much more complicated than that, but you get the idea."

Sam is breathing heavily now. "Are you saying you could do that with me?"

"Theoretically, but we still have to solve a few problems and do a bunch more testing," Frank says.

"Like, what kind of problems?"

"Like from Cage One to Cage Two, Eli lost his tail."

"Who's askin?" Stubbly Beard says.

Ashaki steps further into Max's lodge and the good ole boys form a circle around her. The cabin is dimly lit by several bare bulbs hanging from the wood-beamed ceiling. The smell of spilled beer makes her nose crinkle. "Well fellows, I just wanted to congratulate you on the stunt you pulled off at the Capitol yesterday. Well done," Ashaki says.

Suddenly shotguns and pistols turn up from nowhere and everywhere. Ashaki raises her hands, palms-down. "Relax boys. I'm not with the Feds or any law enforcement. I'm on your side."

Stubbly scowls. "You'd better say your piece right quick before somethin' bad happens."

Ashaki hears the clicks of gun hammers being cocked and rounds being chambered. She smiles calmly. "Boys, boys. I come in peace with a proposition that might make us both a lot of money and stick it to the U.S. Government at the same time. That's why I'd like to talk to Max. Now, which one of you good lookin' fellas is Max?"

A tall man, clean-shaven with pearl-gray eyes, steps through the circle of men, pushing the barrel of one of the boy's shotguns down. "Take it easy, boys." He looks Ashaki up and down. "I'm Max." He smiles broadly. "You don't mind if we make sure you're not carrying. Zak, you do the honors."

Stubbly, aka Zak, grins and licks his lips. He starts patting Ashaki up and down, taking his time passing over her ample breasts and bending down to stroke the inside of her thighs. As his head nears her crotch, she swiftly upraises her knee, striking Zak's nose with full force. Everyone in the room hears the crunch of cartilage collapsing. Zak jumps up, clutching his nose, blood streaming through his fingers. "Oops," Ashaki says. "So sorry. My knee just automatically does that when somebody gets too close to my pussy."

The room goes dead silent for a long moment. Then the rest of the boys, including Max, burst into laughter. Max pats Zak's shoulder, "Looks like you got cock-blocked again. Go clean up."

Zak staggers off to the bar. The bartender hands him a bag of ice.

Max turns to Ashaki. "That's quite an entrance, young lady." He grins. "What can I do you for?"

Ashaki reaches out and shakes hands with Max. "That's quite a welcome you gave me." She smirks. "Let me get to the point why I'm here. I couldn't call ahead and risk the Feds listening in. For all I know, all your phones are tapped. So tell me, how'd you pull off the attack at the Capitol?"

Max strokes his chin. "Who says we did that?"

"I know you did it. I just don't know how. But that's beside the point. I've got a much bigger plan to stick it to them, and I'm looking for a smart, creative guy like you to help me make it happen."

Ashaki watches Max's expression. He seems to feign disinterest, but she's an expert at reading micro-expressions. Max looks up and to the left — he's thinking. She notices a slight swelling in his pants. He's interested in one thing for sure, which is to her advantage.

Max pulls out an unfiltered Camel, flips his Zippo and lights up. He blows a stream of pungent blue smoke just above Ashaki's head. "Tell me about this plan."

Ashaki tilts her head. "Not here, not now. I think we need to talk alone first. You can have your boys stand guard. When you hear what I have to say, you're gonna have to make some decisions as to who you share it with. Get my drift?"

Max widens his grin, showing a big gap between his front teeth. "Yeah, I get it. How 'bout you meet me at the Turkey Tavern in town at six tonight? They got a room in the back. Just tell the bartender you're meeting me and come alone. Maybe we can get to know each other a little better."

"I'll be there, but tame your tiger. Ever hear the expression *Don't dip your pen in the company ink*? I'll just have my driver with me, but we'll meet alone," Ashaki says.

"Works for me, but keep the driver outside. Speakin' of which. He's tied to a post in my yard at the moment," Max says.

Ashaki's expression darkens. *What did I get myself into with these yahoos?*

"Oh, don't worry, honey, he's fine. Just a few cuts and scrapes. You know, we got to be careful."

Ashaki holds herself back. "Yeah, I get it. But if you or your boys put a finger on my man again or you call me *honey* again, I'll shove my fist so far up your ass that my middle finger will be stickin' out between your two front teeth."

Max backs up. "Calm down, little lady. Respect." Max bows at the waist.

"Six tonight." Ashaki turns to leave. "And cut my man down from that post *now*."

Max laughs. "Boys, cut 'em down." Max pivots to Ashaki and winks. "Cost of doin' biznis."

Sam browses the breaking news about the Capitol incident until he gets to the part about the school group from California, Abraham Lincoln Middle School. *My God, that's Evan's school*, he thinks. It's a big school. *What are the odds he was in the group visiting the Capitol?*

Sam's virtual phone rings. It's Monica via Skype. She's crying and gasping for air. "Sam, did you hear about what happened in D.C.?"

Sam can already guess what's coming. "Yes. I saw there was a group from Evan's – "

"Yes! Evan was with the group. I've been calling his cell and his teacher's cell and the school. Nobody answers. I can't believe this."

"Calm down. I can't believe he's hurt, but I'll find out what's going on. I have connections. I'll use them."

"Please hurry. I'm going out of my mind."

"Keep your phone handy. I'll call as soon as I have something." Sam clicks off.

He turns to Frank. "Are you getting this?"

"I'm already pinging all my sources. I'll deep dive DCPD, FBI, and Homeland communications to see what they have. I see names of Congresspeople but not the kids yet," Frank says.

"Please stay on it. I'm calling Rich now."

CHAPTER 6
BODYJACKERS

This is definitely the weirdest place Renata has ever worked. *Maybe they want me because I'm an M.D. and a cryptocurrency expert?* she thinks. She descends three flights of the metal staircase, the sound of her footfalls echoing through the brick stairwell. Pressing her eye to the retinal scanner, the door buzzes open. Inside the dimly lit room, a dozen mostly women sit behind low-walled cubicles, glued to multiple monitors. Maps, CCTV cameras, and text dart across their screens. A large OLED monitor covers most of the front wall, displaying a digital map of Paris and the surrounding area. Over one hundred small blinking red dots move slowly in a random pattern across a grid overlaying the map.

Inspector V, sleeves-rolled-up, stands hunched over a digital table sipping his morning triple-shot espresso. Looking up, he removes his rimless glasses, letting them dangle from a chain around his neck. He puffs on his Gitane then stubs it out. "Welcome back, Ms. Fermi."

Renata laughs. "Where I come from, you can't smoke in offices and why so formal?"

"Mademoiselle, the answer to both your questions is *Paris*. Everybody smokes here, and I address you by your last name out of respect."

"How about you call me Renata and I call you Pierre? Now please tell me – have you got any leads?"

Inspector V points to the massive wall monitor. "All the red dots are bodyjacked people with a digital signature we can follow. There may be others wearing Faraday clothes that block the signal. The ones you see may not all be victims."

"What do you mean? Doesn't bodyjacking by definition mean the victims have unwillingly had their bodies stolen and occupied by body thieves?"

"Yes, some, and maybe for the majority, that's true. But some may have willingly sold or rented their bodies – you know, for money."

"It's still illegal and against the law in the U.S. and the E.U. countries. Do we bring them in?"

"There's too many for our small unit to handle, and I'm not sure what it accomplishes. These bodyjack victims themselves didn't do anything wrong. Until we have a way to restore the bodies to their rightful owners without killing them, we're better off using our limited resources hunting down whomever is behind all this — don't you think? Somebody has stolen the technology and is selling a black market service to give the wealthy, who are dying, new bodies, but you know all that. That's why you're here."

"You know I have a connection to Frank Einstein, who invented the body-reprocessing system. He never intended it to be used this way."

"Mai oui. I'm sure whoever invented AR-15s and AK47s didn't intend they enable the mass killing of innocent women and children either. Once something new and powerful comes along, there will always be evil people eager to exploit it. But I'm, as you say, preaching to the choir. Let's focus. We're tracking all these BJs to see if there is a pattern or if we can track back where they came from?"

"How did you pick up the digital signature in the first place? Can you replay their movements to a starting point?"

"The digital signatures are embedded in the blockchain used to preserve their unique identities. At least Einstein had the forethought to build tracking into the tech. So far, the malicieux have not been able to remove it. Unfortunately, it took our quantum computers two weeks to crack the blockchain to see the digital trail. By then the BJs were far from the originating sources or what we're now calling the *Midwives*."

"Cute. OK, say the midwives create new BJs. Can you pick those up at inception?"

"We believe we can. If and when new dots appear on the screen, we'll be alerted and the AI in our system will automatically track them, IDing their patterns. Only one problem."

"What's that?"

"We've had this tracking system for almost ten days and there have been no new red dots."

"Maybe the midwives know you're tracking them. So they are lying low."

"Or they have something much bigger planned."

"What if we round up a few of the BJs and interrogate them? Maybe they can lead us to the source."

"Already thought of that. Your first interview is in Room 2. Her name is Desiree DeRouen."

It's late morning and a light drizzle begins to fall. The warehouse is in Maisons-Alfort near the Seine. It was once an industrial bakery and much of the equipment is still there covered with white sheets. Although it's been dormant for years, the high-ceilinged space still smells of baked bread. The warehouse is dark except for daylight streaming through the second-story windows. Towards the rear sits a temporary enclosure. It almost looks like an enormous tent with semi-translucent plastic sheeting draped for walls – streaks of light from surgical lamps seep through into the cavernous open space.

The back door swings open and a young, well-built silhouette moves towards the tented enclosure, pulling back a flap. "Are we ready for the next batch?" the man asks.

Two women in white lab coats, bending over two bodies prone on metal tables, look up at the man. The woman with dark hair and large tortoise-shell glasses speaks first. "The new batch looks good, all sixty-seven of them." She waves her hand in the air towards the six rows of male and female bodies lying motionless and naked on their metal trolleys, I.V.s connected to their arms."

"All alive?" the man asks.

The second woman, a short curly-haired redhead, says, "They are in stasis. The crew brought them in last night and we administered the sedatives. We'll have to do the instantiation procedures soon or their vitals could begin to fail. The I.V. fluids may sustain them today, but they'll lose body-tone and perhaps their cognitive functions will diminish by tomorrow."

"I apologize for the delay. We're concerned we are being monitored by the authorities. I'm waiting for an all-clear from our inside man." The man approaches the redhead and grabs her arm tightly. "Your job is to keep them healthy unless you want to become one of them. One of my clients is looking for a young, may I say voluptuous, redhead. You might be perfect. If it weren't for your clinical skills, you'd be on a table right now." He smiles a wide mustached grin. The redhead tries to pull away. The man pulls her closer and licks her ear. "But maybe I'll have a little taste of you first." He laughs and releases her.

She backs up and reflexively lifts a scalpel for protection. The man snorts. "Don't worry, little one. Just do your job. I'll take care of the rest. Get everything ready. You have the digital personality files, correct?"

The dark-haired woman steps in front of Red. "Yes, we have them and we're ready to proceed."

"Wait for my signal. Maybe tonight," the Leopard says.

CHAPTER 7
NANCY LU

Nancy Lu tosses and turns on the couch, another nightmare. The shots. The blood. She bolts up awake swinging her arms, knocking the empty beer bottles onto the floor. Strewn about the apartment are dirty dishes, half-empty pizza boxes, discarded clothes, and the stagnant odor of dead cigarettes. She stumbles into the bathroom and gazes in the mirror at her swollen face and dark circles around her eyes. *This won't do*, she thinks. I can't go on like this. I don't want to go on like this.

She opens the medicine cabinet, searching the mostly empty pill-bottles. She picks one out and shakes it. Nothing. She throws it over her shoulder. With one hand, she sweeps all the bottles from the cabinet. They tumble into the sink and bounce about the floor. Opening the tap, she splashes cold water on her face and combs her hair back with her fingers. She glances at her watch. *Shit, I'm late.* Jogging into the bedroom, she stubs her toe, and starts jumping up and down on one foot. *Fuck, fuck.*

Yanking a pair of inside-out jeans from the bedroom floor, she pulls them up and buttons them around her narrow waist. A green sweatshirt completes the outfit. *The interview won't wait*, she thinks. She seizes the flask from the nightstand, slips it into her back pocket, and pushes her notebook and recorder into her over-sized purse. Careening off the walls, she finds the front door and heads out into the bright Manhattan daylight.

It's 8 AM. Monica took the redeye and her plane taxis up to the gate at Dulles. She flags a cab and forty minutes later arrives at George Washington University Hospital. Out of breath at the Information Desk, she blurts, "Evan, Evan Sunborn. What room?"

The desk volunteer checks her computer. "ICU, 3rd floor. Are you family?"

Monica ignores the question and runs to the elevator. The pervasive disinfectant malodor makes her sneeze.

Evan is lying still, eyes closed, connected to oxygen and multiple beeping monitors. Bending over, she gently kisses his forehead. At the sight of her child, bandaged and bruised, tears fill her eyes.

Her phone vibrates in her pocket. It's Sam. "Honey, are you at the hospital yet?"

She wipes the tears with her sleeve. "I just got here. Evan's asleep. He looks bad. Not sure what the story is yet. I feel so helpless. I want to blame you, but I can't this time."

Sam, in his virtual state, is even more helpless, unable to comfort her. "Monica, put on the video. Let me see him."

She taps the phone and points the camera at Evan. Silence. Finally, Sam says, "I don't know what to say. Frank thinks he can get me back to you again. I'll be there as soon as I can."

"Yeah, and how did that work out last time? This is too much…"

The curtain behind Monica parts. A young, bright-eyed woman, maybe in her early thirties, five and a half feet tall, white coat and stethoscope dangling from her breast pocket, says, "I'm Doctor Susan Potts Sloan. Are you Mrs. Sunborn?"

Monica turns her phone towards the doctor. "Yes and my husband is on the line. How's Evan?"

Dr. Sloan displays a faint smile. "He's stable. We had to remove his spleen. He has several cracked ribs. We're also concerned about head trauma, so we induced a coma."

Sam's voice almost seems robotic. "Doctor, what's the prognosis? Will he recover?"

"We don't know yet. We're going to wait a day or two for the brain swelling to go down. Then, if there aren't further complications, we'll try to wake him and see."

Monica is openly sobbing now. "My God." She drops the phone. It hits the linoleum floor, shattering the screen.

CHAPTER 8

PERFECT GENTLEMAN

At noon, Travis veers the Jeep into the dirt lot next to the Turkey Tavern. Dust kicks up and swirls in the wind. The day is dry and sunny while a cool breeze swoops in from the mountains to blanket the valley below.

"Are you sure you don't want me to come in with you?" Travis asks. He removes his Glock from the glove compartment and lays it on his lap. "I'm not taking any chances, and I'm not getting hog-tied to a post again."

Ashaki smiles, putting a reassuring hand on his thigh. "I'll be fine. At this point, I think they're more interested than dangerous. But just in case..." Ashaki unsnaps three buttons on her shirt and leans toward Travis, revealing the can of pepper spray taped to the inside of her bicep. "I've also got this..." She lifts her pants leg to reveal a twelve-inch SOG Kukri knife fastened to her calve. "But I expect they'll pat me down again and take that. I doubt they'll find the pepper spray."

"Great, hell of a plan," Travis says.

"When you have something people want, it's self-defeating for those people to hurt you."

"Yeah, I know what he wants and it's between your thighs."

"That's a weapon too and I know how to use it. Don't worry." With that, she jumps from the Jeep and heads inside.

The bartender looks her up and down. His grin is barely visible behind the perfectly-groomed handlebar mustache. "Can I help you, ma'am?"

"Max is expecting me."

The bartender's smile evaporates and he points to the rear. She parts a beaded curtain coming face-to-face with Zak and another man she hasn't seen before. Zak instinctively covers his crotch with both hands, which makes Ashaki laugh. No pat down this time. The two men make way and Ashaki enters a smoke-filled room. A single bare bulb hangs over a hexagonal poker table covered in dirty green felt. Max is seated on the far-end. He stands and pulls out a chair. "Have a seat, darlin'."

She smirks. "A perfect gentleman."

"I've been accused of a lot of things, but that ain't one of 'em. Now let's get down to business. What's got your twat in a twist?"

"I guess you didn't take the hint last night. Your limp-dick taunts and come-ons aren't going to work with me. So either you agree to cut that crap out or I'm outta here now." She pauses. "What's it going to be?"

Max raises his hands, palms-forward. "Now, now, I didn't mean nothin' by it. I'm sorry, but you'd better have something special to say or you could be outta here feet-first."

"OK, now that we understand each other. I told you last night I admired what you did in D.C. I wasn't just blowin' smoke up your ass. Now let me tell you what we did. You know the nukes that blew in India and France last year? Or the dengue outbreak in Boston a few months back?" She watches his face, searching for recognition. Max nods and she continues. "What you probably didn't hear about or pay attention to was the destruction of the Seed Vault in Norway or the wiping out of a town in Yemen or the poisoning of crops in Nebraska. They didn't get much press here. But you probably heard about the romaine lettuce recall. That one scared the shit out of a lot of people."

"Are you sayin' you were in on all that stuff?"

"Let's just say that my brothers couldn't have done it without me."

Max looks down at his interlaced fingers and twiddles his thumbs. He seems to be mulling all this. "Supposin' I believe all that. Then you must have some pretty swell resources and people. What do you need me for?"

She strokes the green felt on the table. "Cards on the table? I had a falling out with my brothers and their backers. Besides, both my brothers are dead now. I've got money, lots of it, but I need smart guys like you with connections to make it happen. I can pay for the help."

Max rubs his chin. "Well, depends on what you're talking about."

"It's big, really big. And I figure, aside from the money, we have a common enemy that deserves some payback."

Max leans forward.

She can sense his interest and continues. "How 'bout the Jews, the blacks and the government for starters?"

Max leans back, seeming to relax. "OK, tell me more..."

Renata slams the door of the cold, dark interview room in Paris' UPDC headquarters. The woman chained to the table bites her lip and looks up. Her unwashed hair hangs over her dirty face. Renata places a plastic water bottle in front of the woman. "Parlez vous anglais?"

The woman coughs up some heavy phlegm and spits it on the table. "Un petit peu."

"OK, alors. What is your name?" No answer. Renata raises her voice. "Quel est votre nom?"

Tears well up in the woman's eyes. "Deborah Dumm. Really. C'est vrai."

"Now you're screwing with me," Renata says. "OK, Debbie, how'd you steal this body?" Renata waves up and down at the woman's body." Nothing. "Looks like you got a pretty bad deal to me." Renata puts a pack of Camels on the table. The woman begins to reach for them and Renata pulls them back, takes one out of the package and lights up. She blows a cloud of pungent smoke in Dumm's direction and drops the pack just out of reach of the woman's chained hands. "No, no. Not until you start telling me your story. Your true story. Otherwise, it's retour dans la boîte for you. No cigarettes, no water, rien. Me comprenez-vous?"

The woman nods and suddenly seems to find a smooth, almost sultry voice. "It didn't work out the way I planned. I had terminal cancer. I heard about this procedure where they can put sick people's brains and personalities into new bodies. I checked it out as best I could. They said somebody named Leopard could arrange it. I had money and only a month or less to live. What did I have to lose? Little did I know I'd end up like this."

Renata's stomach starts churning. *Leopard? Maybe, it's true?* "Tell me about this Leopard. How you found him? How you paid him? Where it happened?"

"It's a long story."

"OK, I'm in no hurry and you're not going anywhere. So tell me the story, all of it."

"Une cigarette first," Dumm says.

CHAPTER 9
SWIFT VENGEANCE

Rich and Michelle badge their way into the heavily guarded section of Building 10 at the Walter Reed Medical Center in Bethesda, Maryland. It was only a thirty-minute drive from the Capitol building where the attack took place. The beige walls and linoleum floors are antiseptic clean. The halls are bright and a faint scent of something like Lysol drifts in the air.

Michelle peeks through the green-tinted glass panel outside Room 603 and knocks gently on the door. As they enter, they see a middle-aged African-American man with close-cropped graying hair. He is perched in a lounge chair, only dressed in a hospital gown. Hooked up to an I.V. with an oxygen line necklace hanging around his neck, he looks up, flashing a sunny grin. Michelle likes him right away before he even speaks his first word.

"Directors Little and Hadar, I presume?" Congressman Ball says.

Michelle extends a hand, which the Congressman envelops in both his hands. "So nice to meet you in person, Congressman. I studied your historic work during the Civil Rights Movement in the '60s and the March on Selma. But it seems that you are more active than ever on the Oversight Committee."

"I'm flattered. You know for a while, after Johnson signed the Civil Rights Act in '64, we thought things would get better. When we passed the Voting Rights Act in '65, we thought things would get better. Yet, a couple of years back, the Supreme Court gutted it. Before that, King and Bobby Kennedy and the five thousand known lynchings in the last one hundred years in our country. Now this attack. I don't think it's getting better. Maybe I'm a fool for still thinking someday it will. That's why I keep fighting."

"Well, I hope for the country's sake you continue," Rich says and extends his hand. "How are you feeling?"

"Thanks for asking. I'm having some trouble with my balance and ringing in my ears. Docs think it will go away. It's like I have a bad concussion, they say."

"That's why we're here. We're trying to track down who's responsible. Can you tell us what happened?"

"Sure, as best I can. But tell me, why are *you* here? I mean, you're director-level. Wouldn't you just send some field agents to do this?"

"This is clearly top priority. A domestic attack on Congress with a hate-crime to boot. And to be honest, Michelle and I are hands-on. We like to get out in the field whenever we can," Rich says.

"Speak for yourself there, Batman," Michelle says, and Ball laughs.

Rich's face glows pink. "I guess I shouldn't speak for Robin here. That might be politically incorrect, but I don't give a flying ... "

Michelle squeezes Rich's arm hard.

"Sorry, I can get carried away sometimes. Please, tell us what happened as best you can remember."

"OK. Give me a minute..." He takes a long wheezing breath. "It was about 10:30 AM. We, that is the Congressional Black Caucus, were meeting in the Rayburn Room at the Capitol. We were discussing some controversial legislation pending that would give the U.S. Army the power to intervene in case of a domestic emergency, if declared by Congress or the president. As I'm sure you know, the Posse Comitatus Act prohibits the Army from being employed domestically." The Congressman pauses and sips ice water from a straw. "Sorry, my throat gets parched. Didn't mention that it's almost like I got burned there. Anyway, an aide interrupts the meeting and leads a group of school children into the room. We do this from time-to-time. I love hearing questions from the kids. Not only are they our future, but they'll be in charge of our long-term care someday." He chuckles.

Michelle smiles. "Then what happened?"

"The kids are there for maybe ten minutes. A young girl asks me what it was like facing down the police in Selma. You know by now you can see some of that on YouTube. A good thing, I think. I started to answer when I heard a loud ringing in my ears. Then a headache that's ten times worse than I have ever felt in my life. I throw up all over the table in front of me and fall to the floor. The last thing I remember as I'm lying on the floor, is staring into the dead brown eyes of that little girl lying next to me. After that, it's all a blank until I woke up here."

Michelle is clenching her fists. They sit silently for a long moment. "Congressman, do you remember anything else strange or different about this particular meeting?"

"Hmm, maybe. Before the meeting, I was in my office. You probably know we get a lot of hate mail every day. All CBC members do. Death threats, swastikas. You should be in chains, stuff like that. But that morning, my aide showed me a note that was different. It said…"'On wrongs, swift vengeance waits.'"

"Alexander Pope," Rich says.

"So you know it. We had to look it up," the Congressman says.

"I know it too well. It's clearly a warning," Rich says.

"And maybe a clue. Congressman, do you still have that note?" Michelle asks.

The Congressman fakes searching for the note in his pocketless hospital gown. "Nope, can't seem to find it." They laugh. "But contact Patricia in my office. We save all the correspondence. I always tell my staff to use the hate mail as fuel to keep us going, keep us fighting. The other reason we keep it is just in case something like this happens." His eyes well up. "I lost several good friends and colleagues today."

Rich gently puts his hand on Ball's shoulder. "Thank you, Congressman. This has been helpful."

"Now go find the bastards that did this."

"We will," Rich and Michelle say in harmony.

"I've just got off a call with Renata," Frank says. He seems distracted despite being able to process thousands of things simultaneously in his virtual world.

Sam's heads-down, studying multiple screens of data. "Yes, yes, I was just following the investigation of the Capitol attack."

"Sam, we can talk about that in a minute. Renata and her team are in crisis mode over the expanding bodyjacking problem. I'm really regretting having invented that technology."

"Frank, you can't blame yourself. Alfred Nobel invented dynamite. You can't blame him for how it was used."

"Oh, really? I think you have to look at how new tech is used. If Oppenheimer could have taken back the atomic bomb, knowing the hundreds of thousands of lives lost due to its destructive power, he would have."

"We're good at inventing stuff, not controlling its use."

"Exactly. That's precisely the problem. Somebody has to have a moral compass in all this. Maybe it has to be us."

"I understand, but let's leave the philosophy and ethics for later. What's Renata saying?"

"OK, for now, but we will come back to this. Ethics are real here, not theoretical... Renata says they are trying to track the source of the bodyjacking ring in Paris. They are short on leads and worried about an explosion of new victims. A familiar name has popped up."

"Let me guess..."

"Don't guess. This is not a game. It's the Leopard."

"No, can't be."

"Think about it. If you were saved digitally like you and I were, and apparently the Leopard was, and you had access to or stole our technology for re-instantiating brains into bodies or into minds to be more precise, wouldn't you do it? Wouldn't you be the first to do it?"

Sam snorts. "I was the first to do it and look how that worked out. Here I am back in the digiverse. The Leopard's smarter, testing it out on a few victims first. Then when he felt he could put himself back into a body safely, that's when he'd do it."

"And he'd have the added advantage of not caring whose body he steals. Unlike us, who argued over the ethics of taking over somebody's body, he'd pick a really healthy specimen and hijack him or her."

"That in itself is a partial clue. Whoever's body is housing the Leopard is definitely a healthy one, young, fit, and most likely male. But how would he deal with the conflicting personality problem I had with Juan?"

"Maybe he figured that out and yes, you are probably right about the profile of Leopard 2.0. Renata wants us to help her catch him."

"I'd like to help, but I'm still worried about Evan being in a coma. Getting to the bottom of what happened in D.C. may help me figure out what happened to Evan. Any news on your experiments to get me back there?"

"I think we can do both. We're digital after all and can do a myriad of things at once. So we can certainly help Renata and save Evan at the same time. We've done it before."

"You've done it before. I know digitally we can multitask, but emotionally I can't. For now, I want to use all my multi-tasking abilities on Evan. So, about getting me back?"

"I understand. I did another experiment with the mouse and the cages. Remember, teleporting Eli from one to the other?"

"Yeah, how did that go?"

"Maybe it was a success and maybe it wasn't."

"What do you mean? Either the mouse reappeared in Cage 2 or he didn't, right?"

Frank punches a few keys on his virtual keyboard and swivels his chair around to face me. "Look at your monitor and watch closely."

I focus on the screen. Eli, the little white mouse, is in the cage labeled *#1*. Eli's image seems to slowly blur than disassemble like dust in the wind. My eyes flick back and forth between Cage 1 and Cage 2. Nothing. No Eli in either one.

Frank clears his throat. "Remember Schrodinger's Cat? Eli disappeared, but maybe he didn't."

"What? Where'd he go?"

"I don't know. But if we can find out, we'll know whether my test worked or it didn't."

"Frank, you're losing me."

"Losing you may be the whole point. Losing you may be the way back."

Frank strokes his scraggly beard and turns back to his virtual monitors. "I'll work on both puzzles at the same time. Let me know if you come up with anything on Evan."

Sam throws his hands up in the air and takes a deep virtual breath. "I will. You'll be the first to know."

CHAPTER 10
GARY

Nancy stumbles into the Trader's Deli on Beaver Street, near the DHS office where Gary works. Gary was a level 11 senior engineer, coder, and hacker at Google before the FBI and DHS recruited him. The Bureau had to get a salary exception to match the $150,000 a year Google was paying him. Nancy got to know Gary when he helped Rich and Michelle take down the Leopard in Cambridge and the Cub in Manhattan. She looks out the deli windows facing the street and drums her fingers on the Formica table. *Where's Gary?* She checks her watch – his lunch break should be now. The waitress arrives, holding a pot full of coffee. Nancy slides her cup forward. Just the aroma of coffee seems to revive her.

The waitress fills the cup with a flourish. "Do you want to order something or wait for your boyfriend, hun?"

"Coffee's fine for now and he's not my boyfriend. Just keep the coffee coming, sweetie." Nancy flashes her snarkiest grin.

"Will do, darlin'." The waitress pivots, her pink uniform skirt flaring.

Nancy extracts her flask from her purse and pours a few shots of its contents into her coffee. Hesitating, she pours a little more. The deli door swings open, letting in a cool draft and a short man with thinning red hair. He looks left and right, spots Nancy, and slides into the booth across from her. "Sorry I'm late. Things are pretty nuts in the office. I can't stay long."

Nancy tenderly covers Gary's hand with her warm fingers. She knows how to play this fiddle. "Thanks for coming. I missed you. It's been a while since..."

Gary's eyes water. "I'm so sorry about Al. We all miss her. What's so urgent?"

Nancy pulls her hand away. Unexpectedly, she's thrown back into the memory of that horrible night when her girlfriend and the love of her life was gunned down right in front of her at the Bar None. She still remembers the splatter of blood and brains that sprayed her, Nancy, in the face. She begins to tremble. *Is it the memory or the booze?* "Sorry, it's just the memories came flooding back."

"How are you holding up?"

"Honestly, not great, but I'd rather not talk about me. Listen, I called you because we've helped each other before. You know, with our investigations. You being DHS and me being a reporter, we have the same goal, to solve problems, right?"

"Yeah, but what are you up to this time?"

"I've got two leads. Maybe nothing or maybe something. I could just use your help to point me in the right direction."

"Tell me what you're talking about, and if it's not classified, maybe I can help."

"OK. Number One, somebody in your office, involved in cybersecurity and cyber-warfare, has disappeared. Two, Renata Fermi, whom we both met on the Cub case, was sent to Paris to work on some super-secret project." Nancy puts her hand back on Gary's and looks him directly in the eyes. "Can you tell me about either or both of those two things?"

Eye contact is not Gary's strong-suit. He looks down, averting her gaze and pulls his hand away. "That's classified. I can't talk about either one."

Nancy lifts Gary's chin until she makes their eyes meet again and smiles. "This would be strictly off the record. I just need a little info so I can take the next step."

"Can't do it. No."

"Gary, do you remember how I came up with some valuable information last time that led to killing a known terrorist and stopped a major attack? Do you remember who I gave that information to and who got a promotion as a result? In case you forgot, it was you."

"Yes, I remember. That was a good thing."

"Well, I'd like to do that again. You help me and I'll help you."

Gary hesitates, "Strictly off the record, right? 'Cause if any of this gets back…"

"That's right. I promise. Now, what do you know?"

Gary sucks in some air. "OK. The Renata thing first. You know how Sam came back to life the last time. I mean, he came back in a new body, but there were problems."

"I know, but I wasn't supposed to know. We spent a bunch of time together and since Sam's appearance had changed so radically, he kinda had to tell me."

"So then you know Frank Einstein had come up with a way to put a person back into a human body. What you probably don't know is that someone, and I can't say who, stole that technology and is stealing bodies. Putting people who have died back into other people's bodies. It's called bodyjacking."

"That's a real word, a real thing? What?"

"It's real. There's even a website, bodyjacking.com. And on the dark web, you can buy or rent a body, request what you want, gender, age, big boobs, anything."

"Holy shit. This is really happening."

"Yep. The first reported cases are here and in Paris. The French security agency has set up a top-secret task force, the Bodyjacking Police Unit, to handle it. That's where Renata is now."

"Wow. And the missing DHS hacker?"

Gary is sweating now. The waitress returns and fills his cup. He gulps it down. "She worked for me. I should have seen the signs. Mysterious packages showing up. Stuff like that."

Nancy is scribbling in a notebook. "Signs of what? What's her name?"

"I can't say anymore. Gotta go." Gary jumps up and darts out the door.

Nancy can feel her heart racing. *This is big.* She leaves money for the bill and her half-full flask on the table and rushes out.

CHAPTER 11
IT'S OVER

Gary furrows his brow and walks tentatively over to Ashaki's cubicle.

She's hunched over a Google Earth map. Sensing a presence, she taps a key to darken the screen and swivels her chair towards him. "Hi, boss. I'm back," she says and conjures a smile. Then she lifts half of a peanut butter and jelly sandwich from its foil and takes a bite. Raising the other part of the sandwich, she says, "Want half?" The scent of peanut butter snakes through the air.

Gary crosses his arms, "Back? Adele, where have you been?"

"I took two personal days. Sorry I didn't call you. Family emergency. My head was elsewhere, but I did log it ahead with H.R." Ashaki forgot to do it ahead, so she hacked H.R. and back-dated the personal days this morning.

"I checked H.R. I thought you had bolted. I got nervous."

"Check again. It's all there and I promise to let you know next time. This was unusual. My mom is stable now."

"OK. I'm sorry about your mom. Glad you're back. Rich is on my case to suss out patterns related to the D.C. attack data. Please get on that first thing."

"I will. I was just checking surveillance maps when you came over." *Might as well be careful in case he saw my screen*, she thinks.

"Get on it and let me know when, not if, you find anything."

"Roger that."

Adele, aka Ashaki, waits a few seconds listening for Gary's footfalls to recede. She swivels back to her screen, inserts Bluetooth earbuds, and logs into Skype.

Marsha Hume from the lab in Waltham appears on the screen. "Hello, Ms. LaSalam. Sorry to hear about your brother. We worked closely on the last project. Did you get the package I sent? He said if anything happened to him, I should send the Plan B samples to you. That you'd know what to do with them."

"I got it. Thank you. But I'm going to need a larger quantity to carry out the next project. How long will it take you to provide it?"

"So then we should continue our work? With your brother gone, I wasn't sure we would still be funded."

"Yes. I will provide the money you need. Just let me know the amounts and wire transfer details. But you didn't answer my question, when?" Ashaki catches herself raising her voice. *Am I like my hot-headed brothers? Allah, help me.*

"About a week to get the kind of quantity you'll need."

"That won't do. I need it in two days, delivered to a new address I will give you. Too risky to deliver here. Besides, I have a new distributor, out-of-state."

"But–"

"No buts." Ashaki opens a new window on her screen. It's a black-and-white video monitor. There are young children playing blocks at a school. "I'm looking at the sweet sight of your girls playing at school. They look like they're having fun. Would be a shame if they didn't make it home tonight. What were their names again? Karen and Samantha, I think." She pauses to let the scenario sink in. "Now, about that delivery."

Sam can't concentrate for more than twenty seconds at a time. He's worried sick about Evan. He feels responsible for not being there to protect his son. Rationally, he knows the D.C. attack was not his fault, but emotionally it's a different story. The dark clouds of his inner-self are circling. He's been in that dark hole before, and it feels like he might be falling in again. He decides to call Monica. After three rings, she picks up. "Monica, where are you?"

"Hello to you too. Where do you think I am? I'm still at the hospital with Evan, waiting."

"Sorry, I'm just so worried. How is he? Any change?"

"Nope. I'm next to him in the ICU, watching his heart beating on the monitor. Our son's heartbeat. I can't use a cell here, but I want to talk to you. Hold on. I'm going to step out into the hall."

He waits, not breathing. Ironic, being all-digital, he still has the sensation of holding his breath, like an amputee who still feels his missing limb. The dark clouds are mushrooming.

"I'm back," Monica says out of breath. "You promised to stay out of trouble and keep us safe. Now, this!"

"But I had nothing to do with this. I'm upset and feel helpless just like you do."

"Doesn't matter. You've put us in danger enough times before. Somehow this just feels like a sign. Sam, when this is over, I want a divorce. I can't take it anymore. Maybe you had nothing to do with this, but danger seems to be attracted to you, and Evan and I are on the receiving end. I need some space. I need some time off. So I've made a decision. We need to split. You're gone physically anyway. So what difference does it make?"

Silence. He's stunned. "But I'll be back. Frank has a plan. This will work out. After ten good years... I love you. Please give me a chance, give *us* a chance."

"I'm sorry, Sam. It's over." She clicks off.

The dark clouds close in. The thunder begins.

CHAPTER 12
WHAT'S IN THE BOX?

Tossing her sandwich wrapper into the trash can under her desk, Ashaki peeks over the partition, looking left and right. *No Gary — good*. Her next call goes to Max. She uses a secure VOIP connection and spoofs the Caller ID with a code she gave Max earlier, *Hot Chick*. Max's phone vibrates and wriggles where it sits on the bartop in his Tennessee cabin. Max is outside, so Zak picks up. "Yea, what hot chick to whom might I be speaking?"

"Is Max there?" Ashaki asks.

"Not so fast darlin'. I protect Max if you know what I mean."

"If you don't want another kick in the face, you'll put him on the phone."

"Oh, it's you, Ms. Cunt. He's outside practicing with his whip." Zak opens the cabin door and holds the phone at arm's length out into the fall air.

"Huh?" She hears the repeated cracks of Max's thirty-foot bullwhip as he snaps bottles and cans one-by-one off the fence.

Zak puts the phone back to his face. "Hear it? He's busy."

"Well, get your fat ass out there and put him on the phone or next time it will be your balls instead of your face. As if you could tell the difference. Now!"

Zak instinctively covers his crotch and heads over to Max. He extends the phone and sneers. "It's your new girlfriend."

Max takes the phone. "What? I told you my phone might be tapped."

"Nice speaking with you too," she says. "Your phone is tapped. Only it's me doing it. Nobody else is on the line. I guarantee it."

"Not sure how you're doin' that, but OK. What's up?"

"I told you we had a big plan. What I need from you is distribution. A package is coming my way in the next few days. I'll get it to you. Inside will be several smaller packages and instructions. I need you to get those little packages to your buddies around the country fast."

"Hold on there, honey buns."

"What did I tell you about calling me those names?"

"Sorry, can't help myself sometimes. Guess bein' friendly is just in my nature. But I need to know what's in that package."

"Let's just say that once it's deployed, it will kill a whole lot of people. Put it in the right places, and it will do more damage than a hundred of your D.C. attacks. Maybe kill a million Jew bastards and jungle bunnies. Does that work for you?"

"That's fine, but my buddies wouldn't appreciate themselves gettin' killed now, would they?"

"It's perfectly safe if they keep it in the packages and follow the instructions, or are your buddies too chickenshit to make this happen?"

"They ain't chickenshit. They'se just careful like me. I checked you out and the attacks you told me about. You one dangerous bitch and hotter than a popcorn fart for sure."

"That's why you want me on your side, if you get my drift. So are you in or does this scare you too much?"

"I'm gonna take a good look at that package first. If it don't stink, I'll do it."

"OK, good. Just answer your own fuckin' phone from now on when I call." She clicks off with a sneer.

CHAPTER 13
DARK PARIS

"How'd you like to take a trip to Paris?" Rich says, leaning over Michelle's cubicle inside DHS D.C. headquarters.

"Is this business or pleasure?" Michelle asks.

"Could be both, but business first. From our techs, we now know the only possible source of the microwave equipment used in the D.C. attack is a company in Paris. We could have our local agents check it out, but I'd like to see for myself. Besides, Renata's there. If you don't wanna go, she could be my hot date."

"Very funny. You could just order me to go and I'd have no choice, but I love Paris. So sure, when do we leave?"

Rich looks at his watch. "Wheels up in two hours. I've got the company jet on hold at Reagan."

"You don't mess around."

"Only with you."

Ahmed LaSalam, better known as the Leopard, lies prone on the steel table in the cavernous laboratory. The surrounding space is dark, but he and the man and woman in white lab coats are enclosed in a large plastic tent. Bright surgical lights bathe LaSalam's naked new body. A tinge of antiseptic hangs in the air. "He should wake up soon," Dr. Paul Sebastian says to his young assistant, Charissa.

"This one is special, n'est pas?" Charissa asks.

"Yes, it's our boss and this body is not like the others. It's imported from the U.S. Some government type, but that's all I know."

The body stirs. The eyelids flicker and open. The dark gray eyes race side-to-side. "Did it work?" he asks.

"I believe so, Commander. You have a new body," Sebastian says.

LaSalam runs his hands over his chest and stomach. He feels his head and face. Then he stares at his palms and turns his hands over. "Get me a mirror."

Charissa hands him the mirror and LaSalam stares at his new face, feeling the bristly stubble on his chin. He runs his fingers through his black hair. Tilting his head, he sees the six-inch scar on his neck and gently runs his index finger along it. A big smile, more like a sneer, stretches across his lips. "It appears that I am back. Well done, Docteur." He turns his head, scanning the young woman up and down, focusing on her full breasts that stretch the limits of her white uniform. Then he notices her ample lips and begins to feel aroused, a feeling he hasn't had since being shot in Cambridge and relegated to the virtual world. "And who is this?"

The doctor fidgets a bit at the look in LaSalam's eyes, noticing his visible erection. "Why, it's Charissa, my assistant."

"Well, maybe she could help me up, although perhaps she has already done that." LaSalam looks down, admiring his new tool. "Larger than the last one. Help me up."

Sebastian and Charissa lift LaSalam to a sitting position.

"Get me some clothes."

Charissa leaves to fetch the clothing LaSalam had specified in advance, black pants, gray turtleneck, and navy blue jacket. She hands him the clothes. Slipping on the pants, he carefully accommodates the protrusion. "Wouldn't want to get that caught in the zipper. Charissa, perhaps you can help me with this later. If I didn't have so much to do, I'd enjoy getting to know you better now." He looks towards Sebastian. "Is the office set up with the computers I specified?"

"Yes. If you follow me, I'll show you the way. Now that you have a new body, what shall I call you, Commander?"

"Call me Agent DeMarco. As far as you know, I was on a mission to Paris, disappeared with an old friend for a few hours, and will rejoin my team shortly."

"I don't understand. Who is Agent DeMarco?"

"Agent Don DeMarco of the U.S. Department of Homeland Security."

Frank and Sam are in their virtual office together, facing their virtual monitors, pictures and words swirling in the ether around them. "I've done it. It works!" Frank exclaims.

"What, what is it?" Sam asks. "Monica's ready to leave me. Evan's in critical condition. I've got to get back now. Are you saying we're ready?"

"Yes, it's still risky, but I did just conduct a successful test with the mice. You'd be the first human subject," Frank says.

"I don't see what the risk is. If it fails, you still have digital backups of me. You can just restore me in the virtual world. What have I got to lose that I haven't lost already?"

"Sam, the risk is that your proto-physical self could land up stuck in a bad place or disrupt the physical universe with your unplanned presence. You've heard of the butterfly effect – the flapping wings of a butterfly can lead to a series of events, ya-da, ya-da."

"Yes, and I studied Whitehead in grad school. Every series of new events is the result of all the millions of happenings leading up to this very moment with me in this place at this time."

"Correct and your new presence will create a string of new events that are not part of God's grand plan, if you believe in such a thing."

"Let's say there is, or I believed in a grand plan. How do you know my return isn't part of the plan? And likewise, if there is no master plan and events are not predetermined, then we're just exerting our will to make things happen. Since my intentions are only good and I want to save Evan and my marriage, I don't see the moral issue here."

"I think the keyword you used is *intention*. You may mean well, but the *unintended* consequences could be more catastrophic than either of us has the wisdom to anticipate."

"So, it's... *be careful what you wish for*, right?"

"Something like that. Look, I'm not saying don't do this. I just want you to go in eyes-open, knowing what you don't know, and how dangerous it might be for you, your family, and everyone else you encounter."

Sam takes a deep breath. "I understand. Now let's do it."

CHAPTER 14
RENATA

The nondescript government 727 lands at Charles de Gaulle Airport in Paris. The sky is overcast and there is a cool mist in the air, typical September day in Paris. "OK, so now what?" Michelle asks as she slips on a rain jacket.

"Love these overnight flights." Rich suppresses a yawn and looks at his watch – six AM Paris time. "I didn't order a car. Frankly, I don't want anyone from our side knowing we're here."

"Why? Do we have a leak?"

"We always have a leak. Can't be too careful and this case has a lot of moving parts. I just want to keep it small and simple for now. Let's catch a cab."

About thirty minutes later, the City Cab winds through the narrow streets of the 15th Arrondissement and stops at 12 Rue Fenoux in front of a four-story gray stone townhouse. "I thought we were meeting Renata at *Sécurité Intérieure* headquarters?"

"No, this is it. Trust me," Rich says. He presses the black button on the intercom adjacent to the dark oak front door.

A woman's voice crackles over the speaker. "Speak."

"We have delivery. Pizza," Rich says.

"I didn't order any pizza," the voice says.

"It's from Paulie Gee's with ricotta and spinach. Umm, I can smell the garlic." The door buzzes. They enter.

Renata rushes forward and hugs Rich, then Michelle. "I missed you guys." Her face glows and she looks down. "So where's the pizza? I'm hungry."

"It's seven in the morning. Too early for pizza, but I could use a good French croissant and some coffee," Rich says.

"That I can do. Come in. I've got someone I'd like you to meet."

The home is spacious with high ceilings and elaborate crown moldings. The walls are thick plaster with pinkish off-white paint peeling in places. Renata leads Rich and Michelle into the dining room where a massive mahogany table holds a silver coffee pot, china cups, and a tray of croissants. A middle-aged man with gray hair and pointed goatee rises from his chair. Renata waves her hand towards the man. "This is Inspector Voleurdecor, or as we call him, just V. We are working together on the bodyjacking cases in Paris." They shake hands.

"Bonjour Monsieur Little and Mademoiselle Hadar. Renata has told me much about you. It is a pleasure to finally meet you in person. Enchante."

"You as well, Inspector." Rich stuffs a croissant into his mouth.

"Don't mind him. He's food-obsessed," Michelle says.

"Same old Rich." Renata laughs.

"What? I'm just hungry," Rich says, crumbs spilling from his lips.

 They all laugh.

"Director Little, please tell us how we can help you. Renata didn't tell me much," V says.

"Inspector, I know you are aware of the attack on the Congressional Black Caucus in D.C. We believe we have traced the equipment used to a manufacturer somewhere in Paris. Normally I would send local agents, with your office's cooperation, of course, to check it out. But this is highly sensitive. We wanted to come see for ourselves," Rich says.

"I see. Hands-on, like me. I like you already, but I'm not sure how we can help. Our hands are full with the epidemic of bodyjacking cases, which I'm not sure we can contain," V says.

"We understand, but maybe we can help each other. There may even be a link between your problem and ours." Michelle pauses. "We understand you may have made some connection between the bodyjacking operation and the Leopard. Is that correct?"

"I'm not sure I want to talk further about this. Sharing may compromise our investigation. I have helped the Americans before and been *baiser*. Pardon my French."

"I don't understand." Rich puts his hands out, palms-up.

V rises to leave, and Renata grabs his arm. "He said *fucked-over*. He had a bad experience with a joint-operation that went south. Five of his men and women were killed. He naturally is reluctant to work with the Americans. V, hear them out. These are good people. I have worked with them, and nobody knows more about the Leopard than they do."

V hesitates and returns to his chair. "For Renata, I will listen."

"We promise not to endanger your people. We have a lead we want to check out. We didn't want to do it here without looping you in. If you could spare Renata for a couple of hours, we'd be happy to tell you everything we know about the Leopard and assist you in your investigation," Rich says.

V sits silently with his hands folded for a long minute. "Don't, as you say, bend me over. You take Renata and go. When you return, I'd like to ask you some questions about the Leopard."

"You have a deal," Rich says, jamming another croissant into his mouth.

CHAPTER 15
COMING HOME

Bart looks up from his screen as Loretta puts an arm on his shoulder. "How's it coming?"

Bart and Loretta are working in their office at Digital3000, the company they started with Sam and Frank when Sam and Frank were physically alive. It's a sunny day in California. Ribbons of sunlight stream through the narrow office windows and dance on the walls. Bart sips his lukewarm coffee. "I think we've taken this encryption protocol up another notch. It's needed since Quantum Computers are close to being able to crack the gigabit encryption we invented last year." The encryption program Bart and his team created as a side project while working on the digital immortality program has grown into an industry and government standard. It's made Digital3000 a very successful business. "Yep, I think we're close to having terrabit encryption. Let those hacks try to crack this one."

"Ooh, all that geek talk makes me wet," Loretta says. "Just kidding. Don't get any ideas. Have you heard from Sam lately?"

Skype rings on Bart's screen. An image of Sam pops up. "Did you call me?"

Bart laughs. "Were your ears burning? I smell smoke. Are you still spying on me? Wait till I put this new program in place. No more snooping."

"Don't worry. I think it was a coincidence, synchronicity maybe. I'm not good enough to crack your code. Listen, I have some news."

"Uh, oh. Last time that meant trouble," Bart says.

"Where's the positive attitude? Anyway, I'm coming back, physically. Frank has figured out a new technique."

Silence.

Loretta breaks the spell. "Does this mean we'll have to schlepp to Mexico and retrieve another mental patient for you to inhabit?" Loretta asks. "'Cause that whole experience was dangerous and misguided. Don't you think?"

Bart coughs. "Yeah, and I was scared shitless. We love you and Monica and Evan, but I don't think I can do that again."

"Guys, don't worry. It's nothing like that. You don't have to attach probes to my head, revive me, or sneak me through customs. This is all software. Frank's program. If all goes well, I'll explain it to you when I get back. It's risky and never been done before. So, I'd give it 50/50. But if it works, you'll see my pretty face back in the office soon."

"And how soon is *soon*?" Bart asks.

"In about two hours," Sam says.

CHAPTER 16
AGENT DEMARCO

Jonathan sifts through the mound of reports on the conference room table at the DHS Beaver Street office in lower Manhattan. He looks up as the door opens. "Hey partner, good to see you back. How was the vacation?"

"Paris is amazing, but I wouldn't call hanging out with the trade-negotiators a vacation. Came straight from the airport and I'm a little jet-lagged. It's dinner time there," DeMarco says.

"Had to be better than staring at all this stuff." Jonathan picks up and drops a stack of papers.

"Can I help?"

Jonathan grabs a handful of popcorn from a bowl on his desk. The salty burnt-oil scent fills the room. "Sure. Dig in. Check out these field reports from the D.C. incident. Still trying to figure out who was behind it."

"Yeah, sad thing. I heard another one of the Black Caucus members didn't make it, died in the hospital last night."

"It's sick. These reports are just a bunch of bullshit so far. Michelle and Little are in Paris right now trying to track down the manufacturer of the device that sent the sonic attack bomb or wave or whatever you want to call it."

"Oh, really? Any word?"

"They met up with Renata, my old partner, who's working the bodyjacking case in Paris with the UPDC. She thinks there might be a connection. She should be calling any minute. You haven't met her, but she's good people. Don't say I said this, but she's sexy as hell too."

Jonathan's monitor blinks with the incoming Skype call. He clicks the video icon, launching the image of Renata. "Hey, Jon. How's it going there?" Renata asks.

"I was hoping you or Rich or Michelle had something. All I've got is a lot of paper that's good for wiping my ass. Hey Renata, meet my new partner. He doesn't have all your skills, but he's a good guy. Just came back from Paris himself."

Renata waves to them through the video camera. "Nice introduction. Care to tell me the victim, I mean your new partner's name."

The newcomer enters the video frame and waves back. "My name is Don, Don DeMarco. Nice to meet you." He coughs. "Jonathan has told me a lot about you."

"I bet he has. He's probably still pissed he got stuck doing inventory of the evidence on the Cub's case while I got to travel the world trying to solve it," Renata says.

"No hard feelings. I'm just glad our team here in New York caught and killed the bastard."

DeMarco cringes. His new body is effectively hiding his true identity as the Leopard. Still, they're talking about the Cub, Momar LaSalam, his younger brother. These people cut him down a few months ago in New York. And Momar was unflaggingly loyal, the only person in the world he truly trusted, besides his sister Ashaki. The Leopard, now in the body of Don DeMarco, suspects Ashaki may have somehow been involved in his brother's murder.

"Would love to reminisce, but we're under the gun here. We have a working theory that somehow our old nemesis, the Leopard, has a connection to the bodyjacking and maybe to your D.C. case."

Hmm, DeMarco thinks. I had nothing to do with D.C., but they appear to be on my tail in Paris. Being Agent DeMarco and on the inside is going to be even more helpful than I thought to get my revenge. "Renata, can you tell us more about the Leopard connection. Anything to get us out of paper hell here," DeMarco says.

Renata pivots her head to talk to somebody in the background. Then she turns back to Jonathan and Don. "The NSA apparently picked up some chatter a few months ago before the Cub's takedown. It was a conversation between the Cub and the Leopard about the Leopard returning to a physical body. Somehow the Leopard, Ahmed LaSalam, has stolen Frank Einstein's techniques and schematics for returning virtual beings from the dead into new, or I should say, stolen physical bodies. Hence the outbreak of bodyjacking incidents here in Paris."

She knows more than I expected, the Leopard thinks. "Any leads on where he could be?"

"Not yet. We just know he must have a large space to handle all the bodies and equipment. We also have a way to penetrate the blockchain IDs Frank built into the process of taking over the bodies. So we can track any new bodyjackings back to the source. But once we set up the traces, the bodyjacking stopped. All we know is that they did one more. We raided the facility where we traced it to and it was a large warehouse with some medical equipment left behind. We found some dead bodies, naked and piled up like fish. It was disgusting, but apparently, the operation had packed up and gone."

I'm still a step ahead, DeMarco thought. "And do you know where that one bodyjacked victim went?"

"We think he or she is quite possibly in New York now," Renata says.

Jonathan stands up and starts pacing. "Wow. Here in New York? Text me what you have and we can try to track him down. And how do you make a connection to D.C.?"

"Sure, I'll send you what we have. And yeah, the link to D.C. is a loose assumption for now. The fact that the equipment used in that D.C. attack came from Paris and the bodyjacking outbreak is happening in Paris may be more than a coincidence."

"I get it. Connected or not, I'd like to get out of this office and nail that bastard. Don, ready to hit the streets?" Jonathan puts on his jacket and holsters his Glock.

"I'm with you partner," DeMarco says. *If he only knew.*

CHAPTER 17
THE RETURN

"Are you ready?" Frank swivels in his virtual chair and looks at Sam.

Sam checks his watch, 3:20 PM. His eyelids won't stop twitching. "I'm anxious, but I'm ready. No physical body this time? No waking up in Mexico, night sweats, or multiple personality issues, right?"

"The experience will be totally different this time, but I told you there are risks. This is very new and almost like sci-fi. I'm not sure what problems you may encounter. Just report back to me no matter what."

"OK. When it's done, will I have a body? Will I be able to hold Monica in my arms? Will I be able to read to Evan in bed? Will I be able to feel things?"

"Yes and no. As far as anyone can tell by looking, you will have a physical body. Monica and Evan will be able to touch you and feel you. But in some sense, you will be like a hologram – there and not there. This time we are using our quantum computer, Sylvia, and a crack in time to bring you back. I've based this on quantum objective reduction. That's the theory that the material world is not really made up of material but of information. Simply put, it's *Bits-to-It* and tag, you're *It*. I'm not sure what you will feel, but you will be 99% real."

"Hmm, 99%, really? What's the other 1%?"

"I'm sure you'll find out. Once you are on the other side, I need you to tell me everything – what you see, what you feel, everything. If necessary, I may be able to tune and tweak your experience from here."

"The more we talk, the more I'm questioning this. But Evan's in the hospital and Monica is leaving me. I don't think I have a choice."

"I understand you're anxious. Think of this as a kind of superpower. You may be able to do more than you anticipate."

"And maybe less. But enough of my glass-half-empty anxiety. Let's do it."

"OK. I'm going to have to suspend your digital self to make this work. So for a short time, you will not exist anywhere."

"You mean I'll be dead, dead?"

"In a sense, that's true. However, if all goes well, you will wake up at the Digital3000 office. I had Bart prepare the needed physical equipment on their end to make this happen."

"So it's kind of like a transporter?"

"Not really. We're moving your digital self to a time-based reality. Kind of like a movie where the characters step off the screen. Maybe once you experience it you can come up with a better analogy. Until then..."

Frank swivels back and clicks a few buttons. A green progress bar appears on both his and Sam's screens, inching slowly to the right.

Sam sees, from his reflection on the screen, that his face is turning pale gray. "Wait! What are you...?" His image fades and disappears.

All that remains is an empty chair and the progress bar on the screen – *76% Done*.

CHAPTER 18
DIGITAL3000

It's late afternoon. Bart turns down the fluorescents in the office lab, leaving only a spotlight on the chair. That chair is an antique dentist's chair salvaged from an estate sale, refitted with the wires and circuit boards needed to perform his task. The whole apparatus connects to a scaled-down G-Wave X2 Quantum Computer, affectionately named *Sylvia*, in the environmentally-controlled adjacent room. The computer is kept at near absolute zero or minus 460 degrees Fahrenheit, minus 273 degrees Celsius, to allow for the frictionless super-conductivity of the electrons that will convert Sam's digital-self into the first-ever, time-based lifeform.

Loretta and Juan quietly enter the lab. "Are we ready yet?" Loretta asks.

Bart smirks. "Only if you brought popcorn." He busily checks all the wire connections to the chair. "Just waiting for the signal from Frank. Should only be a few minutes. It's probably best if you stand behind that tungsten partition. You can watch through the small helium filled window." Bart is uncertain of the side-effects or possible radiation from this experiment. Better to be safe.

Loretta and Juan move behind the barrier. Frank Einstein's face flickers to life on the overhead monitor. "Good afternoon, Bart. Are you all set?"

Bart's hands are visibly shaking as he tightens the last connection. "I think so, I mean, I hope so. Are you sure this is going to work?"

"No, but I'd give it a 70% chance based on our experiments with Eli, the mouse. Remember Colin Powell's 40/70 rule?"

"I know if the chance of success is between 40 percent and 70 percent, you should move ahead. Because you may never reach 100 percent certainty, right?"

"And just like in battle, if you wait until you're 100 percent sure, you may lose the war before you even enter the battle."

Bart lets out a deep breath. "OK. We're ready."

"I have Sam in a suspended state. I'm ready for the last step. Get behind the barrier."

Bart looks up and stirs like coming out of a trance. He jogs around the barrier. Loretta grasps his hand tightly. They peer at the monitor through their small window. The screen displays a countdown, 10... 9... 8... "Wait, Wait!" Bart yells.

7... 6... 5... "What is it?" Frank asks in a wavering voice." 4... 3... and the countdown freezes on 2..., the '2' just blinking."

"I smell something burning. Maybe it's a loose wire. Is it safe? Can I fix it?" Bart asks.

"Yes. I see it now. That's a primary. If that remained partially connected, we might have lost Sam forever and you would have been bombarded with deadly neutrinos going right through that barrier."

Bart, still behind the barrier, is sweating now. "You're shitting me?"

Frank half-laughs. "Yeah, I made up that part about the neutrinos, but the danger to Sam is real. You can safely go and fix the wire now. Let's get this thing done."

Bart shuffles with knees wobbling to the dentist's chair. Spotting the half-dangling red wire, he reconnects it. He double-checks the others and darts behind the barrier. "I think we're good now."

"Here we go," Frank says. 2... 1...

Nothing.

"What's happening?" Juan asks.

"I don't know," Bart says. "Looks more like the *Lost Picture Show* than *Invasion of the Body Snatchers*."

"Be patient," Frank snaps. "I need to make a few adjustments. Hopefully, we haven't lost him. Here we go again."

They all focus on the monitor. 5... 4... 3... 2... A faint bluish glow materializes in the dentist's chair. The overhead lights dim and blink as the power surges. A shape starts to take form, yellow around the edges, then blue. Then the room goes dark for a very long six seconds. The lights flicker back on and a man is motionless in the chair. That smell of burning wires is now overwhelming. The man turns his head towards the barrier. "Bart, Loretta, Juan?" he asks.

"Hold your places," Frank insists. "I'm checking the radiation readings in the room. Just one more minute."

"Frank, did I make it?" the man asks.

"Sam, hold still. I'm checking the safety of the room. Once it's clear, Bart and Loretta will come over to check you. Just stay there."

Total silence, except for the audible buzz of the fluorescents.

"OK, it's safe now," Frank says.

Bart and Loretta rush to the chair. "Sam, it's you and it looks like you!" Loretta plants a kiss on Sam's forehead.

Bart smiles and places the flat end of a stethoscope on Sam's chest. His face turns ashen. He looks up at Frank on the monitor. "I don't get it. No heartbeat, just a low humming sound."

"That's what I expected," Frank says. "I think that's *normal*. If I can use that word. Some of his new body is like you and me. He has skin and blood. He should be able to see, feel, and taste. But he has no fingerprints and his heart hums instead of beats. He is the first of his kind, Sam 3.0 if you will. I expect some bugs in his software, hopefully nothing major. I guess we'll find out."

<hr>

I unclose my eyes. The room is out of focus like there is thick morning fog. I hear clicking sounds and footsteps. A face hovers over me. Bart slowly comes into focus. "Am I alive?" I run my hands down my sides and then along the sides of my head and face. "I can feel. It's me, right?"

Frank clears his throat. "99 percent, just like we said it would be. You wanted to *feel* again and now you can. You are alive, just in a different way than the rest of physical humanity."

I swing my legs off the chair and try to stand. My knees buckle, but I steady myself, clasping the arm of the chair. Then standing erect, I take a long slow breath and laugh. "It's good to be back."

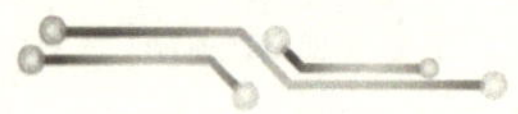

CHAPTER 19
JUAN

"It's good to see you again," Juan says.

I tentatively take some steaming coffee from the office's Keurig. We are sitting in Digital3000's kitchen. "Umm, the taste of coffee. How I missed that." I sniff the aroma swirling from the coffee and take a bigger gulp. I'm all smiles.

"How do you feel?" Juan asks.

"I feel everything. I feel wonderful. I've got to call Monica and tell her if she'll speak to me."

"Is there a problem at home?"

"Yeah, I'd say so. On the last call, she was so exasperated by all this craziness, she actually said she wants to divorce me. I'm going to try to change her mind. I need to change her mind. I have to."

"Good luck, Amigo. But let me know if it doesn't work out. I really like Monica." Juan smirks. I punch him in the arm, hard.

"Ouch, I was only kidding."

"You agreed to stay clear of her. Remember." I take a deep breath. "Now tell me about you. Did you go to Guadalajara and face your old tormentor, Alvarez?"

"I did."

"And?"

"Let's just say he won't be using that asylum to pimp out young children to dirty old men or drug companies anymore."

"Did you kill him?"

"No, that would have been too kind. I wanted him alive enough to reflect on his sins. Oh, and he won't be having any children of his own. Las herramientas se han ido, por así decirlo."

"English, please."

"His tools are gone, if you know what I mean."

I smile. "What goes around..."

"Karma's a bitch," Juan says.

"Your English has gotten pretty good."

"Working for Loretta has taught me a lot and not just English. You know what I'm sayin'."

"Really – you and Loretta? I thought she was married to this place, but I'm glad to hear it."

"Yes, is good. Hey listen, I asked Bart and Loretta about this. You still have enemies out there and as long as you're physically with us, you're going to need protection. They can spare me for a while. So I'd like to offer my services."

"As my bodyguard?"

"Yes, bodyguard and friend. What did you think – as your valet? No gracias." Juan pauses and studies me. "We have a kind of connection, you and me."

"Let me think about that." I hesitate for all of two seconds. "Sounds like a good idea. And this time, I suppose we'll get along better as two people rather than one. OK, I thought about it. Let's do it." I offer my hand and Juan shakes it. I feel a kind of warmth and energy coming through Juan's hand and flowing into me. *Hmm?*

"Y eres mas fuerte," Juan says.

CHAPTER 20

EINSTEIN'S WORLD

Nancy Lu glances at the wall clock, 4:00. Her smiling face appears on the screen. She is sitting at a small table at the Channel 8 Studio in New York, dressed in a dark blue suit, loose low-cut beige blouse and Jimmy Choo shoes. The camera zooms in for a close-up of her face. "Tonight I have the privilege of interviewing Frank Einstein, the father of digital immortality. Dr. Einstein has agreed to speak with me about the benefits and challenges of this new technology. Welcome, Dr. Einstein."

The camera pans up to reveal a monitor above Nancy's table with the face of a tired-looking professor, Frank Einstein. "It's a pleasure to be here."

Lu: Tell me about why and how you created your digital mind and digital immortality.

Dr. E: OK. I have always been fascinated and had a lifelong dream about the possibilities of a brain-to-computer connection. I suppose it's because I grew up reading sci-fi and later became both an M.D. and a neuroscientist. Any scientist worth his or her salt continually asks the question, "What if . . . ?" or "What could be?"

Lu: So, how did that translate into your current work and accomplishments?

Dr. E: I'll try to make a long story very short. Working both as a professor at B.U. and under a DARPA grant, I was studying the possibilities of merging mind and computer. At first, it started as a data puzzle. The mind stores data in the form of facts and memories inside synapses and neurons. The initial problem was how to move brain data into digital form.

Lu: Were you successful and where did that lead?

Dr. E: Umm, unfortunately, as we were making real progress, my wife was killed in a tragic automobile accident. I was consumed by grief for about six months. More importantly, I lost the desire and passion to go on. You need a real fire in the belly to succeed at this kind of research. Susan was the love of my life and my raison *d'etre*. I couldn't stop grieving. Luckily, I still have my daughter, Sarah. Otherwise, I may have just ended it all right then and there.

Lu: What changed that got you back on track?

Dr. E: Right about that time, I met this crazy entrepreneur. He had done some Internet work on a site called InTheEventOfMyDeath. info where members can scrapbook their lives, save last wishes, etc. This wacko guy asked a big *What If* question. "What if we could actually upload people's personalities, memories, and emotions so they could live on digitally forever?" When he heard a little bit about my work, a mutual friend put us together over coffee. I was alive physically then and really loved the aroma and taste of good coffee. Anyway, we hit it off and decided to pursue this utterly fantastic mission of the digital brain together.

Lu: But wait. You were working under a DARPA grant. So I have two questions. First, why was the military interested enough to fund your work? Second, weren't you bound to keep it secret and confidential?

Dr. E: Excellent questions, Ms. Lu. First, the scope of my work, initially with DARPA, was limited to the brain-to-computer data transfer problem. Little did I know at the time, and this is now public knowledge so I can speak about it, that the military really wanted to develop Cyber Warriors. They wanted digital soldiers who could carry out far deadlier attacks by being inside the system than any talented hacker could perform from the outside.

Second, my entrepreneur partner and I realized the real power of this idea was more than just data transfer. If we could upload memories and emotions, in short an entire personality, people might be able to live online digitally forever. Digital Immortality— a real Digital Brain. We both shared a vision to do something good for people, not to create new weapons. With some talented lawyers, I was able to extricate myself from DARPA. Together with my new partner, we started Digital3000, a company devoted to providing digital immortality for the greater good. Could you imagine someday, watching your great, great granddaughter's soccer game? Reading them bedtime stories? Carrying on your research work forever? What if Jonas Salk, Albert Einstein, and Thomas Edison, not to mention Charlie Chaplin, could have lived on forever digitally? Can you imagine what the world would be like now?

Lu: That's a big idea for sure. But then something tragic happened to you. Can you share that with us?

Dr. E: Yes, can you smell wires burning? We formed the company, advanced the research and had already uploaded a few personalities, including mine. I was working on solving one of the many unexpected problems that arose, namely real people going *mshuge* when they met their digital replicas. At that moment, an assassin burst into our lab, shot up the place, and murdered me, at least my physical self, in the process. The next thing I knew, I woke up in the Cloud as a digital form of myself. My partner and Bart had brought me back to life digitally. We were under attack. So we had to shift our focus to tracking down what turned out to be malicious terrorists bent on both ours and the country's destruction. Most of this was in the news, as you know.

Lu: So you are real heroes. As the news reported, you were instrumental in tracking down and stopping the attacks and the attackers.

Dr. E: We may have been heroes, but at significant cost. And, this wasn't in the news, but I don't believe the threat is over. I don't believe we have caught all the attackers, and I wouldn't doubt they are regrouping and working on some other nefarious plan. We are continuing our research but wouldn't be surprised to find ourselves in the middle of another crisis soon.

Lu: Well, that's sobering for sure. You said you are continuing your research. What are you working on?

Dr. E: For both personal and more significant reasons, we are researching how to bring a digital person back to a physical form. This is way more complex than just uploading to the Cloud. It requires translating digital into biological. I think this may be a long, hard, maybe even impossible task. But then again, I've theoretically got forever to figure it out. There's also a host of ethical problems around this, like does it require taking over someone else's body? Is there a class of healthy candidates willing to participate? There are many more issues like this that we could discuss another time.

Lu: Wait, I know that you were able to do this with your partner and bring him back in another's body.

Dr. E: I'd rather not talk about that. It was an experiment. It failed. We had to undo it.

Lu: But isn't it true, Doctor, that whatever you developed to bring people back was stolen and is now in the hands of international terrorists?

Dr E: What? Where did you hear that? I thought we discussed what was going to be in this interview and you never mentioned this.

Lu: Doctor, I'm an investigative reporter. I have sources in Paris that claim your technology is currently being deployed in the crime of bodyjacking. Unwilling victims are having their bodies stolen and taken over by wealthy people willing to pay. Would you like to comment?

Dr. E: I didn't expect this and I can't say I'm happy about it. These reports are just rumors. Our goals at Digital3000 are to develop these technologies for the betterment of humankind. I feel like we are midwives bringing forth something that was going to happen one way or another. I believed if *we* did it, we could build in safeguards against abuse.

Lu: If you built in safeguards, why is this happening? Is it like the discovery of nuclear power? Did the scientists of the Manhattan Project build in safeguards?

Dr E: I don't like what you're suggesting. It's not the same thing, but I will tell you we built in a way to track anyone using our technology. That's all I'm prepared to say for now. This is the last interview you will ever do with me.

Frank Einstein's image on the monitor turns to static white. Nancy Lu's face flushes red momentarily. She gathers herself and swivels her chair towards the camera. "That was Dr. Frank Einstein discussing his controversial inventions. I also think we may have broken some news here tonight. Until next time, this is Nancy Lu for The World Exposed."

The red light on the camera goes dark. Nancy rises and unclasps her lapel mic. Her producer, Ansley Wright, comes over and hugs her. Nancy straightens her skirt and sweeps the hair out of her eyes. "That was rough. I think I may have lost some friends."

"It was just great," Ansley says. "I can't wait to see the ratings and I'm sure it will go viral."

Nancy looks down at her shoes. "Great – just what we all wanted."

CHAPTER 21
SICK

Jonathan throws a stack of papers across the room. The air conditioning kicks in with a thud in the thick-aired conference room at DHS's Beaver Street office. "I'm not sure how much more of this I can handle. Wanna grab a late lunch?"

"Yeah," DeMarco says. "But first there's something I want to catch on the news." He glances at his watch. "Turn on Channel 8."

Jonathan taps the remote and the wall monitor flickers to life. *The World Exposed* logo shows on the screen, an illustration of the earth protruding from an open trench coat. The crawl at the bottom reads *Interview With Frank Einstein Coming Up…* "Why's this interest you?"

"It's relevant, isn't it? He's the scientist that came up with this digital-mind-to-body stuff Renata is working on. Maybe we'll learn something."

Jonathan rocks back on the rear two legs of his chair as the Nancy Lu interview with Dr. Einstein begins. The Leopard's face turns ashen, reliving the horror and frustration from the man behind both his and his brother's deaths. If hate had a color, it would be the Leopard's face.

"You don't look so good, my friend," Jonathan says.

"Must be something I ate," DeMarco says. "I'll be right back." He hurries from the conference room, slamming the door behind him. In the far stall of the men's room, he throws up. *Weak*, he thinks. *He'll pay. They'll all pay.*

DeMarco splashes some cold water on his face and returns. The interview is over, and Jonathan looks up from the mess of papers. "Are you OK?"

"Better now. Anything new?"

"Yeah, I just got a text from Renata on the bodyjacking lead here in New York. Let's go. You probably couldn't eat lunch anyway."

DeMarco grabs his maroon jacket from the chair and looks up at the blank monitor. He stares as if in a trance. Jonathan tugs on his sleeve. "C'mon. Let's go."

DeMarco follows Jonathan down the hall, dodging a janitor mopping the floor, the scent of Lysol interrupting his thoughts. "Where are we going?"

"East Village. I have the address. Not far from here."

They hit a little traffic. Twenty-two minutes later, Jonathan finds a parking spot near the Blind Barber on 10th Street. "It's number 337." They walk a half-block alongside Tompkins Square Park. Jonathan stops and turns, facing a narrow brick four-story walk-up. "This is it—top floor."

There's no security in the building in this yet-to-be-gentrified neighborhood. The muddy black-and-white tiled entrance says 1920s. They climb the steps to the fourth floor, the hallway wreaking of last night's onions. Jonathan points and they straddle the door of apartment 42. Guns drawn, Jonathan nods and DeMarco knocks lightly on the door.

Nothing.

Jonathan knocks harder and they hear footsteps inside, then quiet again. Jonathan swivels facing the door. "I smell smoke, how about you?"

DeMarco smiles. "Beats no warrant."

"Police!" Jonathan kicks in the door and it flies off the hinges. They enter, sweeping left and right. A small curly-haired toddler sits on a blanket, chewing his teddy bear's ear. He starts crying at the sudden intrusion.

"Where's your dad?" Jonathan says, without expecting much. The child continues to whimper.

"Right here." A large man with full-arm tattoos appears from a closet behind them, pointing a double-barrel shotgun. "What the fuck do you want bursting in here like that and scaring us half to death?"

Jonathan and Don pivot, both aiming their Glocks at the man. Jonathan slowly lowers his gun. "We're not here to cause any trouble. We just have a few questions."

The man seems unsure but lowers his weapon a few inches in kind. "This better be good and you guys better fix that door when we're done. This isn't the greatest neighborhood."

"We'll have someone take care of that," Jonathan says. "Is there somewhere we can talk?"

The man waves the gun left and right. "Right here is fine. This gun gots one mother-fuckin' bullet for each of you. So make it quick."

"OK," Jonathan says, lowering his gun to his side. "Please lower your gun, sir. Someone might get hurt." Jonathan looks at Don and he lowers his weapon as well.

The man uncocks the dual hammers on his shotgun. "Now, what is it?"

"I'm not sure how to put this other than to come right out with it. Do you know anything about stolen bodies?"

The man's expression darkens. His skin glows bright red. "What about it?"

DeMarco thinks, *If the man didn't know anything about it, he'd think Jonathan's question was crazy. His response means he knows something. This is trouble.*

"Well, what do you know?" Jonathan persists.

The man doesn't answer for a minute but raises the shotgun slightly. "What's it worth to you?"

Without hesitation, DeMarco raises his Glock and fires three bullets into the man, one to the head and two in the chest. The man's expression is stunned. Amazingly, he is still standing until a few seconds later crumples to the floor. The toddler wails. Jonathan is just as stunned as the victim and fires a knife-sharp stare at DeMarco. "What did you do that for?"

DeMarco raises his voice over the crying child's. "Didn't you see? He was raising his weapon."

"Couldn't you see he wasn't a threat?"

"I couldn't take the chance," DeMarco says.

Jonathan bends over the victim and feels his neck. "Call an ambo. He's still alive. Then call child services." Jonathan puts pressure on the man's chest wounds to slow the bleeding. Warm red blood seeps through his fingers.

DeMarco pretends to call for an ambulance. "We need a bus at 337 10th, apartment 42 ASAP. Victim critical GSW," he says hurriedly into dead air. Then he actually dials child services and gets put on hold. He picks up the child and cradles him in one arm, bouncing lightly to calm him. In the other hand he holds the phone to his ear. He looks at Jonathan and mouths, "On hold." He turns to the child who is now quietly resting his head on the Leopard's shoulder. He purposely blocks the child's view of his father bleeding out on the floor. *I couldn't take the chance.*

CHAPTER 22
LOVELY FACE

Jonathan pushes off with his feet, rolling his chair back towards DeMarco's desk. "Drop your weapon in the bag. Not sure why they didn't take it from you at the scene. You know there will be a review. Boss will want to see you when he gets back. I still don't know what you were thinking."

DeMarco pulls the clip and drops the gun and clip into the bag. "I know. Maybe I panicked a little, but I just kept staring at that shotgun. When he started to raise it again, I reacted." He raises his hand and fakes a tremble.

Jonathan's expression softens. "OK. Why don't you take the rest of the day off? Calm your nerves and be back here first thing tomorrow for the review. Might not see active duty for a bit."

"That's probably a good idea. It's quittin' time anyway. I just want to check something with the analysts on seven first. Then I'll go. Thanks, pal." DeMarco jumps up and heads towards the elevators.

Jonathan swivels back to his desk but suddenly turns back. "Wait, what are you checking?"

DeMarco is already in the elevator with doors closing, out of earshot.

The elevator opens on the seventh floor. It's DeMarco's first time here as a new man, but his tech team told him she'd be here. There is no reception desk, just rows of cubicles surrounded by offices and small conference rooms along the outer walls. On the opposite wall are glass doors through which he sees rows of computer servers on tall racks. He spots a young woman, purple streaked hair and thick pink-rimmed glasses. "Excuse me. Could you tell me where I might find Ms. Lamont?" DeMarco asks.

The woman keeps typing and doesn't look up. "You mean Adele?"

He intentionally acts nervous and shy. "Yes, I think that's her first name."

The woman points a thumb over her shoulder and continues pecking at her keyboard.

DeMarco follows her direction, reading the nameplates one-by-one on the cubicles. The fifth one says A. Lamont. He takes a deep breath. Here dwells his sister whom he hasn't seen in years. He relishes the idea he knows her, but she won't be able to recognize him in his new body. He peeks around the corner of her partition. "Ms. Lamont?"

Ashaki quickly blanks her screen, replacing the surveillance images of Max with a phony spreadsheet screensaver. She looks up with a neutral expression. "Who are you?"

"I'm Don DeMarco from Division 5. We're working a case and I wondered if you could help me." She looks as striking as ever with her hazel eyes and light brown skin. He smiles, remembering their time together when she was younger. *I'd like to taste that again*, he thinks.

She glances at the ID dangling from his shirt pocket. "All requests go through my boss, Gary Conrad. Besides, I'm busy now." Ashaki turns back to her screen.

He finally has what he was looking for, confirmation he's found his sister, the woman who betrayed his brother Momar and is now working for the enemy. He's like a shark who smells blood in the water. "Hmm, busy with what you hid on your screen when I walked in. A little fun and games, I suppose? I wonder if your boss would appreciate that."

Ashaki flushes for a nano-second. "It's none of your business, Top Secret. She hesitates. "... But I don't need the hassle. What do you want?"

He grins. *Got you.* "We're helping Renata Fermi with a case in Paris involving multiple bodyjackings. Do you know what that is?"

"I've heard. So what do you want from me?"

"I'd like you to share any files you have on that with me. Here's my ID and system name."

"I'll have to check your clearance first. I should have it in a few days."

"Unfortunately, that won't do." The Leopard steps forward and drives the heel of his shoe into Ashaki's foot, pinning it to the floor. "This is time-sensitive. Make it a priority and get it to me today or I'll have a little chat with your boss."

Ashaki grimaces. She's dealt with his type before. "I'll see what I can do. Now get off my fucking foot."

He grinds his heel in harder before releasing her foot. "Just make it happen. Put it in my box." He takes a finger and pushes the hair away from Ashaki's eyes. "You have a lovely face." He turns and leaves.

Ashaki slumps down in her chair.

CHAPTER 23
THE PLAN

"You received the package?"

"I was just fixin' dinner. Can you smell the chili?"

"The package, dickwad?"

"I did and I looked inside."

"And?" Ashaki says to the image of Max on her screen.

"Bunch of vials and other shit," Max says through his scraggly beard and beet-red face.

"All you need to do is get it to your guys in the field and then I'll send instructions. Just tell them not to open the vials until they hear from you. I wouldn't want any of you fellas to get hurt."

"Why you're so considerate. Look, I don't mind a little shootin', or burnin', or what have you, but this is dangerous shit you sent."

"You're damn right it is. That's the idea. Are you goin' to chicken out on me now? I thought you had a pair, or was I wrong?"

"Listen darlin', I ain't gettin' any of my boys killed helping you get off on some crazy scheme."

"And here I thought you were a man of your word, a man on a mission to punish those who have infected this great country with their foreign germs. Well, maybe this will help convince you. You can see me on your screen, right?"

"Yeah, I can see you."

"Well then take a look at this..."

Max looks on as the image switches from Ashaki's face to an aerial view of his cabin in Tennessee. "Can you see yourself? Wave."

"What the hell is this?"

"Oh, I didn't tell you I have access to drones? My bad. What you're seeing is my drone's eye view of your cabin. See this button..." The image changes to a view of a red toggle switch next to her keyboard. "I flip this little lever and two Hellfire missiles blow you and your clubhouse to kingdom come. Pretty cool, eh?"

Beads of sweat form on Max's brow. "You are one crazy bitch."

"Why, thank you. That's the nicest thing anyone has said to me all day. So do we have a deal? You will follow through with the plan or ...?"

No answer. Max is stone-cold silent.

Ashaki smiles. "I'll take that as a *yes*." She clicks off.

Don DeMarco takes Jonathan's cue and leaves for the day. He retreats to his small apartment and office on 27th Street. Nothing too fancy or elaborate this time, not like when he had a lab downtown full of computer hackers raining havoc on the U.S. Air Traffic Control system. No, this time, he needs to stay under the radar. No leaks, no complications. He throws his briefcase on the bed and drops into his Aeron chair. The pleasing scent of the lilies in the vase next to his monitor reminds him of something. Shuffling the mouse, he wakes up his computer. He clicks an icon and his untraceable Tor browser comes up. A few more strokes and he enters his Linux environment and logs in. One more click and the image of his sister appears. She's videoconferencing with some bearded weirdo. What's she up to? He listens. *A package, vials, drone, or else.* Hmm. This is quite interesting. She appears to be carrying out her own plan.

Maybe I can use this to my advantage. Perhaps I don't need to kill her yet. The Leopard conjures an image of her as a young girl. How sweet she was. *I thought I'd punch that ticket again and then get rid of her, but this is too good. Maybe two birds with one stone, she being stone number two.* He sets her screen to record and clicks away. A few other adjustments here to keep her from suspecting or tracing him. Good, that should do it. He slaps his hands on his thighs and heads to the bathroom. Splashing cold water on his face, he looks into his new gray eyes and smiles. *I like this new face.*

CHAPTER 24
MONICA

Somehow this new process of returning to a physical body has totally wiped me out. I can't remember fatigue like this before, ever. Hopefully, my exhaustion is temporary and not a chronic state of my new physical form. After some warm hugs and briefly speaking with Bart and Loretta, my first instinct is to go home. But then I remember Monica is still in a D.C. hospital by Evan's side. I've got to get to D.C. and I must go to New York. But I need rest first. Collapsing on the red leather couch in my old office, I do something I have not been able to do while I was digital, fall asleep and dream.

My California home looks comfortably the same. The gravel driveway, the weeping cherry out front, and the pale stucco that always seems to need a paint job. I pull up in my old Jeep that Loretta has thankfully kept for me at the office. Tilting the rearview mirror, this time I look like myself, the man Monica married. Not like Juan or anyone else. My hands tremble. *What will Monica think? Can I save my marriage?*

Ascending the slate steps, I can hear the sounds of laughter inside. I rap the brass knocker on the front door. Monica, still grinning from her tickle session with Evan, swings the thick wooden door open. Her expression morphs. The smile evaporates, replaced by mouth and eyes wide open.

She stops breathing. Then, "Sam!"

Petey, our American Pit Bull Terrier, skids on the tile floor and rushes at me, slamming into my shins, almost knocking me over. I reach down and scratch him behind his ears and under his chin. Petey barks and backs off. A low growl follows.

"Monica, how I've missed you." I step inside and take both of Monica's hands. Tears roll down her cheeks. I try to pull her closer, but she resists. Finally, I relax my grip and she steps forward and wraps her arms around me.

"I thought I'd never see you again, I mean physically, in real life," she says.

"I had the same belief, but I never gave up hope. Frank made it happen and here I am now for good, forever with you if you'll have me."

She backs away and looks me up and down. "Come out back. Let's talk."

"Where's Evan? I want to see him."

"I think he went upstairs. No school today. So he's probably playing video games. We need to talk first."

We head through the kitchen. Smells like a roast is in the oven. Monica slides open the glass door leading to the deck I built last year with my neighbor's help. I look down to inspect the planks. "I think I need to put another coat of sealant on the wood."

"I think we have more important things to discuss, don't you?"

I suck in a deep breath. "I suppose."

"Let's start with how you got back here. What did Frank do?"

"It's complicated, but essentially he was able to trick Time using a quantum computer and pull my body back from the past into the present. At the same time, he updated my physical brain with everything new that had been stored digitally since I was murdered in the lab last year. *Bits-to-It*, as Frank likes to say. But it's me. It's really me." I take Monica's hand. "I can feel your warmth." I raise her hands to my lips and kiss them, "... and you can feel me, I hope."

"It looks like you, the original Sam, and sounds like you, but I don't know what to believe anymore. Your story keeps getting crazier by the minute. I want to believe it's you, but I feel like I need some time."

"But no divorce, right? I mean take as much time as you need, but I love you and need you. I don't want to... I mean I can't lose you."

"We'll see. You can sleep in the spare bedroom for now."

"Not quite what I wished for, but I understand. I'm sorry for all the craziness. Now it will be better. I promise."

"But when does all this crazy shit end?"

"It ends when it ends."

"That makes me feel better. As I said, I just need some time. Now, go see your son. Dinner's in an hour."

I lean forward to kiss Monica and she turns her head away. I back off and head back through the kitchen door. I take one more look at the deck. "I really do need to do something about that floor." Then I wake up.

CHAPTER 25
NYPD

The New York Police Department has yet to set up a unit dedicated solely to bodyjacking. They are aware of the problem and keeping an eye on it, but as far as the brass are concerned, it's France's problem. However, after 9/11, the NYPD built up a counterterrorism task force that rivals its counterparts in entire developed countries. Renata has been in touch with Ann Nickolay in the counterterrorism unit, keeping her informed. She has a hunch New York City is next on the list for the international ring she is tracking. Now she has a hard lead to support her conviction.

"I've gotten authorization to work with you. I can't promise a lot, but I can give you two of my agents from our joint task force, Tony Lizzi and Jackie Tansky. We call them Click and Clack," Ann says.

Renata snorts. "Why Click and Clack?"

"Tony is a computer nerd and Jackie has a keychain with what must be a hundred keys, for no discernible reason, that jangles when she walks. So *Click* and *Clack*."

"Anyway, I was hoping for more, but once your guys see what I've seen in Paris, your boss's tune may change. OK, I texted you a heads-up and now I have an address in Brooklyn," Renata says.

"I'll have my guys check it out after dinner."

"Where's the sense of urgency? You gettin' soft over there? Have them pick up dinner on the way unless you want some zombies shooting up your city."

"Zombies, really? I'm trying to be helpful here. Don't give me a load of crap. We get threats and leads every day. We still gotta eat and sleep."

"You mean like you slept through 9/11?"

"That's a cheap shot. You know how much things have changed here, how much we have ramped up. Just like you guys."

"Well then, act like it and get your guys over there forthwith. I want reports every thirty minutes and sooner if something happens." She clicks off.

Ann speaks into the dead air. "Yes, ma'am... bitch."

Clack steers their black Dodge Charger into a loading zone on Presidents Street in Brooklyn.

Click takes a big bite of his taco. Oil dribbles down his chin onto his white shirt. "Doesn't look like much to me. Just a bunch of warehouses. Quiet as you'd expect at twilight."

"You're gettin' it all over yourself and those onions are stinking up the car. Finish the fucking taco and get the drone ready."

Click looks down at the grease stains on his shirt. "Shit. My wife's going to kill me."

"That's if I don't kill you first."

He takes the last bite and wipes his mouth with his sleeve. Reaching over the back seat and retrieving a small brown box, he holds up the Mavic mini-drone, which is no bigger than a bee. "OK. Bumble ready."

"Hand me the controller. I see an open window on the second story. I'll send her up."

Click opens the passenger-side window and extends his arm with Bumble nestled in his hand. "Ready, Command One."

Clack smiles. "Copy that good buddy." She maneuvers the joystick and Bumble rises and flies to the open window of the brick warehouse across the street. They watch the laptop monitor affixed to the dashboard between them. "Entering location to get a better view."

They both stare in disbelief at the screen. "Holy shit. We better report this," Click says. He types a few commands on the keyboard and dials his cell. "Agent Fermi, it's Tony Lizzi. You need to see this."

"Patch me in," Renata says.

"You're in. First visual. Now thermal," he says.

They all watch silently as Bumble circles the rafters recording the horrific nightmare unfolding before their eyes.

Clack holds Bumble steady with a wide-angle view of the warehouse floor. Rows of bodies lie on silver metal tables covered by white sheets, their faces exposed. "Are they dead?" Clack asks.

"No, not if this is like Paris. Notice their complexions, not white or ashen. They look alive, but they have been drugged. I believe they are awaiting their new personalities," Renata says.

"What. What are you talking about?" Click asks.

Renata hesitates. "I guess you haven't been read in. What kind of clearance do you guys have?"

Click and Clack look at each other. Clack, aka Jackie, answers, "We're Level 3, ma'am."

"I guess this will have to do. This is Top Secret, which means it's above your clearance. But if you're going to be any help here, you need to know what's going on." Renata gives them a two-minute CliffsNotes version of her investigation into bodyjacking.

"Holy crap," Click says. "Computers and cellphones blew my mind when they were invented, but this... This is dystopian sci-fi shit."

"Get a grip," Clack says. "What do we do now, ma'am? Do we move in?"

"Not without backup. Not me," Click says.

Renata puckers her lips. "We watch and we wait. We need to know what's going on and who's coming and going. The goal is to nail the boss so we can bring down the whole operation. Not just this location."

"Are you saying we let them release a whole bunch of these zombies in New York?" Clack says.

"First, they are not zombies. Technically, they are more like Golem, souls planted in other humans' bodies. Second, we can track them, I believe, if they are released from the facility. We may have caught a break. It looks to me like they are just starting the process. Pumping new personalities into the bodies takes time. Then they have to wait until the drugs wear off, wake them, debrief the new entities and there're adjustments from what we can tell."

Renata, Tony, and Jackie are glued to their screens, watching as individual bodies are rolled into what looks like an operating theater. A man and a woman, both in white coats, attach probes and electrodes to the head of the body. They step away, and the body wriggles and writhes. Then it stops. The body's fingers seem to flex, but the eyes are still closed. Two attendants disconnect the probes and roll the gurney to the side. The man and woman then move another body center stage.

"This is nuts," Click and Clack say simultaneously.

"And dangerous," Renata says. "You guys hang there. Record everyone coming or going. Call me immediately if you think you see the big fish. I have to get back to the office. I'll come back as soon as I can. Have an important meeting with an old friend who's back from the dead, so to speak."

CHAPTER 26
MEETING

I take the redeye from SFO to LaGuardia. The airport's still the same shithole I remember from my last visit. The Uber, a clean, vintage Prius, is waiting at the curb. I give the Somali driver the Beaver Street address.

"You have good trip, sir?" the driver asks.

I smirk. "Yes, I feel like a new man."

The driver looks at me through the rear view mirror. "Where you come from?"

"From here and there and another time," I say.

"You an alien, sir?"

"In a sense. I'm from California."

The driver laughs. "Very funny, sir. Very funny."

"Call me Sam. How long 'til we get there?"

"Traffic at Midtown Tunnel. Maybe I go 'nother way."

"Whatever is fastest. I have some important people waiting for me."

"You very important person, sir?"

"No, just in my own mind. Tell me about where you came from."

"I'm from Jubaland in South Somalia. We have bad drought many years. My family try our best, but we need to eat. So I lucky to have cousin here who bring me, my wife and two girls here. Others not so lucky."

"I'm glad you made it here. What can the others do?"

"They get some aide from U.S., and China, but it not enough. So some sell their bodies."

"You mean like for prostitution?"

The driver scowls. "No, nobody have enough money to pay for prostitutes. This man from France, he come. Fancy suit, dark eyes, mustache. He pay families to buy people."

"You mean like he buys children?"

"No, he don't want children. He buys twenty to twenty-five-year-old men and women. He pay a lot. Families have no choice."

"That's terrible. I'm so sorry." *Hmm, just thinking.* "The people I work with may be interested to hear your story. They would pay you for your time."

"I not sell my body! That's why I come here. Here I am free."

"Yes, you are free and you have much courage to come here and start over. You don't understand. My friends are good people who would want to help your people back home. They would pay you just to tell them more about what you told me. How can they reach you? What is your phone number?"

He clutches his cellphone. "I not sure I want to do this. I think about it. You give me your number. I speak to my wife, and maybe I call you, and maybe I don't."

The driver slows and stops in front of the Beaver Street office. I write down my phone number on a twenty-dollar bill and hand it to the driver. "Please call," I say. "At least tell me... What's your name?"

He grins. "My name is Uber Driver."

Exiting the car, I wave and memorize the license plate number.

I take the steel-walled elevator to the third floor. There is a vague odor of cigarettes. Before I can even fully open the clear glass doors in front of me, Renata rushes up and gives me a bear hug. "Sam, it's so good to see you back, but I hardly recognize you."

I can't help laughing. "You're used to seeing Juan or the plastic surgeon's version of me. This time it's the real me and it feels good."

She takes my hand and leads me down the brightly-lit hall. "We'll be meeting with Jonathan, whom you know from our last adventure, and Don, who is new."

We arrive in front of the closed conference room door, and I put a hand out to stop her from entering. "Do they know about my transformation or any details about my return?"

"As far as they know, you were away for months and now you're back. Jonathan knows a bit more because he saw you with a different face, but otherwise, it's all a secret, Top Secret."

"OK, good. Who's this Don?"

"He's Don DeMarco from D.C., an analyst with a strong tech background. He's assisting us with the bodyjacking case. Or I should say, cases."

"Great name, *DeMarco*. Anyway, I was briefed before I left California. Has it gotten any worse?"

"Unfortunately, it has. It's not just Paris anymore. I have two guys staking out a body factory in Brooklyn. If I hadn't seen it with my own eyes, I wouldn't have believed it."

"Somehow, I feel responsible. If I hadn't pushed Frank so hard to develop the technology to put my digital self back in a body, this whole damn bodyjacking business wouldn't be happening."

"If it weren't Frank, somebody else would have figured it out. Not to make you feel worse, but there was one important fact omitted from your briefing."

"Uh, oh." I take a deep breath. "Lay it on me."

"OK. We have strong evidence that the Leopard is behind this wave of bodyjackings."

"No, how is that possible?" I slap my forehead. "Of course, he was digital and wanted to get back into a body as badly as I did. Now we have to contend with that bastard too."

"That's why we called you in. You understand bodyjacking firsthand and you've dealt with the Leopard before."

"How can I help?"

"Let's go inside and talk about it with the team." Renata opens the door to the small conference room. The fluorescent lights shine on an array of photos spread out on the table.

Renata starts, "Don, this is Sam Sunborn."

DeMarco shakes my hand and grins. "Nice to finally meet you, Mr. Sunborn."

A strange chill runs from DeMarco's hand through my body. For a second, I shiver and release his grip. The weird feeling goes away. "Call me Sam. Jonathan, good to see you again, even under these difficult circumstances."

"Glad to have your help again," Jonathan says. He turns to the photos. "Let's get down to it. These are the drone pictures of the body factory in Brooklyn taken last night."

"Shit, those are a lot of bodies," I say.

"We're just waiting for their boss to arrive before we move in. Just catching the worker bees won't stop this."

"I get it. And you think this is the Leopard's doing?"

"We do," Renata says.

DeMarco's expression flickers. "Excuse me a minute, I have to make a call," he says and steps into the hallway, closing the door behind him.

CHAPTER 27
PLAYGROUND

"Clear out. Leave the bodies, take the tools. Stay calm. Don't look frantic. Just move the equipment out to the freight elevator and get out the back way," the Leopard says.

"I don't understand. We're mid-procedure with a body on the table," the man in the white coat says.

"I don't think you heard me. Stop what you're doing now. The feds are parked outside your door. Terminate the guy on the table and get out. I'll hold. Tell me when it's done."

White Coat looks at the beautiful young woman on the table and shakes his head. He fills a syringe with a lime-green fluid and injects her in the stomach. Her body convulses wildly. A frothy foam dribbles from her lips. She goes limp. Her head, with its long brown hair, falls to the side as if disconnected from her body. The putrid stench of her bowels releasing punches the air. White Coat wipes the sweat from his brow. "OK, she's gone. We're leaving."

"Good. Text me when you get to Location 2. Initiate Plan B," DeMarco says.

"I'm not sure I —"

"Just do it, or you'll never see your two girls again. What are their names, Alice and Franny? I do like young girls. I'd probably have some fun with them first. Why waste the opportunity?"

Silence.

"I need confirmation now. I'm watching your cute little girls at the playground at the moment. They seem to be having a wonderful time on the swings. Oh, and they look so much like their mommy. Don't worry, I'd never hurt your wife. What kind of man do you think I am? No, I'd want her alive to blame you for the rest of your life if anything happens to them." The Leopard lets the scenario sink in for a moment. "Your answer?"

There is heavy breathing on the other end of the line. Then, "Location 2, twenty minutes. Stay away from the girls."

"That's better. I'll be looking for your text."

Following Inspector V's directions, Michelle and Rich arrive at the 18th-century granite industrial building in the 13th Arrondissement. The sign above the entrance says Systèmes de Son Electronique. "Makes our colonial buildings back home look ultra-modern," Rich says.

Rich is ready to spring from the car, but Michelle grabs his arm. "Let's talk this through. Maybe this company supplied the equipment used in the D.C. attack. Does that mean they are accomplices or unwitting suppliers?"

"Most likely scenario is they are just vendors or else they wouldn't be hanging out here in the open. Assuming that is correct, I'm more interested in knowing what they sold and to whom," Rich says.

"Yeah, that's kinda obvious, Sherlock. But what's the best way to get that info? We don't have a *mandat* and I doubt identifying ourselves as foreign agents will loosen them up."

"You speak French, but I don't. So I don't know what kind of cover we can use."

"How about we pretend to be potential customers from the U.S. who happen to be here on other business? Otherwise, we would have called in advance. If they buy it, we could learn more about their products."

"OK, I get that, but how does it lead us to who bought and used their products in D.C.?"

"We ask for references and maybe they'll cough up some names."

"Maybe, or maybe they keep their customer names confidential."

"Stop being such a downer. We won't know until we try, will we?"

"Sure. Was just exploring all the scenarios. Last thing, before we make fools of ourselves, we need to know more to sound experienced, like we know what we're talking about in this industry. Either we ask smart questions or it will blow the whole thing."

"OK, Mr. Careful. Let's call Gary and have him feed us the questions. I bet he can bring us up to speed in just a few minutes."

"While Gary is working on that, how about getting something to eat?"

"Some things never change."

"We're in France – *manger et boire sont le passe-temps national.*"

"I thought you don't speak French."

"I'm learning."

"Well, we can't waste much time... so here's French for fast-food... *McDonald's.*"

⊙─────⊙

"Gary says he'll get back to us in a few minutes. That gives you time to grab a bite here," Michelle says.

Rich looks up at le menu. "Oh, great. I'm in Paris and I get to eat a *La Grande Mac.*"

Michelle laughs. "They don't call it that."

"Sounds better than what they have there, the McFirst. What kind of name is that?" The serveuse at the counter takes our order. "I'll have Le Menu McFirst, s'il vous plaît," Rich says.

"Moi aussi," Michelle says. "I just got a text from Gary with intelligent questions. Let's go."

"But–"

"No buts." She turns to the young server, "Faire cet ordre pour emporter."

Rich grabs the bag. "Merci beaucoup. OK, I'm ready to get serious, but I'm still hungry."

Michelle puts their rented Renault in gear. "You've got your food. Just don't drip ketchup et moutarde all over yourself."

"Yes, Mom. Let me see the questions."

Michelle hands Rich her phone. He alternates reading the phone in his left hand and chomping on his Grande Mac in his right. Michelle cracks up. "You're quite a sight."

"I'm multitasking. Look, are you clear on what Gary is suggesting here? We can't be looking at the phone while asking the questions."

"Did you forget I have a photographic memory? I've got all the questions. Let me take the lead and chime in where you think appropriate."

"OK, we're pretty good at improv, partner."

"Damn straight."

They return to the Systèmes de Son Electronique building and enter. Unlike the exterior, the interior of the building and the lobby appear quite modern with bright lights and large contemporary paintings on the museum-white walls. A trim receptionist with close-cropped dark hair and stylish blue-rimmed glasses greets them. "Bonjour, monsieur et mademoiselle comment puis-je vous aider?"

Michelle flashes her friendliest smile. "Bonjour, parlez vous anglais?"

"Oui, how can I help you?"

"We happened to be in Paris for meetings. One of our business partners here recommended your company for some specialized equipment we need for our business back in the U.S. Would there be a manager or someone else available who could speak with us?"

"Let me see," the receptionist picks up her handset and taps some buttons. She speaks rapidly, waits for an answer, then hangs up. "Our sales manager is out visiting with a client — quelle dommage, but fortunately our directeur will be happy to speak with you. If you don't mind waiting for a few minutes..." She waves to the white leather sofas on the other side of the lobby. "Can I get you some coffee?"

Michelle and Rich answer simultaneously.

Michelle: "No, merci." ·

Rich: "Yes, bien sur!"

Michelle gives Rich the death-stare. Rich turns pink. "No, non, merci quand même."

They wait standing near the sofa and survey their surroundings.

"What's this tell you?" Rich whispers.

"Either they are very successful or they are doing something criminal."

"Exactly. Let's find out which."

A fit-looking 50ish man with a full head of gray hair and a tailored Pierre Balmain suit approaches and bows slightly. "Bonjour, monsieur et mademoiselle. I am Frederic Gardin, Le Directeur. So very nice of you to visit."

"Our apologies for not calling ahead. We are in Paris on business from the U.S. and a partner here recommended your company to us. I hope you can spare a few minutes to talk with potential customers," Michelle says.

"But of course. May I ask who recommended you?"

In addition to the questions, Gary anticipated enough to establish some references too. Rich extends his hand. "So nice to make your acquaintance. Talon Trapagnier speaks very highly of you personally and your products."

Gardin raises an eyebrow. "I am delighted to hear that. Talon is an old friend and a good customer. Please, follow me." He leads them up a winding open staircase. Through a two-story picture window, they can see the Eiffel Tower in the distance as they ascend. Gardin's office continues the museum theme with modern art covering the walls and sculptures on pedestals in the corners. He offers them chairs in front of his chrome and glass desk. "Coffee?"

Rich smirks at Michelle. "No, thank you," she says. "Unfortunately, we are on a tight schedule, flying back tonight. Our business is livestock. We have about 80,000 head of cattle on our two ranches in Idaho and Montana. Talon mentioned that you have sonic technology that would allow us to use sound waves to direct the herds, queuing them up for transportation and other purposes. Is that correct?"

"That is what I like about Americans, direct and down to business. In Europe, and France in particular, it seems we must speak of other things — politics, wine, cuisine, travel for maybe an hour or two before we discuss business. Don't misunderstand. This is not a bad thing as it builds trust. You get to know with whom you are dealing before you extend credit. Make sense, non?"

"We understand," Rich says. "I wish we had the time. Your office is such a lovely place to visit. But we must leave soon. I'm sorry if our coming has created any inconvenience."

"Pas du tout. My schedule is quite full today as well. Besides, any friend of Talon's is to be trusted." Gardin turns to Michelle. "To answer your question. Our newest model, the TX2200 is quite effective at using sonic waves, outside our hearing range. It creates a kind of movable barrier which can push animals in any direction that you choose. The parts are made in different countries, but we assemble them here in our plant. If you have the time, I'd be happy to give you a tour."

"That's very kind," Michelle says. "Perhaps, we will take you up on that." She glances at Rich. He doesn't react. "I've heard since this is new technology it is potentially dangerous for the animals."

"I have heard of some injuries caused by some of the devices our competitors sell. However, part of what we include with every sale is operator training. You do need to know how to dial up and dial down the sound to get the desired effect or else..."

"Or else what?" Rich asks. "Could you dial it up too much and harm the animals, even kill them?"

"Monsieur, that is quite extreme. Yes, the TX2200 is very powerful, but we have never had an incident."

"That you know of..."

"Nothing has been reported to us. We have only happy customers."

Michelle puts her hand on top of Rich's hand and squeezes. "Monsieur Gardin, we are prepared to place an order for two of your TX2200s to test its effectiveness at both our ranches. If it performs as you say, we would place a much larger order. Talon told us they are about $100,000 each. Is that correct?"

"Yes and that includes delivery to the U.S. and on-site training of your operators."

"That is very doable," she says. "Before we finalize the order, would you be able to give us any customer references in the U.S? We heard that you may have customers in the eastern or southern U.S. We'd like to hear how your product has worked for them."

"I understand, but our client list is confidential. Our clients do not want anyone knowing their business and we are very careful when it comes to potentially losing clients to competitors."

Rich's leg is bouncing up and down. He can't seem to stop fidgeting. Finally, he stands and leans over the desk. He stares Gardin in the eyes. "You don't understand. We need the names of anyone to whom you have sold the TX2200 in the U.S. and we need it now."

Gardin rolls his chair back away from the desk and stands erect. "You are not cattle ranchers. What are you doing here and what do you want with me?"

Michelle holds Rich's arm, but he shakes it loose. He whips out his wallet. "You are correct Monsieur Gardin. We are with the U.S. Department of Homeland Security. We think one of your customers used your device illegally. We need your cooperation or else..."

Beads of sweat begin to form on Gardin's brow. "I will have to check with our avocate before –"

Rich reaches over the desk, grabs Gardin by his necktie, and drags him around the desk. He pulls his face to within two inches of his nose. "We don't have time for that." Rich holds the knot of Gardin's tie and pulls on the short end, tightening the silk noose. Gardin chokes and turns blue. Rich persists, "Do you understand? Nod if you understand."

Gardin slowly moves his head.

"Good, now let's have it."

CHAPTER 28
TWO POUNDS

South Bend, Indiana, is a friendly Midwestern U.S. town. The downtown is a mix of 1950s storefronts and newer brick and granite buildings. Older buildings have been renovated. The speed limits have been reduced to encourage pedestrians, preserving some of that smaller neighborhood feel. So this Wednesday morning seemed like any other Wednesday when Dale Eberhardt goes to Moxie's Grocery to pick up some vegetables and hamburger meat for dinner.

Behind the meat counter, Moxie smiles when Dale comes through the door, the little bell attached to the door handle ringing behind her. "How are you, Ms. Dale, on this very fine day."

"Don't get too many this nice late September," Dale says. "None of that exotic Australian steak for me today. I'm just lookin' for some hamburger grown in the good old U.S. of A."

"I got some fresh. Picked today right off the hamburger tree. How much would you like?"

Dale laughs. "Moxie, you're as corny as ever. I'll take two pounds. Gotta feed the kids once-in-awhile too."

"How are those little chargers doin'? Cliff playin' Pop Warner yet?"

"This year. He can't wait. We bought him a helmet and he's runnin' around the house like he's playin' in the Super Bowl. He'll have his first concussion before he even starts practice."

"Sounds like he's going to be a star."

And then it happens. Moxie grabs the counter to steady himself.

"My God," Dale says. "You look like you're about to pass out."

Moxie chokes out, "I'll be OK." But he isn't OK. He falls to the floor and begins to writhe. "I can't... I can't breathe." Frothy white bubbles appear on his lips and he vomits a stream of blood.

Dale, who is a nurse by trade, feels Moxie's sweaty neck for a pulse. It's faint.

She pulls out her phone to call 911, but her hand begins to tremble. She tries to steady it with her other hand. Black spots begin to mushroom on the skin of her hands and arms. She looks up and the other half-dozen customers in Moxie's Market are fainting and falling to the floor. She smells the rancid odor of vomit. She's burning up. The trembling gets worse and her phone drops to the floor shattering the screen. Her last words are, "I don't... I don't u-n-d-e-r-s-t-a –"

Ashaki's face appears on Max's screen. "The test seems to have worked. Six dead in twenty minutes."

"Yep, that's my boys in Indiana. They did what you said and it worked. Nasty, that shit of yours."

"Are your boys OK? Did they follow my safety instructions?"

"You bet. They nearly crapped their pants when they read all your warnings. Almost backed out, but I shamed them into it. 'Sides, they owe me."

"I won't ask you what they owe you for, but I'm pleased it worked out. Beats catapulting infected bodies over the wall."

"Huh? Anyway, those folks in the store ain't too happy. Hear it was quite a mess – piss and shit and blood all over the place. HAZMAT and CDC guys in white space suits are crawling all over it."

"Perfect." Ashaki smiles. "Have you got video?"

"Yep, we planted the little camera just the way you asked across the street. Here she is."

A new window appears on Ashaki's screen. First, she spots the local news trucks and the helicopter overhead. She sees the men in suits going in and out of the store carrying HAZMAT cases, presumably full of samples. When the medics start carrying out the bodies on stretchers covered in white sheets, she can't help being aroused. She slides her hand down between her legs and begins to massage herself. She leans back and closes her eyes. *It's so g-o-o-o-d.*

"Are you OK?" Max says.

Ashaki, in her reverie, has forgotten he is even there. She sits back up and puts on a straight face but can't stop the throbbing down there. "Um yeah, I'm OK. Not enough sleep last night, but this is very exciting."

Max furrows his brow. "I mean I's glad it worked out, but are you gettin' off on this?"

"How I feel is none of your fuckin' business." She takes a deep breath. "Sorry, you did a great job. It's that time of month if you know what I mean."

Max snickers. "Yeah, I get it. That's none of my bizness for sure. OK, so when do I give my other boys the OK to go ahead?"

She refocuses on the task at hand. "I just need to check one more thing and I want to make the feds sweat a little. We should be good to go in the next day or two. Just make sure you're ready when I give the signal."

"I like makin' 'em sweat. This is going to be the biggest bend over and take it in the ass these alphabet boys have ever seen. Much bigger than D.C."

Ashaki smiles. "I knew I picked the right guy for the job."

Max purses his lips. "Maybe after this is all over, you and I could git together for a little fun down here, if you know what I mean."

"In your dreams. Keep it in your pants, mister. This is strictly business."

Max raises his hands, palms-up. "I was only joshin'. I'm all business myself."

"Let's keep it that way." Ashaki clicks off and the screen goes dark except for the window with the video feed of the store in South Bend. She takes in a big breath, licks her lips and picks up where she left off. A thought breezes through her mind, *Am I really as bad as my brothers?*, and then it vanishes in an instant.

CHAPTER 29
NINE PLAGUES

"I can't believe it's happening again," President Longford says, gazing out the Oval office window, the sun streaking through afternoon clouds dappling the rose garden. She sniffs as if to smell the roses and turns to the department secretaries sitting on the sofas. "What do we know?"

General Turgidman, the newly appointed director of the FBI, speaks first. "It's like the ten plagues all happened at once in that grocery store, blood, boils, pestilence. Everything except the killing of the firstborn. And who knows, maybe that's next."

"Love your optimism. Let's stick to the facts and what we do know. Save the commentary for later," she says. "Roger, what have you got?"

Roger Brickman from DHS stands. "Madame President, the CDC has the victims' bodies in isolation at their labs. They're doing tests now. They don't have conclusions yet, just educated guesses."

"Roger, this isn't your first time here. You can sit down. Now, what are their educated guesses?"

"I'm not sure how to say this other than to spit it out. Madame President, it's looking something like the plague. You know the Black Death that killed over seventy-five million people in the 1300s."

"I know what the plague was. That happened over seven hundred years ago, how would they possibly have that strain to make the comparison?"

"The CDC has samples of all kinds of epidemic viruses and diseases in Atlanta, including the classic Black Death from undisclosed sources. But it gets worse. They still have more testing to do, but it looks like this virus may have been genetically modified to make it more deadly and act more quickly. If that's the case, we could be looking at a mass casualty scenario."

"Shit, then how could whoever did this have gotten hold of the initial strain, assuming they didn't rob the CDC?"

Turgidman jumps in. "Madame President, if I may... the Ruskies, Chinese, and we believe the Barinians even have their own cache of deadly viruses. There is even a black market in this stuff. I fear this is just a test and a prelude to a much bigger event."

"Did you just say *Ruskies*? What are we, in *Dr. Strangelove* again? Never mind. This gets worse by the minute. So what are we doing about it?"

"We believe this is not an isolated incident and could be followed by much more. So, we have every forensic and biological expert resource on it from CDC, NIH, FBI, Homeland, and a dozen other domestic and foreign intelligence agencies. We are also sharing the data with our closest allies in case there is an international connection," Brickman says.

"During my watch, we've had nuclear attacks, biological terrorism, the attack last week in D.C., and now this. I've only got one year left in my second term and can't seem to catch a break. This is one wild-ass ride." She drops into her chair behind the Resolute Desk. "OK, you keep me posted as this develops. I want hourly updates – make that half-hourly. While we're at it, what's the latest on the D.C. attack?"

Brickman clears his throat. "Rich Little and Michelle Hadar. They have found the manufacturer of the equipment used to blast the Capitol. That is leading them to a list of customers, one of whom is the likely assailant."

President Longford smirks. "Little and Hadar again, hmm. At least *they* know how to get stuff done," she looks the six men in the room in the eyes one-by-one, "unlike some other people I know."

"But Madame President —"

"That's enough! Get out of here and find the assholes attacking us, and do it now."

CHAPTER 30
NO CIGAR

Renata didn't feel the phone vibrate in her pocket the first time or the second time. A few minutes after DeMarco leaves the room, she pulls out her phone to make a call and sees five missed call notifications from this afternoon. She calls back. "What's up?"

"Where the hell have you been? Turn on the feed to the warehouse now," Clack says. "They're clearing out!"

Renata pulls up the mini-drone feed to the warehouse and sees the doctor and his assistant rolling a gurney out of the room."

"What the fuck?" Renata says. Jonathan and I look in her direction. She puts the phone on speaker and places it on the table. "I've got Sam and Jonathan here. We see the video. Can you see anyone exiting the building?"

"No, we've held our position just the way you said we should, but we can't let these bastards get away," Click says.

I can't believe what I'm seeing, the room full of bodies on tables – some white, some black, the operating arena. *Did Frank's bringing me back the last time lead to all this?* My heart sinks. Maybe Monica is right. I've gone off the rails. Now who knows how many people will suffer and die because of it? I bury that thought and focus. "Are you sure they're leaving and not just moving stuff around?"

"See for yourself. What do you think? Should we rush the place and haul them in?" Clack says.

Renata pushes the hair from her eyes. "You're right. They're moving too fast to just be moving stuff around. But don't go in. Follow them when they leave. They may lead us to the source."

"We can't cover all sides of the building at once, and I'm not sure which way they'll exit. Jackie, call for backup. No time, let's go." Click and Clack start to slowly circle the block, turning right on 3rd

Avenue, then right again on Union and finally right again back onto President's Street.

Renata, Jonathan, and I are glued to the video feed. The people, at least the conscious ones, have exited for good it seems. The scene is lifeless. All that remains are the motionless cold-looking bodies. "Have you got them?" Renata asks.

Click blows out a big breath as their Crown Vic rolls to a stop. "No sign of them. I think we lost them."

"Shit," Renata says. "My fault. OK, call in as many meat wagons as you can get and see if you can save any of these poor souls. I'll call you back in a few." A tear rolls down Renata's cheek. She taps off the video. "I blew it big time. What a cluster-fuck."

I put a hand on Renata's shoulder. "Hey, as they say in every cop show, *It's not on you.* But don't you think it's a strange coincidence this DeMarco leaves the room and two minutes later these guys pack up and leave?"

Renata gives me a hard look. "What are you saying?"

I stare back. "You know what I'm saying."

Jonathan starts typing on his phone. "I'm texting Gary to see if he can find out who DeMarco called when he stepped out."

"Yeah, yeah, good idea. I can't believe this," Renata says.

The conference room door swings open and DeMarco returns, sporting a grin. "Any pizza left? What did I miss?"

Gary walks over to Adele's cubicle and hands her his phone. "Take a look at this text from Jonathan. What do you make of it?"

"We've got a mole or worse?" Adele says.

"Do you know this guy, DeMarco?"

"I met him once, unfortunately."

"Why do you say, *unfortunately*?"

She blushes for a nano-second and hesitates. "Oh, um, I guess he rubbed me the wrong way."

"OK, I see. Look, I'm tied up with Rich and this D.C. investigation. Could you take a look into this for me?"

She stands up. "With pleasure. Forward the text to me."

Gary taps his phone. "Done. Let me know what you find."

"Done and done," Adele says.

Gary leaves and Adele, aka Ashaki, swivels back to her screen. She inhales the minty fragrance and takes a sip of her steaming peppermint tea. A little icon of a parhyale insect appears, blinking in the bottom right corner of her monitor. Ashaki stands, scanning up and down the aisles around her. Nobody's lurking. She clicks the icon and Marsha Hume's face appears in a small box. "Good time to talk?"

"I have a couple of minutes," Ashaki says. "What is it?"

"South Bend went well, don't you think?"

"Looks like it. Well done. Any tweaks needed for the *Yersinia pestis* or are we good to go?"

"We had a couple of techs in suits disguised as CDC on-site inspect the results. Apparently, a few customers in the store survived and appeared unaffected. Thinking our techs were official, they allowed us to take blood samples from the survivors. We need to understand why they were immune. If you want 100% success or close to it, we'll need to analyze, go back and gene edit the virus using our CRISPR tools and retest."

Ashaki drums her fingers on the desktop. "How long will that take?"

Hume sucks in a breath. "A week, maybe two."

"We haven't got that long. I need it in three days max. The longer this takes, the greater our risk of getting stopped or caught."

"You could go with the 60% fatality rate we achieved in the test."

"Not good enough. We need 90% plus in three days or less."

"But, but it takes time."

"That is not an option. I know when this issue came up with my brother Momar and you last, he threatened harm to your beautiful girls. What're their names?"

Hume is taking shallow breaths now. She whispers, "Karen and Samantha."

"Let's put it this way. Momar threatened. I act. Check your screen."

An image of the two girls bound, gagged, and blindfolded in a gray concrete cell appears. Hume gasps. "Oh my God. What have you done?"

"Nothing... for the moment. They're fine. Let's just call it insurance. If you deliver my 90% effective toxin in three days, Karen and Samantha will be returned to you unharmed. After three days, they join our less fortunate subjects from South Bend. Understood?"

Hume explodes, "You're even more of a monster than your brother!"

"I'll take that as a compliment. Now calm yourself and answer my question. Can you deliver in three days or not."

Silence. Then, "I will."

"Good, get to work." Ashaki taps her fingernail on her desk like a metronome. "The clock is ticking."

CHAPTER 31
IMAGINE THAT

"That didn't go according to plan," Michelle says as they exit Systèmes de Son Electronique and cross the street.

"We got what we came for, didn't we?" Rich says.

"Yes, a little heavy-handed, but I guess we did. You know we're not in the U.S. and have no jurisdiction here, right?"

Rich smiles. "That's why I had to use an alternative approach, Grasshopper."

Slinked down in the seat of a rental car across from Systèmes is Nancy Lu, watching. When she spots Rich and Michelle, she springs from the vehicle, jogging diagonally up the street to intercept them. She forces a smile. "Fancy meeting you here. What a coincidence?"

Rich puts his hands on his hips. "Imagine that."

Michelle pulls Nancy into a bear hug, smelling the alcohol on her breath. "It's great to see you. Again, I'm so sorry about Al's death. How are you holding up?"

"It was a senseless murder, but to answer your question, not great. I've been drinking instead of eating and sleeping. Not exactly a great health plan, but I'm in Paris. What could be better?"

Rich relents and kisses Nancy on both cheeks.

"Hmm, very French," she says. "Great to see you too."

"Obviously, this is not a coincidence. Why are you here?" Rich asks.

"I won't bullshit you. The one thing that will get me sober and my juices flowing is a good story. I'm on to one here," Nancy says.

"Is that so? How did you know how to find us and what's the story?" Rich asks.

Nancy stifles a laugh. "You first."

"That's not the way this works. If you want anything from us, we need to know what you know. Capisci?"

"That's not French, but OK. A confidential source told me you were here. I can't reveal the source's name, but I will tell you I heard about this bodyjacking thing, like what Frank Einstein invented but has now fallen into the wrong hands. Is that what you're working on?"

Rich and Michelle do sideways glances at each other. Michelle answers, "Rich will want to know about this source of yours later, who by knowing our whereabouts, could be putting us and others in danger. But to your question – No, that's not why we're here."

"Care to expand on that?"

"No," Rich says.

"How about if I share something useful to you or whoever is working the bodyjacking case here, and you share with me what you're working on? Maybe let me tag along like I did in New York? You know I helped."

Rich looks at Michelle again. "Nancy, you go first and if we find it useful, we'll consider your proposal. So what do you know?"

"OK, but I need a little quid pro quo here. So I'll give you some of what I know and if you let me hang with you, I'll give you the rest."

Rich's face purples. "I don't like being extorted, especially by a cub reporter. I ought to throw your ass in a French bastille and then maybe you'll talk."

Michelle grabs Rich's arm and looks at Nancy. "Rich is just a little anxious. I'm sure when he calms down, he'll apologize. Right Rich?"

Rich bites his lip. Michelle continues. "Let's just make this a matter of trust like we did before. Everything on our side is off, way off the record unless we specifically say otherwise. Understood?"

Nancy nods.

"Then go ahead, spew."

Nancy removes a small spiral-bound notebook from her purse and flips the pages. "I know that some criminal mastermind or terrorist has stolen or somehow obtained Frank's technology for putting one person's mind into another person's body. I know this mastermind has placed himself in a new body and that the prime suspect here is the Leopard, aka Ahmed LaSalam. Interesting so far?"

Rich is calm and focused now. "Go on."

"I believe the Leopard, in his new body, is now in New York setting up a similar operation there and perhaps this is only the beginning. He may be building an army."

Rich and Michelle are dead silent. A French taxi goes by, its horn making three high-pitched beeps while blowing a cloud of noxious exhaust their way. "What else?" Rich finally asks.

"I have more, but now it's your turn," Nancy says.

"OK," Michelle says. "Get in the car and we'll talk on the way. We're here on the D.C. attack case, but we were briefed this morning on the bodyjacking case by an Inspector V. You need to share what you know with him. We're following a local lead from the manufacture of the equipment used in the D.C. attack."

"So I can come along? I might be helpful in your case too."

Michelle looks at Rich for a sign. He nods. "Strictly off the record. Repeat that back to me."

"Off the record, absolutely," Nancy says.

CHAPTER 32
UNUNITED NATIONS

When DeMarco returns to the conference room, he senses something is up with Sam, Jonathan, and Renata. He had just stepped out to call his white coats and clear the bodyjacking factory. It took all of ten minutes, but somehow the vibe had changed in the room. He could feel it. He scanned their faces. Blank. Nothing. *Could they be on to him?* "What did I miss?" he says for a second time.

Renata glances quickly at me and turns back to DeMarco. "Nothing. But it looks like the people at the warehouse we've been watching stepped out. Maybe lunch. What do you think?"

DeMarco looks at the screen. "I see the bodies, but it looks like they may have picked up and gone. Any word from Click and Clack?"

"They haven't seen anything either. So we're going to hold still for a while. Why don't you finish off the pizza?"

"Good idea." He picks up a cold slice. "I have to run an errand anyway. Back at 4:00?"

"Sure," Renata says and DeMarco disappears.

She turns to Jonathan and me. "Want to go for a walk?"

I gaze out the window at the cloudless blue sky. "Let's do it. We have lots to catch up on."

<hr>

The Leopard sheds his DHS persona like an ill-fitting coat. He flags a taxi. *It feels good to be Ahmed LaSalam in the flesh again.* The newer, younger body suits him. He stretches his arms just to sense them.

"Where to?" the cabbie asks in a thick, almost comical, Brooklyn accent.

"Drop me at the corner of 43rd and Second."

"Near da' U.N., right?"

"Oh, is it? It's my first time in New York. Just meeting a friend."

"You should check out the U.N. They do tours and stuff. I took my daughter there. Very educational."

"Thanks for the suggestion. Maybe, if I have time, I will." They arrive at their destination and LaSalam pays cash, no traces.

He walks two blocks then down a narrow alley, descending a decrepit brick staircase. The smell of fish from a nearby dumpster permeates the air. He looks up at the single mini-surveillance camera. The door buzzes and he enters. He takes a minute to survey the rows of cubicles with young men and women clicking away.

A short, plump middle-aged man approaches with a smile. "Mr. Merit. This is a surprise. I wasn't expecting you until later today."

LaSalam shakes the man's hand. "Let's move out of earshot." They step a few feet to the side. "I had to move up my schedule. You might call this a surprise inspection."

The man's smile vanishes. "I can assure you everything is in order. You can see how busy everyone is." He waves his hand with pride towards the rows of young men and women tapping away in front of multiple monitors.

"I'm sure they are, but will they be ready?"

"We're tracking all the subjects now, as you can see." The little man gestures to a large wall monitor with a map of Manhattan overlaid with red stick pins and green moving dots.

"It might as well be Pac-Man to me. Tell me what I'm looking at."

"The red pins are the pickup locations. The green dots are your er, *troops.*"

"Only they don't know it yet. They think they have just paid a million dollars for the new bodies they are enjoying."

"But once we invoke the Z protocol, they'll be under our command."

The Leopard corrects him. "*My* command. And you have programmed the target?"

"Yes, as you instructed, General Assembly at 2:00 PM tomorrow."

"Good. And what do all these programmers think they're doing here?"

"They've been told it's a security simulation for the Department of Homeland Security. They're mostly Columbia and NYU computer sci grad students who are happy to earn some money and get the experience."

The Leopard smiles. "Ironic. I could even show them my DHS ID, but I don't think that will be necessary." He turns to leave. "I will check in with you later."

The little man coughs. "Sir, before you leave... a word."

LaSalam turns back. "Yes, what is it?"

"I just wanted to check and make sure. Once this assignment is complete, you will be using your resources as promised to get my family out of Syria."

The Leopard reddens. "I keep my promises. Now just get it done. When it succeeds, your family will be able to rejoin you here next week. I have to go. There are more important things to deal with today other than your family."

The man stammers. "Yes, sir. Thank you, sir. We will succeed."

The Leopard turns back again. "You better. If you fail, you will never see your wife, Jamilla, and little Salwa and Rabab again. In fact, if you fail, I'll give you a choice. Either your wife and children will never see you again or you will never see them again – up to you. Almost makes me want to see you fail just to see what choice you make." The Leopard laughs. "I can make sure of it either way."

He turns and heads for the exit.

The little man wipes his brow. A young man in a cubicle nearby notices. "Are you OK, sir?"

"It's none of your business. Get back to work," the little man snaps.

CHAPTER 33
DECODING

Ashaki stares at her phone, displaying Jonathan's text that Gary forwarded. *DeMarco, Don DeMarco?* Her first encounter with him had been strange, almost perverted. There is something off-kilter with him. She feels like she knows him as a character from a bad dream. Snapping out of her trance, she leans forward and starts typing. She searches the cell phone database DHS maintains for all its government-issued phones. With top-level access, she quickly identifies DeMarco's official phone and opens up the call log. No calls today. *Of course*, she thinks, if he's a mole with half-a-brain, he's not going to make illicit calls with a government phone.

Tapping away some more, she says out loud, "Ah-ha, gotcha!" She previously helped implement a system that clones all phones in the building, government-issued or not. Noting the time the text was sent and filtering all phone activity in the building at precisely 8:38 AM, she gets three hits. She opens up a 3D rendering of the building and rotates it. Three blinking red dots represent the three phones that sent a text or made a voice call on the first, third, and seventh floor. She opens another TOR browser window and sees the meeting DeMarco attended was on the third floor. Her fingers pick up speed as she hones in on her target.

Clicking the dot on the third floor, a virtual phone opens on her screen. All the contacts, calls, and texts are there. Tracing the phone's SIM ID – it's a burner. Identifying the recipient of the 8:38 phone call yields an address. But maybe even more important is all the other activity and contact info. How much should she reveal? *She has to share something or Gary'd be suspicious.* She taps out a text to Gary and Jonathan.

"Traced call made by DeMarco. Time 08:38. Duration 9min 34sec. Address 22.105.66.2.

Burner phone. That's all."

That should keep 'em busy. Now, let's see about these other contacts. She scans the list. Something looks familiar. *How could that be?*

A red icon blinks in the upper left corner of her screen. *Shit, it's Max.* She minimizes the other windows, puts on her headset, and trips the icon. The video window opens. "How are you darlin'? Forget we had a call at 3:00? It's twenty-after and I figured something was wrong."

"I'm OK. Just got tied up with something. Sorry. Listen, your boys did good in South Bend. Nailed a bunch, but a few survived. We're making a few tweaks so we can get 'em all. Should be ready for full distro day-after-tomorrow. Plan to pick up the package as scheduled, same place. Got it?"

"Yes, ma'am. Now about that money –"

"Did you look? It's already in your account."

"Hold a minute. Let me check." Max speaks to someone in the background. Then he returns to the call. "Why thank you so much. It's nice doin' bizness with you."

"And for a good cause. Remember that."

"Sure. Sure. Whatever floats your boat."

"Listen, I got to run. Call me when you get the new package." She hangs up as Max begins to reply.

She reopens the window with DeMarco's call log and contacts. *That number, what is that? How about purchases?* Google tracks everybody's purchases online, all your Amazon purchases, everything going back six years. She punches a few more keys harder now. Rocking back in her chair, the blood drains from her face. *I can't believe it.*

Renata, Jonathan, and I are strolling around Bowling Green Park near the Beaver Street office. The leaves are yellowing and already casting themselves to the wind. The air smells incredibly fresh for the city like it does from the ozone after a thunderstorm. Jonathan's phone dings and he checks the screen. He turns a pale green and silently hands the phone to Renata. She just gazes and her hand begins to tremble.

"What is it?" I ask.

Renata holds up one finger and tries to catch her breath. "I can't tell you. It's government business, classified."

"Hey, you asked for my help. How can I help if I don't know what's going on."

Renata and Jonathan look at each other.

I persist. "Look, either you read me in or I'm out of here." I'm bluffing. No way am I leaving now, but to sell the bluff, I start to turn away.

Renata grabs my arm and pulls me back. "DeMarco is a mole. Adele, who works with Gary, traced the call he made in the hall to the bodyjacker's address we were surveilling in Brooklyn. Let that sink in."

"Shit. So now what?"

"There's a protocol for this kind of treachery," Jonathan says.

Renata is bouncing on her heels. "Fuck protocol. I want to cut his nuts off."

Can't believe I'm the sane one here. "Calm down and think. What can we do with this information by not letting on what we know?"

Renata blows out a long breath and stops the bouncing. "We can find out who he's working with and try to corral them all."

"Exactly," Jonathan says. "So, let's go back like nothing's happened, but tail Don physically and electronically."

Hmm, I think. "If DeMarco is not who he says he is or is an impostor, could he be a bodyjacker? I mean, not just a boss, but another person who took over DeMarco's body?"

"Seems like a leap, but then it kinda makes sense," Renata says. "Assuming DeMarco is a bodyjacking victim, then who is he really?"

I clear my throat. "I may have an idea. Let's get back to the office."

CHAPTER 34
LEAD TWO

Back at the Beaver Street Office, Renata, Jonathan, and I reconvene in the conference room. "Where's DeMarco?" Renata asks.

"Try calling him. Anybody have a mint?" I still have onions lingering from lunch.

"Yes, boss." She smirks, throwing me a pack of Breath Savers. She dials DeMarco's DHS-issued phone. "Nothing. Voicemail."

"He knew we were meeting here again at 4:00," Jonathan says.

"He knows something else," I interject. "He knows we're on to him."

"How do you know that?" Renata asks.

"Because he's the Leopard and he's very, very smart and cunning."

"How do you know he's the Leopard?"

"Think about it. He was killed in Cambridge but digitized before his death. He has expert hacking resources and is highly motivated to return to a physical body. Who else would and could steal the bodyjacking technology and set up an international reincarnation scheme?"

"OK, but that's just a theory, no physical evidence. With you, the Leopard is Batman or should I say, the Joker. So I don't make the connection yet," Renata says.

"Well, here's the kicker. I spoke to Frank about this. He said when he created the tech to download people into others' bodies, he included a physical marker that appears on every victim or volunteer for the procedure."

Renata reddens. "What? Why didn't we know about this sooner?"

"Frank built this in just in case of a problem like this. Do you want to be pissed or do you want to hear what it is?"

Renata shakes her head. "OK, what is it?"

"Everyone who has been re-instantiated into a new body has a scar on their neck. It looks like a tilted letter *T*."

"Holy shit," Jonathan says. "You're right. DeMarco has that mark."

Renata sucks in a big breath and stands. "If that's true, we've got our man or identified him anyway. Now to state the obvious, we've got to stop him."

"Roger that, Kemosabe," I say.

Renata groans. "That's both politically incorrect and offensive."

I guess I watched too much TV as a kid. So what if I liked Tonto? "Sorry, I'm about two steps behind on cultural norms, but I'm trying."

"Try harder. Now Jonathan, maybe Adele can get a location on DeMarco's, or should I say the Leopard's, burner phone. Call her."

"Roger –" Jonathan stops himself. "OK, will do."

"Sam, call Rich. He needs to be in the loop on this. He believed the Leopard could be behind the bodyjacking but now needs to know about our mole, DeMarco, is the Leopard in a new physical form. We need more resources on this. We can't forget we're on the D.C. attack case too."

I just nod this time.

Ashaki's phone vibrates, gyrating on her desk. A text from Jonathan,

"Priority One: Need loc on DeMarco's burner. Any other info, contacts, calls?"

Ashaki swivels to her screen with the virtual image of DeMarco's burner. It appears to be offline or deactivated. She responds,

"Phone dead. Maybe ditched. Have tons of data here. Read me in + tell me what u looking 4 + I can scan for it."

"Will call u. Need clearance 1st," Jonathan replies.

Ashaki sweeps her hair back and ties it with a rubber band. This is getting interesting.

Her phone rings – it's Jonathan. "Look, Adele, this is strictly confidential, understood?'

"Of course. What's going on?"

"Remember that big takedown last year, where we stopped a nuke attack and nailed a big terrorist."

"Sure. It was all over the news."

"Well, he's back. Ahmed LaSalam, aka the Leopard, is back."

"Wait, how's that possible? I thought he was dead."

"He was, but in a sense, he's been reincarnated as DeMarco."

Ashaki gasps. *I knew it. My brother who abused and tortured me and even toyed with me in this office. How do I handle this?*

"Adele, are you there?"

"Yes, yes. I'm just shocked by the news. Reincarnated?"

"I can't get into that now. I need you to get me a list of anyone he's contacted in the last three days. We think he's planning something big and we need to track him down before he pulls the trigger."

"Understood. I'll do what I can."

"Do it fast." He clicks off.

My brother does need to be stopped for good, but I want to get to him first. I want to look him in the eyes when he goes down. But reincarnated? What the hell is that about?

CHAPTER 35
CLUSTER F*CK

"OK. We've got a cluster fuck." Rich yawns. "Sorry, jet-lag from the flight back home. But we're stepping all over each other here." The sun streaks through the blinds in their conference room at the Beaver Street office. The smell of cinnamon buns bounces in the air.

Rich swivels his head, making eye contact in turn with Michelle, Jonathan, Renata, and me. Then he looks up at digital Frank on the monitor. "Good morning, Professor. Glad you could join us."

Frank smiles. He's wearing his professorial clothes and visage – tweed sports jacket, thick glasses, and disheveled gray hair. "Happy to help. As you know, being digital, there's no need for sleep or yawning. I just go 24/7, which is great. But I do miss the taste of good coffee in the morning. I'll have to figure out a way to simulate that."

Rich throws an intense look my way. "Look, we've got to get down to business. We're dealing with assaults from all sides – the D.C. attack, the chem-bio strike in Indiana, and all this bodyjacking crap. There's plenty else going on in this building, but these three things are our priority, and I don't want you tripping over each other. It's getting a little nuts. So here's the plan —"

Renata interrupts. "Don't forget our missing mole, DeMarco."

Rich continues. "That's all part of the bodyjacking stuff."

I can't help myself. "The Leopard is on the loose."

"Cute," Rich says. "The scary part is we don't know what comes next. Unless we get our shit together, we'll get caught flat-footed again. Listen, I've got a call with the White House in five minutes. So this is how it's going to go. Michelle, you and Jonathan are to follow up on the chemical attack leads. Call in any help you need. I'll authorize it. Renata, you, Sam, and Frank get back on the D.C. microwave case."

Frank coughs. "You forget that being digital, I can handle a thousand things at once, unlike you one-track humans."

"Well, put your thousand tracks on D.C. I'm getting extra heat on that one. If you're needed on the other cases, we will call you," Rich says.

"What about the bodyjacking cases?" Michelle says. "Renata's been on it since day one. She has the most knowledge. Why put her on something totally new? Who's going to chase down the Leopard, you?"

Rich raises his hands, palms out. "Chill out. I just want fresh eyes on everything. We haven't gotten very far on any of these yet. Plus, we're suspecting connections between them and your knowledge of one case may help in the others. Trust me. I know what I'm doing."

"Sometimes," Michelle says and then bites her lip. "Most of the time, but you still haven't said who's pursuing the bodyjackers."

"I'm bringing in Hamed and Swan. They'll work with me. Renata can bring them up to speed on Paris and Jonathan can fill them in on New York. Got it?" Rich searches our faces. We all nod.

He slaps the table and stands. "Good. Gotta go."

○━━━━━○

It's five o'clock. President Longford, General Turgidman, Brickman, Hagar, Osborne, Kennedy, and the Joint Chiefs, along with staff and several others in uniform, fill the Situation Room. It's standing room only. A thin cloud of pungent smoke floats above the long mahogany table. Longford stubs out her cigarette. "Sorry, executive privilege. OK, we've got a shit storm going on. Where's Little? I want to know what's happening."

"We'll have him in a minute," a young marine says, pecking away at a laptop.

They collectively stare at the world map on the monitor. There are red stick pins on Paris, New York, and South Bend.

A voice breaks the silence as Rich Little's face pops in a corner of the monitor. "Madame President, gentlemen and ladies. How can I help?"

"Deputy Secretary Little, we need an update from the field. What's going on with D.C., the dead people in Indiana, and the bodyhustling in New York?" Longford asks.

Brickman interrupts, "Deputy Secretary Little has briefed me as his boss and head of DHS. Perhaps I should brief the group?"

"Roger, we all know you're very important, but I want to hear it directly from the people on the ground."

"But –"

"Roger, just shut up and listen. Rich, please proceed," Longford says.

Brickman slides down in his chair.

"Madame President, we have teams and forensics on the ground in South Bend. Michelle Hadar is heading up that team. I'm sure you remember her."

"I certainly do. She's saved our asses more than once. But what do you know so far?"

"We know it's a deadly, genetically-engineered bio-weapon with a high, quick-kill rate. We're trying to track down its source."

"I heard what it does to peoples' skin. Just awful. And D.C.?"

"I just got back from Paris, where we tracked down the equipment used to create the sonar blast. The owner somewhat reluctantly gave us info on his customers in the U.S., Renata Fermi and Sam Sunborn are on that one."

"Sunborn's like poop. He's everywhere," Longford says.

Some of the staffers stifle a laugh.

"Yes, ma'am. He's been very helpful."

"And the bodyhustlers?"

"Actually, we're using the term *bodyjacking*. With Sam's help and other evidence, we have concluded the Leopard is behind the whole scheme. To make matters worse, he used the technology himself to bring himself back in the body of a DHS agent, Don DeMarco. He used DeMarco's body as a disguise to spy on the investigation and steal some DHS resources."

"How bad?"

"Bad, Madame President. DeMarco, aka the Leopard, is on the run. We're trying to assess what he may have stolen."

Turgidman grumbles and stands. "Madame President, I can have troops on the ground in less than twenty-four hours at all locations."

"Sit down, General. We're not there yet, but we may be soon if Deputy Secretary Little can't produce results and stop these terrorists. You have twelve hours before I declare a national emergency, and we throw everything we have at the problems. See what sticks."

Kennedy from State slams a fist on the table. "Madame President, we must do whatever we can to avoid causing the kind of chaos and panic that deploying the military domestically might cause."

"Daniel, which would you prefer, to be scared or dead?" Longford asks.

Brickman sits up. "For once I agree with Daniel, let cool heads prevail, investigate and stop the attackers. We've done it before. We can do it again here."

Longford snorts. "That's why I'm giving your cool heads twelve hours. If they don't show results by then, we'll let the hotheads have at it. Understood?"

The directors in the room answer in unison. "Yes, Madame President."

She looks at her watch. "Listen, I've got to run, meeting with the Gang of Eight now. I'll have to brief them on all of this, then jump on a chopper. Speaking at the U.N. tomorrow, but this is the priority. Deputy Secretary Little, we'll expect reports on the hour. Godspeed."

"Yes, Madame President. Thank you."

CHAPTER 36
THOUGHT EXPERIMENT

"I need a minute," I say as we head up 3rd Avenue. Something's wrong. I can feel it. "There's a Starbucks right up there on 23rd Street, quick stop."

Renata swings in front and I jump out. "Don't worry. I'll be right back". I beeline for the restroom. There're a young woman and a basketball-tall, bearded man on line in front of me. I've had bathroom emergencies a few times in my life, but this is different, way different. I am waiting, bouncing on my toes. The restroom door opens and the young woman goes in. This feels interminable. I look back through the window at Renata in the waiting car. I wonder what she's thinking. I look down at my hands. What? They're blurry. Is it my eyes? Can't be. The walls and floor are in focus. What's happening? Will anyone else notice? I put my hands in my pockets. Finally, it's my turn. I lock the door and look in the mirror. My face is fading in and out, blinking like an old black-and-white TV. I'm feeling nausea like I've never felt before. Sweat soaks through my shirt.

My hand shakes as I grip the phone to call Frank. He answers on the first ring. "Sam, how are you? I see you're at Starbucks. Enjoying the coffee?"

Frank has a tracker on me and loves to let me know it. "Trouble..." I try to stay calm and describe the problem to him.

"You're having a Time phase synchronization issue," Frank says.

"English, please."

"You are disappearing."

"What? Can you fix it?"

"I may be able to tweak the quantum entanglement sequence, but it's really going to be more up to you."

"What have I got to do with this? You and your science brought me back. What's up to me?"

"Sam, we're in unique territory here. Nobody's ever done this before. But what we're doing is quantum time phasing combined with a force of will, your will."

"I don't get it. What does that mean?"

"It means you have to will yourself into existence. Just like normal physical people have to force themselves to 'be present.' You have to take what I've given you and will yourself to be here, now. Did something happen that particularly stressed you recently?"

"You mean the fact that the Leopard is back and probably about to launch a catastrophic attack and Monica wants to leave me? Nope, besides that, no stress."

"I get it. Stress can weaken the will, the will to live. But you wanted to return to the physical world. Has that changed?"

"No, it hasn't."

"Then exert your will. Make yourself present."

"I'm not sure how to do that."

"What's the most important thing to you in the physical world?"

"Evan, my son."

"Then whenever you experience this slippage coming on, focus on Evan. It should bring you back."

"Frank, are you serious? My wife and son are not a thought experiment. I can't be here and afford to be in and out. That just won't do."

"Sam, look at it this way. Everybody's life is a thought experiment. We choose to be present and in the moment, listening and interacting with others, sucking up the beauty and wonder of every moment or we choose to be distracted and elsewhere, unfocused, mind in the future or past, locked in the world of worry. The only difference is the average human's body can be visible and 100% present, while their mind and attention are a million miles away. In your case, your physical appearance or lack thereof reflects your mental presence. So you're right. You can't afford a thought experiment. You need to be right here, right now..."

"At every moment or I'll fade or flicker or disappear?"

"That's right. It's going to require a huge effort at first, but you'll get the hang of it. Then it will become a habit. You'll be the way *you are* all the time."

I look again in the mirror and my face and body gradually come into focus. I am clear, distinct, seemingly normal. I look down at my hands. They are steady and not flickering. "I understand now. Thank you, Frank, I think."

"You can do this, Sam. Go on. Renata's waiting."

I return to the car. Renata gives me a furrowed brow. "Are you OK? I was getting worried."

"I'm fine now. I just wasn't feeling myself."

She swerves into traffic and hits the gas.

CHAPTER 37

SCENT OF A WOMAN

The Leopard looks both ways and dashes down the dark, narrow alley leading to their headquarters near the U.N. He does an eye scan and the rusted metal door buzzes and unlocks. He slips in and wipes the sweat from his brow with his sleeve. Ninety-five degrees and humid, Indian summer in New York is terrible enough. His rushing and double-backs to elude any tails just made it worse.

The little man greets him. "Mr. Merit. I wasn't expecting you back so soon." He studies the Leopard's sweaty face. "Are you OK?"

"It's just hotter outside than the desert back home. Are we still good for the operation tomorrow?"

The little man stammers. "Yes, I believe so."

"That's good, but we may have to advance the timeline. The General Assembly is meeting for the keynote speech tomorrow from President Longford at 11:00 AM, not 2:00 PM. Could you be ready if we need to execute earlier?"

The little man looks at his watch. "That's three hours less. I'm not sure."

"Well, make sure. I'll let you know if it's a *GO*. For now, take me to a computer I can use."

"Yes, sir – over here," the little man says, leading Mr. Merit to a cubicle.

"No, I need something more private."

"You can use my office. Follow me."

They enter a small, cluttered office in the corner of the windowless space. "This will do. Close the door," the Leopard says. He sits down at the little man's terminal and logs into their secure servers. Then he accesses the DHS servers and enters his password credentials. *Good, they haven't blocked my access yet.* His high-level clearance lets him look up Adele Lamont, aka Ashaki LaSalam, his sister. *That bitch is mine, a pump and dump.* He feels himself getting aroused by the memory of taking her as a child. Delicious. He licks his lips. He types a few more strokes that surreptitiously activate the webcam at her terminal. She's there at her desk, looking as lovely as ever. He can almost smell the lavender perfume she likes to wear. If she's onto him and the team suspects him, he can't go back. But he can stay a step ahead, execute the plan and then maybe get a new body. For now, he's going to stay in the shadows. He logs off.

The little man is standing nearby when the Leopard opens the office door. "I got what I needed."

"About the operation, Mr. Merit. We will be –"

"Ready? Great. I'll be back in touch shortly. I have to take care of something. No need to show me out. I'll just use the restroom and go."

"Ah, OK," the little man says.

The Leopard smirks and lifts the little man's chin. "Remember your family. They're counting on you."

The little man backs away, nods, and heads for his office.

The Leopard locks the restroom door and studies his face, DeMarco's face in the mirror. He smiles. *It's good to be alive,* he thinks. He rinses his face seven times with cold water, an ayurvedic practice he adopted from time spent in India. Opening a locked cabinet near the mirror, he withdraws some dark makeup, a shaggy toupee, and tinted glasses. He looks again, rechecking his reflection. Taking a small stone from the cabinet, he puts it in his shoe to force a limp, changing his gait. *Good enough.*

He opens the restroom door slowly and checks. The little man is in his office, head-down on the computer. The Leopard turns and exits onto 43rd Street.

CHAPTER 38
QUEEN TO ROOK FIVE

Ashaki jostles amidst the rush hour commuters, ascending the steps from the Nostrand Avenue subway station into the Bed-Stuy Brooklyn neighborhood. She scans her phone. The video loop of her working at her DHS workstation is still running in case anyone checks. She taps and sees there has been one viewer. *Hmm? I'll have to check on that later.* She walks two blocks to a worn brownstone on Herkimer Street. Unlatching the wrought-iron gate next to the stone steps, she descends the half flight to a basement apartment. The sweet-pungent aroma of weed seeps through the door. She knocks four times, then once, then twice. The security camera nestled in a corner above blinks red.

The door opens a crack revealing only a red nose and scraggly red beard. "What the fuck are you doing here?" the man, only known as X, says.

Ashaki grins. "Let me in dick-wad or I won't be the only one who knows where you live."

Silence, then the door opens to a dark, cramped space only illuminated by a bank of computer monitors. She enters and grabs X's genitals, squeezing hard. "Glad to see you too." She lets go and pecks him on the cheek.

"What do you want?"

"We've never met in person. I thought it was about time. Ever since I watched you crack the Moscow power-grid, I've been an admirer. You're hotter than I thought."

X, who looks more like a troll with pock-marked skin, wild hair and a beer-belly, blushes. "You're not bad yourself." He smiles.

Ashaki notices a small bulge growing in his trousers. *Perfect.* "Listen, hon. I need your help. It's a little sticky."

"Why me? You have access to everything DHS has."

"This can't be DHS and can't leave breadcrumbs. There's a rogue DHS agent named Don DeMarco. I need you to find him."

"What's so important about this guy?"

"He's planning something big and destructive, but I don't really care about that. My agency does and I'd score some points if I could stop him. But to me, there is something more important. I have a score to settle and I want to take him off the board."

"Sounds like a pretty bad dude. OK, if I do this, what do I get?"

"I'll owe you. You'll make out in the long run."

"The long run is a really long time. I need something now."

She hesitates. "How about... you do this for me and you get to see me naked."

The bulge grows larger. "And?"

"I'll take care of that thing growing in your shorts." *Hmm*, she thinks. Isn't she just exchanging one abuser for another? No, this time, she's in charge. She's the chess master and this nerdy hacker is just a useful tool, a pawn. Anyway, she can get what she wants and maybe have some fun too. *Men are so easy.*

Beads of sweat form on X's upper lip. "Where do we start? Tell me what you know about this DeMarco."

CHAPTER 39
CHEN

Not sure why Chen's ME office and lab has to be two stories underground in a windowless bunker. Must be something symbolic there. When Renata and I arrive, he's bent over a dark-skinned corpse illuminated by bright spotlights. He's wearing those black rim bifocals with little magnifiers on the lenses. When he looks up, he reminds me of a 1940s vintage alien. "Good to see you again, Sam. Looking like your old self," Chen says.

"It's only an illusion," I say, which is half right.

"And who is this?" Chen grins.

"Agent Renata Fermi." She extends a hand.

Chen looks down at his blue latex covered hand and blushes. "Maybe we can shake hands later."

Renata smiles. "You know why we're here. What have you got?"

Chen waves at the corpse. "Meet Congressman Jones. He was one of the unfortunate attendees of the infamous Black Caucus meeting. Either they had too many bodies or they know how good I am, so they sent him to me, here in New York."

My moral compass goes into the red zone. "The meeting wasn't infamous. The attack was."

"I stand corrected. I've never seen anything exactly like this before. It's as if somebody shredded his spinal cord cartilage and blew up his blood vessels from the inside."

"We think some kind of sonic beam was aimed at the meeting from a distance," Renata says.

Chen shakes his head. "I suppose if the beam was focused enough and the right frequency, it could explain it, but that seems like a stretch to me."

"Then what could explain it?" I ask.

"What do you know about the room they were meeting in?"

Renata taps a few times on her tablet. "Here, see for yourself."

Chen studies the 3D view of the mahogany-paneled room in which the CBC met that day. He swivels the tablet side-to-side, and the augmented reality view pans the room. "Looks pretty standard, conference table, side tables. Wait. There are three monitors and a sound system on the wall."

Renata and I watch over Chen's shoulder. "Do you have any idea what was on those monitors, or playing through the sound system, during the meeting?" he asks.

Renata and I look at each other. "I'm not sure," she says, taking the tablet back and swiping through the incident files. "I can't find anything."

Chen rubs his nose. "Well, maybe you should look harder. I pulled out this article for you on how somebody managed to weaponize one of those popular ASMR videos, you know, Autonomous Sensory Meridian Response – whispering and crackling and brushing. Dumb stuff like that."

"Yes, they drive me crazy," Renata says.

"Many people have that reaction. Now let's ask, what would happen if they could be more than just soothing? What if they could actually do damage? And what if that were combined with the longer distance sonic attack, creating a synchronized resonant frequency effect? You know, like the famous Tacoma bridge collapse. The sound waves stack up rupturing blood vessels and pulverizing spinal cartilage? Just a theory. Humans naturally look for one single cause for a problem. But when two or more things that by themselves are harmless, act in combination to create a horrendous result, it can be the hardest kind of mystery to solve. Our one-track, one-solution minds usually can't do it."

I punch him gently in the arm. "But you can?"

He grins. "I'm a genius, remember?"

"I was waiting for your sense of humor to appear."

"It's not funny. It's dead serious — no pun intended. Your next step should be to test my theory. Recreate the scene and see if you can make it work," Chen says.

"I'm not sure we have the time or resources for that," Renata says.

"Do you have the time or resources for another attack?

CHAPTER 40
PRIORITIES

"Are you OK?" Monica asks, trying to catch her breath. "Had to run to the bathroom down the hall from Evan's room to answer the phone. No cell phones allowed in the I.C.U."

"I'm fine. Still in New York, but I'll be there as soon as I can. How's Evan?" I ask.

"He's awake, thank God. He's a tough little guy. He may need a ton of P.T., but he should recover."

"That's a huge relief. How are you?"

"I'm still pissed at you and need a little more time, but I do care, you know."

"I know you do. I just wish I could come there now."

"Don't kid yourself and me. If you really wanted to be here, you wouldn't be in New York chasing the terrorist du jour."

"Interesting choice of words. I'm doing it for our country, for all of us."

"But why does it have to be you? There are plenty of capable people like Rich and Michelle and Renata that can fight this fight. Why not let them? What makes you so special?"

"First, if everybody said 'Let someone else do it,' we'd have nobody protecting us. Second, I am special. I have super-powers."

Monica snickers. "Umm, huh. Like what?"

"I can time travel."

Monica laughs. "Oh, really?"

I smile. "Sort of. Anyway, I hate to tell you this, but the Leopard is back and I am uniquely qualified to track him down. I did it before, didn't I?"

"How's that possible? He's dead. Rich and you killed him in Cambridge."

"Remember how I came back last year in Juan Valiente's body? Well, LaSalam stole Frank's technology. Apparently, he found a good chunk of the hardware Bart used to bring me back left behind in a Mexican airport restroom. Not only has the Leopard come back, but he has bodyjacked unsuspecting victims, stolen their bodies, and turned them into an enemy army."

"*Bodyjacked?* This is crazy."

"We think he's planning something big and I need to help stop it. You know the attack in D.C. and the incident in South Bend? We think he may be behind one or both. That it's only the beginning of something bigger, much bigger."

"Oh my God. Does this mean Evan and I are in danger again?"

"Look out your window."

"What?"

"Just look out the hospital window."

Monica steps to the window, clutching the phone. "Your old Jeep is there. What's it doing here? I thought you left it at the office. And who's that inside?"

"It's Juan. I've asked him to keep an eye on you both, just in case."

"Juan? Sam, I swear I'm going to take Evan and disappear. You'll never see either of us again. If –"

"Calm down, honey. It's just a precaution. I doubt you're in any immediate peril."

"Great. That's just great. I feel so much better now. You keep doing this, putting us in danger while you imagine yourself saving the world. You need to get your priorities straight, mister."

"Monica, it will be OK. I promise. Please stay put. You'll be safe at the hospital. I'll be there as soon as this is over and we can talk. Promise me you won't leave me."

"Sorry, Sam. At this point, I won't promise anything. At least one of us has their priorities straight. Mine is Evan's safety. We're only staying until Evan's healthy enough to leave. Then we're outta here."

I let out a long breath. "I don't know what to do or say. I love you and Evan more than anything. I don't want to lose you."

"That's your problem, Sam. You don't know what to do or say. So let me make it easier for you. You've already lost us. Goodbye, Sam." Monica hangs up.

"Monica!"

*   *   *

Maybe I am lost, the dark clouds of my genetic depression circling. The wind is picking up. A cloud burst seems imminent. I call my best friend.

"Sam, how's it going in New York?" Loretta asks.

"We have leads, but we're really mostly just chasing our tails. You and Bart may be able to help, but first I've got a problem with Monica... I could use your advice."

"OK, what is it?"

"She can't seem to handle the crises and danger I seem to dump on her. She's tried, but she's given up. She's left me and she's taking Evan."

"So it's her fault?"

"Not you too! I thought you of all people, you would give me a little sympathy and support. What should I do?"

"You won't have my sympathy. You can keep the woe-is-me self-pity to yourself. But you will always have my support. So here's my advice. Drop what you're doing and go to her now if you want any chance of salvaging your marriage."

"I will. I told her as soon as I'm done here, I'm hers."

"Are you listening to yourself? Life is all about decisions and choices. You have a life-changing choice to make right now. What's it going to be — family or country?"

"I want both. Is that too much to ask?"

"Yes, in your bizarre case. So?"

"I can't leave. I've got to see this through. Then I'll go to her and try to pick up the pieces."

"Good luck. I'll still love you, but I'm busy too. We're testing Bart's new terabit encryption program. You know quantum computers are running millions of permutations a second and cracking standard encryption. The government needs this upgrade or its systems are toast. So buck up. What do you need in New York? I've got Bart on the line."

"Hey buddy, I miss you," I say.

"I miss you too, but we're swamped. Government's up my ass about quantum computers cracking their gigabit encryption. Worried about attacks on government systems and national security," Bart says.

"Little stuff like that? The U.S. government's our biggest customer. Better take good care of them," I say.

"Yeah, I am. Doing the final testing on the new program that should keep the bad guys out. Got a few minutes while the code compiles. What do you need?"

"OK. I could use your help in the investigation. I feel in my bones these attacks are somehow LaSalam related."

"How could it be? You killed him. Not *you* personally, I mean. Oh, you know what I mean."

"Second time I've had that question today. Look, since we're all short on time, I can fill you in on the Leopard's resurrection later. Just trust me — he's alive and in the body of a DHS agent named Don DeMarco."

"So you need us to track him down."

"No, DHS is all over that. Here's what I'd need you to hunt and kill. There's still a big loose end from the Fulton Street incident last year. Remember when Rich received an anonymous phone call revealing Momar LaSalam's, aka the Cub's, plans? The caller also saved Rich's life by pointing him to a hidden IED. Who tipped off Rich about the Cub? Who's still alive that might have been working with him? I'll admit that the Black Caucus incident looks racially motivated. Still, the chem attack in South Bend has LaSalam or his cohorts written all over it. And whoever tipped Rich then, might know about LaSalam now. Had to be somebody on the inside. Can you find him or her?"

"Where do we start?"

"I've got nothing on that. I'm going to send you a link to the text and phone records between the mysterious informant and Rich regarding the Cub. Do your magic and see what you can trace."

"Where'd you get this link?"

"Professor Frank Einstein. Who else? He's expecting your call. I can't think of three people better equipped, whom I trust, to figure this out."

Loretta looks at Bart. He shrugs. "We're on it, boss."

CHAPTER 41
CLUB SODA

The midday heat and intense sun on the streets of Manhattan can be suffocating, not at all like the cool Paris she just left. Nancy Lu slips into The Dead Lizard bar on Water Street. Maybe not such a good idea since she's been on the wagon only for a couple of days. No Red Chip yet. As soon as she enters, the dim light almost blinds her. She halts for a minute to let her eyes adjust. As the aroma of beer on tap hits her, she feels a pang deep in her gut – that longing for just one drink. No, not today.

She boosts herself up onto the leather barstool. Sometimes she just hates being short. There are a few people at the tables but nobody besides her at the bar. The heavily tattooed bartender washing glasses ignores her.

She waits patiently at first. Still no acknowledgment. *Great, another racist pig.* She slams her hand on the bar. "Hey, bar-hole."

He turns his head. "In a minute."

"Now! I work for the Times. I'd love to write an article about this shithole, but a Yelp review will be a good place to start."

"Sorry, love. What can I get you?" He grins.

"I'm not your love. I'll take a seltzer and lime."

He shoots the seltzer into a glass, drops in the lime and slides it to her. "Big drinker, eh?"

"Fuck-you-very-much."

The bartender shrugs and goes back to his glass washing.

The ice-cold drink and bubbles feel good going down. Nancy puckers her lips, *I love a good fight.*

The door opens and an attractive, thirty-something brunette grabs a stool two-away from Nancy. Nancy studies her six-inch red heels and tight pants. *Hmm, I could do that*, she thinks. The stranger turns and smiles at Nancy. "Hotter than a witch's tongue out there."

Nancy smiles back. She knows the stranger's semi-dark skin is going to be a problem for her new acquaintance in this place. She slaps the bar again. "Bar-hole, you have another customer."

He looks at Nancy. "Now there's two of you. My lucky day." He turns to the stranger. "Sorry, dear. What can I get you?"

"Give me a whiskey on the rocks. Make it a double, but wash your hands first. I don't want your germs."

The bartender shoots her a look and makes the drink. Nancy snickers. "Tough day?"

The stranger grins. "Ain't he a piece of work. Yeah, my boss is on my back. Working a tough case."

"Case? What do you do?" Nancy asks.

The stranger slides onto the stool next to Nancy and extends a hand. "I'm Adele. Adele Lamont. Work at DHS down the street. She leans over and whispers, "But don't tell anybody."

Nancy takes Adele's warm, soft hand and continues to hold it. She looks at both of Adele's hands. No rings. "I'm Nancy Lu. Just had to get out of the heat."

Adele laughs. "By the looks of it, you didn't come here to get drunk like me."

"I wish I could, but I'm a month sober." Just a little lie.

"And Ms. Lu, what do you do?" Adele chuckles at the inadvertent rhyme.

"I work for the Times. I'm a reporter. Funny coincidence. I was just in your office, working on a story."

"Really? What's the story about?"

"I'm following up on the D.C. attack and some of the other crazy stuff happening lately. I can't say any more than that now. What department are you in over there?"

"I'm an analyst. I know about those cases too."

"Uh, huh. Maybe I can ask you a few questions."

Adele takes a sip of her whiskey and smacks her lips. "What I do is strictly confidential. If I talked, they'd fire my ass."

Nancy checks out Adele again. "And a nice ass it is. I'd hate to see something happen to it." Then she whispers, "But I understand."

Adele chugs the rest of her drink and slaps the glass on the bar. "Tell you what. You show me yours and I'll show you mine."

Nancy blinks. "My ass or my story?"

Adele retakes Nancy's hand. "How about both?"

Nancy looks up, remembering Al. *Forgive me*, she thinks. Dropping a twenty on the bar, she gazes back at Adele Lamont, née Ashaki LaSalam. "OK, let's go."

CHAPTER 42
NICE ASS

"First your ass, then the story," Adele says, leading Nancy into the bedroom of Nancy's apartment.

It's getting dark earlier as summer succumbs to fall. Nancy closes the blinds and turns to her new friend. "No, I'm an eager reporter. I want the story first."

Adele tilts her head and smiles. "I bet if you knew the story, you wouldn't be able to think of anything else. So no ass, no story."

"OK, OK," Nancy says, grinning back.

Clothes go flying. Limbs get tangled and wet. The room spins. Time stops. It's feverish, passionate, even hungry, and then... then it's over. Nancy stares at Adele, sweaty, and satisfied. The sweet-sour bouquet of sex drifts in the air. She takes a deep breath. "OK, what's the story?"

Adele snorts. "So soon. You are eager. I see why you must be good at your job. You first."

What's the harm – she's DHS? Nancy thinks. "OK... " She proceeds to fill Adele in on her working with Michelle and Rich, what she knows about D.C., the bio-attack, and even bodyjacking. She can't seem to stop herself. *Is she saying too much?* She relates their theories about the Leopard's connection to all these incidents. Finally, breathless, "I've probably said too much. Your turn..."

"Fair enough. You've been so forthcoming." Another smile, another pun. "OK, I'll tell you this. I don't know much about bodyjacking, but I'm really interested. I'll have to check that out further. But I do believe we have a mole, named Don DeMarco, who we suspect is the reincarnated Leopard. But they're wrong on the D.C. and bio-attacks. I know who did them."

Nancy darts upright. "Oh my God, who?"

Adele smirks. "If I told you, I'd have to kill you."

"That old trope? Quit messing around. I told you everything I know. Spew."

"OK, your choice. The D.C. attack was done by a bunch of very smart hillbillies from Tennessee using neuro-weapons built in France."

"Really? Give me names. Who was behind it?"

"A guy named Max Werner."

Nancy is already scribbling notes in her notebook.

Adele looks at the notebook. "I like it, old school."

Nancy glances up briefly and then continues writing excitedly. "It's been a habit since I was a kid. And what do you know about the bio-attack?"

"I know who's behind it."

"Who? Tell me."

Adele deadpans it. "I am."

Nancy looks up from her notes. All the color drains from her face. She suddenly feels a chill like she has never felt before. "What?"

"I did it as a test to see if it would work. We're just tweaking it to make it better and then I have something much bigger planned."

"Oh, my God." Nancy chokes on her words. "Why are you telling me this?"

With that, Ashaki swings her hand out from behind her back and pulls a piano wire taught against Nancy's neck. Nancy thrashes her naked body from side-to-side, but Ashaki's grip on the wire is too taut. It cuts through Nancy's skin, tracing a line of blood across her throat. Nancy gags and struggles harder. Ashaki pulls the wire through Nancy's windpipe all the way through to her spine. The thrashing stops. The last fleeting image in Nancy's mind is of Al lying next to her, smiling.

Ashaki releases the wire and looks at the red marks on her hands, then down at Nancy's lifeless body. "I told you if you asked, I'd have to kill you. But thanks for this afternoon."

Ashaki swings her legs off the bed, slides on her black pants, and gets dressed. After slipping on her shoes, she reaches across Nancy's bare torso for the notebook. Holding it up, she flicks on her Zippo. The notebook goes up in flames. Ashaki drops it on the sheets, which immediately ignite, the flames spreading outward and then up the walls. The dancing light show is hypnotic.

Ashaki, like a black widow, heads for the door, taking one last look back. "Very nice ass indeed."

CHAPTER 43
LOVERLY

The gravel driveway is long and winding up to the Riverdale Assisted Living Center in Scarsdale. Rich gets out of his Crown Vic and takes a minute to take in the puffy morning clouds doing their slow dance in the early fall sky. The scent of freshly cut grass lingers in the air. *Life is short and bittersweet*, he thinks. Scarsdale is one of the most affluent towns in America, not that it matters in this case. What matters is that it's close to where his sister Margaret lives, so she can check on Mom regularly. Rich feels pangs of guilt for visiting so infrequently, but being assigned with DHS to California and then D.C. has made it harder.

Rich's mother, Alice, is in Stage 5 of her Alzheimer's journey. Her trip down this path is mostly pleasant but sometimes scary and confusing. She has good days and bad, according to Samantha, her nurse. There is no earthly light at the end of this road. Hopefully, there is a divine one.

Rich checks in with Samantha. "How is she today?"

"Today is a good day. She may remember you. Why don't you see if she'll go outside? The morning is cool enough and the fresh air may do her some good."

Rich takes Samantha's hand. "Thanks for being so kind to her."

"It's not hard. She's a sweetheart."

"I miss the way she was, but I'm sure you hear that all the time."

"Getting older is about adapting, Alzheimer's or not."

"I understand. It's just a loss. That's all."

"Yes, and despite the series of losses we suffer from age, there is much left to appreciate and enjoy. Try focusing on that." Samantha gestures towards the hall. "She's in her room."

"I will," Rich says. Samantha pivots and saunters towards the reception desk. Rich can't help noticing the gentle sway of her hips.

He heads down the hall and knocks gently on the open door to Alice's room. His mother is in a rocking chair, attempting to knit something, which looks like a tangle of knots. She looks up. "Rich, you're home from school. How was your day?"

Rich forces a smile. "It was good, Mom. Would you like to go for a walk outside? It's an extra-special day."

She smiles broadly. "You remembered what I always taught my students that every day is an extra-special day." She turns back to her chaotic knitting.

He reaches over to lightly take her arm. She recoils. "Don't touch me. You took advantage of me once. Shame on me. You won't do it again."

Rich wonders what cruel memory she is reliving. "It's me, Mom, Rich, your son. I saw they are serving ice cream outside. Would you like some?"

Her demeanor instantly changes. "Ice cream. I love ice cream. Do you think they have chocolate sprinkles?"

"I bet they do. Come, let's go see."

She drops her knitting in a nearby garbage can. "Let's go. I want vanilla with chocolate sprinkles." She stands, but still slightly stooped, heads for the door.

Rich circles behind her as she heads out, retrieves the knitting, and puts it on her chair. He hears her from the hallway. "C'mon. What are you waiting for?"

He hurries into the hallway, gently guiding Alice downstairs and onto the expansive lawn. There is a Good Humor truck ringing its bell, last call. Rich buys two ice cream cones, one with sprinkles and hands it to his mother. They share a bench in a white gazebo on the edge of the woods. A cardinal alights on the railing and chirps a few notes.

"Rich, what was that song we used to sing when we did the dinner dishes at night?"

"We sang lots of songs, Mom. Mostly show tunes."

And as if she is a blossom opening up to the sun and not failing at all, she launches into... "All I want is a room somewhere/ Far away from the cold night air/ With one enormous chair/ Oh, wouldn't it be loverly?"

Rich joins in. "Lots of chocolate for me to eat/ Lots of coal makin' lots of heat/ Warm face, warm hands, warm feet/ Oh, wouldn't it be loverly?..."

Then Alice stops abruptly and seems to shrink back into herself, like a tulip closing at the end of the day. "What did you say your name was?"

Rich's eyes water. "Rich, your son, Mom."

"Oh, Rich, yes. Did that bully pick on you again at school today?"

"Yes, Mom. He did."

"Remember, bullies are just weaklings in disguise, trying to make up for their small penises. You stand up to him. Show him who's the better man."

Rich blushes and smiles for real this time. "I'm trying every day, Mom."

"Good," she says as a tear runs down her cheek. "Because today is an extra-special day."

CHAPTER 44
FLICKERING

Unbelievable, I slept last night like a normal person, dreams, pee breaks, and all. Early this morning, Renata and I are riding Amtrak somewhere between Trenton and Wilmington, to our destination, Union Station in D.C. "Why are we doing this?" I ask.

The train rocks side to side and clatters on the outdated tracks. Renata waits for the clamor to die down. "As I said, we should review the evidence and forensics in person," Renata says.

"I don't get it. We have all of it online in New York, images, video, all that stuff."

"You've been living in the digital world too long. There's another dimension when you can physically touch the objects, feel their weight, and manipulate them. It's almost like they speak to me somehow."

"OK, I get it, like Sherlock Holmes."

"Exactly, Watson." She grins.

My cell vibrates and without me answering, Frank's face appears on the screen. "Ah, I miss riding the train," Frank says. "There's almost something Zen-like about the rhythm of it. I've done some of my best work on trains."

"Yes, it's great to be back. I have you to thank for that, Frank. I'm sorry you can't really experience this in the Cloud," I say. "So why'd you call or are you just spying on me again?"

"OK. There's one particular object I'd like both of you to look at in D.C. It may seem odd but find Object ID 908274. It's a pencil eraser."

"Why that?" Renata asks.

"Because an eraser is to sound, like rock is to fossils. It captures an imprint, particularly if the sonic blast is of high intensity."

"Really? That raises a couple of curious questions. First, how do we see the imprint and if we do see it, what do we do with the resulting data?" Renata asks.

"If my resonant frequency theory is correct, using software I developed to work with an electron microscope, we will see the intersecting waves from the two sources merging in the eraser. The same way they merged inside the brains of the unfortunate victims."

"Very cool. OK, say that works. Where does that leave us?" I ask.

"It leaves you with a new set of leads. First, you review the crime-scene photos of where the object was found and how it was oriented during the attack. Then, with the wave pattern, you can triangulate the location of the original two signals. That may open a whole new can of leads."

"Makes sense. We'll do it," Renata says.

"Excuse me a minute. I've got to hit the head." I look down at Frank on my screen. "I guess you're coming with me."

I move quickly up the aisle between the seats, steadying myself against the sway of the car. Thank God, the W.C. is free. Opening the door, the intense odor of disinfectant hits me. I lock the door and check the mirror. My face seems to pixelate, then blur. "Frank, it's happening again. Look!" I put the phone camera in selfie-mode."

"I see. Stay calm," Frank says. "Have you been focusing and exerting your will to be present the way we discussed?"

"Yes, yes I have. And I thought I was getting the hang of it. I wasn't stressed or losing focus just sitting on the train. I don't get it. I can't go back out there like this or continue working with Renata or, more important, return to Monica and Evan. Not like this. You've got to do something."

Frank reappears on the screen, stroking his goatee. "Hmm, maybe it has something to do with the train, being inside a metal box like that for an extended period. I think it's more likely the movement of the train is disrupting the spacetime algorithm in the re-engagement program I wrote to bring you back."

"Spacetime? What are you talking about?"

"Most people believe Space and Time are separate, different dimensions. Right?"

"Well, aren't they? That's what we've all been taught."

"No, not exactly. Take the fact that you're traveling on a train. About how fast is the train traveling now?"

I look out the small restroom window. "About fifty miles-per-hour, I'd say."

"That's how it would appear to someone standing on the ground looking at the train. Now, how fast is the train going relative to you?"

"Relative to me, the train is standing still."

"Exactly, fundamental physics, you have a different frame of reference from the person outside, watching the train go by. Now, which reality is the real one, yours or the outside observers?"

"That's an absurd question. They're both real."

"Are you sure? You only know what you know, standing where you are, in the bathroom. When you consider reality, in quantum time, we have to merge space and time to create the true reality. That way, you can be both moving zero miles-per-hour while moving fifty on the train. And don't forget the train tracks are on earth, which is rotating at a thousand miles-per-hour while circling the sun at 67,000 miles-per-hour."

"That's all very informative, but what's it got to do with me?"

"It seems that the train is altering your spacetime in a way I hadn't accounted for."

Can you fix it?"

"I'm not sure."

"Not sure? Frank, I'm counting on you. Please!"

"Hang on. Stay in the bathroom. I'll figure something out, make a few adjustments."

There's rapid knocking on the bathroom door. I ignore it. Knocking again, more insistent this time. I have to answer, "I'm sick. Please use the restroom in another car." I'm feeling nauseous. Not sure if it's the rocking train or my flickering state. More knocking. "Go away," I shout.

CHAPTER 45
NEXT STOP

The Leopard stares out the basement window at his new pop-up office on Willow Street in Brooklyn. The odor of burning wires greets him as he enters. "How's it looking?"

The little man crawls out from under the desk, beads of sweat on his brow. "Last feed is connected. I think we're back in business."

"My apologies for the sudden change of plan and the rushed move. Security, you understand."

"No explanation needed. I do what I'm told."

The Leopard pats the little man on his shoulder. "Right thinking, my little man." Then he grasps the man's shoulder and digs his thumb into the soft spot just under the collarbone.

The little man winces, "What? What did I do?"

"Nothing. I just felt like inflicting some pain. I feel better now. Thank you." The Leopard releases his grip.

The little man backs up two steps. *I'm working for a psychopath, but what choice do I have?* he thinks.

"I understand a brief time delay on account of the move, but we still need to make the window when the president's addressing the General Assembly tomorrow. Are we still on track?"

The little man stammers, "I think... I think so."

"That's not the answer I am looking for." The Leopard swings his hand up and out like he's about to strike and just as suddenly pulls it pack, stroking his perfectly coiffed hair. An old playground taunt that has the desired effect. The little man flinches.

"Yes, I mean, *yes.* We'll be ready."

"That's better. Because you understand the consequences of failure."

The little man pictures his wife, Jamilla, and his two small daughters. The sweat now soaks through his white shirt. "Yes." *I can't be near this man. I'll lose it*, he thinks. "Excuse me, sir. I have much more to do to be ready." He pivots and heads for the large closet, which now houses their sixteen triginti-core servers.

Ahmed LaSalam, the Leopard, removes a photo from his pocket. It is an image of the little man and his family standing on a beach. The little man is holding Rabab in his arms. The other girl, Salwa, holds his free hand. His wife has an arm around his waist and her head leans on his shoulder. They are all smiling except for Salwa. She projects a distant stare. Maybe she has a whiff of the future. Perhaps not. The Leopard props the photo up on the desk and leans it against the computer monitor.

A grin crosses his face. He turns for the door.

A few long minutes later, I plunk down on the toilet of the rocking train in a cold sweat. An announcement comes crackling over the loudspeaker. "Wilmington, next stop Wilmington." What's Renata think about my prolonged absence? I'm sure she'll come and check any minute now. If I wasn't stressed before, I sure am now. Look at my hands – they're still fulgurating. I can't stand it. I ping Frank again. His face appears on my screen. "Frank, what's happening – any progress?"

"It's only been a few minutes, son. I'm working the problem. Be patient."

I check my watch, which is solidly in focus, despite my wrist underneath fading in and out. "It's 9:15, been almost ten minutes. I thought you could work super-fast in the Cloud."

"I can. I do. Hold on a sec. I think I've got something."

"Hurry, please."

"OK, I've made some adjustments to the latest update of the quantum spacetime software. It should just take a couple of minutes more to kick in. Then we'll see if your virtuality problem goes away."

"Wait, I don't understand. How can you do something there that affects me here? I thought I was autonomous in my new body. Do you have some kind of remote control? Now you're really spooking me."

"Don't worry. It's nothing like that. Sam, have you ever had a Reiki treatment? You know where the therapist moves her hands over your body but doesn't actually touch you."

"No. Sounds creepy."

"It's not. It's quite amazing. I used to get regular treatments for my back and it really helped, better than anything else I tried."

"And she never touched you?"

"That's right. It gets better. You don't even have to be in the same room, and a skilled Reiki practitioner can still heal you from a distance."

"No way. That's like Voodoo, Frank."

"In a way. I even tested it from miles away. I asked the Reiki practitioner to do her thing without telling me exactly when she did it. Then when I felt the effects, I called her up and checked the time. She sent her remote healing at me at the exact time I felt the effects. I was so fascinated by this phenomenon that I had to understand it and see if I could mimic the power of it digitally. And I have. I've been able to tap into and manipulate the Etheric and Emotional fields the Reiki people use for remote treatments. I call this communication aspect of the spacetime code, Remote Regeneration. Your fields were disrupted. I think I've been able to fix that. You should start seeing the results about now. Oh, and I implanted a receiver in your thigh just in case Reiki stuff didn't work."

"Very funny. You can be exasperating sometimes."

"Humor has magical healing powers too, you know."

"Thanks, I'll keep that in mind." I close my eyes, afraid to look. Finally, I take a deep breath and unclose my eyes. My wrists and arms come into focus. I turn them over. They look normal. I go to the mirror. My face is back, clear and distinct. I splash on some cold water. It feels good. I double-check the mirror. It's OK. I'm OK."

"Sam, are you there? What's happening?"

I pick up my phone. The screen is filled with Frank's concerned expression. "I'm OK. It seems to have worked. Amazing. Will it last?"

"I hope so. It's the first time I've ever applied this code fix. Let me see you."

I move the camera up and down. "I hope you've solved the problem for good. Otherwise, I can't go on. You know that, right?"

"I'm fully aware. Now go back to Renata. She's probably worried by now. Call me when you get to D.C. and have that eraser."

"OK, and yes, she's probably more than a little concerned." I click off and return through the swaying car to my seat.

"Sam, where the hell have you been? I looked all over the train. I thought you jumped."

"I went to the restroom. I told you that."

"I know. I knocked on the door several times. I tried your cell. Nobody answered."

"I'm sorry." I force a smile. "I just had to fix my makeup."

She punches me hard in the arm. "Don't do that to me again."

"Ouch, that hurt. From now on, I'll try to be present at all times."

"You better."

We ride in silence for almost an hour. I nibble at a stale Danish pastry. Then the loudspeaker blares, "Next stop, Washington, D.C., Union Station."

CHAPTER 46
MY GIRL

The Leopard ascends the steps to Willow Street. He dons his Yankees hat and sunglasses to blend in. DHS will be looking for DeMarco. Back at the office, he had slipped the pebble in his shoe to fake a limp. A precaution in case DHS is using forensic gait analysis software that identifies the unique way a person walks. He looks up, checking his mental to-do list. *Call Ashaki.* She answers on the first ring.

"Guess who this is?" the Leopard says.

"Sorry, no time for games," Ashaki moves her finger to disconnect.

"Don't hang up. It's Ahmed."

She thinks fast. "I thought you were dead, killed in Cambridge by those DHS agents."

"I was, no thanks to you. Turning on our brother was not a healthy idea. Unlike him, I saved myself to digital and now I'm back. We need to meet."

She knows by now that he's back in DeMarco's body. But he doesn't know that she knows. Ashaki taps a few keys on her phone to start a trace. "Why should I meet you? You'll only try to exact revenge. I know you."

"I miss you. I'm willing to forgive and forget."

"I doubt that. So tell me what you want."

"I've grown. I've become a better man."

"I think the only thing that grows with you is in your pants."

"Now, now. I know you've grown too into a smart and beautiful woman."

"You make my skin crawl. So cut out the bullshit and tell me why you're calling."

"Ah, you've also become very direct, like the Americans you work for. Speaking of which, if you refuse to meet me, they might just be interested in your little moonlighting gig. You know, like planning a terror attack with your hillbilly lover. What's his name, Max? Is he as good in bed as I was?"

Ashaki's jaw drops. She feels a chill. Opening her mouth, nothing comes out.

"It seems I have your attention," the Leopard smirks. "You don't have to answer my questions. Like a good lawyer, I already know the answers. I will text you a location to meet in one hour. Don't be late or else... And don't worry, I need your help with a little project of mine and maybe I'll help you with yours. We made a powerful team before. As they say here, 'I'd like to get the band back together.' Maybe even have a little fun backstage after. What do you say?"

Ashaki tastes vomit reflux on her tongue. Her mind is racing. *What can I do here? How do I stop this maniac?* She remembers her Aikido training. *Maybe I can turn his own energy against him?* "OK," she whispers.

"That's my girl." He clicks off.

CHAPTER 47
YOU, FIRST

Busy. WUP? Ashaki texts.

Have juicy info U asked me to dig up re LaSalam, X replies.

GD. Let's have it.

Nope. Question of payment first. Remember, U naked? U know my ADDY. MIRL 1 hour if U want what I have.

Ashaki looks at her watch.

Have other meeting in an hour. Nearby. Meet in 10?

X licks his lips,

TSTB.

Ashaki rounds the corner on Lincoln Place, checking both ways. There's no reason for anyone to follow her, but you never know. She finds the number, opens the wrought-iron gate, and descends to the basement apartment. She notices the bars on the windows and the garbage bags covering the glass from the inside. No need to knock – she knows he's watching. The door buzzes and she enters the dimly-lit, claustrophobic room lined with computer monitors and servers. The odor of burnt popcorn suffuses the air.

X appears from behind a server, his red hair still wet from the shower. A Hawaiian patterned shirt hangs over his football-size belly. He's been getting ready like this is his first date. "How do you like my place?"

"Been here before, remember? Listen, I've got an important meeting to get to. I don't have much time. So tell me what you've got."

"And?"

"And what?"

"You're going to show me what you've got. Tell you what. I'll tell you one thing for every piece of clothing you remove. Let's start with the blouse."

What the fuck? she thinks. She unbuttons her blouse and tosses it on a chair. "I'm waiting."

X clears his throat. "LaSalam had an office and a bunch of hackers near the U.N. DHS got wind of it, so he relocated in a hurry before they got there."

"And you know this how?"

"Because one of my coding buddies works for him."

"Nice, and where's the new location?"

"That will cost you your pants."

She snorts, wriggles out of her tight pants, and turns, revealing a red silk thong taut between her cheeks. She rotates back, noticing the lump growing in X's pants. "OK, let's have it."

Staring, X chokes on his words. "It's... it's 32 Willow Street in Brooklyn."

She tilts her slender hips and smiles. "Did you find out what he's planning?"

"Now the bra." He beams.

She loosens the bra and turns her back to him. She holds it out between her thumb and forefinger. Dangling it by its strap, she lets it fall to the floor.

"Now turn around."

"Tell me what you know first and then I might."

X is breathing heavily now. "All my friend could tell me is they are planning something big. Something at the U.N. today."

"Anything else?"

"Nope, that's all I have. Now let me see those gorgeous melons."

Without turning, she retrieves her pants from the floor and slips them on.

"Hey, a deal's a deal."

She zips her fly and reaches into her pocket. Cradling a Naruto throwing knife in her hand and nestling it behind her wrist, she turns back to face X. "What do you think?"

His eyes pop. "Unbelievable."

In one swift motion, she swings her arm while expertly flicking her wrist. The knife sails end-over-end through the air between them, landing its razor-sharp point in X's neck. Blood gushes rhythmically from his pierced jugular. A look of wonder crosses his face. He tries to reach for the blade but collapses first to the floor.

Ashaki quickly dresses. Looking at X, she says, "Thanks for the info. Like you said, *a deal's a deal.*"

***

"Sam, how are you? I've been worried," Monica says

My eyes water as I look at her radiant smile on my phone. "I'm glad. Oh, I don't mean I'm glad that you're worried. I just mean, I'm glad you still care enough to worry. I'm OK. In D.C. in a rental car with Renata. We're on our way to the hospital to see you and Evan. Then we have to go check something out."

"Of course, I care. I always will. But we checked out of the hospital a couple of hours ago. We're at the airport, heading home. I just can't risk Evan's safety for your adventures."

"I wouldn't call them *adventures.*"

"Then I don't know what they are. I mean, what are you trying to prove? Why can't you stay home and go to work like a normal person?"

"Maybe because, for the first time in my life, I feel like I'm making a difference. I mean going to work, building stuff for clients, and making money are all good. Don't get me wrong. But protecting millions of people from death and disaster is really making a difference. I know it's risky, but it feels right."

"So you're making a choice – your family or your adventure."

"As I said before, when this is over, I'm done. I'll come home if you'll still have me. As Frank would say, I'm exercising *counterfactual regret minimization*."

"What the heck is that?"

"It means I know I screwed up and I'm learning from my mistakes. How long until your flight? Can I come see you at the airport?"

"They've started boarding. There's not enough time."

"Can I come home this weekend to spend a little time with Evan... and maybe you?"

"You're still sleeping on the couch."

"I under —"

Renata is driving us through the intersection at D Street NW and 7th Street. Suddenly, a garbage truck runs a red light, slamming full speed into the driver's side of our car. Glass and shrapnel fly in all directions. The truck driver gets out and flees down the nearby metro station stairs. Renata lies unconscious. Her head, bleeding from her mouth and eyes, rests on my lap. The smell of gasoline invades the car. I feel like I'm a feather floating. My body seems to drift upwards through the roof of the car. I'm circling above, a drone's eye view of a horrible accident scene. Sirens wail in the distance, growing louder. Then nothing.

"Sam. Sam! Are you there? What's happening? Answer me..." Monica shouts.

CHAPTER 48
NAKED TRUTH

Ashaki wasn't alone when she went to X's apartment. Green knew how to be a ghost. He learned the skills of camouflage and evasion as a sniper in Afghanistan. But in the city, you can't wear a ghillie. In urban warfare, you dress in gray with maybe a few paprika accents that blend in with brick and granite walls. Green was on Ashaki's tail from the time she left her office to the Nostram Ave station to X's apartment, always in the shadows, always blending in.

Once Ashaki entered the apartment, Green's next challenge was to get ears on her meeting. Fortunately, he had brought his infrared wall-penetrating listening device. With it, he could listen through walls from across the street. As Ashaki's striptease encounter with X unfolded through Green's headset, he felt a stirring he had long ago suppressed. Was the sweat soaking through his clothes from the heat of the day or from what he was hearing? He wasn't sure.

When the man with Ashaki revealed his boss's location, he was stunned. He listened even more intently. Then 'unbelievable' and a gurgling sound. He knew that sound from his experience in hand-to-hand combat. When you slice open a man's throat, you never forget that sound.

Green drops the earphone from one ear and dials. Before he can even speak, the Leopard barks, "What is it?"

Green instinctively knows how to keep it short and sweet. "She knows your location."

The Leopard snickers. "What's she doing now?"

"She's exiting the apartment. I think she killed her informant."

"Tying up loose ends. That's what I'd do. I think I know where she's going but follow her anyway. The mouse thinks she knows where the cat is. Won't she be surprised? Game on."

My eyes flutter open again into the nightmare I left. The smell of gasoline is everywhere. I'm still strapped in. Looking down, I see Renata unconscious and bleeding. Her blouse is ripped open, her full breasts exposed and blood-splattered. Instinct moves my hand to cover her up. Her eyes flicker. "Don't touch me, you perv." Then she fades out again, her head lolling to the side.

I stretch to reach my phone on the floor, pain slashing through me. The seatbelt is stuck. My outstretched arm flickers like before. I feel my blood pressure skyrocket and my face burning. People are approaching the car, presumably to help. What happens if they see me like this? Renata, I've got to save Renata. Inching the phone forward with my fingertips, I finally grasp it and call 911. Sirens wailing already, help is on the way.

A twenty-something man in baggy shorts with an afro peers through the car window and tugs on the door handle. A flame bursts out from beneath the car. The gathered crowd of good Samaritans and onlookers backs away. Smoke fills the car. I'm coughing, choking. I slam my elbow into the car window, but it won't give. Feeling stuck and helpless, I see my waving and blurry image in the vanity mirror. Is this it? Does it all end here? As I try to focus my eyes on the fading mirror, my face totally disappears. Gone.

CHAPTER 49

SCHRODINGER ME, BABY

"I retrieved you just in time or you and your problem would have been discovered," Frank says.

I look down and sideways, but I can't see anything. A rush of images from the distant past, the present, the accident, Monica, Bart, Loretta, Evan, a clock striking twelve, choking on thick smoke, tires burning, all rush through me. Then it hits me. I'm all digital again, no body, no flesh, no feeling – just a bunch of electrons in the Cloud. "What happened?"

"You were in an accident. I had to pull you back from the brink of death and maybe worse. So you are back with me in our cozy digital world."

"And Renata?"

"They got her out right before the car exploded. She's in critical condition at Georgetown University Hospital."

Frank turns back to his virtual monitors. I am sitting on a virtual sofa trying to wrap my head around all this. "This was a deal-breaker. I understand. I couldn't be exposed in the flickering state, or I don't know what would have happened. Media attention? Monica leaves me for good? Feds lock me up? What?"

"I'll make some adjustments to your settings and we could put you back, but I can't guarantee it won't happen again. Think of it this way, you'll be like old guys, like me. Younger people don't even notice we're there."

"Great. That's very reassuring. I already have PTSD from our other recent encounters with the Cub and Leopard. I just don't know if I literally have the guts do this anymore. Tell me how this works. What are you actually doing to me?"

"I am using Quantum Life as the science behind getting you back into a physical body. Sometime around 2018, scientists were able to simulate the evolution of life from inorganic to organic, from inert material to living cells. Probably the biggest existential question of all time – how did life evolve from just molecules and atoms? The traditional myth is that lightning struck at just the right time and was a catalyst transforming the dead to the living. Well, that's probably about as crazy as the Adam and Eve story. Don't get me wrong. The initial Quantum Life scientists didn't actually solve the big question of that magical transformative moment, but they got close enough for me to extrapolate their work and answer it myself."

I am transfixed but anxious to know how this story ends too. "Frank, how's this work?"

"Patience, Grasshopper. Now you know since I'm digital, I can put a thousand or ten thousand instances of myself to work on the problem 24/7 – don't need sleep after all. And that's exactly what I did. Because I had to take that moment of inception and evolve it all the way to a physical Sam. Fortunately, I had your digital DNA. That gave us a map of you and voila, a million man hours of work later and there you are, Sam Sunborn in the flesh, so to speak. I say 'so to speak' because part of this miracle is a form of projection. You are like Schrodinger's Cat – here and not here – you are truly quantum life like a quantum particle, space and time merged into one – you can be both here and not here at the same time."

"It's beyond me, but I've got to do this. What's next?"

"What I'm calling Quantum Flickering is the problem. Your space and time were partially out of synch. Part of you was in the train's restroom moving at fifty miles-per-hour and the other part was the observer standing outside and watching the train go by. You weren't one hundred percent in that one place at one time. You were essentially split between two places, but I'm working on that problem. Once I solve it, you can go back."

"I don't think I can wait that long. Renata is hurt, LaSalam is probably planning to kill thousands, and my wife might leave me for good. I need to go back now and take my chances. You keep working on the problem and when you've figured it out, maybe you can upload an update to me."

Frank chortles. "This isn't like doing a Windows update. I'll probably need to pull you back again to apply the fix."

"When you're ready and that time comes, do what you have to do."

"OK, but be careful. I've implanted a more powerful tracking chip in you so I can not only follow you for your own safety, but it also has audio capability. I can hear you and what's going on around you. Stop frowning, you can turn the sound off when you're with Monica or want me to butt out."

"That's kinda creepy."

"Sorry about that, but it's the only way I will agree to send you back. Your choice."

"I don't think I have a real choice. Send me back."

"You always have a choice," Frank says.

CHAPTER 50
FIVE BLOCK

Ashaki's cab deposits her on Clark Street, four blocks from the address X gave her before his untimely demise. She instinctively looks both ways and mentally plans a switch-back, evasive route to her destination. She spots a homeless man covered in newspapers next to a shopping cart with his possessions wrapped in black garbage bags. The odor of sweat and cigarettes blasts her senses.

She turns and heads down Hicks Street and turns right on Pineapple Street, ducking into a doorway. She checks her watch, 12:15, and waits.

Meanwhile, the homeless man stands and sheds the newspapers. He slips out of his soiled urban camouflage and picks up Ashaki's trail. It's Green. His sniper's camouflage skills come in handy again. He looks around the corner of Hicks and Pineapple and ducks back when he doesn't see his prey or anyone else. He points his audio scanner surreptitiously around the corner of the granite wall facing down the block and inserts the earbuds. He waits. Nothing, just the ceaseless ambient noise of Manhattan.

Then footsteps. She's on the move again. Green counts to five then follows. Pulling out his phone, he sends a quick text. Ashaki makes another right on Henry Street. She's doubling back, standard tradecraft.

Coming towards her is a man in a trench coat and baseball hat, brim pulled down. Something's not right. The coat makes no sense on a warm day. She turns back, but a large muscular man is jogging toward her. *Shit, what is this?* She turns again and the other man in the trench coat raises the brim of his hat.

"DeMarco, what are you doing here?" she says with a quiver in her voice.

"I could ask you the same thing, but I'm here following a lead. I heard that one of our suspects may be in this neighborhood," DeMarco says.

How does she play this? *Does he know what I know?*

Green is now stopped two feet behind her.

She stares at DeMarco and points her thumb over her shoulder at Green. "Who's this guy? He's not agency."

"No, he's my guy. A private contractor, you might say." DeMarco is like a cat that likes to tease and paw at injured prey. "So, I repeat, what are you doing here?"

Ashaki looks up and to the left. "I was following a lead too."

"That's strange. I thought you were an analyst glued to your computer. I suspect you're um, fabricating."

Think. "I'm not. I'm meeting Little and Hadar any minute. Their phones are off and I have some important information for them."

"I'm working with them too. Tell me."

"Don, I think you know why I can't tell you."

DeMarco flashes a wide grin. "You mean we can cut the charade now, sister?"

Ashaki's mouth drops open. She pivots and plants a back-leg side kick into Green's groin. Green doubles over. She starts to make a break for it when 30,000 volts course through her body and drop her to the ground face up.

The Leopard hovers over his sister, her eyes bulging. She's conscious but temporarily paralyzed.

DeMarco, aka the Leopard, aka Ahmed LaSalam, bends over his stricken victim, removing the TASER's prongs. Her eyes widen even more. The Leopard snickers. "First, we're going to find out what you know. Then..." he licks his lips. "Then we're going to make up for lost time. I can't wait. Can you?" He lays a wet kiss on her frozen lips.

Green staggers over with flex cuffs but first delivers a three-point kick to her ribs. "Bitch."

Ashaki groans through her semi-conscious state.

The Leopard grabs Green's arm. "Just cuff her and let's get out of here. You can do whatever you want with her when I'm done."

Green cuffs her wrists and ankles extra-tight. A white unmarked van screeches to a halt at the curb in front of them. Red jumps out.

A tall man with baggy shorts and a headset approaches the Leopard. "Hey, are you guys cops? Whatcha doin' to her?"

The Leopard without hesitation whips out a Sig Sauer 9mm pistol from his trench coat pocket. The man backs up. "Yeah, we're cops." LaSalam fires a bullet into the man's head and two to the chest. The man crumbles to the ground, blood oozing towards the gutter.

LaSalam looks both ways. "Clear."

Ashaki, reviving, starts to fight her restraints. Red and Green drag her kicking through the side door of the van. Green throws a right hook to her jaw and she crumbles. Red gets behind the wheel. LaSalam slides into the passenger seat and Red punches the gas pedal, peeling out onto Henry Street. The cat has the mouse.

CHAPTER 51
SINGLEHANDED

I make my way through the crowded corridors of Georgetown University Hospital. Patients in beds line the hallway. I sidestep gurneys whisking by. The faint scent of failing disinfectant drifts by. The 6th floor is much quieter, the corridors empty. The only sound comes from the soft beeping of monitors coming from patients' rooms.

I head for the nurse's station. The one nurse present is on the phone. Staring at the back of her hand, admiring her nails, she doesn't acknowledge my presence. It's clear from her smile and animated lips she's on a personal call. Pacing back and forth in front of her, I try to be patient, never my strong suit. She continues her engaging conversation while I remain invisible.

Finally, I slam my fist on the counter. She flinches and looks up. She flushes momentarily and cups the phone. "What?"

"Renata Fermi, what room?"

She raises an index finger and goes back to her conversation as is if I am an illusion.

I reach over the counter and push the disconnect button. "Jeez, what did you do that for?"

"I'm sure he'll be there when you call back. Now, what room?"

"What, who?"

"Renata Fermi, what room?"

"We're nurses. You get the room numbers from reception in the lobby. We take care of patients here."

"I'm sure that was a patient on the phone, right? Do they allow you to make personal calls? Couldn't you get in trouble for that? Now just tell me in which room *you care* for Renata Fermi?"

Her eyes shoot darts at me. If thoughts were bullets, I'd be swiss cheese. "Down the hall, Sipowicz. It's the one with the uniform in front."

I spot the patrolman in a chair outside the door. Breezing by him, I get the door half-open when he yanks me back into the hall. "Who are you?"

Renata's voice comes from inside. "It's OK, let him in. He's a friend."

The officer lets go. I shoot him a look and enter. "I'm so glad to see you alive. I mean awake. You know what I mean."

Renata laughs. "I'm glad to see you too. I'm trying to remember what happened, but it's pretty fuzzy. Maybe you can help fill me in."

"Yeah, but first, I gather by the guard at the door, somebody suspects foul play and you're in danger."

"A precaution, just in case."

"Probably a good idea, but with that Nurse Ratched in the hall, the bad guys are unlikely to find you."

"What?"

"Never mind. I'm just glad to see you're OK."

"Me too. I'm banged up, sore, and look like the victim in a slasher movie. My injuries look much worse than they actually are thankfully."

"When do they let you out of here? We've still got those leads to track down and bad guys to catch."

"Probably tomorrow. I had some internal injuries they're keeping an eye on. What happened to you? I just remember you disappearing like in a dream."

"Uh, the NYFD pulled me out of the car and the paramedics patched me up – only had a few scrapes. They checked me out and let me go. Since you were seated on the impact side, I feared we'd lost you."

"No such luck, partner. But I did have a weird dream–like you were touching me, trying to feel me up."

"Funny, that's my dream too."

She throws her plastic water cup at me, striking me in the forehead. I recoil, faking injury. "Good shot, partner. I think you're ready for duty. Listen, Monica would kill me – so don't worry. I tried to feel your neck for a pulse. You pushed my hand away and then I got yanked from the wreck. That accident sure looked intentional. Who do you think did this?"

"It did seem premeditated by what I've been told. My memory is still hazy. My guess is that we might have been getting too close. So somebody decided to stop us."

"They may not have stopped us, but they sure slowed us down. That's why I'm going to pick up from where we left off until you get out of here."

"It's dangerous. I said I'll be discharged tomorrow."

"You just get better. The clock is ticking and the Leopard may strike at any moment. So, it can't wait."

"They have other people on this now. You don't have to single-handedly try to save the world."

"That's what Monica tells me all the time."

"Maybe if you listened, your marriage wouldn't be .... Sorry. That's none of my business."

"You're right and you're right. But by the time somebody else gets up to speed, we could all be toast, the Leopard's toast. Let me know when they plan to release you and I'll pick you up. Meanwhile, I'm heading out."

Renata snorts. "You're a lot like me, a dog with a bone who won't let go."

"I know we can stop this bastard. We did it before and we can do it again."

"Go then. Be safe and call me if you find anything."

"You'll be the first. Now get better. I need you. We need you."

"I know."

CHAPTER 52
LET'S BE FRANK

The Star Wars ringtone rouses Renata from her dream. She dreamed she was back in Afghanistan with Nad Maji, her interpreter, attempting to recruit a Taliban asset in a Kabul Cafe. The coffee was strong and bitter. She'd grown fond of Nad, who had helped her through some pretty dicey encounters in that hostile land. She got to know his wife and young son. A cloud of dust kicks up in a breeze. Something seems off. Nad falls backward in his chair. Bloodstains growing on his white payraan. Sniper! She dove for the floor. The asset was gone. It was a setup.

The phone rings again and now she is fully awake. She wipes the cold sweat from her forehead. Where am I? Still in the hospital. OK. I'm OK. Caller ID *Unknown*. Great. She picks up. "Fermi, speak."

"Hi, it's Frank. How are you?"

"You should know. Aren't you watching everybody and everything?"

"Nice to talk to you too. And yes, I can see you are in a bed at Georgetown Hospital, but I was worried about you. I called to see how you're feeling."

"Thanks. Sorry I snapped. Bad dream. I'm doing OK. Nothing too serious. Hopefully, they'll let me out of here tomorrow. We need to stop the Leopard or who knows what shit is coming down. Plus Sam's out there on his own and liable to get himself killed... again."

"What do you know so far? I've been trying to track him, but LaSalam's a wizard at disguising his whereabouts."

"We raided his warehouse come laboratory. Chased him from a location near the U.N. We were back on the D.C. attack case in Washington, hoping to pick up another lead when the accident happened. You know, we were going to look at the forensics and that eraser thing you wanted."

"It wasn't an accident."

"I assumed he was on to us and wanted to slow us down. It worked."

"My wife got killed in a car crash, another supposed accident. I never solved that one, but I believe it was meant for me. I still haven't gotten over it."

"I'm sorry about your wife. Did you see all the bodies piled up in the lab? Do you have any idea of the scope of his gruesome bodyjacking activities?"

"I saw the video feed. It's all my fault, my invention. Those poor people, my wife. All my fault. I truly am better off dead," Frank says.

Renata looks at Frank's tired eyes on her screen. Tears are running down his virtual cheeks, his face contorted. "In case you haven't noticed, you are dead physically anyway. You can't blame yourself for being a brilliant scientist any more than they can blame Oppenheimer for the 200,000 killed at Hiroshima and Nagasaki."

"He did blame himself as did all the other scientists. For the rest of their lives they regretted the horror that resulted from their work. What if they failed or stopped their work? Those people would have lived. Their families would have thrived and grown. Instead –"

"Cut it out. If they failed, you might be bowing to the emperor right now. As for the body instantiations, the New Life Foundation is pairing good brains with willing partners. Your invention is doing some good."

"But does the good outweigh the shlekht, especially if LaSalam bodyjacks thousands into his zombie army."

"Frank, snap out of it. I don't have time for your self-pity. It's time for action. Can you help us stop the Leopard or not?"

Frank wipes away the tears and sits up. "I kept a backdoor into the software behind the process."

"Does that mean you can turn it off?"

"I think I can, but it may be an all or nothing switch. Meaning all those good people downloaded into new bodies might be instantly removed along with the Leopard and his minions. I'll look at it, but I don't think I can be selective."

"When will you know?"

"Let me work on it. If I can find a solution, you, Sam, and I will talk again before I flip the switch on it. Otherwise, we may have to shut it all down for everybody."

"OK, then who makes that decision?"

"Well, do you want to leave it up to the politicians or the scientists this time?" Frank asks and pauses. Then, "I'll get back to you."

CHAPTER 53
BOB AND RAY

"Sam, where are you?" Renata asks from her phone. She stands up from the wheelchair and walks out into the late afternoon Indian summer air. Funny, it almost smells like spring.

"I'm in D.C. Well, Virginia, to be exact."

"What? I thought you were going to forensics there?"

"I am. I'm standing outside Quantico, going to check out a hunch I have at FBI forensics. In the meantime, you should go back to New York, get some backup, and follow the Leopard lead to Brooklyn."

"Thanks, boss. I appreciate the direction."

"Look, I stayed out of trouble like you told me to and Juan is with me. I doubt there's much danger to us in forensics."

"You'd be surprised, but you're right about back up. I heard Swan and Hamed are in town. I'll tap them for backup. Juan? I thought he was watching Monica."

"I was not comfortable with that. He's got a thing for her. Besides, I need backup too. Stan or Jerry is with Monica."

"Sounds like you're being sensible for a change."

"Thanks for the compliment, I think. I'll let you know what I find here."

"You better."

"Stay safe and keep me posted, *please*. I feel like something will break soon."

"It's got to. The clock is ticking."

I'm standing outside the imposing Quantico complex with Juan. What was I thinking? I don't have a badge or credentials, but I'm a good talker. Using a letter from Rich, I get through the sentry at the entry gate. We enter the Forensic Science Research and Training Center, pass through a scanner and approach the two guards at the reception desk. They are dressed like G-men in dark gray suits, starched white shirts and red ties. For some odd reason, they remind me of Bob and Ray, the old-time comedy duo.

"Gentlemen, we'd like to visit your forensics lab."

"Do you have an appointment?" Bob asks.

"Let's see some ID," Ray says.

Juan and I hand over our passports. "We're here on official business, we're working with DHS."

Bob scowls. "And how do we know that?"

"Good point. You can call DHS Deputy Secretary Rich Little to verify." I show him Rich's letter.

"We're not calling anyone. This guy with you is Mexican. If you want a tour, you can contact your Congresswoman for a D.C. FBI visit. We don't do tours here," Ray says and scans my passport.

"Good to know. Give me a minute." I step aside to make way for two people behind me.

Juan looks ready to beat the shit out of them. "Les daré una gira a estos estadounidenses."

I hold Juan's arm and call Rich. He answers on the first ring. "Sam, what are you up to now?"

"I'm in Virginia with Juan at Quantico. I need you to get us into forensics. I have an idea."

"You're what? What did I say in our meeting about coordinating efforts and not stepping all over each other?"

"Rich, we don't have much time. We'll be in and out in twenty. But if I'm right, this could be a big break in the D.C. case. And who knows where that might lead and what we might stop next?"

Silence.

I persist. "I've never steered you wrong, have I?"

Rich takes a beat. "OK, I'll make a call."

"Thanks, I'm at the front desk with Bob and Ray."

"Who? Never mind." He clicks off.

The front desk is now clear. Bob makes a come hither gesture with his index finger. "Time for you to leave, sir." He hands back our passports.

"Just give it a minute," I say.

Ray taps his foot and looks at his watch. Their desk phone rings. Bob answers and listens. He looks up at me. "Yes. Yes, sir. Yes, I understand. Right away. Yes, sir. No, my name is not Bob or Ray... Thank you, sir."

I can't help smiling. I know it's a national security thing and Bob and Ray are just doing their jobs. Still, it feels like we face a giant bureaucracy every day. Unless you know somebody, you might as well be Franz Kafka or just bend over and take it.

Bob hangs up the phone and turns pink. All he says is, "Third floor and ask for Dr. Wu. But the Mexican stays here. Take this." He hands me a visitor's badge.

Juan seems to have a slight tremor, but he nods. No benefit in picking another fight. "I'll be back soon. Go get some coffee and meet me in the car. I'm buying," I say to Juan. He does a double take and heads for the door.

I turn back to Bob. "OK. Thank you." I tip my imaginary hat and beeline for the elevators.

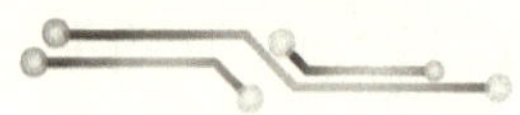

CHAPTER 54
SAM SPADE

Another guard greets me on the third floor. He glances at my passport and studies my face. After wanding my Visitor's badge, he swings open the frosted glass door. A young woman, maybe five-feet tall, in a white lab coat greets me. "Mr. Sunborn, follow me."

I glimpse her badge. *Jennifer Potter.* We proceed down a sterile green-tiled hallway. "Any relation to Harry?"

She grunts. "Oh, that's the first time I've heard that."

"Sorry, dad joke. I'm here to see Dr. Naz Yingling."

"Yes, we're very aware. He's interrupting a hectic day to speak with you."

At the end of the hall, Jennifer hands me a mask, puts one on herself, and pushes through the metal doors. There must be a dozen bodies on metal tables, all under spotlights with masked doctors prying at them. "Dr. Yingling," she says.

A middle-aged man, wearing inch-thick glasses, removes his mask. "Mr. Sunborn? Welcome to my office." He pulls off a latex glove to shake my hand.

It's then that the odor of formaldehyde slams me. "Thanks for seeing me on such short notice."

"Either you or whatever you've come for must be quite urgent to yank me away from a top-priority national security case."

"Yes, it is. Is there somewhere we can talk?"

"Follow me. Thanks, Jennifer."

She disappears and we enter a small office with 1940s government-issued metal furniture. The office has a picture window overlooking the examination floor.

Naz removes his mask and settles his considerable bulk into a chair behind the desk and waves me to the chair in front. "OK, what can I help you with?"

"I'm working with DHS on the D.C. attack case."

"Funny, so am I. Can I get you a drink?"

"Oh, a drink, yeah. Hot day. What do you have?"

"I have water and water." He swings open a metal mini-fridge behind him and hands me a frosty bottle.

"Perfect. Thanks. Then you are familiar with the case and may be able to answer a couple of questions?"

"I'll try. Shoot."

"Did you or your staff examine all the fatalities from the D.C. attack?"

"Yeah, took a while, but we're finishing up now."

"Good. Was there any particular victim who seemed more damaged than the others? Does one stand out for you?"

"There was one. A congresswoman actually." He flips through some files on his desk, finds one and thumbs through the contents. "Here it is. Josette Thomas from Tennessee."

"Really? What made her injuries worse than the others?"

Naz puts down his glasses and rubs the bridge of his nose. "The others displayed damage to the frontal lobe, the auditory nerve and the aorta. The Congresswoman had all those indications, maybe a bit more than the others. However, she also had severe vaginal trauma. As if a bull had raped her. I've seen nothing like it."

My brain is on fire. "I can look it up, but does it say what district in Tennessee she represented?"

"Just says the 7th district. I'm not sure what that covers, but I'm sure you can look that up too."

I stand and reach out a hand. "Thank you, Doctor. This has been extremely helpful. Again my apologies for interrupting your work, but I think you may have just given us an invaluable clue."

Naz smiles for the first time. "I'd say call me *anytime*, but I wouldn't mean it."

I return the grin. "Understood."

Juan greets me with an iced coffee as I exit the building. "You 'da man," I say as I gulp the cold drink.

"So, what happened, gringo?"

"Let's get in the car. I'll call Rich and you'll hear the whole story."

"Where are we going?" Juan asks.

"Tennessee, my friend."

CHAPTER 55
TENNESSEE

I drive, because frankly, I'm a control freak and I rarely trust other people with my safety. It's a fault, a limitation, I know. Or maybe I'm reluctant because Juan is a relatively new driver. But then exhaustion outweighs my usual paranoia and this time I'm happy to switch off and let Juan drive. Given where he grew up, drugged out in an asylum, he relishes the freedom of the road. His wide grin makes me smile too.

Dark clouds gather as we wind our way through the Unaka mountains. Lightning does its random dance on the horizon. Then small raindrops turn into torrents. Hail pelts the car as visibility drops to zero. "Juan, pull over."

"I'm doing OK."

"You can't see shit." I see a rest area. "Pull in there."

The phone vibrates in my shirt pocket. It's Rich. "OK. Sorry, I couldn't take your call before. Something big's going on in New York. Where are you now?"

I check the GPS. "We're pulled off on Route 40 in Tennessee."

"Tennessee? What the fuck, Sam? And what's that noise? Sounds like you're under fire."

"It's hail pounding us. Maybe God's trying to tell me something."

"Like you're losing your mind and going off the rails."

"No, that happened a long time ago. More like I got a lead from forensics that our D.C. attacker may be in Tennessee." I fill him in on the visit with Dr. Yingling and the late Congresswoman Thomas. "My guess is that the especially malicious wounds imply a particular home style form of vengeance against the Congresswoman. You'd have to be from Tennessee to even know who she is, right?"

"Maybe, but Tennessee is a big state, over 400 miles wide. How do you know where to look?"

"I asked our resident geek, Gary, to cross reference the Congresswoman's district with likely white nationalist groups and bing, we got a few hits. There's the United Klans, Vanguard America, and the NNN. The state's big, but her district is manageable size-wise. So we'll pay a few house calls."

Silence.

"Don't worry. Juan's with me and we're prepared."

"I'm not even going to ask, but you need to check in with the FBI field office in Memphis. Let them know you're there and what you're working on. They'll check the deconfliction database and make sure you're not stepping on another investigation or compromising any assets. They can also be there for backup if you get your asses in a sling."

"Glad to see you have your priorities straight."

"And don't go all cowboy on me. If you suspect something, back out and call."

"Will do."

"No bullshit, no ready-fire-aim. Promise you'll call first."

Juan nods at me. "I promise."

"Good. Now call Monica. She's been calling me looking for you. She's worried. Why don't you take her calls?"

"I've been busy."

"Sure. Divorced man's advice, call her now."

"Thanks. I will."

<hr>

"It's about time. I've been trying and trying to reach you. Are you OK?" Monica asks.

"Yeah, I'm fine. Sorry. I've just been crazy busy," I say. *That's mostly true.*

"Where are you now?"

I check the GPS for the second time in as many minutes. "Let's see. I'm on Route 40 in the lovely mountains of Tennessee, just waiting for this wicked hail storm to die down."

"What are you doing there?"

"It's classified."

"What a load of crap. In this marriage, nothing is classified. I have marriage-or-else highest level clearance. So read me in."

I clear my throat. "So I'm still in our marriage?"

"For the moment. Spill it."

"We're tracking down a lead we got that may take us to the perpetrators of the D.C. attack. I'm really just following a hunch."

"And if you find these people, then what?"

"We call Rich and the local FBI office first."

"And what's second? You don't confront them, right?"

"I have Juan with me. He's a black belt, remember? We're prepared."

"Sam, Evan needs his father."

"What about you? Do you need your husband?"

"I do, but I already feel like I'm grieving my loss of you in advance. So I'm burying my feelings, trying not to care. I can't get hurt again."

"But you do care?"

"After twenty-two years of marriage, how could I not care? Just get your —"

Static fills my ear. The call drops. Lightning hits a tree right in front of us with a simultaneous explosion of thunder. Juan floors the car as a massive falling oak grazes the side of our Toyota.

CHAPTER 56
DEVIL'S BIANGLE

The van turns right into a narrow alley and rumbles to a halt alongside a metal dumpster. The smell of trash in the summer heat pervades.

The Leopard turns his head to face Ashaki who is bound but fully awake in the backseat. "I have to keep moving locations because of you and your friends at DHS. It's getting tiresome."

"Your weariness is my first consideration," Ashaki says, launching a gob of spit into her brother's eye.

He wipes it off with his sleeve. "So that's how it's going to be. You were always a feisty one. I like that."

LaSalam nods to Red and Green. They each grab an arm and haul Ashaki from the van through an unmarked metal door. Instinctively, the Leopard looks up and down the brick-walled alley before joining them. The room is dark and dank. Green flips a switch and a hanging bare bulb dimly illuminates the storage room.

"Not very luxurious, I know. But you'll be comfortable on the couch."

Red pushes Ashaki, whose feet are zip-tied. She falls like a bowling pin onto the couch.

The Leopard flashes a demonic grin. "So now I'd like to know what you're up to. I'm getting blamed for the D.C. and Indiana attacks. Mind you, I don't really care. As my father said, 'If anything good happens within eight miles, take credit for it.' But I suspect you have a hand in some of this."

"I don't know what you're talking about," she says.

"I thought you might need a little coaxing. That's why I've prepared this especially for you." The Leopard holds up a syringe with a four-inch needle. He gently taps the plunger and it emits a few milky-amber drops. "You could either just talk or with my special nerve agent, we'll see how much pain you can stand."

Ashaki flinches.

"So how do you like it, hard or easy? Tell me what I want to know and then –"

Ashaki glares. "Then what?"

He caresses her soft cheek. She swivels her head and bites his hand like a bear trap snapping shut. He groans and tries to pull away, but she bites harder, drawing blood. He slaps her hard with his free hand. She bites harder still. He balls his free hand into a fist and punches her full force in the temple. She releases her bite, her head lolling to the side.

LaSalam licks the blood from his wounded hand and turns to Green. "Tie her down. It seems she's chosen the hard way."

CHAPTER 57
SOUTH

The clouds finally part, I see patches of blue as we descend from the mountains. I crack the window to take in the dewy ozone, post-storm air.

"OK, now where are you?" Rich asks.

"If I didn't know better, I'd think you are worried about us," I say. "Don't be. The sky is finally clearing. We should pass through Memphis shortly."

"Perfect. I'm on my way there on the company jet. Should land at Memphis International Airport in about an hour. It's just north of Memphis. Meet me there."

"But –"

"No buts. You're not doing this alone. Got it?"

"OK, I guess."

"That's not a request."

"Yeah, yeah. I've watched enough cop shows. 'It's an order.'"

"No, it's national security and personal... If anything happens to you, Monica will kill me."

"She's not vindictive. She'd just cut your balls off and feed them to our dog, Petey."

"Nice. Somehow I can't unsee that image. But *you* need a woman like that to keep you in line."

"You understand me so well, partner."

"So, at the airport in sixty, right?"

Juan is tapping the GPS and nods.

"Yeah, we'll be there," I say.

LaSalam gently strokes Ashaki's cheek. This time he's covered her mouth with duct tape. "I can't tell you how good it feels to see my sister again."

She is still bound head and foot to a chair with snap ties. She doesn't flinch. She fires a laser-like stare that bores a cosmic hole through her brother.

The Leopard picks up the syringe again. "OK. So let's get down to business. Hopefully I won't need to use this." He ejects a few more drops from the long needle and rips the duct tape from her mouth. "I'll get to the point. What do you know about me and my hypothetical plans?"

"I know that at best you're a pedophile. And your plan is to express your weakness by abusing and attacking others. Close?" She grins.

"That wasn't exactly the cooperation I was looking for." He gently places the syringe on a table, whirls, and slaps her hard across her left cheek.

Her head jerks to the side. A red welt blooms.

"If you didn't tie me down here and have Beavis and Butthead protecting you, you wouldn't be so tough, such a man." Ashaki spits blood and saliva onto her brother's shoe.

His face seems to rupture. "Ok, so now it's time for a little fun." He moves in and with one motion rips her blouse wide-open.

Pushing the limits of her restraints, she skull butts him. He wobbles back, holding his forehead. She angles forward, knees bent, and jumps, breaking the ties on her feet. She kicks him hard in the crotch. He falls to one knee, groaning and cursing. "I've still got you, you little bitch."

With her hands and arms still bound to the chair, she rotates fast, hitting him with the legs of the chair. She leans forward and then jumps up, pulling her feet in and smashing the chair to the floor. The snap ties break off, leaving rings of blood on her wrists. She slams a foot into her brother's face, breaking his nose. Blood sprays across the floor. There's pounding at the door, then loud thuds as Red and Green try to break in.

The Leopard shouts, "Get in here! She's loose."

Ashaki shoves a chair under the doorknob and rubs her sore, bleeding wrists. Picking up another chair, she hurls it through the back window. The glass shatters. Red and Green are still ramming the door, the hinges giving way. Ashaki has one foot out the window but turns back. She rushes over to her brother, who is semi-conscious on the floor. Grabbing the syringe, she plunges it into his neck. "See you later, brother."

Ashaki leaps through the shattered window just as the door flies off its hinges. Carried by their momentum, Red and Green stumble forward. While LaSalam writhes on the concrete floor in his own blood and feces, Red vomits.

CHAPTER 58
PLAN C

Ashaki feels shaken but not stirred by her kidnapping and violent, yet narrow escape. Nothing is going according to plan. She can't go back to DHS - her cover and identity are probably blown. She hides by a doorway behind a bar. The door opens a crack and the smell of beer rushes out. As they said on the old TV Westerns she'd watched when trying to learn English, *Time to get out of Dodge. I think I'll go to Tennessee and make sure Max carries out the mission. Besides, he's kinda cute in a redneck sorta way*, she thinks.

But first to tie up a loose end. She types an anonymous text to Renata,

> By now u know Don DeMarco is Ahmed LaSalam, the Leopard. He organized the bodyjacking ring, the D.C. attack and the bio-attack. If you hurry, you might catch him at this addy 241 41st Brooklyn. I hurt him, but didn't kill him. Maybe I should have. You can try to track me, but it will be fruitless.

Renata talked her way out of the hospital a day early and is back on the road. She hears the ping and checks her screen - *Unknown*. She opens the message and swerves, almost hitting an oncoming bus. She takes a deep breath and pulls to the curb, then types a reply.

> Who are you and why are you telling me this?

Ashaki turns over an answer in her head, then replies.

> My only interest is in helping. If I get more info, I'll send it along. TTYL

The best lies are 90% truth, she thinks and clicks SEND. *That should keep them busy for a while and put an end to my brother.*

Renata tries to process this latest wrinkle in an already bizarre case. She checks her watch, almost 5:00. Sucking in a deep breath, she wrenches the steering wheel hard to the left, cutting off traffic. She pops a flashing turret onto the roof and guns it. Ten minutes out.

"Rich, it's Renata. I just got a tip."

Rich holds the phone tight to his ear to block the jet engine noise. "What? Where are you? What tip?"

"I got a text with his address. I'm close."

"I thought you were in the hospital."

"I'm fine. They released me a couple of hours ago and I hopped the first shuttle back to JFK. I was following up an earlier lead, which puts me heading to Brooklyn already."

"Where'd the tip come from?"

"Dunno - unknown."

"Ask Adele to trace it."

"Tried her. She's MIA."

"Huh. Try Gary then."

"Look, I can do that after. I've got to focus now."

"Understood. Is anybody with you?"

"Nope. I got this."

"Call for backup – that's an order."

"No time. Gotta go. Bye."

Renata turns into oncoming traffic on the Manhattan bridge, dodging approaching cars and blaring horns. I've got to nail this bastard once and for all.

Renata and Sam's phones ring simultaneously. It's Frank. "It looks like you two are busy. My trackers tell me that Sam, you're in Tennessee and Renata, you're on the Van Wyke heading from the airport to Brooklyn, correct?"

Renata is trying to weave through slow traffic and talk at the same time. "Listen Frank, I'm in the middle of a white-knuckle ride to an address where the Leopard is supposedly injured. I really can't talk now."

"Then just listen. Sam, what's your status?"

"I'm in Memphis waiting for Rich's plane to land. We may have triangulated the location of the D.C. attacker."

"Good. Listen, both of you. I think I may have figured out a way to stop or at least neutralize the bodyjacking," Frank says.

I duck into a corner of the private terminal to block out the airplane noise and jet fuel odor. "Rich's plane is landing. Please give us the short version."

Frank grumbles. "I know what you are doing is urgent, but this is important and I'll need your help to pull it off."

"We're listening," Renata and I say in unison.

Frank starts. "It involves capturing the bodyjacked victims, attaching the probes, and uploading their personalities to a private server I set up. Then we remove the invading personality from the victim and give them their lives back. You'd do the physical part of restraining the victims and hooking them up. I'd do the rest."

"Whoa," Renata says. "That's a whole lot of tracking and capturing. We'd need an army to do that. We don't even know for sure how many bodyjack victims there are, do we?"

"I know," Frank says. "I have an exact count from the blockchain tags I built into the original program."

"OK, so how many?" I ask.

"Seven hundred and thirty-eight so far, but that number is growing. That's why we've got to stop it now," Frank says.

"That's what I'm trying to do. In a few minutes, I'll hopefully capture the asshole behind all this," Renata says, veering the Audi onto the sidewalk to get around a smelly garbage truck.

"Not to diminish your prowess, Renata, but I believe your odds of capturing the Leopard are under 30%, 23.6% to be exact," Frank says.

"And how do you know that?" Renata asks, blowing through a red light.

"I'm an Einstein, remember. Explanations later. Let me get to the point before I lose you. You need to capture the bodyjack victims. DHS has how many employees, 240,000? They should be able to spare a few thousand to round these people up. I'm sure the FBI could kick in a couple hundred more of their 35,000 employees if needed. Anyway, you capture them and bring them to the labs I have set up in Paris and Manhattan. Before you ask, I may live virtually in the Cloud, but I can still pay physical people to get done what I need done."

"And then we torture them for info?" I ask.

"We need not be so groyzam, we just read their data," Frank says.

"But then we still have their digital personas roving the Cloud and creating havoc, right?"

"I have a solution for that too. In the labs, we'll upload their personalities to my private server which we will then take offline. They'll be fully contained, air-gapped. There we can extract from our digital captive, his or her digital DNA and then –"

"Digital DNA, what's that?" Renata shouts as she side-swipes a parked Maserati.

Frank continues. "It's their unique markers and data patterns. We also have blockchain markers that will be useful."

"OK. If we have their digital DNA, then what?" I ask.

"This is the big leap." Frank's voice rises. "We can find that data, like using Google. Do an Internet-wide search for those DNA markers. There could be thousands we don't even know about. But I can write a script to delete forever those entities with the matching DNA and thus free up and return the bodies to their original owners. This is hairy because a mistaken match and deletion would be like murder."

"Is it worth the risk?" I ask. "And if you move ahead, when can we use this?"

"You know me. I have to test and make sure it's safe and there aren't errors or other unintended consequences."

"OK, but when? We've got this psychopath, the Leopard I'm trying to stop, and maybe many others plotting our destruction. We need to act fast before the shit hits the fan and we don't want to be the fan," Renata says.

"I think I've heard that one before." Frank laughs. "As Sam knows from our coding a hack to stop one of the Leopard's earlier apocalyptic plans, it will be ready when it's ready."

"Can't you just throw all those thousands of copies of yourself into testing?"

"I already have and that's helpful, but it's like a pregnant woman. Even if you have nine women working on it, they won't birth a baby in a month. The baby will still take nine months, not one, to come. Testing is like that."

"I've heard that one before too," I say. "It's called the Myth Of The Man Month, but it's always frustrated the hell out of me. Always felt like a way for programmers to keep control and a thumb on us mere mortals. But don't worry Renata. Frank doesn't have control issues. He just likes to under promise and over deliver. He'll find a way safely, I hope."

"Yeah, I'll find a way. That's how entrepreneurs like Sam encourage us programmers to do the impossible. I get it."

"Let's cut the geek shit and get it done. I'm at the Leopard's supposed address. Keep me posted." She clicks off.

I laugh. "She doesn't mince words, but I know she appreciates your efforts. Look, I gotta go too. Rich is here. I'll update him on your plan."

"Stay safe," Frank says.

"That's part of the plan," I say.

CHAPTER 59
BUGS

To avoid being tracked, Ashaki pays cash for a cab to LaGuardia Airport. *Talk about shit holes*, she thinks. Hitting the ladies' restroom, it seems like a good time to check in with Marsha Hume. "I'm on my way to meet our distributor, how's it coming?"

"Just a sec." Hume drops her safety goggles and retreats to her office to take the call. She slams the door. "I think our babies are almost ready for prime time. Let's switch to video. I'll show you."

Hume points her cell camera at a diagram on her screen and explains the altered-DNA virus-carrying bugs.

"OK, Professor, nice explanation, but I don't give a shit how the engine works. I just need the car to get me there. So, once you have these bugs configured, how many can you breed and how quickly?" Ashaki asks.

"How's several million by next week?"

"How's day after tomorrow?"

"They're organisms. They take time to reproduce and grow."

"You're an organism too and organisms can die or be killed if you know what I mean. Get 'em the fuck faster. Give 'em Viagra. Do whatever you have to do." Ashaki lowers her voice to a whisper. "This is not being capricious or arbitrary like my brothers were. I think DHS and the Feds could be on to us. So the window is closing fast. We don't have a week. We might not have two days. So make it happen."

"Assuming I could do it, and even if my life depends on it, I'm not sure I can. What about distribution? The crop-dusters Momar tried just don't cover enough ground to mean much and you don't have the resources for that kind of covert air force anyway."

Ashaki turns scarlet. Breathing fast, almost panting, she says, "Don't tell me what resources I have. I'll handle the distribution. That's why I'm taking this damn trip to Tennessee. You just do your fucking job." She hangs up but wishes she could slam the phone like she used to. She stops herself. *Am I really like my brothers?*

I click off the call with Frank and Renata as Rich enters the small private terminal waiting room at Memphis International Airport. I extend a hand. "Good to see you, Rich."

"Same here. Hope you've stayed out of trouble since we last spoke," Rich says.

"As ordered, I waited for you so we could both get in trouble together."

Rich laughs. "Where's Juan?"

"He's probably hitting on a flight attendant, knowing him. Listen, I spoke to the FBI field office in Memphis as you suggested." I check my Fitbit, 5:30. "An agent should be meeting us about now."

A short woman with curly red hair and freckles dressed in a dark suit and white blouse stumbles through the entrance. She looks down at the curled mat that tripped her, cursing under her breath. Since we are the only ones in the waiting room, she heads straight for us. "Deputy Secretary Little and Sam Sunborn, I'm Agent Tiffany Sly." We shake hands. Her vise grip almost makes me cringe.

Rich looks around. "Good detective work. You ID'd us."

"It's one of my superpowers," Tiffany says.

I like her already. "Rich, I filled Tiffany in on my lead and the NNN."

She interrupts. "NNN has been on our radar along with thirty-five other hate groups in Tennessee."

"What does on the radar mean?" I ask.

"Casual surveillance. Some interviews, but our best bet is the guy we have inside. He can't communicate with us or he'll lose his cover, but we have a meet set up in an hour. Lucky, we just do this once a week at a set time, since I can't contact him directly to schedule anything," she says.

"That's promising, but I'd like to go out to NNN's place and have a look for myself," Rich says.

"I understand but it's dangerous. Let's have a conversation with Mic first. It may make your visit more productive."

"And less dangerous," I say.

"We're meeting him at Crutchfield's Bar-B-Q nearby."

"Good, I'm starved," Rich says.

"You're always hungry," I remind him.

Rich snorts. "Just give me some of those grits and fried biscuits."

"OK, our car's out back," I offer.

Tiffany cackles. "That junker yours? Ain't gonna make it. 'Sides if we go to the NNN's place, we're heading up some pretty shitty roads. We'll take my Jeep with 4-wheel."

"I guess we know who's in charge." Rich grins. "Let's get Juan and head out."

"Roger that," I say.

CHAPTER 60
SOMETHING DEADLY

Ashaki flies Delta, connecting through Atlanta and arrives at Memphis International Airport twenty minutes after Rich, Sam, and Tiffany drove off. She rents a car under a fake ID. She had a GO bag ready just for an emergency like this. The bag holds stolen IDs and fake licenses, passports, credit cards, cash, clothes, and toiletries. The picture ID on one of the passports matches her changed, smoky-black hair color. She added tortoise-shell glasses. Unlike what most people think of disguises, you only need to make a few subtle changes and it alters people's perceptions, unless someone is using facial recognition. To block cameras, she dons a baseball cap. Otherwise, plastic surgery is the only sure disguise. Although she couldn't bring a weapon on the plane, they're easy enough to buy in Tennessee.

She drives a little over an hour north on Route 51 towards Fort Pillow near the Lower Hatchie Wildlife refuge. From there, it's dirt roads into the woods. No maps, no GPS, but she knows the way. She sees the smoke of a wood fire burning, parks the rental five-hundred yards away and walks. Spotting the trip wires and light beam sensors, she follows a circuitous path so as not to trigger some booby trap or spring-loaded weapon. *You never know with these guys.*

She finally makes it to the cabin where Max is chopping wood. He's covered with sweat soaking through his stained, strapped T-shirt. An odor like bear piss drifts her way.

He looks up, axe firmly gripped in both hands. "Well, hello honey. I wish I knew you were coming." He looks down at his filthy T-shirt. "I'd 'a put on my tux or something for you. Looks like somebody roughed you up pretty good. What happened?"

"Didn't want to risk a call. I'm avoiding the authorities at the moment." Ashaki points to her bruised face, "As for this, you should've seen the other guy."

Max flashes his gapped pearly whites. "What happened? I thought you worked for the feds."

"It's a long story. I just made a sudden career change, if you know what I mean."

"Uh, I been there, sweetie. You can crash here if you like. I'll keep you safe, if 'in you don't mind there's only one bed."

She needs him right now. If she has to play to the little brain between his legs, so be it. She grins. "If 'in you take a shower, I might consider it."

"Hot diggity dog. I was wantin' some of your sweetness since the day I first lays eyes on you."

"Not so fast. How are we set with the distribution?"

"Always bizness with you. I got my crews 'round the country. Maybe a thousand, maybe more on Harleys, ready to go. They'd just be looking for that money you promised."

"That's not a problem. You'll have it and how you split it is up to you, but don't fuck with me or you'll regret it."

"I seen what you did to my boy, Zak, before. I knows you can be a mean bitch. I just wanna fuck you, not fuck with you."

"A distinction without a difference."

"Huh? No matter. But my boys wants to know what they be carrying."

"Something deadly. That's all I can say."

"Better say more, pardner, or it's no deal. I got a reputation, you know."

Ashaki hesitates. *What choice do I have? They will find out sooner or later.* "I'll tell you, but if you tell a soul, I'll have to kill you and that's not a movie line. They'll find you with your balls cut off and stuffed in your mouth."

"That's not a pretty picture." He draws his finger across his zipped lips.

Ashaki gives him a non-technical explanation of what Hume has developed and what it can do.

"Hoo-wee, you can do that with bugs? That's the craziest thing I ever heard, but I believe you." He slaps his knee and grabs his crotch. "I loves it. I'm gettin' hard just thinkin' about it. I'll tells my boys it's some kind of poison or something."

"That'll work. Now when I get the packages to you, how are you going to distribute them and keep it quiet?"

"We got our own little underground railroad. It's secret. Just leave it to me. I got this. Now when're the bugs coming here?"

"UPS Air to a UPS store in Millington. You must pick it up there."

"That's how, but when?"

Ashaki looks at her watch. "In 42 hours," she says. But she's anxious about Hume delivering. Hume better be ready. *The window of opportunity is closing fast.*

"We'll be ready, but how about that little bit o' fun you promised me first?"

Ashaki groans inside. He's not so cute after all, but she knows what she has to do. They're all alike, her brothers and Max – useful idiots if you give them a little taste. *I'd still rather cut all their balls off. Maybe when this is over, I'll get my chance.*

CHAPTER 61
SWEETENER

Rich, Tiffany, and I take a corner table at Crutchfield's Bar-B-Q. The red-checked tablecloth and the aroma of hot sauce remind me of something from the distant past, but I can't quite put my finger on what. The rotund waitress, with her hair tied in a bun and a pencil behind her ear, hands us the plastic menus.

"I guess plastic on the menus is a good idea in case we get messy," I say.

"Or throw up," Rich says.

"Lighten' up. This is some good southern barbecue and it's dinnertime," Tiffany says. "I wouldn't have brought y'all here otherwise."

I look down at the menu and notice my right hand starting to fade. *Oh, shit.* I stand up. "Gotta go to the little boys' room."

"Who says that?" Rich says. "You don't need permission."

I put my fading hand into my pocket. "Thanks, I wasn't sure."

Moving quickly to the rear of the restaurant, I lock myself in the single stall wood-paneled restroom. It smells like the person before me had a sick stomach. Too much Bar-B-Q be'd my guess. Hitting speed dial, I say, "Frank, it's happening again."

"Slow down, Sam. What are you talking about?"

"The fading, the flickering. You know. I'm here with Rich and an FBI agent. You said you'd fix this. What do I do?"

"Look, I've been working on a software update and bug fix, but I'm not quite there yet. You need to do what we discussed before. Focus your mind. Be present. Put your worries and anxieties in a box and lock them in a mental cupboard. Whatever works for you."

"Great. You've got to make this work soon or I'll either get found out or have to hide until you do."

"Just a little longer. You can do this."

"Right. OK, I'll try. Have little choice again." I click off.

I splash cold water on my face like last time. Something to shock me or bring me back. Putting down the toilet seat, I sit and close my eyes. I think of Monica and the first time we met. It was at an ice cream stand on the boardwalk by the ocean in Wildwood. The Ferris wheel and spinning cups were whirling by in the background. Suddenly she appears holding a little girl's hand. We're teenagers, so I doubt she's the girl's mother. Monica has long wavy auburn hair and hazel eyes. Those eyes just suck me in. And without a word, I knew. She's the one. I can't remember how the conversation started, but I'm sure I said something stupid and it made her laugh. We walked together with the little girl, her charge as a nanny for the summer. We went on our first date that night and I never looked back.

And there was Evan, born a decade later and it was love at first sight again. Monica had to have a C-section. Evan came out large and purple-skinned. His first act was to pee on the doctor, an early indicator of his future personality.

Back to now, I can feel myself smiling and look down at my hands. No flickering. Rubbing them together, I feel whole again. I suck in a deep breath and return to the table.

"You OK? You looked a little pale before," Rich says as he knocks over his coffee cup into his lap. He leaps to his feet, flapping his necktie. "Shit. The pants will be OK, but this is a brand new tie."

We all grab napkins to mop up the mess. Rich pats his tie and his pants with napkins. The waitress returns with a rag and wipes the table. She looks at Tiffany and nods towards Rich. "Yankee, be'd my guess?"

Tiffany touches the side of her nose. They both laugh.

"Let's not attract attention, right Rich?" I snort.

"Fuck you."

I hand him two packets of Sweet n' Low. "Here, rub this on the tie. It'll take the stain out. Just rub it on and let it sit there for a bit."

Rich sits back down. "You're shittin' me."

"Just try it. What have you got to lose?" I say.

He sniffs and starts rubbing the white powder on the stain. "If you're pranking me, Sunborn."

The waitress comes back and takes our order, BBQ chicken, brisket, and a dozen wings. She looks at Rich and shakes her head. "Nice tie."

"Glad I could make your day. Don't you have other customers?" Rich asks.

"None as much fun as y'all." She refills our coffee cups and moves on to the next table.

"OK Rich, brush off the powder," I say.

He flicks the Sweet n' Low from his tie. "I can't believe it. The stain's gone. How did you come up with that?"

"Nobody, except you, wears ties anymore. But back in the old days, I wore them to work every day and my ties were like soup magnets. I figured I needed something to absorb the stain, like a drying agent. So I grabbed the nearest thing, which was Sweet n' Low and damn if it didn't work. It's almost like a magic trick. Right?"

"Yeah. You're spooky sometimes."

"Interestingly enough, this only works with Sweet n' Low. Subsequently, I tried the other artificial sweeteners, the yellow one and the blue one, and they didn't work. Just this stuff." I hold up a pink packet.

"That could be the geekiest thing I've ever heard," he says.

"Thanks. I'll take that as a compliment."

"This is all fascinating, but we've got to pay and go meet Mic," Tiffany says.

"I thought he was meeting us here," I say.

"He just texted me. He thinks he might have a tail. So he's changed locations. Let's go."

The waitress drops a check. Rich stops her. "Can I get a to-go cup for your coffee?"

I can't contain the mouth full of coffee I have and a laugh at the same time. I burst out laughing and spit the coffee up in a spray, barely missing everybody. "That was close."

"Send in the clowns," Tiffany says.

CHAPTER 62
MIC

After a six-minute drive, we meet Mic on a gravel turnoff in Frayser Park. The sun is setting, turning the clouds a pale pink. The scent of fresh-cut pine surrounds us. A rusty door creaks as Mic gets out of his 1968 Ford pickup. He's tall and lean, wearing torn jeans and a cowboy hat, no shirt. He looks like the Marlboro Man. Tiffany does the introductions. Mic keeps looking over his shoulder. If he's always this jumpy, I'm not sure how he maintains his cover.

"Listen, I can't stay long. Things are heating up. They think I'm just picking up some booze and paranoia runs in their veins," Mic says.

Tiffany gently puts a hand on Mic's shoulder. "Calm down. I've never seen you like this. If you're like this with them, you're toast. We're toast."

Mic's head bobs up and down. "Yeah, yeah I know. Here's what happened a few days ago. Max's brother and a crew were working on some equipment in the shed and testing it. They brought some ray gun looking device, hooked up to a power source, and pointed it at a raccoon in a tree. The poor thing keeled over, fell on the ground and then wandered in circles like it was drunk – them laughing. I knew something was up. Next day they disappear in a white van. Came back later celebratin'."

"Who's Max?" I ask.

"Max Werner. He's the head of the NNN. Mic, go on," Tiffany says.

"See they take all us guys' phones and electronics. We're off the grid, 'ceptin' the one I got hidden. But the next night they turned on their one TV to watch the news. Although they didn't fess up in front of us, they gave each other smirking glances and elbows. It was them."

Rich knows, but he wants to hear Mic say it. "It was them what?"

Mic takes a long breath. "It was them that killed those black congressmen in D.C."

Tiffany knows Mic well and seems to sense there's more to the story. "What else?"

"That night some woman drives up. Spends a long time talking to Max. The car was probably a rental. Here's the plate number." Mic hands a scrap of paper to Tiffany.

She immediately texts the number to the office. "Can you describe her?"

"Yeah, 'bout five-six, green eyes, brown hair. She looked tough, but kinda sexy at the same time."

"*Kinda sexy* really narrows it down," Tiffany scoffs.

Mic draws a toe through the gravel. "You know what I mean. So Max has a meetin' with this gal, but I wasn't invited. There's a scuffle, but in the end they shake hands and she and the guy she came with leave. Couldn't get much of a look at him."

"So now all we got to do is take these guys down, right?" Rich says.

"Ain't going to be that easy," Mic says. "These guys is heavily armed. I even seen RPGs like the ones we used in 'ghanistan."

"... and we want to know what the woman and this Max are up to next. If we move in now, we might not be able to stop it," Tiffany says.

"OK, so we watch them and send out alerts. Tiffany, can you call in the cavalry if we need them?" Rich asks.

Tiffany's eyes are down on her screen. "Yeah, I got a fuckin' battalion ready. We've been waiting two years to do this. Just got a text with an ID on the car renter. Diane in the office cross-checked the license to the social. Looks like a stolen, bullshit ID for some eighty-year-old woman in Wisconsin."

"Another reason to watch and wait," I say.

"But I want to go out there now," Rich says.

Mic's bouncing on his heels. "I better get going. I picked up some beer and whiskey in town for them and I better get back. The sooner we can end this, the sooner I can get back to my family. I haven't seen my wife or kid in six months. She's probably losing patience or fucking another guy by now."

I can't help myself. "I know how that goes."

"Hopefully you guys will shut this down sooner," Mic says.

"Otherwise, Mic, next week, same time?" Tiffany says.

"Yeah, if I make it until then."

"Thanks for your help. Be careful," Rich says.

"You too." Mic tips his hat and heads back to the pickup.

CHAPTER 63
I LIED

The early autumn sky fades to black. The Leopard is back at his latest headquarters on Willow Street in Brooklyn with Red and Green in the cramped conference room. On the other side of the glass conference room door, a dozen other youngish men are staring at their monitors. For LaSalam right here, right now, it's about regrouping and pushing ahead with his plan.

"At least the bleeding's stopped. Do you want me to get some ice for your nose?" Red asks.

The Leopard waves him away. "I'll deal with that bitch later. In the meantime, we have work to do. I can't risk going back to DHS. I'm sure the whore has leaked my identity." He points through the glass at his chief engineer, X, in front of an array of ten monitors and turns to Green. "Get him in here."

X stumbles through the door. "Yes, you wanted to see me, but I have to get back soon. I've just completed compiling a bunch of code."

"I don't care if you've completed a pile of shit. How do we look to deploy Phase 1? And what happened to you? You look like somebody beat the shit out of you."

X puts a hand on his bandaged neck. "Uh, my girlfriend tried to kill me. I was lucky a friend came by just in time to save me, but I don't want to talk about it. I'm still setting up the relays and masking addresses so when we deploy they won't be able to trace it back to us," X says.

"That's all well and good but doesn't answer my question. Maybe plain English will help. When can we flip the fucking switch?"

"Three days should be enough time."

"My dear boy, I don't think you're getting my drift. With Ashaki, DHS, and the Feds after us, we are out of time."

"I understand, but we're talking about the largest hack in history. There are literally thousands of entry points that need to be hit simultaneously. We're debugging over two million lines of code at the same time"

The Leopard snarls. He whips out a ballistic knife and touches the razor-sharp point to the underside of X's chin. "Understand this." A drop of blood runs down the shimmering blade. "Tomorrow noon. Nod if you understand."

X trembles, beads of sweat growing on his forehead. He whispers, "Fuck, if I nod, you'll cut deeper."

"Nod."

X nods and more blood seeps from his neck. The odor of his sweat punctuates the nightmare. LaSalam flashes a toothy grin. "Good. I will be here tomorrow well before 11:00 ready to go." He removes the knife, licks the blade, and replaces it in the sheath.

X exhales. "But you said noon."

"I lied. Be ready at 11:00."

CHAPTER 64
NOW WHAT?

The headlights barely pierce the fog and darkness. I sit in the back with Juan, Rich riding shotgun as Tiffany maneuvers her Jeep over some rough dirt and rock roads. Driving off the road, she parks under some pine trees, suitable cover and out of sight, a half-mile from NNN headquarters. A pleasant wisp of chimney smoke floats by. Rich is glued to his tablet. "I called in a domestic drone. We're not supposed to use them over our soil, but um, this time is an exception."

"I have a feeling there are a lot of exceptions," Juan says.

"That's classified, but look here," Rich says. He turns the tablet first to Tiffany and then towards me in the backseat. "Mic is returning."

They see Mic walking back from his truck through the drone's lens, hovering 18,000 feet above. The image is a bit grainy, but little graphic squares hover above Mic and Max with their names in mini-call-outs. There are several other unidentified NNN members working around the property. A few carrying guns are clearly visible. I see Mic hold up a bag, presumably with the whiskey and beer he bought in town. Max waves his arm and follows Mic inside the cabin.

"What do we do now?" I ask Rich.

Rich pulls the tablet back. "We watch and wait."

"I'm nervous about this. Should I call in our teams?" Sly asks.

Rich is breathing heavily, "Let's give it a few minutes."

I check my cell – no signal. "Since we're sitting on our hands, I should call Monica. Rich, let me use your SAT phone."

Rich smirks. "Is this official business?"

His humor pisses me off sometimes. "Just give me the fucking phone."

"Lighten up, Sam." Rich hands the phone to me. "But seriously, make it quick. We might need that phone any minute."

I stick my tongue out and step out of the car. "Thanks. I'll let you know if anybody important calls."

I wade through some brush to put some distance between me and the others.

Monica picks up on the first ring. "Sam, I'm glad you called. How are you? Where are you?"

OK, truth or lie? Considering the state of my marriage, I'm not sure which is best. I opt for my default, truth. "You can't repeat this. We're in the backwoods of Tennessee with eyes on a domestic terror group that may have been responsible for the D.C. attack."

"Sam! What? You –"

"Before you say it. I'm here with Rich, the FBI. We have serious backup and firepower coming. I'm an observer." I stall on the word *observer,* thinking about my flickering state in the restaurant. Am I the observer or the observed? In quantum physics, I know the observer is part of the quantum state he or she observes. That's really what this is like. I observe, but I am the observed at the same time. This is all me. Is it in my head?

Monica's labored breathing is audible. "OK, OK. This will be over soon?"

"One way or the other." I smack myself in the forehead. *What a dumb thing to say.*

"Great. Here we go again."

"Tell me about Evan. What is he doing today?" *Try to change the subject.*

Monica hesitates. "He enjoyed his soccer game via Skype from home. His team won for a change. All the kids were very excited. He really missed being there, but I think he'll be up for the robotics competition tomorrow, if his energy holds up. He really wishes his dad could be here."

"Me too. I'd say I'll try, but I can't promise that. I really believe it won't be much longer."

"Good. I gotta go. The hot UPS delivery man just got here."

I snort. "Great. I love you." I wait, hoping for a certain reply.

"Stay safe." She clicks off.

As I return to the Jeep, the echo of gunshots pierce the night. Where'd that come from? Tiffany and Juan leap from the car. Rich is pinging the drone pilot. "Did you guys see anything?"

"Our ShotSpotter pinpointed the sound as coming from the barn," the drone pilot reports.

Rich is glued to the drone image of the barn on his screen. The smell of cordite wafts up from the valley. A few seconds later, Mic staggers out the barn door and drops to the dirt. The drone camera zooms in. His head is cocked at a weird angle. Blood stains bloom on his shirt. Rich ducks his head out the window. "Tiffany, call in the troops. We can't wait any longer."

Rich's phone vibrates again. Caller ID shows Roger Brickman. Rich answers. "Not now. We're hot."

Brickman ignores the greeting. "The president wants an update."

"Our inside man was murdered. We're on the NNN now. I'll call in." He hangs up.

Two seconds later another call. It's Michelle. "Hi. What's going on there?"

"Shit's hitting the fan and this time, we are the fan. We just lost our inside guy."

"What do you mean? You mean you can't find him?"

"No, I mean like he's dead. We saw it all through the drone camera. FBI is bringing in backup now. We're going in. Update me on your end."

"We're playing cat and mouse around the city with LaSalam. Lots of strange shit happening. Frank is working on shutting down the bodyjacking software. Sounds like a long shot to me. Besides, we're now certain DeMarco is the new stolen body for the Leopard. Strangely, that analyst, Adele from the seventh floor, is MIA. We're looking into her background. Yet, with her hacking abilities, I suspect she could invent a back story and we wouldn't know the difference."

"Yeah, keep me posted. We're gearing up here. We'll reconnect after this all goes down."

"OK, wear your vest. I want you back in one piece."

"That's the plan."

"You once told me plans are for pussies."

Rich laughs. "Forget I said that. I always come back. A little bruised maybe, but you can't get rid of me that easily."

"OK, be smart." She's gone.

Rich updates me on New York and LaSalam. My mind is racing. "Somehow this all fits together. I'm just not sure how yet," I say.

"We better figure it out fast or else… " Rich says.

Tiffany coughs. "I've got gear and weapons, enough for all of us in the trunk. C'mon, let's get ready. Our guys are about ten minutes out."

Oh shit. If I don't get killed now, Monica will finish me off. I can't tell her about this.

We put on vests and helmets. Having FBI stenciled on my chest makes me feel like Superman for about twenty seconds. Moments later, anxiety exerts its gravitational pull again.

Rich looks like RoboCop with his helmet and night-vision goggles. Juan is fumbling with his vest.

"Let's do this," Tiffany says.

CHAPTER 65
REAL MENSCH

Renata arranges the conference call with Inspector V and Frank.

"Bonjour Inspector," she says.

"Bonjour. Don't you ever sleep? Since it's five hours later here, it must be 2:00 AM there," V answers.

"Time is relative," Frank says.

"OK, and I don't have much of it. Frank, you asked me to set up this call. What's happening?" Renata asks.

"I completed the programming. I programmed the OFF switch for the bodyjackers. We might do all of them at once, but the good news is it doesn't need to be an all-or-nothing proposition. Utilizing the blockchain ID built into the system, I believe I can use the unique identifier and selectively turn off specific body invaders, freeing up the individual victim bodies."

A million ideas are racing through Renata's brain. Her pulse is pounding. "You said you *believe* you can do it. What's that mean? You're not sure?"

"It means I must test it first on a real bodyjacked victim to be sure. It's risky. The program might kill them, but it's better to risk one than all or many to be sure. Don't you agree?"

Inspector V clears his throat. "So we're stuck in a classic dilemma. Sacrificing one for the good of the rest. That is *très cher* for the one."

"I'm 90% sure it will not harm the test victim, I mean subject," Frank says.

Renata's palms are sweating. "Here's another case of what choice do we have? If we don't do this, the Leopard, who is still on the loose, could steal thousands more bodies and build a bigger zombie army beholding to him. We've got to stop him and save those who have already been afflicted."

"You need to understand I cannot guarantee this," Frank says. "Remember that Sam was the very first bodyjack test case and it failed, sort of."

"Yeah, he only helped save thousands, if not millions, of lives in Juan's body, as I recall."

"The problem was that Juan's mind and personality were still in that body. Sam had a serious case of Multiple Personality Disorder until he voluntarily gave the body back to Juan," Frank says.

"I know that was hard, but Sam's a real mensch," she says.

Frank laughs. "Now you're talking my language. Yes, he is."

"How did you bring him back this time?" Inspector V asks.

Frank exhales. "That's a story for another time. I think we're agreed we need to move forward. So to get our test subject, I either have to create a new bodyjacked subject, which I'd rather not do or..."

"Or what?" Renata asks.

"Or one of you needs to capture a victim and get them to a safe location. You will also need to restrain them."

"Lovely," Inspector V says. "Well, Ms. Fermi, *c'est moi or vous?*"

"You both should try. It will double our chances and speed things up. Using our tracking data, I have just texted you both possible locations of subjects near you. It's now up to you. Let me know as soon as you have someone."

"Kinda like Tinder," Renata says.

"What's that?" Inspector V asks.

"That's for another time too. Frank, your plan makes sense, but I'm hot on the Leopard's trail. I'll forward the list to Michelle and see if she can pick it up. Maybe we should send several people on this hunt?"

"No, I believe two is enough. More will trip over each other and cause more harm than is necessary. Two of you should be able to capture a subject in the next hour or two."

"I appreciate your optimism," Renata says.

"Just confidence in your talents. Now you've got work to do. Get me a victim subject, preferably alive this time," Frank says.

CHAPTER 66
HOOYAH!

Rich, Tiffany, and I walk about twenty yards into a dense stand of pines to get out of plain sight. The pine scent is both invigorating and arouses some deep primal feelings in me. Maybe it's from all the time spent fly-fishing on rivers meandering through pine forests. "What now?" I ask.

"We wait," Rich says, " ...for Tiffany's backup to arrive. Waiting is a big part of fieldwork."

"'bout 90%," Tiffany says.

Rich's SAT phone rings again, an old-fashioned telephone ringtone, Caller Unknown. "Little, speak."

"It's Secretary Brickman for you," an assistant says.

Rich waits for the click. "Yes, Mr. Secretary. Sorry to be so short before. I've got a few minutes now while we wait for FBI backup."

"Good. I'm in the Sit Room with President Longford, Turgidman, Osborne, Kennedy, and staff. We've got the drone's eye on the big screen. I will conference you in and you need to update everybody. Understood? Hold... "

"Great," Rich says under his breath.

Brickman continues to the group, "I've got Rich Little on the scene about a click outside the NNN compound. Rich, can you hear us?"

"I'm here, Madame President and gentlemen. Let me get right to it as we're expecting FBI backup any minute. Once they're here, we plan to breach the NNN compound."

President Longford interrupts. "Deputy Assistant Director Little, I'm glad you're there. We want these guys, preferably alive. But what I don't want is another Waco on my hands for moral, strategic, and political reasons."

Turgidman coughs loudly. "Madame President, I doubt anybody'd blame you if you wiped these suckers off the face of the earth. Hell, I'd bet the country'd love it."

"General, that's not what I was thinking. We need to confirm 100% that NNN did the D.C. neuro attack. If so, did they act alone or who else or what other groups might be in on this?"

Turdgidman reddens and jumps up from his seat. "We can handle it, Madame President. Let us go round up these rascals. We won't kill 'em, just bruise 'em a bit."

"General, sit down. Rich, do you know how many we're dealing with? We can only spot about a dozen from the drone," Longford says.

"FBI Agent Sly is with me. She and her team have been monitoring this group for a couple of years out of Memphis. I'll put her on."

Sly gives Rich her middle finger. Rich hands her the phone. "Madame President, this is Agent Tiffany Sly, FBI Memphis. It's an honor. This group has somewhere north of 150 members. As you can see from the drone image, there are several outbuildings. As best we can tell, there are a few workshops, an armory, mess hall, barns, and a clubhouse. There could be a hundred people. Heat signatures show a mess of people inside. I'd guess eighty to a hundred. They have grenades, rocket launchers, hundreds of AKs and even a 50 Cal mounted on a Jeep. If they get wind of us coming, they could be locked and loaded in under a minute."

Longford looks at her staff. "Why haven't we taken this group out before? How can we allow them to be so heavily armed?"

Brickman chimes in, "With all due respect, there are hundreds of groups across the country with the same or more firepower. Unless we want a full scale war, we just keep track of them. As long as they can buy semi-automatic weapons at gun shows without background checks using phony IDs, you will have a *well-armed* nation."

"Yep, when the 1994 assault weapons ban expired in '04, there were Chinese cargo ships waiting offshore loaded with assault weapons. At 12:01 they docked and started offloading military style weapons. I know. I was in a do-nothing Congress back then," Osborne says.

"It's been awhile since we've had a do-something congress," Kennedy says.

"OK, I understand," Longford says. No point bitchin' and moanin'. Let's deal with the situation at hand. Agent Sly, is your backup sufficient to handle this?"

"Honestly, I don't know. If there are a hundred armed men, we'd probably need more on our side," Sly says.

Rich takes the phone back. "How long would it take to get some Delta or Seals in here to assist?"

"Hooyah!" Turgidman exclaims.

"That's Marines," Osborne says.

"That's where I come from, son. Let's gear up. I'll have my boys there in 2 to 4."

"Give me a minute," Rich says and looks at Tiffany, "What do you think?"

"We wait and do this right," Tiffany says.

Rich looks at me. "I agree with Tiffany. I will use the time to get Frank and his team on this. We may be able to get some useful info that will get us what we want without killing them or us."

"OK, we wait." Rich gets back on the phone. "Send your boys, but tactically we want to go in before daylight."

Turgidman is out of his seat again. He appears to have a puffiness in his pants. "We're on our way if Madame President so orders."

Osborne stands up. "Madame President, you understand we have the Posse Comitatus Act, which prevents the armed forces from engaging in domestic activities."

"I'm making a national security exception. We'll declare Marshall Law if we need to."

"It requires an Act of Congress to make the exception. You can't authorize it," Osborne says.

"Don't tell me what I can and can't do. If we wait for Congress, we could all be dead. Since you're the expert, what's the penalty for violating this Posse Act?"

"A fine or up to two years in prison or both."

"I'll take my chances. We're not fucking around this time. Go ahead, General, so ordered."

Rich nods to us. "Please keep us posted on their ETA and other details and thank you, I think."

CHAPTER 67
LOCATION, LOCATION

At 2:40 AM, Renata calls Inspector V back after talking with Frank. "OK, what do you think – what's the fastest way for us to track down a bodyjack victim, alive this time?" she says.

V strokes his goatee. "I've got a half-dozen in the morgue, but I guess that won't help. Do Frank's blockchain tags on the bodyjacked track locations?"

"My understanding is there's a latency, a lag time of at least thirty minutes and there is a bug in the tracking code. Seems there's some kind of programming conflict between the security and the tracking. According to Frank, it's like in electricity, they are shorting each other out."

"OK, here's an alternative. We have ID and an address for one of the dead victims brought in today. They lived near the entrance to the Catacombs. I'll head over there. Why don't you check out Adele's leads and put out a BOLO," V says.

"You know I work with you, not for you, right? This is not my first rodeo, I know how to do fieldwork, and I don't appreciate being ordered around," Renata says.

"Je suis désolé. I'm used to being in charge and working with less competent people than you."

"Apology accepted."

"So what do you plan to do?"

"I will follow Adele's leads for whatever they're worth and put out a BOLO, of course." They both laugh.

"But what identifiers can you put in a BOLO? They have to have something to go on."

"That distinct mark on the victims' necks may be enough. Oh, and they all smell like lavender, probably from the disinfectant soap the bodyjackers used to clean the bodies. You never know, a patrol person might catch it on a traffic stop or pick up the scent, so to speak. We might just get lucky."

"C'est simple comme bonjour! Worth a shot. Bonne idée."

Renata laughs again. "Merci, boss. When can I catch some sleep?"

"When this is over, you can snooze like Rip Van Winkle. Until then, grab some coffee and keep me in the loop if anything at all develops, 24/7. I'll do the same. That's an order."

"I love you too." She clicks off.

CHAPTER 68
CLOSING IN

"That was sweet last night, darlin'," Max says as he pours two cups of coffee.

"Glad you're happy. That's a one and only, hun. We've got work to do," Ashaki says, taking the cup from Max. She checks her watch, 5:10 AM.

"We better get to the clubhouse or the boys'll be wondering."

Ashaki takes a last gulp of the coffee and hoists her backpack over one arm. "Let's go."

They cross the dusty yard between buildings, and Elroy runs up to them. "Boss, you need to see this." He tugs on Max's checkered shirt. Max and Ashaki follow to a different out building, the tech shed. Three young men in torn overalls and baseball caps are glued to monitors.

Elroy points to the middle screen. "Look at that."

The boy in front of the screen swivels his chair to the side. "Hey, what is she doing here?"

"None of your business," Max snaps. "Now what am I looking at?"

The boy shrinks in his chair. Elroy hovers over Max's shoulder. "You're looking at an image from one of our DJI Phantom drones. This is about a quarter mile up the road." He puts a hand on the boy's shoulder. "Rewind and show them what you showed me."

The boy shrugs, taps a few keys, and the image of a Jeep appears. Four people, three men and a woman exit the car, talk for a minute and then walk into the woods.

"Impressive," Ashaki says.

"Can't be too careful," Max says. "We have four drones, souped-up with hydrogen fuel cells for extra distance and air time, circling the property. We may be rednecks, but that don't mean we're stupid. Nowadays you can get just about anything on the Internet. Feds ain't the only ones got high tech."

Ashaki grins. "Guess not. Can you go back and zoom in on their faces?"

The boy looks at Max for approval. Max nods and the boy grabs a joystick like this is a video game, rewinds and zooms in.

Ashaki's face turns blue. Max notices and grabs Ashaki's shoulder. "What's the matter sweetie pie? You looks like you just seen a ghost."

"Ain't no ghost. I recognize the guy on the left. He's a top dog at DHS. They're on to us."

Max's face darkens and his back stiffens. "Elroy, this is Code One. Get all the men to the arsenal and gear up. We got a fight comin'." He turns to Ashaki. "Follow me."

He leads Ashaki back across the yard to a small unkempt shed. His men are already moving to their armory building, but at a casual pace as Max trained them. In their Code One plan, the assumption is they would be watched and would not want to alert anyone they were getting ready for battle.

Max and Ashaki enter the shed. The musty odor crinkles Ashaki's nose. Furniture and other dusty, unwanted items are stacked around the walls. Ashaki scratches her head. "What are we doing here?"

Max is already leaning into an old wooden banker's desk. "Just help me move this and you'll see."

They push together and slide the bulky desk to the side. Pillars of dust rise into the air. Max moves to the side and kicks up a handle in the floor. He yanks on a wooden trapdoor that blends perfectly into the floor. "Our way out. El Chapo ain't the only one who can do this."

They descend onto a ladder. Max reaches up and slams the trapdoor behind them. It's pitch black until he flips a switch, illuminating a string of dangling Edison bulbs. "Looks like a party, don't it?" Max grins. "Got these lights online, dirt cheap."

They climb down twenty more rungs to the dirt floor of a tunnel. Ashaki has to stoop not to hit her head. Max just clears the ceiling standing up. *Guess this tunnel was custom made for him*, she thinks. "How far do we have to go?" she asks.

"Far enough to get clear o' here," he says. "Took us darn near a year, but my boys dug this beauty the better part of a mile."

"You continue to surprise me," Ashaki says.

"Why thank you darlin'," Max says. Half an hour later, soaked with sweat and laden with dirt, they shimmy out through an opening under a large boulder. Max looks back at the house-size rock overhanging the dark crawl space exit. "Think a bear lived in there once."

Ashaki peers around at the dense forest surrounding them. "Where are we?"

"We're a good ways from those federales. We're going this way..."

They arrive at a small clearing next to a gravel road. Max strolls over to a group of pines tugging at branches until he uncovers a small beat-looking Toyota pickup. "Here's our ride," he says.

A ringing from Ashaki's backpack breaks the silence. She perches her pack on the truck and extracts her SAT phone. It's Hume calling. Ashaki answers with yeses and grunts and then hangs up.

"What is it?" Max asks.

"You know that package we've been talking about? It's at UPS in Millington. Let's go get it. Are your delivery boys ready?"

"They be ready when we have the goods."

"Good. Then we're a go. What do you think's happening back at your place?"

Max laughs. "Our boys been waitin' and practicin' for this day. The Feds won't know what hit 'em." He licks his lips. "Gonna spill some blood back there, but we got a job to do, right?"

Who or what have I gotten into bed with? she asks herself. Ashaki swallows hard... "Right."

CHAPTER 69
I HAVE THE ANSWER

It's 5:30 AM. Through the glass door, X can see LaSalam's face darken. He's poking a finger into the little man's chest. This can't be good. The little man collapses into a chair. LaSalam's arms are waving wildly in the air. The Leopard pivots, leaving the small conference room and slamming the door behind him. X ducks back behind his monitor, pretending to be focused on his code.

LaSalam approaches and plants his hand firmly on X's shoulder. "How's it coming? Will you be ready?"

Better to lie than provoke. X learned that lesson the hard way from his drunken father and the sting of a leather belt. "Yes, sir. We'll be ready."

"What you don't realize, my talented young man, is that I have a finely tuned bullshit detector. Fabrication is not your strong suit. Prove to me that you're ready."

X flashes on the memory of his father, belt-in-hand, ready to strike. "It's code sir. It wouldn't mean anything to you," X says, voice trembling.

"Show me!" LaSalam shouts. Other heads in the room turn in their direction. LaSalam sprays the room with a sneer, and they all turn back to their screens. He softens his tone. "Now, please."

"OK, I said I *will* be ready. I'm close enough to be certain of meeting your deadline." X punches a few keys. "Here you see we have hacked the security cameras inside the U.N." He scrolls through dozens of images including the General Assembly hall that seats 193 nations, the Security Council Room, several hallways and offices." X swivels to a second monitor. "Here is a diagram of the power grid around the U.N. complex. The red blinking dots are our intercept points. The yellow dots are the access points we are working on and should be able to tap shortly. When you give the signal, we shut it all down."

"Very good. So, explain to me the lack of confidence I picked up in your voice. And remember, if you bullshit me, I'll know."

"OK." X points to a third monitor. "You see the green squares overlaid on the grid?"

"Yes, what are they?"

"They are backup generators that will automatically kick on when the power goes off. They are not connected to the Internet. So we cannot get to them directly. However, I will try to disable the automatic fail-over switches. I was working on that when you inter – I mean when you came over here. That's why I was nervous when you asked."

"I understand now, but when will you be able to disable the switches?"

"I estimate twenty to thirty minutes, but you never know with these things."

LaSalam digs his razor-sharp fingernails harder into X's shoulder. X winces. "*Never know* does not work for me. Get it done. You understand the price of failure by now, right?"

X chokes on his words. "Yes sir, I do. I will get it done, sir."

"Is there anything else you're not telling me? I don't like surprises. 'Surprise' to me is just another word for failure."

"No..." X hesitates. "But there is one constraint you should prepare for. When we shut down the local grid and disable the generator switches, someone in maintenance at the U.N. will figure out the problem and will manually engage the generators. That would narrow the blackout window to between five and ten minutes. Will that give you enough time?"

LaSalam loosens his grip. "It will and I appreciate you're giving me an honest picture." He smirks. "I know I can be a bit pushy sometimes. But what you are doing is critical to our success. I also know that failures occur when you plan too close-to-the-limit. Just in case five to ten minutes is too close, I assume these generators operate on diesel fuel."

X nods.

"Then show me on your diagram where the diesel fuel tanks are located."

X punches a few more keys and four blue rectangles appear near the generator icons. "These tanks are sealed in concrete two-stories down."

"Ah, but they must have a way to refuel them, no? Can you tell me where the proverbial gas caps are?"

X pages through more layers of the diagrams he pilfered from the offices of the U.N.'s architects. He rotates the image to get a 3-D view. Gray pipes attached to the fuel tanks come into view. He traces his finger along the serpentine pipes to ground level. "They are here, here, here, and here."

"Very good. Please text me their exact locations and I will take it from there."

X taps a few more. "There, done."

LaSalam pats X on the back. "Well done. Be ready for my signal." He looks at his watch. "In about three and a half hours."

It's raining in Paris as it often does. There's a slight chill in the air signaling the end of summer. Inspector V parks his car at an angle on a cobblestone street near a Cabinet de Medicine Chinoise. The anonymous clue to a potential bodyjack victim leads here. He questions coming alone without backup, but protests on the Champs-Elysees have sapped the department's resources. Removing a crowbar from the trunk of his Renault, he looks both ways and positions himself over a manhole. He leverages the crowbar and leans his full weight. It breaks loose. This is a little-known entrance to the secret world of the Parisian Catacombs. He's been here before, but it still creeps him out. Six million Parisians are buried down there. Their bones and skulls are neatly stacked floor-to-ceiling along the walls. In the 1700s when Paris's cemeteries were overflowing, the solution was to consolidate the remains of centuries of Parisians in the three hundred kilometers of tunnels that already existed.

Inspector V descends the ladder one tentative step at a time. Since it's five stories down, it takes nearly twenty minutes to reach the bottom. He pulls out his Pamas G1 9mm pistol and flicks on the attached flashlight. The musty odor of dampness and death is almost overwhelming. Sweeping the beam side to side along the ghostly ossified walls, the only sight is bones and more bones. *Why here? Why would someone, anyone be here unless they were already dead? There's an irony to all this, the catacombs and bodyjacking,* he thinks. But he just can't quite put his finger on the connection.

Then it happens. A shot rings out. A sudden blurriness in his vision, V stumbles and leans against one of the skulls embedded in the wall. *What happened? I feel weak but no pain. Like I want to go to sleep. Yes, sleep.* V falls to his knees and then on to his side. The blood oozes from his left ear and mixes with a murky pool of water on the floor. *Yes, now I understand. I have the answer. But who can I –?*

CHAPTER 70
ASSAULT

Renata parks on Lawrence Street, two blocks from her destination. Attempting to hide her bulky Kevlar vest, she zips her navy blue unmarked parka over it. Now she just looks fat or pregnant, neither of which she ever hopes to be. She pats her waist to make sure she has both her Glock 19 and her TASER. Always double-check. A vibration in her breast pocket, a text from V, only one word... "Snipe_"

She knows in her gut what it means. *Amazing how one word or part of a word can have so many meanings*, she thinks, ducking into a doorway. Checking on V will have to wait. The rooftops seem clear. What about the windows across the street? Nothing. Walk in and out of doorways, scan the buildings, the people. Wait. Breathe. Backup? No time for that. Go or retreat? Both could be dangerous. So GO. Carefully, fast and slow. Keep breathing. Now, there – fourth-floor window. A rifle barrel and scope. Does he see me or is he waiting? Does the bulky vest give me away? Only one way to find out. Be smart. A store.

She ducks into Macy's. A few minutes later, she emerges, pushing a baby carriage with a wrapped doll in it. *They're going to love this on the expense account if I make it that far.* The new Mets hat shields her face. It's a risk, but she had to lose the vest. It's tucked under the doll. *At least the doll'll be safe.*

OK, time to cross the street. Deep breath. Don't look up. She laughs grimly to herself at a memory, *serpentine, serpentine*. So far so good. Parking the stroller in the lobby, she flashes her ID to the security guard at the desk. "What's on the fourth floor?"

The guard stutters. "J-just, it's bein' renovated. Nobody's there. New, n-n-n—new tenant soon."

"Stairs or elevator?"

He points to the right. "B-b-both."

"OK, don't let anybody in or out of the building until I come back." *Good luck with that one*, she thinks.

Elevator's too noisy and slow. Take the stairs. She heads up the steps, ducking around corners. The stuttering guard makes a call. Second floor is law offices. Fast and slow. Third floor, a printing company. This is it. She starts up the flight to the fourth floor. A muffled ping and a nick in the wall two inches from her left ear. Down she goes. Several more shots bounce off the metal railing and concrete steps. *What the fuck, how'd he know?*

Earplugs in, goggles on, she steps out and lobs a Kareem-like left hook. The flash-bang loops up and over the fourth floor railing landing at the feet of her assailant. It momentarily stuns the shooter. She races up the steps, leveling her gun at him. He rubs his eyes and raises his TAC-338 rifle. She fires. Two at his legs. He crumbles. She leaps the last few steps and kicks the rifle free.

The unknown assailant rolls over. She yanks off his masked beanie and sees the distinctive neck mark, a bodyjack victim, and the long hair. It's not a *he*. It's a *she*. The injured woman murmurs, "What? Where-am-I?" She looks down and sees the blood. "Oh my God, I'm hit. Shit. Who are you?"

"Renata Fermi, DHS. Who are you?"

"I don't know. I was Diana Searby. I'm a mother. Where's Jack, my son? I was walking him to school and now I'm here. P—p-part of the army?"

"What army?"

"It's like a dream. I think he called it the Leopard's army."

◦━━━◦

"Frank, I've got one," Renata says into her cell while leaning over Diana and checking her wounds.

"What? Tell me," Frank says.

"Her name is Diana. She's a bodyjack victim as you requested. She seems dazed and confused, like her original personality has reemerged, but she has some memories of the invading one. Can you do the extraction you need to do?"

"You must take her to the Hilton Brooklyn where Bart has set up a temporary lab. He flew in from California last night with the equipment. He should be ready for you."

"Diana has lost a lot of blood. I have a med kit and will do the best I can. Helps that I'm a doctor, but she may need a hospital."

"Get one of your emergency medical teams to the hotel. I've ordered a private ambulance to your location. Better get going."

"OK, I'll call you soon." She clicks off and looks down at Diana. "I'm going to patch you up. An ambulance is on the way. Hey, how did you learn to shoot like that?"

She coughs, some blood dribbles from her lips. "I'm a –" She coughs again. "I'm a forward observer for the ATF."

"You're a sniper?"

She smiles weakly. "And proud of it."

"Help is on the way," Renata says.

Diana's eyes close as her head lolls sideways.

CHAPTER 71
UPSTATE

It's 6:25 AM. The dawn sun rises over the New York Thruway overpass near Newburgh. The Leopard took a short flight from Teterboro to Stewart Airport to inspect the training facility. Red and Green picked him up. He misses his long-time friend and bodyguard, Viktor, who was gunned down last year by the infidels in Cambridge. He really doesn't have any other friends. For now, Red and Green will suffice. Viktor and the Leopard's late brother, Momar, were the only ones he could trust. Ashaki is a disloyal traitor. With all he did for her, she was upset by having to satisfy his needs from time-to-time. It is a paradox how women are more trouble than they're worth, but he needs them, especially the young ones. Some women he has bodyjacked tried to pleasure him, but it's not the same. They are just useful zombies that bring no real heat, not like the girls he's had. His mouth waters at the memories.

A short ride from the Thruway exit, they turn right into an industrial park he recently purchased with the help of his good friends in Barin and the stolen bitcoin his hackers so deftly purloined. *I wonder how much those nerds kept for themselves? Cost of doing business,* he thinks.

The industrial park comprises eight neatly arranged free-standing warehouses of forty to fifty thousand square feet each. It would be foolish to do training out in the open with American drones and satellites overhead. Bin Laden made that mistake in Afghanistan. He was just lucky that two American presidents were too cautious or too weak to take him out before 9/11. But LaSalam's training facilities are right in their backyard disguised as light industrial facilities, forklifts and all. Trucks arrive and leave as they normally would in the course of business. But in his case, they carry weapons, armor, and gear. His warehouse workers are bodyjacked homeless U.S. veterans, skilled marksmen, explosive experts, programmers, and trainers who will not be missed, at least not until this mission is over. Then he will shut them all down with the flip of a switch. This is Phase One – New York and Paris. The Phase Two plan—go global.

The Leopard's experts have enhanced Frank Einstein's body reactivation technology. He can now kidnap and inject a new personality into the unwitting victim's body. However, his code modification goes a step further, exerting a kind of mind control. And in the Leopard's Bodyjacking 2.1 software, the recruits, as he calls them, have no fear of death. Like Kamikazes, that makes them especially lethal. Here in Newburgh, he has amassed an army of zombie-like bodyjacked vets that will follow his every command, and they already come with significant skills built into their muscle memory.

So far, they haven't all worked out. Some rebel, probably a bug in the code. For the defective ones, he has an industrial incinerator on-site. Fortunately, there were only a few that fought the power of his body commands. The Newburgh facility allows him to test and train them to operate as a group. One warehouse, Building #7, functions as an infirmary and rehab center. Some vets he bodyjacked off the streets and from under bridges were in pretty bad shape with PTSD and addiction issues. But they met his criteria, were skilled, and have no family to miss them. The doctors and nurses at his infirmary brought most of them back, sobered them up, and got them healthy in time to perform. For those who failed, a hot oven awaited.

The tall, gray-haired director of the facility, Ron McNerney, greets them at the small reception area in Building #1. He extends a hand. "Welcome, Mr. Merit. Jolly good to see you."

Red and Green flank LaSalam in a protective stance. The Leopard grins, baring his teeth. "This is not a social call. What is the status of our trainees?"

McNerney waves a hand towards the front door. "Let me show you." He leads LaSalam across a dusty, pot-holed driveway to Building #2. The interior is barely lit by fluorescents and industrial skylights twenty feet above. "I'll show you around."

LaSalam nods. The near side of the facility is a well-equipped gym with the latest isometric machines. Men are lifting weights. Women are doing pull-ups. Others are sprinting around a synthetic rubber track that runs along the periphery of the floor. McNerney's face lights up with pride. "The firing range is out back." They proceed halfway across the building. McNerney pulls back a heavy sliding steel door, releasing the loud clatter of gunfire. The odor of cordite washes over them. The ceiling is lower and the lighting much brighter in the long, narrow range. About a dozen men and women are firing automatic weapons at remote targets. McNerney hands LaSalam noise-canceling headphones with built-in walkie-talkies. McNerney dons another pair and waves his hand in the air. Red and Green, always prepared, extract earplugs from their pockets. The bearded training instructor pushes a button on the sidewall. A red beacon lights and spins. The trainees cease firing and the paper targets slide on carrier tracks back towards the marks-people. McNerney and LaSalam stroll along the row of trainees and see neat clusters of bullet holes in the heads and chests of the human silhouettes on the paper. McNerney speaks through his microphone. "What do you think?"

The Leopard smirks. "Very impressive, but I asked for their status. When will they be ready?"

McNerney loses his smile. "They are making very good progress. They should be ready in about a week."

LaSalam snorts and looks at his watch. "Get them ready in an hour. Two chartered buses will be here to pick them up. They have about a two-hour ride to their destination. Mystee Pulcine will be on board with the mobile command module. Understood?"

McNerney begins to speak, looks at Red and Green, then seems to think better of it. "Yes, I understand."

"Make sure they gear up and eat first. They won't have time later. I need them fully charged and ready to go. There will be a restroom on the bus should they need it. Make sure to load all the gear from the Plan on the second bus."

"We just received the night-vision goggles from Barin. The RPGs and AKs are combat-ready.

"You seem to have thought of everything, sir."

"You better have as well."

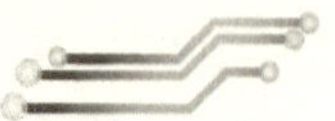

CHAPTER 72
GFUDS

The cloaked and silenced Blackhawks hover two feet above the road, one hundred yards from our position. We wouldn't have known they were there unless a sudden wind kicked up in our direction. The normally deafening sound of Blackhawk rotors is a low murmur. Out of two seemingly invisible doors, a dozen fully equipped Delta Force operators appear. They jog toward our position, hugging the side of the road.

A fortyish man with short-cropped gray hair and piercing blue eyes halts in front of Rich. "Deputy Secretary Little I presume?"

"Correct, thanks for getting here so fast. You are?"

"Major Robert Morton, sir. What have we got?"

"Eighty to a hundred heavily armed. We need their leader alive and the woman he's with. You've seen the drone shots, I assume?"

Morton extracts a tablet from his vest. "Yes, sir. If you have no objections, I'd like to send two of my recon guys ahead before we make any moves."

"It's your show, Major."

Morton waves his arm in a circle and two operators, one male one female, jog ahead wearing augmented reality goggles that display maps, coordinates, and drone images overlaid on their present position. They proceed up the road towards NNN without further instructions. Morton checks his watch, 6:30 AM. "We should have a closer look shortly."

"We want to go in with you. This is FBI Agent Sly and Sam Sunborn," Rich says. Sly smiles. I'm already soaked with sweat and catastrophizing.

"Deputy Secretary Little, I'm afraid those are not my orders," Morton says.

"You mean us going along is not in your orders, but your orders don't preclude it. Is that correct?" Rich says.

"That is correct, but I am now in charge here. I don't plan on losing any civilians on my watch."

"We are not civilians. We are armed and armored. Besides, we can ID the two we want alive. I don't care about the rest."

"What about him?" Morton asks, pointing at me.

Rich chuckles. "You'd be surprised how much combat he's seen. Besides, he's our intel man. Look, I can make a call and bother General Turgidman or you can make a command decision in the field. Which is it going to be?" Rich says.

Morton snorts. "I don't want to deal with that old bat. OK, but you stay behind us when we go. Got it?"

Rich nods. "As I said, you're in charge. Think of us as your backup."

"Sure, but don't bullshit me and do as I say."

"Roger that."

"Should be soon. I'd rather use the dark as our friend and move now." Morton points to the night-vision goggle perched on his forehead. "We have these, but I doubt those assholes do. And if they do, we have GFUDs." He sees Rich scratch his head. "Goggle-Fuck-Up-Devices. We switch our goggles from active illumination to thermal, then throw the GFUDs at them. They're basically like flash-bangs that will blind them."

"Sounds good. So what's the plan, full on assault?"

"That's what we do. We fuck people up, sir."

CHAPTER 73
KABOOM

At about 6:45, the last moments of pitch dark before dawn, it's time. Delta moves with stealth into position, clustering like the planets around the sun as their target. The two dozen operators all understand their roles. Three with night-vision binoculars in infra-red mode ID the targets and call out numbers to their comrades via their coms.

"A1 in position. Fifteen tadpoles in my one-eighty."

"B2- Group signature in building number-two."

"C1 - we've got buildings one and three."

"Alpha Dog - be ready on my command."

Rich, Sly, and I are hunched behind a loose-stone wall. The major is standing nearby with his night-vision binoculars focused on NNN's courtyard. I look up and see a small commercial drone circling a hundred feet above us. I tap Rich on the shoulder and point up.

"Shit," Rich whispers. He crawls over to the Major, who shifts his focus to where Rich is pointing skyward.

The Major clicks his com. "All teams, they know we're here. Prepare to take out any UAVs in your visual. Once they hear shots, it's game on. So it's on GO command. Down the UAVs, take out the long targets and move in."

A chorus of replies. "Roger that."

"What about the two we want to keep alive?" Rich asks.

"We've got digital signatures on those two and my guys know to save them if and when they see them. The others are toast," the Major says.

"Sounds good to me," Rich says.

I think I'm holding my breath. I force myself to breathe. The silence seems interminable. Rich and I stare at our Drone image from almost three miles above. Small red, digital squares lock on the glowing infrared human signatures moving about in the NNN courtyard.

Then the major says, "Be safe. Take 'em down." Several shots ring out from the HK 417 rifles, their cracking sound bouncing in echoes across the valley. The UAV I had spotted drops in pieces a few feet from us. The Major shot it down. I swivel back to the screen and see flashes coming from the woods surrounding the NNN compound. Several squares on the screen drop to the ground, but then flashes of return fire come from the NNN combatants. A vehicle that looks like a Hummer erupts from one of the barns and sprays fifty caliber rounds from a homemade armored-turret mounted on top.

The Major looks at us as he starts over the wall. "This ain't gonna be easy. You guys stay here."

"Fuck that," Sly says, standing up. "We're behind you."

Rich looks at me and says, "Gear up, partner."

We rise and follow Sly and the Major zig-zagging down a hill through the thick trees and heavy undergrowth. The sound of gunfire is non-stop. A bullet flies by my ear, chipping off the bark of a pine two feet away. I raise the Sig Sauer P229 Rich gave me, prepared for who-knows-what. The Major raises a hand to stop us at the edge of the woods. The fifty cal is spraying bullets in our direction. We're hunched low behind trees. We look right as one of our operators shoulders a PSRL, Airtronic Precision Shoulder-fired Rocket Launcher. He fires, missing the Humvee but hitting the building behind it. The structure explodes in flames. The gun shots pause briefly and then resume even more furiously. The operator's partner loads another PSRL round. This one hits the Humvee. The explosion throws the gunner clear as the Humvee bounces up in the air and lands on its side.

The Major waves again. "Let's go."

We stay low and head for cover in the courtyard behind any available vehicle, piece of equipment, or outcropping. NNN members in full gear with vests, helmets, and rifles stream out of a third building firing on full-auto. Delta snipers methodically pick off every third-one. The Delta operators near us hook shot grenades into the melee. As the grenades explode, Rich, Sly, and I rise from our cover and shoot at whatever moves. I hit two men, one in the head and the other in the chest. They fall like Raggedy-Ann dolls to the ground. I don't know what planet I'm on or what movie I'm in, but I fire like a madman and then take cover when a volley of bullets come back at me. It feels like my heart is thumping out of my chest. Adrenalin shoots through me like an electric current.

More grenades, more shooting. Then a massive explosion as our drone's Tomahawk missile obliterates another building. The ground rocks from the intensity of the blast. That overwhelming firepower changes everything. The gunshots die down. The Major hits the com and barks, "Hold your fire."

We slowly emerge from our cover and see the few remaining men alive in the courtyard raising their rifles over their heads in surrender. Knowing what to do, the Delta operators move in, sweeping their weapons side-to-side. Two shots ring out from a window in the only remaining building. I see one of the Delta guys tumble backwards. The others drop to the ground and take aim at the sniper. I feel a thump as if someone punched me in the shoulder. Something wet just under my Kevlar vest. The PSRL operator takes aim and blasts the window where the shooter is perched. It goes silent again. Dust and the smell of death fill the air. The operators and the living NNN members slowly rise again. The operators seize the NNN weapons and flex cuff the remaining men, stepping over bloody bodies to restrain the living.

The Major clicks the com again. "Any IDs on our two prizes?"

A collective "Nope" comes from the operators and the drone circling above.

Rich looks over at me. "You're hit."

"I'm what?" I feel like I'm spinning. There's no ground under my feet. All sound fades and then nothing.

CHAPTER 74
LIGHTS OUT

At 7:30, Rich checks his phone as the dust and smoke clear. Dawn brightens the eastern sky while EMTs swarm the scene of the dead and injured. A voice mail from Roger Brickman tells us, "The president wants answers and she wants them now."

"What is it?" Sly asks.

"I guess I can't avoid this call. It's the White House. Stay with Sam. I'll meet you at the hospital," Rich says. He walks a few steps out of earshot and glances back as I'm hoisted on a stretcher into an idling ambulance.

"Good, it's you. You're on speaker," Brickman says. "I'm in the SIT room with the president, Kennedy, Osborn, and Turgidman. We've been watching from above. It looks like a real shitshow. Did you secure the prize? Um, I mean is everybody OK?"

"No and No, but I'll give the good news first. I'd estimate we took out almost a hundred sworn enemies of the U.S. I'm sure you can see the casualties on your screen. We lost two of ours in the gunfire and Sam Sunborn was hit."

"And...?"

"And Werner and the woman slipped us. I think Sunborn will be OK. If you can direct the UAV to scan the surrounding area, maybe you can spot the two that got away."

Brickman motions to a staffer who lurches at the phone. "What else?"

"We'll take it from here and track down those S.O.B.s."

President Longford slams a fist on the mahogany table and says, "Why do I feel like we're cats chasing our own tails? If I understand the situation correctly, we're running out of time." She hesitates and wipes a tear from her eye. I'm sorry about our two lost boys. Roger, get me the names. I'll call the families."

General Turgidman coughs. "Madame President, with all due respect, they're my guys. I'll make the call. But first, we've got to stop whatever's coming at us."

"Rich, who's this woman we're chasing?" President Longford asks.

"We believe she was one of ours, an Adele Lamont, and that she somehow has a connection to the Leopard. We're still trying to piece that together. But obviously she is working with this Max Werner and has some connection to the incidents in D.C. or Indiana or both."

"So it's still a fuckin' jumble, and you have no idea what you're doing. Is that about it?" Turgidman says.

Rich's face grows hot. He takes a deep breath. "General, we just took out an entire group of domestic terrorists, we have several leads, and we know a lot more than we did yesterday. Nobody said this isn't a messy business, but we'll get it done."

"You better," Turgidman says.

"Hold up Turdman. We've got this," Brickman says. "I'd appreciate it if you didn't shit on our guys."

"Watch the language," Osborne says.

For a few moments, the SIT Room lights flicker and the room goes into blind darkness. "What the fuck?" Turgidman says.

A few seconds later, the back-up generators kick in. The lights flicker back to life. Two suited secret service agents enter the room. The gray-haired fifty-ish male agent speaks first. "Madame President, please come with us."

"What's going on?" Longford says as she reluctantly rises from her seat.

The auburn-haired female agent, Debbie Rodriguez, replies, "There's an unknown intrusion to the power system. This is just a precaution. Gentlemen, if you will follow me." They all rise to file out.

The last to leave is General Turgidman. Rodriguez puts a hand on his chest. "Not you."

"What? What are you talking about? Where they go, I go."

"You're not on the list," she says.

CHAPTER 75
ROUND 2

At 8:15, I unclose my eyes. Trees flash by in a blur through the window of the speeding ambulance. I glance down at my blood-stained shirt and say, "Was I hit?"

"Stay still, Mr. Sunborn. You've lost a lot of blood." Marlene Claire, the EMT says as she dials up the I.V.

"Where?" I say.

"You were lucky. The shoulder, a through-and-through."

There's a large gauze bandage on my chest with crisscrossing tape below my right collarbone. I start peeling the edge of the tape off.

"What are you doing?" Marlene asks, her face contorted. She extends her hand to stop me. I have a good grip now and rip the dressing off in one swift motion. The bandage is soaked in blood.

My eyes widen. Marlene's mouth opens wide as if to scream, but nothing comes out. We both stare down at the wound in shocked silence. There is no wound, just some dried blood. The skin is not broken. "What?" Marlene says. "I saw it myself, a gushing gash the size of a silver dollar." She cleans off the dried blood with an alcohol wipe. No wound.

The strong medicinal alcohol malodor seems to clear the fog from my brain. "Maybe it was the other shoulder?" I say in a faint whisper, but I know.

Marlene tears the blanket off my left shoulder. No wound there either.

"I'm a quick healer," I offer.

"I don't get it. Am I losing my mind?" she says.

"Do you have my cell phone?" I ask.

Marlene hesitates and fumbles through a plastic bag with my effects – no, I mean belongings. She hands me the phone. I dial Rich. He picks up on the first ring. "Sam?"

"Yeah, it's me. How are you?"

"Me? You were shot. It looked bad. How are you talking to me right now?"

"It only grazed me, I guess. Lot of blood, but no hole."

"What? That makes no sense."

"I'll explain when I see you. Where are you now?"

He takes a minute to answer. "We're wrapping up at the scene. We have a live one to interview. I'd take him back to Memphis, but I don't think we have much time. There's been a major blackout in D.C. I think something's about to go down." Rich turns to Sly. "Where can we interrogate this asshole nearby?"

I hear Sly talking in the background, but I can't make out what she's saying. "What is it? What's she say?"

"We're taking him to South Covington. Sly says there's an Applebee's on Route 51 with a backroom we can commandeer. About ten minutes out," Rich says.

"I'll meet you there." I click off before Rich can protest. I turn to Marlene. "Take me to –"

"I can't release you just like that. You're wounded," Marlene says.

"Do you see a wound? This is a national emergency. That was Deputy Secretary Richard Little of the Department of Homeland Security," I say, looking into her eyes. She seems unmoved. "Look. You can come with me if you like. Just get me there or there will be a lot more blood on your hands."

Marlene Claire looks down at her hands covered in blood, my blood. She turns to the ambulance driver and shouts, "Do what the man says."

⊶——⊷

Rich and Sly stand outside Applebee's awaiting the sheriff with their suspect-witness-captive in tow. But first the ambulance veers to the curb. Marlene spots the man and woman in dark suits. The man has dark hair with gray streaks and radiant blue eyes. The woman appears to be five and a half feet tall, muscular, and intense. Marlene unlocks and exits the rear door of the ambulance. She scans Rich and Sly up and down and says, "Are you Director Little or do I have a psycho magician in my bus?"

Rich extends a hand. "I am Deputy Secretary Little and you are?"

Marlene demurs, offering a fist pump. "Who I am ain't important. The vic in my wagon is bloody, but his wound totally disappeared. If I hadn't seen it for myself, I wouldn't believe it. Then he tells me some cockamamie tale and demands I bring him here. Says it's a national emergency. Is that true?"

"Yes, that's true. Is he OK? I mean, does he need to go to the hospital?"

"He seems perfectly fine, 'cepting those bloody, pukey clothes he should burn. I strapped him down on the gurney to restrain him until I could check out his story."

"You can unstrap him. We need him, if he's OK and can walk."

Marlene climbs back in the ambo and unstraps me. I sit up and rub my arms where the restraints dug in. "Nurse Ratched has nothing on you," I say.

"Who's that?" she asks.

"Never mind, thanks for the lift." I slide down the rear bumper of the ambulance. Feeling shaky, I hold on to the rear door for a minute. Rich and Sly seem to study me with concern. "I'm OK. Let's go talk to your witness."

Rich throws me a clean shirt. "Wash up first and put this on. We'll meet you in five in the backroom."

"You got it. Thanks." I hesitate to let go of the ambulance door, fearing I might fall down.

Marlene grabs my elbow and leads me to the curb. "C'mon Rambo. I just got a call. Got to go help some normal folks caught in a fire. It's been real."

No, it hasn't, I think.

Sly takes over from Marlene, helps me inside, and says, "You're a real piece of work, and you smell like shit warmed over. The restroom's over there. Wash up real good. The back room's down the hall."

I regain my balance and head to the restroom. The bloody shirt goes right into the garbage. My pants look like I slid into third base ten times on a rainy day, but they'll have to do. I almost don't recognize myself in the mirror with the dirt and blood on my face and torso. But no wound. *What's that all about?*

I suspect I know, but I call Frank. He answers without a ring. "Sam, are you OK?"

I snicker. "I might be more than OK. I got shot and bled, but the bullet wound disappeared. I thought I was physically alive again. Want to fill me in?"

"You want the long version or the short version?" Frank asks.

"Rich is waiting on me to interview an NNN guy upstairs. Check that–he's probably not waiting. Better make it quick."

"Remember, I said you were 99% alive. Well, you are, and you aren't. Like a quantum particle, you're present, and you're not. I also mentioned before that Time is involved. An hour ago you were shot and had a bullet hole in you. But you didn't always have a bullet hole in you. The other part of your quantum self doesn't have a wound in its shoulder. I was watching the whole battle with the NNN go down, tapping into the drone and into yours and Rich's cell phone cameras. I saw you get shot and loaded into the ambulance. Fortunately, my nifty new program allowed me to swap out the injured you for your uninjured other quantum self. Try saying that three times fast."

I'm stunned. What kind of being am I now? "I don't know what to say."

Frank laughs. "How about, 'Remote control is a beautiful thing'?"

CHAPTER 76
RALLY

Juan burst into the Applebee's men's room as I finish drying my face. "Are you OK?" he asks.

I give him a Cheshire smile. "Where were you? You're supposed to protect me."

"I did. You almost got killed, but I tackled the gunman behind you and gutted him with my kukri knife before he could swiss cheese you. Then everything went dark. Not sure what happened, but I have this shiner to show for it. Wait a minute. You're bloody but not injured?"

"I cleaned most of the blood off. Am I presentable?" I run fingers through my hair and do a mock twirl.

"But I saw you get shot?"

"Just a graze, but that's a story for another time. I want to get to that interview with Rich and the NNN guy down the hall. You look like shit. Clean yourself up. Join us when you're done, but stand in the back and say nothing. And Juan, thank you."

Juan gives me a hug. I check myself again in the mirror. Not great, but it will have to do. I knock lightly on the back room door and enter, taking a seat next to Rich and Sly. Sitting across the table is a young man in his twenties, covered in mud and blood. He looks worse than me by a mile. He wriggles in his seat, either fighting against or trying to get comfortable with the snap ties tightly binding him to the chair. A Tennessee Highway Patrolwoman stands in the shadows two feet behind.

Sly looks at me. "Good, you're looking better. Still smell like shit, but at least you're alive."

"Yeah, I'm grateful for the little things," I quip.

Rich puts a hand on my arm and looks at our prisoner. "OK. Let's do this." He places his phone on the table and starts his Otter audio recording app. "I'm Richard Little from DHS. Seated next to me are Tiffany Sly, FBI, and Sam Sunborn..." he hesitates, "... consultant. Also in the room is Patrolwoman Cheryl Walton. We are interviewing a suspect we captured at the NNN compound this morning. The time is 9:20 AM, Eastern Daylight Time." Rich stares into the captive's eyes. "And your name is?"

The bedraggled man spits, "I ain't tellin' you shit."

Sly jumps in, "It's been a tough day for all of us. Listen, we have your fingerprints and your DNA. Between that and facial recognition, we'll figure out who you are, but you're in control. You can make this easy and maybe do less time at Northwest Correctional or make it hard and spend the rest of your life at Riverbend Super Max — your choice."

Silence follows. The man seems to be mulling it over. One thing top negotiators and interrogators learn is the power of silence. Another way to think of it is, *he who speaks first loses.* So we wait quietly. A long few minutes pass. The lull is excruciating because every minute is precious if we're to prevent the next shoe from dropping. Yet, Rich and Sly sit lips-zipped.

Finally the prisoner speaks, "It's Zak, but that's all I'm sayin'."

"OK, Zak. That's a start. Thank you for cooperating," Rich says.

"I ain't cooperatin'. No way, no how."

"Either way, that's not what your buddies will say when you get out of here," Sly says. "I'll make sure of that. I've heard they're not a very forgiving bunch." Sly turns to Rich. "What have you heard?"

Rich smirks. "That your leader... What's his name, Max, is pretty darn good with a whip. Can you imagine being tied to a post naked and having Max take aim at your testicles? Oh, ouch. Just the thought of it..."

Good cop Sly tag teams. "But we can protect you if you help us."

Zak sneers. "Just like you protected those Afro-Congressmen the other day? How did that —" Zak stops himself as if he's already said too much.

"So you're confirming that NNN pulled off the D.C. attack?" Rich asks.

"I ain't confirming nothin'."

Juan enters the room quietly and stands behind us.

Zak looks alarmed. "What's that guy doing here? He's a crazy man, like Bruce Lee. He must've killed or sliced up ten of our guys."

Rich lights up. "Zak, meet Juan Valiente. He works for us off-the-books, if you know what I mean. He was a star in Afghanistan before Obama banned torture. So we brought him here for special situations like this."

Of course, Rich is making this Juan stuff up. But by looking at Zak, it seems to have some effect. "So, Zak, if you don't speak to us willingly, we're all going to leave the room, including Patrolwoman Walton, but Juan will stay. He has ways to get people like you to spill their guts, literally and figuratively."

Juan breaks into a wide grin. He seems to love this.

After another long silent minute, Zak whispers, "I help and you'll protect me, right?"

"That's correct," Sly says.

Zak closes his eyes like he's thinking things over. "All I knows is that we built an escape tunnel for Max. He, and that bitch he's porkin', most likely ran out da' tunnel.

"Where would they go? What do they have planned?" Rich asks, growing red faced.

"That's all I's know,"

Rich looks at his watch and loses it. He jumps across the table knocking Zak, lashed to the chair, backwards onto the floor. He steps on Zak's neck. "You know. Tell us."

Zak spits and coughs as Rich leans his shoe with more weight on Zak's neck. Sly pulls Rich away. Patrolwoman Walton lifts Zak and the chair upright. Blood seeps from Zak's lips. Rich paces behind us.

Something deep inside me takes over and I say, "Listen, Zak. You can see these guys are serious. We believe Max and that woman have something planned that may kill many more people. But I can promise you if you don't give us something useful right now, you'll be the first to die." I glance at Juan. "And it will be an extremely painful first."

"I'm just a worker bee, not a boss. They don't tell me squat."

"Did you overhear anything?" I say.

Zak looks up and to the left. "I might have, but I can't remember what."

"If you could remember what you overheard, what would it be?" I say. Sounds like a dumb question, but it's surprising how often "if you could" works.

Zak takes a deep breath. "The bitch's got some kinda bug or virus. Max is gonna help her get it out."

"How's he going to get it out?" I ask.

"Not sure. If I had to guess, we got bikers all over that could move things."

"Like you do with drugs now, right?" Sly asks.

"Yeah, that's right."

"OK, so where are Max and the woman? Where would Max go?" I ask.

Zak looks up at the ceiling. "Hmm, let me think about that."

"Think fast," Rich says.

CHAPTER 77
PRAY

It's 9:40 at the White House. Osborne, Hagar, Brickman, and Turgidman sit on the two sofas in the Oval Office while Longford paces in front of the Resolute Desk. "At least the power's back," she says. "I've got to get on the chopper to the U.N. for my speech." She looks at her watch. "Supposed to be at 11:00 but looks like I'll be late."

"Since we pay most of the U.N.'s bills and you're the leader of the free world, I assume they'll wait for you," Osborne says.

"Not to state the obvious." She glares at Osborne. "OK, so where are we?"

"The NNN breach was a success, but their leader and his accomplice got away. Rich Little is interrogating one of the NNN people now. I just got a text from him. The NNN captive as much as admitted that NNN was behind the D.C. attack," Brickman says.

"Sounds like progress, but what about this bodyjacking crap in New York and the Indiana attack?" she asks.

"Uh, we're tracking down leads," Brickman says.

"In other words, you've got bupkis," Longford says.

Turgidman bolts upright. "Madame President. I've got 5000 troops plus Delta locked and loaded at Fort Dix in New Jersey. Just give me the green light, and we'll be on the ground in New York in thirty."

"Cool your jets. Let's give Roger's New York team a little more time. Besides, we don't have enough information to direct you where to deploy. Am I right about that, Roger?" Longford asks.

"That's correct, Madame President. Give us a little more time before we go nuclear," Brickman says.

"I like the sound of that," Turgidman says with a straight face.

"Buck, sometimes I don't know what planet you came from. Look, I've got to go. You can reach me at any time. Interrupt my U.N. speech if you have to, but keep me in the loop and don't go off half-cocked. Remember, I am the commander in chief, right?"

"Yes, Madame President," they stand and say in unison.

Michelle, Renata, and Jonathan sit silently around the small conference room table in the Beaver Street office, staring up at the clock, 10:00 AM. "What have we got?" Michelle asks.

"Dead ends," Renata says. "But at least Rich and Sam have stopped the NNN."

"That's like popping a pimple," Jon says. "With the Leopard about to strike who-knows-where and the NNN leader out there, we could be one minute from midnight on a major attack."

"You're right," Michelle says. "But –"

Michelle's cell lights up with a text from Unknown:

Anytime now. International incident TTYL

Renata stares over Michelle's shoulder. "What the heck does that mean?"

"I bet it's from the same anonymous tipster that gave us the lead before," Michelle says.

Jonathan grumbles. "Not helpful, That's all we fuckin' need is a riddle at the eleventh hour."

"Yes, but she wouldn't have sent this unless she wanted us to act," Michelle says.

"Then why not just come out and say it?" Renata asks.

"Maybe she's being watched," Michelle adds.

"Or maybe she only has part of the answer and needs us to figure out the rest," Jonathan says.

"Let's go with that – she has incomplete information herself and needs our help," Michelle says.

"OK, so the 'Anytime now' is obviously very soon. We need to decipher 'International incident.' Since 'incident' could mean a range of bad acts. Let's focus on 'International' – what's that tell us?" Renata asks.

"So we know the *when* is any minute. How about the *where?*" Jonathan asks.

"Let's assume to start it's New York. Could it be an assassination attempt? That would be *international*," Michelle says.

"Whoa, the president is addressing the U.N today," Renata says. She taps in a quick Google query. "... at 11:00 AM. Shit."

All three shoot looks at the wall clock, 10:35. Then all the lights go out.

○——————○

Michelle and Renata hit their cell phone flashlights. Jonathan is stunned, either by Renata's revelation or the blackout or both. "What the fuck?" he says.

"We've got to act on this and do it fast," Michelle says. "Renata, you call the head of NYPD Counterterrorism." She snaps her fingers twice. "What's his name?"

"Riley Reed. On it," Renata says.

"I'll call U.N. security," Jonathan says.

"Good. I'll call Rich, but let's do it on our way there. Let's go."

The hallway is lit with emergency lights. The three of them run and talk into their phones at the same time. They pass the large, open, now dark, office space filled with cubicles. The only light comes from computer monitors running on UPS battery backups. Michelle stops running in the middle of the room. Rich answers her call. "What's going on?"

"Listen," Michelle says. She holds the phone at arm's length so Rich can hear and raises her voice to the whole room. "Listen up, everybody. Stop what you're doing and pay attention. I'm declaring a Code Red. We have a credible threat at the U.N. The president is due to speak there any minute. This power outage may be related. Get every available resource on this now. Send FBI SWAT and coordinate through CTF. We're headed there now."

There's a shout from an agent at the back of the room. "The power is out on the entire eastside of Manhattan, including the U.N."

"Great. Rich, did you get all that?" Michelle asks.

Rich is still wrapping up the interrogation in Tennessee. "Yeah. Where'd this all come from?"

Michelle starts running again. Elevator is out. She heads for the stairs, taking them two at-a-time. "Our mystery informant. It all fits. I'm heading over there. Call in the cavalry."

"I'll call Brickman right now," Rich says. "Stay safe."

"And, Rich —"

"Yeah?"

"Pray."

CHAPTER 78
9/12

Michelle's response to emergencies is a focused calm. Her next call is to Gary. "Dude, are you on this?"

"Yeah, looks like the power-outage is a cyber-attack for sure. Where are you?"

"I just left the building. We're on our way to the U.N., but traffic's a bitch even with sirens."

"Ah, I've got your location. Take 1st Avenue. I'll turn all the red lights green."

"Thanks, that'll help. We are Code Red, credible threat to the president and maybe the whole General Assembly. We're working the theory that the power outage is a cover for an impending attack. You've got to get the power back, especially at the U.N."

"How much time do we have?"

Michelle glances at the dashboard clock and says, "Twenty minutes or less."

"Shit. We're on it."

Michelle can hear the furious clicking keyboards in the background. "Keep me posted."

"Go, go, go," Gary says and clicks off.

It's 9/12. Dates can be symbols. Counterterrorism units around the world step up their efforts on the anniversary of that fateful day, 9/11. The Leopard chose 9/12 not only because his enemies might be less wary and alert the day after 9/11, but 9/12 seems to have a poetic cleverness—it's the "next day" when the next shoe should drop.

X is sweating buckets as he checks his watch, 10:50. The Leopard steps behind him and squeezes his shoulder a little too hard, saying, "Nicely done on the blackout. Were you able to disable the U.N.'s backup generators?"

X wipes his brow with his sleeve. "Yeah, they're off. But some maintenance engineer at the U.N. will figure out somebody disabled the fail-over switch, and he'll manually kick on the generators."

"Then we better not wait until 11:00. Send the signal now."

"Are you sure you want to do this? Hundreds or thousands could die?"

"What do you think? That I'm going to change my mind now? After months of planning and personal risk? You must either believe I'm crazy or you don't get it. Don't waste my time. Do it now!"

X's face turns an icy blue. He swivels back to his keyboard and types a few keys. "It's done."

The Leopard strokes the back of X's neck and says, "Bring up the cameras. I want to see."

X's three monitors fill with dozens of palm-sized images from security cameras placed around the outside and the inside of the U.N., covering the Plaza, the lobby, the General Assembly, conference rooms, and hallways.

A drop of drool trickles down the Leopard's chin. "Ah, it's starting. This is quite exciting, isn't it?"

X drops his head, and the Leopard grabs the arm of X's chair to spin him around so he can see his face. He lifts X's chin, looking him in the eyes. "You've done an excellent job, my friend. So, I will give you a bonus."

X grimaces. The Leopard reaches down as if to scratch his ankle and reveals a Beretta 92X compact 9 millimeter pistol. "This is for you." In one quick motion, Ahmed LaSalam raises the gun and fires a clean shot into X's forehead. X's eyes go wide. He falls forward and the Leopard catches X's collar, lowering him to the floor.

LaSalam takes X's chair, sits, swivels around, focusing on the camera feeds and says to no one, "I wish I had some popcorn." He hears gunshots behind him in the office, but he seems oblivious, absorbed in the images on the monitors. Without looking away, he reaches across the desk for a gas mask and straps it on. *If this goes as planned, it will only be the beginning, a deadly distraction. Many of my recruits will die, but I can make more, thousands more, and the next attack will be one hundred times bigger.*

CHAPTER 79
EBB AND FLOW

At 10:55, dark clouds race quickly overhead. Light rain dapples the U.N. plaza. A fog rising from the East River envelops the plaza and the darkened 39-story Secretariat Building in a cloud. The two Decamp buses parked at the curb appear to be like all the other tour buses that deposit curious visitors throughout the day. The signal X sent reaches its destination and green beacons alight inside the buses. The reincarnated, retrained, and fearless veterans jolt upright as if hit by an electric shock the second the remotely signaled auto-pilot kicks in. Filing out in silence, they fan out in a semi-circle surrounding U.N. headquarters. Armed with AK 47s, grenades, and rocket-launchers, they move in. One group approaches the 1800-seat General Assembly Building and the other veers off to the Secretariat Building.

A scattering of half-dozen tourists—women and children, and a gaggle of men in Italian-made suits turn towards the approaching militia. The women scream, the children hide behind their mothers, and the men drop their briefcases and sprint towards the tall tower. The apparent leader of the armed group lifts, then lowers his right arm. The insurgents send a five-second burst of gunfire at the tourists and men in suits. They drop like ten-pins, all toppling, not one standing—a strike, not a spare. The odor of smoke and burnt flesh fills the still air.

A few blocks away, the Leopard is glued to X's monitors, barely making out the movement in the fog. He has to tilt his head to see through the smallish window in his gas mask. Through a gap in the mist, he sees women and children lying in pools of blood and the dark shapes of the troops moving deliberately towards the building's entrance. He grins and feels strangely aroused. The game is on.

Three security guards emerge from the glass doors of the General Assembly, carrying automatic weapons. They get off a few rounds before being pummeled with a deadly barrage. They dance like rag dolls, their guns still firing in all directions as they tumble to the pavement.

The armed leader wheels his arm in a large circle, urging his charges forward. One of the armed men takes a knee and shoulders an Airtronic rocket launcher. The others make way, moving right and left. The rocket soars between them, leaving a trail of smoke. It strikes the glass entrance to the General Assembly, exploding the door. Shards of glass and metal fly in all directions. The uniformed men and women duck and cover their eyes as the glass shower washes over them. There's a moment of silence. Nobody moves. Then the intruders all rise and snap on the LED lights affixed to their helmets. All at once, they rush the blown-open entrance.

The power is still out. In the darkened atrium lobby, the Leopard can make out the headlamps sweeping about and sporadic muzzle flashes dropping bodies.

⊶━━━━━○

Michelle, Renata, and Jonathan drive up over the curb onto the Plaza. Michelle slams the brakes inches in front of a child's tattered body, lying with his head on the belly of a lifeless woman, her dangling arm encircling the boy's head.

"Oh my God," Renata says.

Michelle dials Rich and puts him on speaker. He answers before the first ring. "Mayday," she blurts. "Bloodbath at the U.N. Dead all over the Plaza. Front entrance blown wide-open. Hearing automatic weapon fire."

"Stay where you are. Helos will be there in two," Rich says.

There is an explosion from inside the General Assembly and another in the tower. The ground vibrates beneath their feet. Renata leans over the phone. "It may be too late. Where's the president?"

"Not sure. There were over one hundred and eighty international leaders inside plus maybe fifteen hundred staff including translators and attaches. The General assembly was in session. Don't know what they did when the lights went out," Rich says.

Michelle and Renata are in the front seat of the Audi. Jonathan is in back when the car's back door opens. Michelle drops the phone and the three of them draw their Glocks.

The intruder raises her palms and slides in next to Jonathan. "Chill out. You guys are awfully jumpy," Ann Nickolay says.

"What are you doing here?" Michelle asks.

"I'm on the NYPD Counterterrorism Taskforce. You were supposed to keep me in the loop, remember? No matter, I've been following you. I had a tip this was going down. You know this is the Leopard's bodyjacked army out there, right?" Ann says.

"What the fuck, you are sneaky," Renata says.

"No, but I have good sources. Listen, what's more important is that I have a location for the Leopard. There isn't much you can do here. Let's go get him."

"Who put you in charge?" Jonathan says. "Can't you see what's going on here? We can't just leave."

"If we charge in there now, it would be a suicide mission," Michelle says. "I fought too hard to get to this country and survive the last attack. I want to help, but only if I can make a difference and not die trying. Besides, I have more than national security reasons for wanting to get that son-of-a-bitch, LaSalam."

Rich's voice comes through the phone Michelle had hastily dropped on the seat. She picks up the phone and raises the volume. "Rich, we have an unexpected visitor. Ann Nickolay showed up and says she knows where the Leopard is." Another explosion from inside the building. "What should we do?"

Rich's answer is drowned out by the thundering rotor-blades of three Blackhawk helicopters approaching overhead. The helicopters land. Delta Force operators stream out, split up, and run into the General Assembly and Secretariat Buildings.

The rotor blades die down to a soft whirr.

Michelle says, "Rich, I didn't hear what you said, but Delta just got here and rushed the buildings. Here's what we'll do. Renata and Jonathan, get out and stay in the plaza. Don't enter the buildings, but hang back as backup and liaisons to us. You'll be our eyes and ears.

Ann, you stay with me. We're going to hunt the Leopard. Copy that, Rich?"

"Copy," Rich says.

Jonathan and Renata shoot fiery looks at each other, nod, and get out of the car. Ann follows and jumps in the front seat. "Three blocks up, then two blocks over," she says.

CHAPTER 80
WHAT NOW?

Renata checks her watch. It's only a little past eleven, and it already feels like they're in the middle of World War III. She rings Gary. "Any progress on getting the lights back on, at least at the U.N.? We've got dead bodies all over the place." A stench like burning tires wafts across the Plaza.

Gary is breathing heavily. "Close. I figured out how they disabled the backup generators. I'm reversing what they did. Hold on."

Jonathan bounces on his toes. "We can't just stand here. We've got to do something."

Renata holds up a finger. "Gary, what is it?" She looks up and floor-by-floor in the Secretariat Building, the U.N lights up. Except for the bombed out lobby, the rest of the building looks normal, offices and meeting rooms clearly displayed in the windows. "Well done. I hope it's not too late," she says and clicks off.

"Let's go," Jonathan says and jogs towards the General Assembly.

Renata takes a deep breath and follows behind.

The Leopard observes the ruins of the U.N. Plaza and sees the explosions and gunfire inside. How many dead? The president? He can't tell. He can't reach McNerney for a report. Either coms are down or he's intentionally radio silent. With Delta in there, there probably won't be much left of them anyway. Just as well. Ties up loose ends. *There isn't much more I can do here*, he thinks, and stands. He sees the little man lying face down on his desk with a bullet hole in his temple. The cubicles are empty except for the bodies of the young men and women strewn about on the floor, their mouths wide-open, eyes gaping. The Leopard removes his gas mask and tosses it on top of a twenty-something dark-haired Asian woman. "Here," he says, "you could have used this." He reaches down and strokes her soft hair. Then he reaches under her skirt, still warm and wet. *I could have done her*, he thinks. Too bad.

As he stands he sees two women, one he recognizes like a bad dream, standing in the doorway, "You again," he says to Michelle. "Have you come back for more? We didn't get to finish what we started last year in Cambridge."

"Oh, we're finished. You're finished," Michelle says.

"Is that so?" the Leopard says. "And who's that lovely young lady with you? Oh, I know. It's the dyke from the NYPD. They must be desperate if they're bringing in the B Team."

He raises his Beretta and fires. Michelle ducks. Ann rolls behind a desk. They both draw their weapons. The Leopard presses his back behind a partition and pivots out to fire two rounds. They miss. Michelle fires back. Ann moves left to get a better angle.

"Fuck, my gun jammed," Ann says. She lifts her vest, unfolding a Strider SMF knife. "Under twenty away, a knife beats a gun."

"What are you doing, don't!" Michelle barks.

But Ann erupts like a volcano with supernatural force. She charges across the room towards LaSalam. He fires three rounds at her, missing her once and hitting her with the second bullet in the leg and the third in the shoulder, but she keeps charging. The Leopard hesitates in wonder at the whirlwind coming his way. He points his gun again, but this time he lurches forward as a red plume erupts from his chest. He stutter-steps and falls to the floor. Michelle looks toward the unexpected shooter. She recognizes her.

Standing near the exit door is Adele Lamont, aka Ashaki LaSalam. "He had it coming," Ashaki says. "Take care of your friend and remember, I am a*ll rivers at once, *" she says and disappears out the exit.

Michelle stares in disbelief. Ann crawls towards the Leopard, blood soaking her white blouse. Michelle runs to Ann. "Are you OK?"

Ann loses steam and crumbles next to LaSalam. "I don't know. I feel numb. Is he dead?" she whispers.

Michelle kneels and puts pressure on Ann's chest wound with one hand and thumb-types 911 with the other hand. She looks over at LaSalam, blood dripping from his lips.

LaSalam chokes and mutters, "It's not over. You know I'll be back."

"Not if we can help it," Michelle says.

Now the Leopard laughs and coughs, but then comes the faltering voice of the real Agent Don DeMarco. "What's happening? Help me."

The demonic laugh returns and the Leopard stretches under a desk for his Beretta. Michelle raises her weapon, but then LaSalam reverses direction, putting the tip of the barrel under his chin, and fires. His head erupts like a burst balloon, gray matter flying, hitting Michelle in the face and blanketing Ann.

Michelle freezes and then asks, "Fuck, what now?"

CHAPTER 81
WHAT A DAY

By 11:30, ambulances and police cars, lights flashing, clog First Avenue from 40th to 45th Street. Renata and Jonathan watch as the line of gurneys pass by. Their faces are covered in soot from the fire and smoke inside the General Assembly Building. Acrid smoke is still rising while FDNY fireboats in the East River lob streams of water onto the U.N. buildings. Several of the Delta Force Soldiers limp across the plaza to their choppers, supporting their wounded brothers and sisters.

Renata's phone vibrates. It's Michelle on secure Skype. "What's happening there?"

"Take a look for yourself." Renata pans the cell phone camera across the U.N. Plaza. "Massive shitstorm cleanup. And you?"

"The Leopard's dead. You've got all the ambulances so I'm driving Ann to New York Presbyterian. It's close."

"What happened to Nickolay? Is she OK?"

"She's lost a lot of blood, but I believe she'll make it."

"I hope you beat the crowd that's coming to their ER any minute."

"Are you guys OK? What happened to the president?"

"We're fine. We saw some bodies in the General Assembly. The president was rushed off the podium when the lights went out. Not sure what happened after that."

The loud thumping of the Blackhawk rotors drowns out the conversation. The three helicopters rise in formation, start north, and make a slow right bank over the East River heading south. The roar briefly subsides, but starts up again. Marine One hovers overhead, then gently touches down in front of the General Assembly. Renata and Jonathan stare as a line of Secret Service agents hustle out, followed by a jogging woman with blonde hair in a red overcoat, her hair blowing in the stiff wind.

Renata shouts over the roar, "Looks like the president is OK."

"Listen," Michelle shouts back. "Go to the office where Ann and I were. Get forensics there. Process the Leopard. Get Gary there too to see what he or his team can get off the computers."

Marine One lifts off, following the same one-eighty degree arc over the river. "One other thing," Michelle says. "There's a bunch of dead people there. But I left two of the Leopard's guards tied up in the conference room. They're called Red and Green. It looks like they both shot and gassed all the others in the office. Sick. Haul them down to Beaver Street. I'll meet you there once I get Ann taken care of."

"Roger that."

Jonathan drives, trying to get around the traffic snarl on the East Side. Red and Green are zip-tied in the backseat. Renata clips her phone onto the dashboard mount. Just as she lets go, Frank's face appears.

"I see you have Monsieurs Green and Red as your guests," Frank says.

"I wouldn't exactly call them guests," Renata says.

"Either way, their presence is timely. But first, are you both all right?"

"We're fine, but the Leopard shot Ann."

"Yes, I know, I've been following that. Did Michelle tell you who shot and killed LaSalam?"

"No, I assumed she did."

"Reminds me of a song, *I Shot the Sheriff*, but no she didn't. I'll let her fill you in on that one. Let's get back to Red and Green."

"Now you've really got my curiosity piqued, but I'll let it go for now. What about Red and Green?" Renata asks.

"I've completed testing the bodyjack-reversal program. That program really needs a better name. Can you think of one?"

"Frank, get to the point."

"I'd like to try the new program on Red and Green. They're among the first of the Leopard's bodyjack victims. How about calling it *dejackification*?"

"Really?" Jonathan says. He turns and looks at Red and Green. "We weren't even thinking about that with all this other crap happening."

"That's all I've been thinking about and working on," Frank says. "If I hadn't created the body transference technology and the Leopard hadn't stolen it, there'd be a lot more good people who didn't deserve to die, alive today. Anyhow, where are you taking them?"

"Back to Beaver Street Headquarters," Renata says. "We're on 34th Street heading to the West Side to get around the traffic. Then we'll head downtown. Should be there in thirty minutes or less."

"Good. I'll have one of my associates, Derek Hollis, meet you there with the equipment. Please make sure they let him in and he gets to you."

"I must get clearance for this," Renata says.

"I spoke to Rich. It's cleared. Just set it up... please."

"Since you asked so nicely, I will. How's Sam?"

"He's recovering rapidly. They may have nixed the NNN, but they've got to stop some crazies with a killer virus," Frank says.

"What a day," Renata says.

"Vos a tog, indeed," Frank says.

CHAPTER 82
A GOOD LIFE

At 1:00, Rich with Sly riding shotgun, screeches to a halt in front of Baptist Memorial Hospital. I'm waiting at the front door in a wheelchair. I don't need the wheelchair, but you know hospitals. I stand and skip to their car, sliding into the backseat.

"You look like shit. How are you feeling?" Rich asks.

"I love you too. If you've got a clean shirt, I'd look better without this bloody one on," I say.

"Better to look good than feel good, huh?" Sly says.

"I'm fine. I saw what happened in New York on CNN," I say.

"Yeah, Michelle's handling it. What you probably didn't see on the news is that the Leopard is dead, for now anyway," Rich says and steps on the gas.

"Frank clued me in on that too. Where're we going?" I ask.

"Highway Patrol picked up a lead on Max at a gas station outside Covington. They got ID from plates on a Toyota. He probably had the vehicle stashed like a GO-bag for emergency escapes like this," Sly says. "I dispatched a chopper to follow him. We should be able to intercept him on Highway 54."

"Sounds like a plan," I say, looking down. It's happening again. My hands are turning blurry. They fade in and out of focus. *Not now, please.* A cold-sweat washes over me. My own body odor hits me like smelling salts. "Can one of you lend me a cell phone? I need to call Frank."

Sly hands a phone over her shoulder to me in the backseat without looking back, fortunately. Frank's image pops on the screen. I wave my hand in front of the phone's camera and whisper, "Frank, look. It's happening again."

"Sorry, Sam, I can't talk now. I'm setting up our first dejackification," he says.

"What? I thought you could do a thousand things at once. I'm in the car with Rich and Sly. I need to be right. I mean whole. You know what I mean."

"When it's important, I'm totally focused. I don't have the bandwidth for you now. You're smart. Figure it out." Frank rings off.

I glance down and see my legs begin to fade again. "Shit," I say out loud, not meaning to.

Rich glances up at the rearview mirror. "Sam, what the fuck is happening to you?"

Sly turns around and her jaw drops. "He's – he's fading in and out."

The sweat has now soaked through my clothes. "I can explain, sort of."

Rich slams the brakes and veers off onto the shoulder. "I've seen some weird shit in my day, but this takes the cake. Spill. What is it?"

I explain what I experienced back at the diner and on the train and what Frank said was happening.

"And you can control this?" Sly asks.

"Frank says that if I focus on being present, the fading will stop. It takes a constant force of will to pull it off. Yet, if I get anxious or distracted, this happens." I hold up my disappearing arms with the hands almost invisible.

"Christ," Rich says. "That probably explains your disappearing gunshot wound too."

I put my hands down. "Yeah, Frank says I'm here and not here at the same time like quantum particles."

"OK, so now we know. Good. We've got to focus too and catch this son-of-a-bitch NNN weirdo. So do your thing. Be present and we'll talk more about this later," Rich says.

"So that's it? That's all you have to say?" I ask.

"That's it. We're prioritizing," Rich says, peeling out from the shoulder.

We ride in silence for about twenty minutes while I focus all my attention on being present. I watch as my hands and legs slowly reappear. They seem normal again.

Sly's phone beeps and she starts giving Rich turn-by-turn directions relayed from the chopper overhead.

A few minutes later, she says, "There. Up ahead. That's him." Rich floors it and the 400HP V8 easily overtakes the Jeep, forcing it off onto the shoulder next to a steep cliff.

Rich and Sly jump out, guns drawn. Sly takes a few tentative steps forward. "Put your hands out the window where we can see them."

"Should we wait for Michelle?" Jonathan asks back at the Beaver Street office.

"I don't think we can afford to wait," Renata says.

Red and Green are cuffed to steel chairs in the tight conference room.

Derek Hollis exits the elevator led by a tall security guard. Hollis pulls a large, black roller bag behind him and approaches. The guard puts a halting hand on Hollis's chest and turns to Renata. "Agent Fermi. Were you expecting a Mr. Derek Hollis?"

Renata smiles. "Yes, let him through and thank you. You can go now."

Hollis tries to catch his breath. "Sorry it took so long. Your guards downstairs made me take my suitcase apart and attempt to explain all the equipment. Then I had to put everything back together. Anyway, here I am. Where're the subjects?"

"Follow me," Jonathan says and they squeeze into the conference room with Red and Green.

"Hi boys," Renata says. "Since you weren't very talkative on the ride down here, I'm going to assume you are either mute or uncooperative. That's OK. This gentleman is here to help return you to your original selves."

Red furrows his brow. Green's eyes narrow.

Renata holds up a syringe. "You can either remain calm and let Poindexter here attach some probes to your head or I can inject you with some of this." She depresses the syringe, letting a few drops of amber liquid squirt from the needle.

"My name isn't Poindexter," Hollis says.

Renata ignores him and looks at Red and Green. "What will it be?"

They both wriggle and strain against the cuffs. Renata sighs. "I guess I have my answer." She looks at Jonathan and Hollis. Hold them down."

They restrain Red and Green while Renata injects them both. In seconds, their heads loll to the side. "OK Poindexter. Do your thing."

"I'm calling Dr. Einstein first. The whole procedure should take maybe fifteen or twenty minutes after I attach the probes. There's no need for you to hang out. I could use a coffee, black-no-sugar."

Jonathan grunts. "I'll get it. Renata, want anything?"

"No, I'm staying. I want to watch what happens."

CHAPTER 83
CHECK'S IN THE MAIL

"OK, keep your hands where I can see them and get out of the car," Sly demands.

Max opens the Toyota's door and slides down.

"Now turn around and put your hands on the vehicle," Sly says.

"I know how this goes, hun. This ain't my first rodeo." Max grins and turns facing her.

"I said, put your hands on the car."

"I can feel my heart giving out. Can I reach for a pill in my pocket?"

Sly looks at Rich. He nods. "Go ahead, but do it slowly."

Max reaches into his shirt pocket, extracts a small red pill.

Sly recognizes the oblong pill. "Wait, stop!" She grabs Max's wrist.

Max dips his head forward, sucking the pill into his mouth. He smiles. "Shouldn't take long now. I've had a good life, not to mention the piece of ass I got last night." Max's knees buckle.

Rich rushes to him, catching him before he hits the pavement and says, "What the fuck did you do?"

Max whispers, "I took a sleeping pill–only I ain't never goin' wake up."

"Shit!" Rich says. "Where's the woman with you?"

"She's in my dreams." Max's voice trails off. His eyes close.

Max is still breathing. Rich lowers him to the pavement and asks, "The packages, where did you send them? What were you planning?"

Max's voice is so soft Rich puts his ear to Max's lips. Max laughs, making a sickly gurgle. Bile foams on his lips, his bowels let loose. He coughs and sputters his final words. "Check's in the mail, hombre."

Rich and Sly stand silently over Max's motionless corpse. The scent of mountain pines fills the cool air wafting up from the valley below.

"Now what?" Sly asks.

Rich's phone vibrates. "I've got to take this. You call Highway Patrol. They can deal with this scene. We've gotta get out of here."

Sly steps away to make the call.

Rich answers his phone, "Margaret, what is it?"

Rich's sister answers in a broken voice, "I'm sorry. It's Mom. She died this morning. Come home."

Rich spins and looks up at the sky as if asking God a question, but there is no answer. He buries his head in his forearm, leaning on the roof of the Charger.

"Rich, are you there?" she asks.

Rich sucks in a deep breath. "I'm here, but I can't leave yet. A maniac's on the loose who's about to kill thousands of people. Should be another day or two and then I'll come straight home."

"There's always a maniac on the loose. It's your mother, for God's sake."

"I know, but she should be the only other death I have to deal with today."

"What do you mean by *other* death?"

"It's a long story. I'll tell you when I see you. Meantime, can you start making the arrangements? I'll do the rest when I get home... please."

Margaret hesitates and sighs. "I will, but you'll owe me big time."

"You know I always repay my debts," Rich says.

"I'm counting on it," she says.

"What's happening there?" Michelle asks. She hears coughing and puffing on the phone. "Rich. Are you OK?"

"Nothing." He seems to gasp for air. "I've had some bad news. Where are you now?"

"I'm at Columbia Presbyterian. Ann seems stable now. I'm heading back to the office... What bad news?"

Silence, then, "It's my mother. She's gone."

"I'm so sorry. Do you want to talk about it?"

"No. Listen, we just cornered Max and he killed himself. Somewhere out there is the woman he was working with, Adele or Ashaki, whatever her name is, and she's about to release a deadly bio-weapon. His last words were, 'Check's in the mail,' which probably means it's on its way to their intended targets."

"I'm not sure how this is possible or why she did it, but Ashaki is the one who shot LaSalam and probably saved our lives."

"How the worm turns? You need to find her. She can tell us where the targets are."

"She's smart and she's savvy. Even if we can catch her, I doubt she'll tell us anything."

"Make her tell us. Look, I don't think we have much time — maybe a day, two at the most. Do what you have to do. I'll get with Sam and Sly and figure out what we can do from here," Rich says.

"OK. Again, I'm sorry about your mother."

"Thanks, but I'll grieve later. We've got work to do now and not much time to do it."

CHAPTER 84
FALSE VICTORY

I put an arm on Rich's shoulder, trying to comfort him. "I'm so sorry, Rich. I don't know what to say."

"Nobody ever knows what to say, do they?" Rich says.

"No, they don't. Everybody struggles with death. It's probably why Frank and I started Digital3000 and invented uploading personalities to the Cloud. You know, so at least you can live digitally forever," I say.

Rich smirks. "How'd that work out?"

"So far, it's been one of those 'Be careful what you wish for' things."

"OK, listen, the Leopard's dead. We've got to focus on stopping Ashaki's plan."

Without any prompting, a voice speaks from the phone in my shirt pocket. Removing the phone, I can see his face. It's Frank. "Rich, I heard that. LaSalam may be dead for now, but he's probably trying to come back. I'm tracking new activity on the reinstatiation program he stole from me. It looks like they're getting ready to do some more bodyjacking. I'd bet anything the Leopard would be the first to steal a new body."

Sly, who is looking over my shoulder at Frank's professorial image, asks, "Can you stop him? We've got enough threats to deal with at the moment."

"Couldn't have said it better," Rich says.

Silence. "Frank, did you hear the question?" I say.

"I heard it. While I'm talking to you, I'm working the problem in a thousand other places. I do love multitasking," Frank says.

Rich is tapping his foot. "Frank, please answer the question."

"There!" Frank blurts. "I've implanted something like the Stuxnet virus in the program. It will at least stop them from stealing bodies temporarily until they figure out they've been hacked, then can counteract the virus. So you better deal with your other issues quickly before LaSalam rears his ugly head again."

"Thanks, Frank. We're short on time for other reasons," I say. "Please let us know if anything changes, if we need to watch our backs, or if you figure out a permanent fix to the bodyjacking problem, maybe, hopefully."

"Your thoughts are in my prayers." Frank's image disappears from my phone.

Hollis is just finishing his procedure on Red and Green. Both are out cold, still zip-tied to their chairs. He removes the eighteen probes from each of their skulls just as Jonathan returns to the room. The wall clock swings past 2:30.

Jonathan hands a hot paper cup to Hollis. He takes a big sniff before sipping the coffee. "I love the aroma of coffee, even crappy coffee like this."

"That's good to know, but what's with Grin and Bearit here? They look half-dead," Renata says.

"If all goes well, they'll wake up in a few minutes as new men or, I should say, as their original selves," Hollis answers.

"Whatever state they're in, I hope they have something helpful to share. Otherwise, I don't really give a shit about them," Renata says.

"One of the many things I love about you, you don't sugarcoat it," Jonathan says.

A few minutes pass. Red begins to move his head and then Green stirs. Their four eyes pop open at the same time, going wide, like they've just seen ghosts. In a way, they have. "Welcome back to the real world," Renata says. "May I have your names please."

Jonathan picks up on their seemingly stunned disorientation. "You are in New York City with law enforcement. You're not in trouble. You've been through some kind of trauma. We'd just like to know what you remember, starting with your names." The "Not in trouble" part might be a bit of a stretch.

Red turns, looking at Green, not showing any recognition. "My name is Mathew Erwin. The last thing I remember was kissing my wife goodbye before work."

"And where do you work?" Renata asks.

"I'm an MP at the Picatinny Arsenal in New Jersey," Erwin says.

"And how about you?" Jonathan asks, looking at Green.

"Can I get some water, please?" Green says.

Jonathan digs into a mini-fridge and hands Green a Poland Springs bottle. Green gulps down half then speaks. "My name is Ted Berggren. I work at a lab in Waltham, Massachusetts."

Renata and Jonathan look at each other. "What kind of lab?" Renata asks.

"They do bioengineering, gene editing, stuff like that, but it's classified. I can't say anymore," Berggren says.

"You can and you will," Renata says. "We're with Homeland Security. You're in our headquarters, and this is a matter of national security. So you will tell us everything you know. But let's start with an easy unclassified question, what's your boss's name and what's the address of the lab?"

"That's two questions," Jonathan says. Renata gives him a withering stare. "Sorry," he says.

Berggren takes a beat. "The director of the lab is Marsha Hume. It's on School Street in Waltham."

CHAPTER 85
NEXT DAY DELIVERY

With the Waltham lead, Renata heads off Michelle, diverting her to Teterboro Airport where a DHS jet is fueled and ready for the short flight to Massachusetts. Meanwhile, Rich, Sly, and I are trying to figure out how to track the package or packages Ashaki and Max sent out. Rich contacts Gary to track all packages sent today from the local post offices.

"I should try following UPS and FedEx too. That could be tricky since they pick up all over the place," Gary says.

"Hi, Gary. This is Sam. You're on speaker. Given the precious nature of what's in those packages, I'd assume they would walk them into UPS Stores and FedEx Centers to distribute them. They wouldn't want the extra risk of local pickups. So you could narrow the search to post offices, UPS Stores, and FedEx drop offs."

"Makes sense," Gary says. "How big a radius are we talking?"

"Gary, this is FBI agent Tiffany Sly. Do a 20-mile radius out from Fort Pillow, Tennessee. I'd think they'd want to move fast and wouldn't make a long drive."

"OK, suppose I round up all this data in the next couple of hours. What do you want me to do with it?" Gary asks.

"Sort it all by destinations and send it to me, Sly, and Sam. We'll take it from there. Oh, and Gary, a couple of hours won't do. Make it thirty minutes," Rich says.

Something else occurs to me. "Gary, one other thing. Give us a separate file with a narrower search. Take the full dataset and filter it by those marked for next day delivery. Our culprits, knowing that we are close on their heels, would be in a hurry. The cost of expedited delivery wouldn't matter to them."

"Got it. That should narrow it way down," Gary says. "Anything else?"

I put my hands up. *I've got nothing.*

"That gives us a place to start," Rich says. "What are you waiting for?"

"Dinner?" Gary says.

"I'll owe you one," Rich says and clicks off.

* * *

"I'm in Waltham at the lab. It's almost 6:00. I see a few lights on," Michelle says. "Maybe somebody's working late or maybe they're just gone for the day. Any suggestions?"

Rich puts his phone on speaker again. "Call for some local backup. I'd suggest FBI Boston and a heads up to the local PD."

"I'll alert them, but I'd rather go in alone, low-key first."

"OK," Rich says. "We're working on how to stop distribution. I think your goal has to be to figure out what kind of bug we're dealing with, bio, nuclear, viral, what?"

"Will do," Michelle says.

* * *

Michelle approaches the renovated brick building, refashioned from an 1800s textile mill. No surprise, the doors are locked. She taps the intercom and a man's voice answers, "It's after hours here. What do you want?"

"I have an urgent message from Ted Berggren."

"Ted Berggren? He just up and disappeared a few weeks ago," the man says. "Perhaps, I should call the police."

"No, I saw him today. He gave me a message and said I'm to deliver it to a Doctor Hume in person. Is she there?"

"This is highly irregular. There are only a few people working late. I'll check."

A few minutes later, a woman's voice comes over the intercom. "This is Doctor Hume, who is this?"

"Doctor Hume, this is Michelle Hadar from Homeland Security." Michelle holds up her ID wallet to the camera embedded in the intercom. "It's important that I speak with you tonight."

"That's what my husband says too. We're closed for the day and I'm late leaving. Call me tomorrow," Hume says.

"Doctor Hume, either I can have FBI and local PD surround the building, get an expedited search warrant, and tear your lab apart or you can let me in alone to have a simple conversation. Your choice," Michelle says.

The door buzzes and Michelle enters.

CHAPTER 86
DEADLINE

"Madame President, I'm so glad you made it back safely," Osborne says, taking his seat on the sofa next to Brickman in the Oval. The dark night seems to press in through the windows.

President Longford picks a rose from a vase on her credenza, sniffing its sweet scent. "I don't think I've ever been so scared in my life. My ears are still ringing from the explosions. So you will need to speak up."

General Turgidman clears his throat. "Have you been checked?"

"Yes, the medical team was all over me. If they poked and prodded anymore, I'd probably need a pregnancy test. They'll monitor me for any percussive aftershock. General, your Delta Force did a marvelous job shutting down what could have been an international disaster. Let me know who I should call to thank personally."

Turgidman puffs his chest. "Thank you, Madame President. My aide will send your secretary a list."

"I wouldn't say we got off scot-free. One hundred and ninety-seven people died, including some foreign staff members," Brickman says.

"Don't be such a downer," Kennedy says. "It could have been worse."

Longford reddens. "I hate that expression, 'It could have been worse.' Every time we have an attack or a school-shooting and our brave first responders intervene and people die, some politician says, 'It could have been worse.' Which is another way of saying, it wasn't so bad—no need to do anything about preventing the next attack. If people die, it is *worse*. Do you think the husband, wife, or child who loses a loved one says, 'It could have been worse?' No. For them, it is *the* worst. Sorry for the rant, but that bullshit, from do-nothing leaders, just pisses me off. So now what? Where's Little? What's the update?"

"I have Rich Little dialing in, ma'am," DHS Secretary Brickman says. "If I may…" Brickman stands, bends over the Resolute Desk, and punches the speaker button on the phone. "Rich, we have the president and General Turgidman and Secretaries Kennedy and Osborne here on speaker. What's your status?"

"Madame President, gentlemen, as you should know by now, the Leopard is dead."

"Yes, but he keeps coming back like a bad penny," Longford says. "What's stopping him from bodyjacking another innocent victim and plotting more death and destruction?"

"Frank Einstein may have found a way to shut down bodyjacking all together so it will not happen again. We're awaiting word on that," Rich says.

"But doesn't this body reinstatiation process do some good, giving deserving people a second chance?" Osborne asks.

"Let's not get wrapped around the axle on that one, George," Longford says. "For national security, just shut the whole fucking thing down. I don't want to see that LaSalam or his family again. Then after this whole thing settles down, we can have another look at it."

"Speaking of family, we may be safe from the Leopard now, but his sister, Ashaki LaSalam, has set in motion what could be a deadlier plan. I am still in Tennessee with Sam Sunborn and Agent Sly. We are working with our cyber-team to trace packages containing mass-destruction bio-weapons. My assistant, Michelle Hadar, is in Massachusetts as we speak, trying to find out the nature of this weapon," Rich says.

President Longford stands and paces, staring out the window into the night. She turns back. "I don't know what to say other than we're counting on you. Is there anything else you need from us?"

"I think we have all the resources we need, but thank you," Rich says.

"What's our deadline?" Longford asks.

"Unfortunate, but accurate choice of words," Rich says. "Tomorrow is the dead-line."

CHAPTER 87
HEAD-FAKE

Michelle follows Marsha Hume into her office on the second floor. Before entering, Michelle scans the laboratory floor outside Hume's office, making a mental note of the twenty-seven lab benches, workstations. microscopes, and computers, barely visible in the low light of the evening hiatus.

Hume closes the door and they both sit, Michelle in a club chair across from Hume behind her desk. "What's this about?" Hume asks?

Michelle notices the framed picture on Hume's desk of two young girls on a jungle gym, grinning ear-to-ear. "Beautiful girls. Yours?" Michelle asks.

Hume's eyes widen. "Yes. Now, please tell me why you're here." She looks at her watch, 6:30. "I need to get home."

Michelle leans over the desk, invading Hume's personal space. "Tell me, Dr. Hume, what is it that you do here?"

Hume leans back. "Genetic research. We have grants from the local universities."

"And do you do any gene-editing, specifically to create bio or chemical weapons?"

There is a long pause. Hume lowers her gaze. "We have done some research for DARPA, but not much."

"How about for private individuals?" Michelle takes a beat. "Like Ashaki LaSalam?"

Hume swallows and Michelle recognizes the tell. "I don't know anyone by that name."

"Oh, really?" Michelle says. She taps a few times on her cell phone and turns the screen towards Hume. A surveillance video plays. "So, who is this entering your building a few days ago?"

"Uh, I'm not sure. She could have been making a delivery or meeting with one of my staff," Hume says.

"Nice try, but not really. There's only one thing that will stop me from slapping cuffs on you right now and calling in my forensic people to tear this place apart. Can you guess what that is?"

Silence.

Michelle smirks. "Nothing? Let me put it another way–is there someone else who can raise your girls while their mother is in prison?"

That does it. "What do you want?" Hume asks, her eyes twitching.

"Just tell me what you were making and how much for Ashaki LaSalam. While you're at it, describe the effect on humans of your creation and any possible antidote."

"But my girls... she threatened my girls if I didn't..." Hume drops her head, tears tumbling onto her desk like raindrops. "I'm a mother. I had to protect them."

"You have a choice if you ever want to see your girls again. I can guarantee the girls witness protection, a new name, a new identity, a new home for the girls, and if they survive, they can visit you at the Federal Pen. What's it going to be?"

<hr>

Rich, Michelle, Renata, Jonathan, and I are back at the Beaver Street DHS office.

"Who's taking the lunch order?" Rich, ever-hungry says, and we all look at Jonathan.

"OK, just write down what you want from Trader's Deli and I'll run across the street to get it." Jonathan pushes a pad and pen to me.

"I don't get it," Renata says. "It's been five days, we notified all the hospitals on what to look for, and no reported attacks or unusual illnesses, other than the Indiana incident that we now know came from this toxin. Unless something breaks, I have a flight booked tonight to Paris for Inspector V's funeral."

"Michelle, did Hume say anything about an incubation period for this bug?" Rich asks.

"She said it's a gnat that they genetically modified with what's called a gene-drive. They planted a deadly virus in the genes of gnats, which is bad enough, but they took it a step further. The gene drive in the gnat means their modification includes both the CRISPR editing machinery together with the toxic gene it's tied to. The result is kind of a super dominant gene carried by 90% of the offspring of the gnats born from one parent carrying the same gene drive."

"Holy shit," I say. "So that means what Hume developed is a bunch of Patient Zeros for now gnats and future generations of killer gnats, and the symptoms are?"

"The virus they carry attacks the nervous system. It spreads on contact with the skin. The effect is almost immediate and she expects a 90% fatality rate within twenty-four hours of contact with the victim. So no, no delay."

"Where'd it go?" I ask. "We failed to intercept anything at the post office or other carrier facilities."

Jonathan picks up the completed lunch order list, stands, and says, "Maybe, her plot failed or it was a dud or a head-fake. Be back in a few with lunch."

"Head-fake, huh? Maybe. Remember the ketchup and hot sauce this time," Rich says.

"Roger that," Jonathan says, heading out the door.

"And no word on Ashaki? Just poof, she's gone?" Renata says.

"Or she's playing chess and we're playing checkers," Michelle says.

"It's a mystery, but I have a feeling the plot twist is still ahead," I say.

Suddenly, the door swings open and Jonathan rushes in, panting.

"What, they ran out of bread?" Rich asks.

Jonathan raises a hand and says, "No, but we have our first reported case with symptoms that Hume described—sweats, high fever, hives all over. It's a child whose parents brought her to the ER at Mass General thirty minutes ago."

"Uh, oh," Rich says. "Renata, cancel your flight."

CHAPTER 88
PRIORITY MAIL

The packages arrive in unmarked cardboard boxes. Ashaki has hacked the addresses and information from several ancestry websites. The target recipients are young children, ages three to eight. The gifts are trucks for the boys and dolls for the girls. The packages include a note; the messages vary. Some say, "Just thinking of you…" others, "For my special niece…. Love Aunt –" Ashaki culled the names of aunts and uncles paired to their nieces and nephews in the ancestry databases. The personal notes, tinged with the faint scent of lilacs, ease any concern or paranoia on the part of parents who happily turn over the gifts to their children. Once the child opens the gift, the hardly visible gnats escape landing on the children first, then the parents and household pets, later mating with ordinary gnats, producing, with the help of the gene drive, a new generation of killer gnats.

Ashaki's clever instructions to the biker distributors were to hold packages for four days on the assumption that the heat from law enforcement would die down. She was right. Just as DHS, FBI, and other agencies ceased carefully scanning for Ashaki's packages, the bikers delivered them to local post offices, and UPS, and FedEx drop-offs around the country. A few days later, the "gifts" started arriving. After Jonathan's first report and before Rich and his team could eat lunch, the reports started pouring in from around the country, children with high fevers, vomiting, and skin rashes arriving at local hospitals. Sixty-two died so far.

Although Ashaki's plan was to release the killer gnats far and wide, Max made a little modification to the instructions he forwarded to his biker distributors. He filtered the addresses to target minorities and people of color in urban areas as well as any names ending with –berg, –stein, and –man.

Still in the DHS conference room, Rich calls his group back an hour later. "Renata, you're our resident M.D. How do we know these reported illnesses and deaths connect to what Ashaki and Hume developed and distributed?"

Renata shuffles a few papers and extracts two photographs. "Normally, it takes blood tests and some forensic finesse to connect the dots, all of which take time. Here, two ERs found these gnat larvae under the skin of their victims. Apparently, our friendly bugs, upon biting their prey, deposit their larvae to germinate under the epidermis of their human hosts. Look at this picture." She hands Rich a bug larvae photo and he passes it around. "This was taken from Patient One at Mass General. And this one..." She hands me the second almost identical photo, "...is from a sample at Hume's lab. They're the same."

"OK, so at least we know what we're dealing with," Rich says.

"I don't think you've fully grasped what we're dealing with," I say. "These little buggers with implanted gene drives will replicate untold generations of killers. We stop this soon, I mean like now. If it's a month from now, we'd have to kill every gnat on earth to stop a doomsday scenario."

"I think we get that," Michelle says. "But what's the endgame? I mean, this could become a worldwide epidemic. Unless it's a kamikaze mission, how would Ashaki protect herself and her followers?"

"Maybe she has an antidote or a vaccine? Did Hume tell you anything about that?" I ask Michelle.

"She stopped talking at that point. She said that once she and her daughters are safely tucked away in witness protection, she'd say more."

"I don't see how we give her that choice. Time is the enemy here and people are dying," Rich says.

"While you guys deal with that one, let's figure out how to stop more infected packages from landing. I've been in touch with Frank. We have a theory that there may be trackers in those packages, so Ashaki would know what hit and where. If we're correct. Let's examine the packages the victims have already received and see if we can find some kind of tracking devices. If we do, then maybe we can hack her system and track down the remaining packages."

"Good idea. I'll send some local agents to contact the victims' families so we can look closely at those packages," Rich says. "Meanwhile, Renata, head to Boston and Mass General. Interview Patient One and get a hold of their package. See what you can make of it."

"Keep in mind tracking devices are made as small as a particle of dust, if it's RFID or the size of a quarter, if it's GPS. So they need to really examine the packages closely," I say.

"The CDC is already quarantining everyone who has come into contact with the known packages or the victims," Jonathan says.

Rich slaps the table and rises. "We may be on the verge of mass panic with that going on. I better call Brickman and the president." Meeting over.

CHAPTER 89
ALL IS LOST

The sky's dusty dawn light brightens over the Washington Mall, sharing a sliver through the windows of the Oval Office. President Longford and the usual suspects are assembled.

"How big an outbreak are we talking about now?" Longford asks the men, tamping out her cigarette in the ashtray on the Resolute Desk.

Brickman looks at the others. *Tag, I guess I'm it*, he thinks. "Madame President, we have reported cases of what we're calling Bestiola-21 Virus in thirty-three cities, mostly in African-American and Latino neighborhoods. It seems our doer is targeting minorities."

"Except, I understand it affects some white, mostly Jewish, Americans as well," Osborne from CIA says.

"Great. There's a pattern here, or am I crazy?" Longford says.

"Yes, we know Max Werner is involved in this plot as well as the attack on the CBC. But he was working with Ashaki LaSalam, and we don't see her just targeting minorities. Sunborn figures Max altered Ashaki's intended targets to meet his own sick agenda," Brickman says.

"That may be a moot point if this Bestiola-21 is as contagious as it seems. Anybody and everybody could eventually get it. And the packages keep showing up," Longford says.

General Turgidman jumps up and starts pacing. "We've got to shut down the postal service right now."

"The stock market's already dropped fifty percent and we closed that down. Shut down eleven thousand post office branches and I can't imagine what happens to us," Longford says.

"Let's bomb the fucking post office and put an end to it," Turgidman says.

"General, are you nuts?" Osborne says.

"I'd evacuate them first, of course," Turgidman says.

Longford grabs the ashtray and throws it at him, barely missing his head. "General, sit down and shut up." She turns to the others. "What are we realistically doing to stop this?"

Brickman stands. "We're looking for a way to track and intercept the packages. The CDC is testing the infected patients, who haven't died, to see if they can isolate their immuno-resistance."

"English please," Longford says.

"From the surviving victims' blood and genetic analysis, they hope to develop a vaccine or an antidote or both like we did with Covid-19," Brickman says.

"Makes sense," Longford says. "But that takes time. What can we do now?"

"People in surgical masks are lining up at banks to withdraw their money. They're cleaning out the grocery stores and the gun shops. You must address the nation, calm people down, tell them to stay indoors, not open packages, etcetera," Kennedy says.

Turgidman laughs. "Ever the diplomat. Remember when a former president told us to go out and buy duct tape and plastic wrap to seal off our houses from anthrax? How'd that work?"

"The point is to give people something they can do to help protect their families and prevent further panic," Brickman says.

"So give them some pointless tasks?" Turgidman says.

"George is right," Longford says. "This is a national emergency and I'm in charge." She punches a button on her phone. "I need Kimberly Gray and the whole communications staff in my office right now."

All eyes are on the president. She lights up another Marlboro, blows the pungent blue smoke at the ceiling, and then glares back at the men in the room. "What are you waiting for? Get to work and stop this thing."

"What are you talking about?" Monica asks.

"I've booked you and Evan on a flight to Calgary. I had to pull some strings to get you both seats. Pack your bags with enough for a couple of weeks. The flight leaves in two hours. You've seen the news?" I say.

"Are you in the middle of this again?" Monica asks.

"You say that like it's my fault. I'm trying to stop it. Listen, you don't have much time. If you don't catch this flight, I expect travel restrictions will go into effect and you'll be stuck."

"I've had enough running and hiding. I have plenty of food. We'll stay home until this blows over like the many other scares we've had," Monica says.

"This is not like the others. I've seen what this virus can do and it's not pretty. This has the potential to kill off a large part of our population. I love you both too much – I can't lose you."

"Come home. Let's be together. That's how you can protect us."

"I can't, not yet. Once we stop the threat, I'll come home for good. This is the last time I get involved."

"I've heard that before. Listen, we'll be fine."

I sense a cold sweat coming on. Something like the smell of burning wires fills my nostrils. My stomach sinks. "I don't know. I feel helpless to protect you."

"Tell me about it. Call me when you're coming home. Goodbye, Sam." She rings off.

I hope the finality of those last words is not what I'm feeling in my gut right now.

<hr>

Two hours later, Michelle dials in from Boston. Rich calls Renata, Jonathan, and me back to the conference room. "We found a tracker in the first package," Michelle says.

First, how's our Patient One doing?" Rich asks and lifts his coffee mug.

"His name is Daniel Colmenares. He's seven years old and hanging on by a thread. They have him on a respirator and ECMO. This virus makes Coronavirus look like a runny nose."

"And the tracker?" I ask.

"I'm glad I brought Gary with me. He's on the line with Frank now. The little bugger is about the size of a quarter, including the battery and GPS chip. So far, we figure it sends out a signal every twenty seconds. Gary and Frank are trying to figure out where the receiver is," she says.

"But isn't that impossible? I mean, when NPR broadcasts radio into the air, they can't track who's listening on the other end," Renata says.

"That's true, but we're hoping there is something unique about the signal that will give us a clue. More like when one cell phone calls another. If you have the recipient's number, you can track it. Only one other problem," Michelle says.

"What's that?" Rich asks.

"The signal is encrypted. Gary and Frank need to decrypt it before they can try to trace it to Ashaki. Irony is the device is using Sam's company's Digital3000 terabit encryption program. You know, like the NSA, CIA, and others are using. So far, it's been uncrackable."

I gulp. *Somehow we're responsible for a part of this?* "That may not be all bad news. If our team, Frank and Bart, developed the encryption, they may have a leg up on cracking it," I say.

"You mean like a backdoor?" Rich asks.

"That would be unethical to sell the government leading edge security, but keep a backdoor for ourselves," I say but secretly hope the opposite is true.

"Keep us posted," Rich says and turns to Renata whose mind seems elsewhere. "Renata, wake up. Any progress with Hume on an antidote?"

Renata snaps out of her haze. "Not yet, but we're securing her daughters and trying to assure her enough to talk."

Jonathan blinks and says, "Why don't I just beat the shit out of her? If there ever was an exception to the no-torture rule, this would be it."

"I'm trying to keep her trust. If that doesn't work, you can go downstairs and do your thing," Renata says.

"I'll call Frank. Let's see if we can't find a better way," I say.

"OK," Rich says. "Michelle, you've probably done all you can do there. Gary and Frank can work on the tracker. Do you have any other leads?"

"I just might," Michelle says.

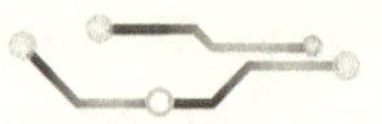

CHAPTER 90
OK, GENIUS

It's late morning and Michelle's in a middle seat, scrunched between two extra-large men on a United flight back to New York. She calls Jonathan from her computer using the plane's WIFI. "Can you pick me up at LaGuardia in thirty?"

"What's going on?" Jonathan asks.

"Remember, I mentioned having a lead to Rich. It's those mysterious text messages I'd been receiving. I think they were coming from Ashaki. I'd like to see if we can track her down and stop the virus that way."

The two big men both turn at once, glaring at Michelle. She smiles and switches to texting.

Can't talk now. Just pick me up at terminal B

A half-hour later, Jonathan is waiting at the curb in front of United Arrivals, Door 11. He has to badge-off airport security that shoos cars away that stand too long. Michelle hurries through the automatic doors, pulling a roller bag, phone wedged between her shoulder and ear. "Yes, yes," she says and drops off.

Jonathan shoots her a broad grin and opens the rear passenger-side door. "Mi deh ya, where to?" he says in a thick-Jamaican accent.

She punches him in the arm. "Like old times, huh? Next you'll offer me a joint." She slams the rear door and jumps in the front seat instead.

"Jamaica's finest, ma'an," he says, sliding in beside her and extending a hand-rolled stodgy.

"You're a piece of work. You can drop the accent and put away the ganja. We've got work to do."

Jonathan laughs. "Everything criss, just wanted to make you skin dem teeth, ma'an. What have we got?"

"It's about those texts I got presumably from Ashaki."

"I thought they came from an unknown address, untraceable."

"For mere mortals and your average hacker, they are untraceable. But that was Gary on the phone. He tracked it and has an address for us. It's in Brooklyn."

Jonathan punches the address into his GPS. "Everything's in Brooklyn." He stomps on the gas and reaches out the window to place a flasher on the roof. "I love doing that."

"Just kill the flasher and siren a few blocks before we get there."

"Yes, ma'an."

I pace the conference room. *Think*. I'm startled by a voice out of nowhere.

"You seem concerned," Frank says.

I look down to see Frank's face, or at least his digital professor persona face, staring back at me from my phone's screen. "Don't you ever knock?" I say. "No wonder, people are worried about privacy."

"We don't have time for privacy, do we?" Frank says.

"No, I guess not. Any luck with the package trackers?"

"Bart and I did a helluva job on that terabit encryption she's using. Gary, Bart, Jazzle – we're all working on it, but no luck so far. Any ideas?"

I can feel the answer just out of reach, like the name of a book or movie from the past that escapes memory no matter how hard you try to retrieve it. "If we knew the answer, what would it be?"

"Are you asking me that question or yourself?" Frank asks.

"It's just my way of coming at a problem from a different direction."

"OK," Frank says. "I'll play along. If we knew the answer, it would probably be something simple, like a code. Remember when you figured out the secret code to the elevator buttons that took you to a hidden floor in that building in lower Manhattan?"

"Yeah, it was a matter of pressing nine and eleven at the same time. That got us to the Leopard's hideout."

"It's probably something like that."

"Like a password that's easy to remember. And if Ashaki is anything like her brother, the code or password has some symbolic meaning," I say.

"You're on to something. We've been trying to jackhammer the encryption program because we're techies and we worship code."

"Have a hammer and everything looks like a nail. Is there a password field?"

"Yes, and our quantum computer, Sylvia, is running every combination of letters, numbers, and symbols, uppercase and lowercase to crack it. But even with all that computing power, it may take days to crack it and we don't have days."

"So let's use some human brain-power and treat it like a riddle. It could be faster than your brute-force approach."

"OK, genius. So what's the answer?" Frank asks.

"Let's start with... what's the riddle?" I say.

CHAPTER 91
THE HORSE AND THE BARN

"New York, WNYS – The Bestiola-21 Virus outbreak may be reaching pandemic proportions soon. The recently discovered deadly killer seems to spread faster with a higher fatality rate than both the Ebola outbreak in 2014 and the Coronavirus scourge of 2020. Reports just in of postal workers being infected and collapsing at their workstations. The CDC with the cooperation of local authorities and the Postmaster General have quarantined over thirty thousand post office branches, supplying cots and provisions to surviving postal workers to remain on site for twenty-one days until they can be cleared.

President Longford has declared a national emergency. She has ordered a three-day postal holiday to assess the situation, stop or slow the distribution of packages carrying the virus, and protect postal workers. With the weekend, that means all mail will be frozen for five days at a minimum. She has also closed the stock market, which dropped 50% today on pandemic scares. With the exception of first responders and essential personnel, citizens are required to stay indoors.

Apparently, the virus victims experience high fevers, severe rashes, and intense joint pain. Scientists are working frantically on trying to develop a vaccine and a cure. There has been a run on duct tape and plastic at Home Depot and Lowe's with homeowners attempting to seal their houses off from the invader. Banks are also closed until further notice.

Despite the risk of spreading the virus, protesters wearing surgical masks have jammed the streets and public malls to protest the government's seemingly slow response to the crisis. We expect President Longford to address the nation at 7:00PM tonight. It seems doubtful she can calm the fear and panic that has embraced the nation.

Most stores are closed to protect employees, but extensive looting has been reported in over a dozen cities. The targets are mostly grocery and hardware stores, although the looters have attacked several pharmacies too. Street vendors, taking advantage of shortages, are selling bottled water for upwards of ten dollars per bottle and surgical masks for a hundred dollars each. Premium masks with vents and gas masks go for up to a thousand dollars each.

This reporter and my colleagues are working remotely until it's safe to return to our offices. We wish all of our readers and all the citizens of our great nation Godspeed. The message from our New York Senior Senator, Rose Leatherman, 'Please take every precaution and be safe out there.'"

Michelle turns off the news report on the car radio. It's 1:00 PM. "This sounds terrible and it's getting worse. I'm not sure even if we find Ashaki and track all the packages, that we can stop this thing from spreading everywhere."

Jonathan turns off the flashers and siren. "I probably didn't need those. The streets are almost empty."

"It's good to see you have your priorities straight. Pull over. This is the address."

Jonathan parks the Charger a few doors down from an old Brooklyn brownstone on 11th Street in Park Slope. "How do you want to do this?" he asks.

"Protocol says we wait for backup or call in SWAT, but fuck that. We're *all* running out of time, literally."

"Ooh, watch your language. You've been hanging around Rich too long."

"Will you get serious? I'll call this in now, but we won't wait. The back up can either save our asses or haul away our bodies. You take the back door and I'll take the front. I'll make the call while you get in position. If she's there, I'll try to spook her into running out the back and you grab her. We need her alive."

"You know this is a bad plan, right?"

"Yeah, but we're going to do it anyway," Michelle says.

Jonathan grabs his vest from the trunk and creeps slowly down the alley alongside the brownstone. He surveys the postage stamp sized backyard and tucks himself into a corner under the rear stoop. Michelle finishes her call for backup and opens the trunk, looks at her vest, and leaves it. *That's all I need is to approach the house in a vest with three scary letters on it.* After tucking her Glock in the waistband behind her back, she throws her holster into the trunk and slams the lid. She takes a deep breath and climbs the stoop. Above the door is a CCTV camera with a red blinking light. *Press the buzzer.* Nothing. Ten seconds pass. She puts her ear to the door. She smells onions cooking. Pzing... Pzing. Two bullets pierce the door. One comes so close to Michelle's head, it brushes her hair aside. The other grazes her left upper arm. *Shit!* She grabs her arm and ducks to the side. Two more bullet holes appear in the door. She pulls out the Glock and waits. *Ugh, that hurts like hell, but we really need her alive.*

The sound of garbage cans crashing comes from the backyard, then shouting and more gunshots. Michelle descends the stoop, clutching the Glock in her right hand and pressing the same hand against the wound in her arm. She lopes down the alley to find Jonathan standing over a zip-cuffed woman.

Michelle instinctively points her weapon at the bound suspect, her sweaty index finger trembling against the trigger. "It's so tempting..." She turns to Jonathan. "Get Ms. LaSalam up. Let's take her inside and see what we can find."

Jonathan ties Ashaki to a chair while Michelle heads for a laptop on the kitchen table.

"You found me. I guess I fucked up, but it's too late now," Ashaki says. "I erased the hard drive."

Michelle opens the laptop and sees *Drive C: reformat complete.*

"It is... how do you Americans say it... The horse is out of the barn," Ashaki says. "No need to torture me. I'm done and I know it, but you all will suffer greatly for your crimes against my family and my people. Go ahead. Ask me questions. I'll answer them all except where to find the packages and how to stop the virus."

"Well, that's mighty helpful," Jonathan says and slaps Ashaki hard across the face. Her head snaps to the side and red welts emerge on her cheek where his ring had sliced her skin.

Ashaki smiles, a small trickle of blood dribbling from her lips. "Feel better?" she asks.

"So there is a way to stop the virus?" Michelle asks, glancing at her own blood-soaked sleeve.

"I didn't say that. But if you want to know why I did it, I'll tell you." She pauses. "And if you don't want to know, I'll tell you anyway. I want you to know. I want you all to know. Ahmed, whom you call the Leopard, is actually my half-brother. His desire was to avenge the loss of his innocent Barinian family to your demonic drone strikes. The only survivor was our mother. Her side of the family were Kurds. Kurds who fought valiantly beside you during the Gulf War, only to be abandoned by your president, left to the vengeful Saddam Hussein, who unleashed his chemical weapons on my mother's family, killing some and maiming many. Years later we forgave you and fought again, spilling blood and defeating ISIS, only to be abandoned again. This time your soldiers stood by and watched as the Turks moved in, destroying our homes. My mother had bad timing and made the unfortunate mistake of moving back from Barin to live among her people just before you turned-tail and ran. Just before we were going to build tunnels and defenses and you assured us you would defend us. "Don't build the tunnels," you said, and we trusted you. My mother was raped, beaten, and killed by the Turks. So you can chalk up what I'm doing to karma — what goes around, comes around." Ashaki spits in Jonathan's face, hitting him squarely in the eye.

He wipes the spit away. "Maybe she's right that she can't help. Which makes her and this a dead issue." He puts the barrel of his Glock to Ashaki's head.

"She's right about the Kurds and I'm truly sorry for your loss, but why punish us, all these innocent people, for the foolishness or cowardice of our leaders?"

"In your country you elect the leaders, right? Then who should be responsible for your leaders?"

I can't answer that, Michelle thinks. *I guess this is a dead issue.* "Jonathan, leave her be. Killing her is not our way. She'll spend the rest of her life in prison if the virus doesn't kill her and us first, but that gives me an idea. I have to make a call."

Jonathan puts the pistol back in his shoulder holster. "Make your call on the way to the hospital. An NYFD ambo just arrived and our NYPD friends at the front door can take our guest away somewhere nice and cozy."

Ashaki lowers her head and murmurs, "I guess all I have left is Quietness."

CHAPTER 92
HOW MANY TIMES?

"Frank, I just hung up with Rich. Michelle and Jonathan captured Ashaki, but they couldn't get anything useful out of her," I say.

"I'm not surprised. We've been running the password cracker on the Quantum Computer. It's already tried several billion combinations, but no luck. I guess the encryption we built is too good. We never thought it would be used against us," Frank says.

"I'm sure the atomic scientists on the Manhattan Project thought that too."

"That makes me feel much better. Any progress on your human solution, Sherlock?" Frank asks.

"Wait, don't most password logins limit you to a certain number of unsuccessful tries, like three times or ten times or something like that? Once you hit that threshold, the program locks itself down and will accept no further attempts?"

"Yes, most logon scripts do that, but although the password is eluding us, we were able to block that limitation. But as you say, that's tech dreck. Tell me what you've found out."

"OK. Rich shared the story Ashaki told Michelle about her mother and the Kurds."

"And?"

"If we're looking for something symbolic to crack the password, it would have some deep personal significance for Ashaki. What are the Kurds famous for?"

"Mainly their struggle for a homeland and their prowess as fighters?"

"That's true. Also, most Kurds are Sunni Muslims and among them are many who practice Sufism. Based on the town where Ashaki's mother came from, I believe she is a Sufi."

"OK, so what does that tell us?"

"Sufis are big into mysticism, and Ashaki said something puzzling to Michelle yesterday when she shot LaSalam. What she said was that little thing just beyond my grasp. She said, 'I am all rivers at once.'"

"So did you figure it out, that thing you couldn't grasp?"

"Again, maybe. The most famous Sufi poet, Jalaluddin Muhammad Balkhi better known as Rumi, wrote a poem in the 13th century called *All Rivers at Once*. Coincidence?"

"I don't believe in coincidence."

"Neither do I. It's a short poem. Here's how it goes...

What is the body? Endurance.

What is love? Gratitude.

What is hidden in our chests? Laughter.

What else? Compassion.

"OK, doesn't sound like a terrorist to me."

"Nobody's born a terrorist. In this case, trauma and loss created a twisted, or at least a tortured, soul."

"Or brainwashing caused it."

"Not in her case."

"Too bad she is so damn clever and driven, not a schmendrick."

"Maybe too clever. Whether or not she meant to, I think she gave us a clue."

"Which is?"

"Try Endurance, Gratitude, Laughter, and Compassion as passwords. Run those words alone and in combination. Run them in English and Arabic. Maybe, just maybe, one combination will work."

Renata holds the phone up so Marsha Hume can view her daughters clapping hands and singing *Patty Cake, Patty Cake, Baker's Man...* They are in a living room somewhere with 1950s decor, a plaid couch and shag carpet. An FBI-looking man in a dark suit, starched white shirt, sits in a chair behind the girls, a blank expression on his face, blowing lazy blue smoke rings into the air.

"Look, I told you the girls are safe now," Renata says.

Marsha Hume is past her first youth, the wrinkles around her eyes growing into gray canyons. "I want to visit them."

"You know you are a co-conspirator in murder and terrorism, right?" Renata leans forward. "Tell me what you know about an antidote or vaccine for Bestiola-21 and I'll arrange for you to visit your daughters. If you don't, you may never see them again, sorry to say."

"I'm afraid to talk. You don't know who you're dealing with. If I say anything, somehow she'll find my girls and she'll – I don't want to think about it. She's already threatened them."

"That woman is Ashaki LaSalam and we have her in custody. She can't hurt you or them now."

Hume hisses. "What kind of fool do you think I am? She doesn't work alone. She has a network of evil-doers just like her. One word from her and my girls are dead."

Renata's phone vibrates. She checks the screen. "I've got to take this." She stands and paces. All Hume can hear is Renata's side of the conversation. "Are you sure? That seems drastic. I guess we have no choice. I understand, Michelle. I'll tell her." Renata rings off and turns to face Hume. Renata's face is an icy gray. She taps a few more buttons on her phone and the image of Hume's daughters playing reappears. Renata turns the screen so Hume can see. The agent stubs out his cigarette and rises from the couch. He stoops down, whispering softly to one of the girls. Neither Renata nor Hume can make out what he's saying.

The agent removes a syringe from his pocket and injects a dark amber liquid into young Samantha's arm. He then hands her a lollipop.

Hume's face reddens. "What's he doing? What is that?"

Renata doesn't answer, and Hume struggles against the steel cuffs holding her arms to the table. Her wrists begin to bleed. "Tell me. What's he doing?"

The agent beckons the other girl, Karen, and repeats the procedure. The needle, the injection, the lollipop. When he's done, he nods to the camera. The girls resume playing. Hume is thrashing in her seat, tears running down her cheeks. "What? Please tell me."

Renata remains silent for a long minute. "He's injected your daughters with the Bestiola-21 Virus. Now, will you tell us about the antidote? Their lives depend upon it."

"You're insane. You can't do this. This is the U.S.A. It's illegal."

"And what you did wasn't illegal and cruel?" Renata checks her watch, 1:45. "Talk or they're dead or will be dead soon."

Hume's words are garbled through the tears. She shakes her head. "I don't understand how you could do this? They're little girls."

"If there was any other way..." Renata trails off. "I could justify it as national security and we wouldn't be wrong, but we're plain desperate and running out of time, not just for your daughters, but millions of others. So talk *now*."

First Samantha, then Karen, crumble like rag dolls toppling to the floor.

CHAPTER 93
EXTERMINATORS

Next to the bed, Frank's face lights up on my phone's screen. "Sam, Sam, wake up."

"What, huh? I must have fallen asleep." I checked into the nearest hotel I could find in the middle of the night in New York. It's already 2:00 PM. It seemed like days since I'd slept or showered. I didn't make it to the shower.

"We tried thousands of combinations of Rumi's poem to get the password to the package trackers," Frank says.

"And?"

"We took the keywords from the poem, *endurance* and *compassion*. Each word forms a seven-letter anagram, *unearned* and *casinos*. We set our quantum computer to solving it."

"Wait, I can see Ashaki's mind working the symbols here. To her, *compassion* for us is *unearned* and we are a *casino* culture where luck tries to replace hard work but usually fails miserably."

"But that's as far as we got. Our computer ran thousands of combinations, but we still can't solve it. Any ideas?"

I love puzzles, words, numbers. My mind involuntarily works any puzzle or problem it faces. Now I feel like fireworks are going off in my brain. "We know Ashaki is smart, brilliant in fact, particularly with computer code. So, I think you need to take this puzzle two steps further. Let's take unearned and casinos and make an anagram from the two of them. What's the longest real word you can make from those two?"

"I can go run that one through Sylvia."

"Don't bother. You come up with several eleven-letter words, like *unreadiness*, *renaissance* and *secondaries*. But there is a better one that fits Ashaki's and the Leopard's story."

"Which is?"

I can feel it now. I'm in the zone, *"Reascension*. Like rising from the ashes. What does that remind you of?"

"A Phoenix."

"Correct, a new life rising from the ashes of its predecessor, like Ashaki rising from her brother's ashes."

"Wow, that just seems so far out, even for a genius like Ashaki."

"It is far out, but so is she. Now for the last step. You've been trying different letter and number combinations to no avail, correct?"

"Literally, billions of them."

"How about feeding the program an image instead? The image of a Phoenix."

"OK, I suppose we can decode a phoenix image into a very long string of numbers, but which image. There must be hundreds, if not thousands of them."

I can't help smiling. "Have your genius computer Sylvia decode every phoenix image she can find. I bet one will work."

"We'll try it. What have we got to lose?"

"Time and human lives," I say.

"That wasn't a question," Frank says.

"It's the biggest question," I say.

I slowly drift off, back to sleep. A dream image overtakes me, Monica and I walking down the beach, holding hands, the smell of salt air, the cool waves splashing over our bare feet as they sink into the soft sand. Zing, Frank's image and voice awaken me again. "That was quick. So you got in?" I mumble.

"Yes, and while you were getting your beauty sleep. With the cracked password, we tracked all the packages. I forwarded the data to Rich. He's dispatching HAZMAT teams to all the known locations to secure and isolate the packages."

"That's very good news." I sit up and stare into the mirror above the dresser. The morning sun peeks through a crack in the curtains to give me just enough light to see my reflection. I check my watch. "I think I've only slept for twenty-one minutes. So I'm far from beautiful. I look like somebody hit me in the face with a two-by-four."

"I was only kidding about the beauty sleep. If it wasn't for your brilliant detective work, finding and analyzing the poem and anagrams, we'd still be beating our heads against the wall."

"Well thanks, I appreciate that, but there's still a problem. You said *known* trackers. What if they didn't put trackers in every package? Then there could be hundreds of untracked packages out there."

"That occurred to me too, and I asked Rich that question. Apparently, they are using an FBI profiler, Donald McGill, who has analyzed Ashaki. McGill believes Ashaki has fairly pronounced OCD and that her drive for exactness and tidiness wouldn't allow her to send out untracked packages. Her need to know and control points to a high probability that all the packages have trackers. That OCD can be both a strength and a weakness. In this case, it may be a failure that allows us to foil her plot."

"I hope he's right. Now we have the other problem. The gnats are out there. They are spreading the contagion. But just before I conked out, I spoke to Michelle. She was interrogating Hume." An image flashed into my head. I'm not sure where it came from, a medieval painting maybe. There is a hand pushcart with dead bodies piled on it. The cart is on a cobblestoned street in front of a dilapidated row of two-story mud-brick buildings. The undertaker is holding the handles of the cart and shouting something. Now I remember. It was a painting titled *Bring Out Your Dead*.

⊷———⊶

"I'll tell you. I'll tell you, but please give some to my daughters. There isn't much time," Hume urges through her tears.

Michelle relays the information to the DHS and FBI agents already crawling Hume's Waltham lab for clues. Michelle stays on the phone as two agents carefully remove ceiling tiles in Hume's office. There, secured only by a bungee cord, is a plastic gallon container of red liquid, the antidote.

"We have it," Michelle says and turns the phone toward Hume. "This is the antidote, correct?"

"Yes, yes that's it," Hume says.

"And how do we make more of it?"

"The formula is on a thumb drive."

"Where's the thumb drive?"

"It's in a waterproof bag inside the gallon container you found. Now hurry, please. My daughters."

Michelle barks some orders to the agent holding the gallon of antidote. She rings off and turns back to Hume. "We're not going to give Samantha and Karen the antidote."

Hume seems to find renewed strength and tries to jump from her chair, but the restraints hold her back, cutting deeper into her wrists. "What? But you said– You can't do this. How cruel can you be?"

Michelle waits for Hume to slump back into her chair, seemingly resigned to her tragic fate. Michelle lets the silence crowd the room and then, "How cruel can we be? You were willing to kill millions. Don't you think the victims have mothers and fathers? Daughters and sons? What about them? You only cared about yourself. Screw everybody else."

Hume lifts her graying face and speaks not to Michelle, but to the air or to some higher power, a plea, an explanation before the judge's sentence. "I had no choice."

"You always have a choice," Michelle says. "But don't worry, we're not giving Samantha and Karen the antidote because we didn't give them the virus to begin with."

Hume's eyes widen. "What, what are you talking about?"

"You see, we are not as cruel as Ashaki or you. We would never poison or infect innocent children. We just gave them a sedative. They'll wake up soon and be fine."

"So, you tricked me with a cold-blooded deception?"

"No, we helped you make the right choice. I was in a bind like yours once, my family or my country, with millions of lives at stake. I made a different decision. That's why I'm standing here and you're sitting there."

CHAPTER 94
THE OFF SWITCH

"We did it!" Frank says.

Back at DHS on Beaver Street, the sun has set and the aroma from the fresh pot of coffee I put on fills the conference room air. "What?" I ask. "You're on speaker with Rich, Renata, and Jonathan."

"We've used our backdoor into the bodyjacking program and disabled it," Frank says.

"What does that mean?" Renata asks.

"It means that the Leopard, and nobody else for that matter, can victimize more healthy people and steal their bodies," Frank says.

"So no more unwitting recruits for the Leopard's army, but what about the remaining victims out there? Can you stop them with your program?" Renata asks.

"Yes and no," Frank says. "We could, but it's an all-or-nothing proposition. We could shut them all down with the flip of a proverbial switch. They'd drop like flies doused in Raid. But then the many good people who got a second chance at a good life, resurrected in willing bodies, would die too. Do you see the dilemma?"

"Frank, this is Jonathan here." He looks at Rich while addressing Frank. "You have to figure that we probably killed or captured most of the Leopard's bodyjacked army in the U.N. assault. That seems to have been his big play. If there are any left, we could go after them like we would any other criminal."

"For me, it's not a dilemma," Frank says. "I won't kill them off as long as there is one good soul among them."

"Kind of like Sodom and Gomorrah," I say. Frank is like Abraham in *Genesis* who pleads the case to God of the good few among the many bad to save the city.

"But who is God in this case?" Jonathan asks.

"Well, it's Rich, of course," Renata says and we all laugh.

"No, I think in this case Frank is both God and Abraham and I can't argue his logic. We stopped Ashaki and the Leopard. Hopefully, we've thwarted the virus. So now it's back to some good old-fashioned police work to track down any stragglers from the Leopard's grand experiment. Renata, if you leave now, you still might be able to make it to Paris in time for Inspector V's funeral. The company jet is on hold for you at Teterboro."

"Thanks, Rich. I'm outta here." Renata clutches the handle of a roller bag parked against the wall and trots out the door.

"OK, where do we start?" I say.

Rich glances at his watch. "First, we have Nancy's funeral in the morning. I'm really going to miss her."

My eyes suddenly tear up, "I think we all will."

Rich places a gentle hand on my shoulder. "Second, you don't start anywhere. You want to save your marriage? After the funeral, hop the next plane to California. We've got it from here."

Like a splash of ice-cold water to the face, I realize he's right. Time to go home and make things right with Monica, if it's not too late.

"What's the status of the infected?" President Longford asks. She glances at the wall clock, 9:30 PM.

Besides Brickman, Turgidman, Kennedy, Osborne and staff, Tashia Jennings, head of the CDC has joined them in the Situation Room. "Fortunately, we were able to quickly decipher the formula of the antidote on Dr. Hume's thumb drive and the antidote's components are readily available ingredients. We sent the formula to our two hundred labs around the country and a half-dozen pharmaceutical companies that can produce it. They estimate they can produce up to 100,000 doses per day starting in a few days."

"How many souls have we lost so far?" she asks.

Roger Brickman clears his throat and says, "Two thousand, six hundred and twenty. We expect we may lose five hundred to a thousand more for whom the antidote will be too late."

Longford slams her fist on the table. "Dammit, pull out all stops, spend whatever you have to get that antidote out to everyone who needs it not in a few days, tomorrow. Understood?"

Everyone nods. "We are coordinating all domestic military vehicles and aircraft in an effort to speed up deliveries," General Turgidman says.

"We've also ramped up the postal service and all 200,000 of their vehicles, together with FedEx and UPS to get supplies where they need to go," Brickman says.

"Good. Any other threats I need to know about, or are we good for now?" Longford asks.

"We're good for the moment. Rich and his team are tracking any residual members of the Leopard's bodyjacked army. Ashaki's in custody and the Leopard is dead," Brickman says.

"For now," Longford says.

"Yes, for now," Brickman says.

CHAPTER 95
WHERE'VE YOU BEEN?

"It's good to be home," Michelle says as she sips her double-espresso outside the Hard Times Cafe in Old Town Alexandria. The air is unseasonably warm, the sky turquoise, and aroma of fresh-baked bread lingers.

"I love that silk dress. I think you're having a major fashion moment," Rich says.

Michelle grins. "Where'd you get that line from?"

"One of my favorite shows, *Access Hollywood.*"

She can't stop herself and sprays her mouth full of coffee in Rich's direction. Rich pushes back his chair, partly missing the oncoming liquid. "Hey!" he says, wiping, more like spreading, drops of espresso from his white shirt."

Michelle laughs through her words. "I'm, I'm so sorry. I couldn't help it. That is one of the funniest things I've heard in some time. You never stop surprising me, but I like you despite that."

"Like?"

She puts both her hands on his and stares into his eyes.

"It's too early yet, you know, with Anita's passing and all. The other night was a mistake," Rich says.

Michelle tilts her head and smiles. "I understand. Let me know when you're ready. Remember dial one for a kiss, two for a hug, and three for more options."

A not-unhappy silence falls between them.

"You know you might be too old for me," he says.

She throws her cranberry muffin at him, hitting right above his left eye.

Rich beams. "Just like back in the day. Your aim's still good, I see."

"Yeah, you old fart, and I'm ten years younger than you."

They sit quietly, the gentle breeze pushing Michelle's dark hair across her face. "Oh, I forgot to check. Ashaki said something about *Quietness*?"

"Another Rumi poem? I heard what Sam did to solve the puzzle with the Rumi poem. Google it, Rumi's *Quietness*."

Michelle taps in her search. Her face flushes.

"What is it?" Rich asks.

She turns the screen so Rich can read it:

Become the sky.

Take an axe to the prison wall

Escape.

Walk out like someone suddenly born into color.

Do it now.

The house looks the same from the outside, but it feels like a memory from the distant past. A little paint is peeling above the door. I need to fix that. Never mind its flaws, I love this house. It says *home* to my soul.

I have a key, but I decide to knock. Nothing. I take a deep breath and knock harder. Footsteps. The door slowly opens and there's the face, the smile that melts my heart. I'm home.

It's an awkward moment, just the two of us standing there. What's she thinking? Finally, she launches herself at me, burying her face into my chest, hugging me so hard my ribs hurt. I close my eyes, enfolding her in my arms. Petey, our dog, runs and slides across the wood floor, panting and smashing into my legs. I bend down and scratch him behind his ears. I realize he's a dog, but I can swear I hear him purring.

Finally, Monica says, "Where've you been?"

"I think you know, sorta." I hesitate. "What's for lunch? Is that chicken soup I smell? I'm starving."

She ignores my diversion. "Is it over?"

"For now."

She breaks away from our embrace. "What do you mean *for now*? Does that mean you're going back?"

I hesitate a second too long. "I'm not going back. I'm here and I'm staying. Going back to work with Bart and Loretta and coming home for dinner to you and Evan is all I need. If anything, this last escapade has taught me how to be *present*. And I am present, here and now with you."

She lifts an eyebrow. "And if Rich calls you?"

"I can't say I won't help him over the phone or from the office, but I'm not leaving. I promise."

"This is it, your last chance, our last chance," she says.

"I know and I love you. I'm sorry for all I put you through. My adventure days are over. You and Evan come first and always."

I pull Monica back into a tight embrace. I can sense the moisture from her tears against my skin. I hear Evan's footsteps coming down the stairs before seeing him. Then, a sinking feeling seems to wash over me as if my will is slipping away.

Monica backs away, her jaw dropping. I glance down at my arms as they flicker and then fade. The last thing I hear is Monica's gasp.

Evan runs to Monica, who is openly weeping. "Where's Dad?" he asks.

Frozen, Monica stammers, "He's... he's gone."

The End

AUTHOR'S PERSONAL NOTE

If you have gotten to this point in reading NOT SO DONE, I thank you for sticking with it. I hope you enjoyed reading it as much as I did writing it. The title has extra personal significance for me as I lived an unexpected writing roller coaster ride along the way.

I thought of subtitling this novel *Sam Sunborn's Last Novel*, but that would have given away the ending. And we don't really know what the ending is anyway, do we? I thought about this during my crazy, parallel real life adventure. Last November, I was diagnosed with cancer, which I wrote about on my blog in *A Not-So-Usual Thanksgiving*. After receiving that dreadful news, my prognosis was unclear. With the knowledge the end might be near, it compelled this clarifying question: what's most important in my life and what do I want to do with your remaining time on Earth? Besides spending time with my loved ones, family, and friends, a top priority was to finish writing the novel you just completed. Why? While my mild OCD doesn't tolerate loose ends, more importantly I felt I had a story to share and something to say.

Fortunately, the cancer surgery was successful and the subsequent tests are clear. So, maybe there will be a sequel to NOT SO DONE. But wait, another uh-oh hit just as I was about to send the finished book to my editor. Covid-19 took us all by surprise and turned the world upside down. I could write at length about this tragedy, the lives lost, the mistakes made, how much we still don't know, and what the uncertain future holds. I probably will at some point. However, the immediate and oddly prescient concern for creating NOT SO DONE was that I had written about a pandemic that could kill thousands, close businesses, crush the markets, and instill fear and panic across the world. The scenario that my character Ashaki brings about was happening as I had written it.

What to do? I updated the pandemic plot to take into account what happened and is happening with the Coronavirus but kept the essence of it the same as what I wrote before any of us had even contemplated Covid-19. It's a mixed blessing for a writer to predict the future only a short time before it actually happens. It isn't like it hasn't happened before with the Bubonic Plague, Smallpox, the Spanish Flu, Polio, and AIDS, but we seem to collectively have a very short-term memory, limited to our own personal experience–previous history being a kind of fiction relegated to the collective unconscious. The world, as those alive today know it, has radically changed. May we survive it, learn from it, and grab the small pleasures of life like reading a good book.

As Samuel Beckett wrote in 1963 to the New York theater director Alan Schneider, whose father had died, "So I offer you only my deeply affectionate and compassionate thoughts and wish for you only that the strange thing may never fail you, whatever it is, that gives us the strength to live on and on with our wounds. Ever Sam."

Beckett's sentiment resonates with me, and I like that *Ever Sam*.

FACT REFERENCES AND FURTHER READING

All the science and technology in this book is currently available and being deployed. The exception is the uploading and downloading of personalities, which is "in development" and may arrive in the near future. If you're curious, as I was, about some of this amazing stuff, here are some links to further information and insights on the topics mentioned in the book.

Bodyjacking:
https://en.wiktionary.org/wiki/bodyjack

Tor Super-Secure Browser:
https://www.torproject.org/

Bits to It:
https://blogs.scientificamerican.com/cross-check/a-super-simple-non-quantum-theory-of-eternal-consciousness

NYPD Drones:
https://www.cnn.com/2018/12/04/us/nypd-drones/index.html

History of the Plague:
https://www.cdc.gov/plague/history/index.html

Google Purchase Tracking:
https://www.nytimes.com/2019/06/04/opinion/google-purchases.html

Tacoma Bridge Collapse - Resonant Frequencies:
https://www.youtube.com/watch?v=j-zczJXSxnw

ShotSpotter:
https://www.shotspotter.com/

Sound Hidden in Objects:
https://www.npr.org/2016/03/18/470514319/how-can-hidden-sounds-be-captured-by-everyday-objects

Forensic Gait Analysis:
https://www.policechiefmagazine.org/gait-footprints-and-footwear-how-forensic-podiatry-can-identify-criminals/

Spacetime - Are the Past and Future Real?
https://www.forbes.com/sites/fernandezelizabeth/2019/11/10/are-the-past-and-future-real-the-physics-and-philosophy-of-time/amp/

Reiki remote healing:
https://www.mindbodygreen.com/0-17652/what-is-distance-reiki-does-it-really-work.html

Infrared wall-penetrating listening devices:
https://hackaday.com/2010/09/25/laser-mic-makes-eavesdropping-remarkably-simple/

Quantum Life:
https://www.digitaltrends.com/cool-tech/artificial-life-quantum-computing/?amp

Forbidden Paris - The Secret World of the Parisian Catacombs:
https://theculturetrip.com/europe/france/paris/articles/forbidden-paris-the-secret-world-of-the-parisian-catacombs/

Hydrogen Powered Drones:
https://impakter.com/hes-hycopter-hydrogen-powered-drone/

Gene Drives:
https://www.nytimes.com/2020/01/08/magazine/gene-drive-mosquitoes.html

ECMO - Extracorporeal Membrane Oxygenation:
https://www.ucsfhealth.org/treatments/extracorporeal-membrane-oxygenation

RFID trackers, the size of dust:
https://www.livescience.com/4372-scary-small-tracking-chip-size-dust-grain.html

Liked NOT SO DONE?

Check out more adventures of Sam, Michelle, Rich and Al in NOT SO DEAD and NOT SO GONE by Charles Levin.

If you enjoyed NOT SO DONE, please consider leaving an unbiased review on Amazon,Audible Goodreads or Bookbub to help spread the word.

You can learn more about this book and contact the author at charleslevin.com

Contact or follow the author at Facebook: facebook.com/Charles.Levin.Author

Twitter: @charlielevin

Instagram: @charleslevinauthor

Bookbub: bookbub.com/authors/charles-levin

ACKNOWLEDGEMENTS

Although writing a novel is a solo effort, it takes a team of talented people to bring it to life. From my dedicated and critical readers Steve Bennett, Amy Levin, and Ann Keeran to the editors Judy Roth and Gabriella Swartwood to the skillful book cover designer Jessica Marony and video producer Luis Socorro to the Audiobook Narrator Daniel Greenberg, I can't thank you enough.

ABOUT THE AUTHOR

Charlie is an author who has written the bestselling thriller novels, NOT SO DEAD and NOT SO GONE. Charlie's 26 year background in tech, degree in philosophy and love of fast-paced thrillers are the brew that created NOT SO DONE.

He lives in New Jersey with his wife, Amy, and has two sons, too far away in California.